ALL MY LOVE, DETRICK

All My Love, Detrick
BOOK ONE

ROBERTA KAGAN

2nd Edition

ISBN (eBook): 978-1-957207-35-3
ISBN (Paperback): 978-1-957207-36-0
ISBN (Hardcover): 978-1-957207-37-7

Title Production by The Book Whisperer

PROLOGUE

INGA HASWELL SIPPED STEAMING tea from a chipped china cup as she gazed at the second-hand bicycle. It stood with its front wheel slightly turned in the middle of her sparsely furnished living room. It seemed to be tilting its metal head and staring back at her. Her fingers, red and covered with open lesions from scrubbing, folded and unfolded a ragged dishtowel. As the mild aroma of the tea wafted to her nose, she thought it more like hot water than tea, and she wished she'd saved a bit of sugar to sweeten it up. Sugar was difficult to obtain for anyone, but a doctor's wife she did laundry for gave her just enough for the recipe for her son's birthday cake.

Today her son, Detrick, turned seven. She shook her head and marveled at how quickly the years had passed. In her mind, she recalled the boy as he'd been a tiny infant, reaching up and tangling his small fingers in her wheat-colored hair. It had been so long ago felt like a moment to her. As she allowed her mind the indulgence of drifting into the past, her memory of girlhood returned. She'd been such a shy and sheltered child with very little experience outside of her home.

It had seemed strange to everyone that Hans Haswell had shown an interest in her. She smiled. Had he been so handsome before the drink had seduced him like an unfaithful lover and taken over his life? Detrick resembled his father. In fact, both he and his sister, Helga, had their father's good looks. In her youth, she'd been slender with a plain face, not ugly, just ordinary. Thoughts of Hans brought an empty ache to her chest. Once, he'd been the brightest star she'd ever known and such an athlete. Inga recalled the first time she'd seen him. He'd been playing football in the park. With his blond hair shining like polished gold, he'd caught the sun's rays, seeming to light up the entire field. He looked over to find her staring at him, and he smiled a bright, white-toothed smile that captured her immediately. Even now, she recalled how foolish she'd felt, how her face had grown hot as she'd looked away in embarrassment. It came as a shock that she should have the attention of one of the most popular boys in school. There could be no doubt that he had his choice of girls, but he'd chosen her. She smiled at the memory, the skin around her eyes sinking into dark, cavernous crevices.

They'd fallen in love that summer and married early that fall. Well, he'd fallen in love that summer, but her love had been instantaneous. Then the war came, poisoning the country's young men with dreams of heroism.

Hans enlisted, leading a large group of his friends to follow. With passion and patriotic conviction, he'd walked through the city wearing his uniform, inspiring awe throughout his neighborhood. Hans basked in the glory—reveled in it, in fact. Their friends and families hosted dinners where the liquor flowed freely, and toasts to his honor continued throughout the night. There she had been, right at his side, her heart swelling with pride. This brave and astounding man belonged to her—little, insignificant Inga. The feeling had been so powerful and consuming that she could recall it as if it were yesterday. When his company marched out of Berlin, her world went dark as if the entire universe had been lit by a single candle that now lay extinguished, leaving only drifting smoke in its wake.

She grew serious, unable to laugh, and had no heart to accompany her friends when they attended parties or picnics. Instead, she wrote long letters filled with emotion, holding them tightly to her heart before sending them to her beloved. While Hans engaged in battle somewhere far away, she worried incessantly. He'd only returned home on leave once, two years after he'd left. When she saw him, Inga cried and laughed and wanted to hold him so tightly that he would be unable to leave again. However, Hans had stayed for only a few days, but it was long enough for Inga to become pregnant. The war raged on, and friends and neighbors returned monthly from the battlefield crippled or maimed. Then there was the unthinkable: those who were buried on the battlefield and did not return. She knelt beside her bed every night, begging God to deliver her husband home safely. Hans was not there when his son was born, but Inga had been able to get a letter to him to inform him he would be a father. She'd labored for sixteen terrible hours, but then, with the help of a midwife, she'd given birth to a little boy. She named the child Detrick, and he became her reason for living while she waited and prayed for Hans, uncertain of her husband's fate. Detrick was a good baby. He brought Inga back to life and made her smile. Finally, her prayers were answered. Hans survived unscathed but not completely. Only his physical body remained intact.

Germany had lost the war.

Hans Haswell returned from fighting an outside enemy, only to find himself fighting one within. Now, he was at the bottom of a pit of scruffy, starving, unemployed men. Fits of unpredictable rage replaced the gentle words he'd once spoken to Inga. Haunted by visions of battle, he'd awoken nightly, bathed in sweat, the sheets twisted around his writhing body. Sitting up with a start, he'd cried out names she'd never heard. When he was awake, his hands shook, and sometimes he had trouble swallowing his soup, which leaked out the side of his mouth and onto his chin. Although his appearance remained the same, he had changed—completely.

Somewhere out in the fields, as bullets broke through the quiet of the morning, leaving his comrades torn to shreds in pools of their own blood, he'd been stripped of the confidence of the athlete she'd married and transformed into a frightened, troubled soul.

When Hans first saw his son, he cried. It broke Inga's heart to see him so filled with emotion. At the time, she believed that he was overcome with love. However, the blessing of a child could not save Hans from his tortured mind. It only added to the weight of his responsibilities. Even though Hans had no idea how to go about it, he knew he must find a way to provide for his family. He questioned his own worth. Instead of the fierce, protective provider instinct taking over, he sank even deeper into his depression. Accompanied by thousands of others who had returned from the war, he went out scraping and scrounging for work, only to find his way back to the local tavern in defeat.

When Detrick got an earache, he cried all night, and it only amplified Hans's sense of frustration, and Hans shouted at Inga, "Get that child out of here! I can't stand it when he cries!"

Inga took the boy where Hans could not criticize him and cradled little Detrick in her arms, rocking him until he slept. From the moment Detrick took his first breath and let out a lusty cry, she'd adored him. Now Hans and his aura of despair faded in the illumining joy the boy brought to her. Her little man amused her continuously as he held her heart in his little fist.

Helga, Inga's second child, came later that year. Inga loved her, but nothing had ever captivated her as completely as little Detrick. In a way, she felt that Detrick had saved her. She feared she might have taken her own life If Detrick had not come along. However, the baby had only served to reinforce Hans's inability to support his family with a devastating effect. It broke what was left of his spirit, and he began to manifest a strong resentment toward his children. He'd wandered the streets for over a year, begging for spare change and seeking day labor. When he earned any wage, he drank most of it away to fill the vast emptiness within.

Finally, with no education or skills, he'd chanced upon a bit of good fortune. Inga's brother had found him work as a janitor at the Hausladen Insurance Company. Although Inga felt they'd been blessed, Hans found the job humiliating. He could not accept the idea of himself sweeping up the day's mess or on his knees fixing toilets. She had also hoped that Hans would bring home money to help her with food and rent, but he did not. Hyperinflation caused most wives to get their husband's daily pay in the morning and rush to buy food before the prices went up and the food was gone, but Hans did not allow it. He had his employer pay him his wages at the end of the day at the currency's value at day's end so he could take it to the tavern. As time passed, his inner demons grew, and he lost interest in his family entirely. He thought only of the end of the day when he would take his suitcase full of nearly worthless money and head for the only comfort he could find at the bottom of a bottle. The responsibility to keep them from starving or being evicted fell entirely on Inga, who struggled to feed them by taking in laundry. She did not have time to wait in line at the stores like the other wives, so she bartered her services whenever she could for food, taking cash only to pay the rent.

Lost in her thoughts of the past and gazing out the window, Inga did not see seven-year-old Detrick as he entered the apartment, returning from school. His aqua-blue eyes filled with light as he looked at the bicycle.

"Mama!" He ran into her arms.

"Happy birthday, sweetheart." She hugged him and ruffled his golden hair as it fell softly over his left eye.

"For me? Really?" He stared at the bike and then back at her in disbelief.

"Yes, for you." She kissed his forehead and held him close.

Detrick walked over to the bike and gently touched the handlebars. Then he walked around it twice and stopped to touch the seat, his eyes wide with wonder.

"Can I take it for a ride?"

"Yes, but please be careful. I know it is yours, but your father will want to use it sometimes to ride to work. Of course, only if that is all right with you." She knew Hans would take the bike whenever he felt like it, but she also knew Detrick would never deny his father, and she wanted him to feel as if the gift were his.

"Of course, he can use it whenever he likes."

Tears threatened to spring from the corner of Inga's eyes. She wished Hans could learn to love their son. If only he could see what a treasure God had given him in this generous and kind little boy.

The door opened, and a lovely girl who would be four years old in November with long, golden curls entered the room.

"Hi, Mama. Hi, Detrick." Helga looked over at the bike. "Is that Detrick's birthday gift?"

"Yes, dear, it is."

"Happy birthday, Det. It looks pretty bad."

She ran her hand over the dent on the wheel cover and frowned at the faded black paint.

Inga shook her head, marveling at how different her children were. Detrick would never notice the imperfections. And Helga... well, things had to be the finest quality to satisfy her.

"I think it's beautiful!" Detrick smiled at his sister. "And when you get bigger, I'll teach you how to ride."

"Thanks, Det, but no, thanks," she said suspiciously, eyeing the beat-up old bike. "Can you ride it?"

"Yes, I learned on Konrad's bike."

Helga went to her room to change clothes before meeting her girlfriends in the courtyard of the building to play.

"Helga, make sure Heidi is in the courtyard watching her little sister, or you come right back."

"Yes, Mama."

His mother could not help but smile when she looked at the young face filled with joy. "Now I have to get back to the wash. Mrs. Reitman will be expecting me to deliver it by this afternoon. You two run along and play. And Detrick, if you are going to ride, try to be home by six. I've baked a surprise for you. I want to serve it after dinner. Your father will probably not be home until very late, but if he is not here, we will enjoy the cake without him, yes?" With a wink of her eye, Inga assured her son that his birthday would be a celebration, regardless of his father's presence. When she allowed herself to indulge in wishes, she thought of Hans. If only he would offer to carry some of the financial burdens of raising a family instead of taking his daily wages to the bar as he undoubtedly would tonight. If he made some effort, she might be able to spend less time scrubbing dirty clothes from early morning until late at night.

Detrick turned to Inga. "I love you, Mother." He hugged her. "Thank you so very, very much for this wonderful birthday. I will never forget it—ever."

"All right then, my darling. You promise to be cautious? Now don't be gone too long. I will worry if you are." Inga held him tightly for a moment, inhaling the essence of him, then kissed the top of his golden hair. "Put on your jacket. There is a chill in the air."

"Yes, Mama, I promise to be careful, and I'll be back by six." He cautiously guided the bike by its handlebars, down the staircase, and into the bustling street.

It was late afternoon and a time when the sun cast the last of her warm rays upon the earth, illuminating it with a gilded haze. October's crisp winds rustled the colorful blanket of leaves that covered the ground. Detrick was filled with excitement. When he looked at the bicycle, a smile immediately came to his face. He caressed the handlebar for a moment, then jumped on the bike with ease. His golden hair fell gently over his left eye as he began to ride, swerving past people, trees, and an occasional new machine they called the automobile. The blaring of horns from the vehicles brought a previously unheard sound to Berlin.

Evidence of Germany's terrible economy and rising inflation were everywhere. Army veterans, many with loss of limbs, sat on the concrete sidewalk still in uniform, holding cups and begging for food or spare change. *Hausfraus* stood in long lines outside the bakery or the butcher shop, each holding suitcases filled with the pay their husbands had earned for the day. The suitcase had to be returned the next day because the suitcase was more valuable than the paper money inside. The wives were waiting and hoping to buy food for the night. They prayed that the price would not rise beyond their ability to pay, and that the shopkeeper would not be sold out before they reached the front of the store. Detrick glanced across the street to make sure it was safe to cross, and he saw a mother with her young child coming out of one of the homeless shelters. The little

boy waved to him, and Detrick waved back. The dull-black metal of
the handlebars glistened in the afternoon light, seeming to grin at
the boy as if they knew a secret. Something within Detrick tingled
and stirred as he felt a divine hand on his shoulder. So strong was
the presence of touch that he turned to look. The wind whistled, but
he saw nothing. It was a mystery that a child his age could not
possibly understand.

As the park came into view, he glanced over to see if his friends
were playing soccer on the field. From the front of the park, he did
not see anyone, so he decided to go around to the back and check
there. As he turned a sharp corner, Detrick was not looking forward.
He was studying the park, so he did not see an old woman hobbling
across the street in front of him. Left with no choice, Detrick
swerved to miss her, only to find he'd come right into the path of a
junk collector with a horse and wagon. His heart pounded as he
maneuvered the bike to the right. 'Hurry!' his heart said, 'just a few
feet to be out of danger!' Sweat trickled down Detrick's brow. The
horse snorted and then tossed its head. The animal whinnied, trying
desperately to stop. Detrick never heard a thing. The intense
thunder of his heartbeat filled his ears, drowning out all sound. His
legs pumped the pedals. Harder... Move... Faster! Then a tremendous blow knocked the wind out of his lungs as the horse plowed
headlong into his back tire. The sound of crushed metal broke
through him. Thrown from the bike, Detrick was catapulted into the
air, flying across the road. It felt as if he were watching himself
instead of living this nightmare. What seemed like hours took mere
seconds. As he hit the ground with a thud, the pavement assaulted
his face, hands, and knees, leaving him with bloody scratches and
scrapes. At first, he could feel nothing, only numb shock, but then
his body ached with bruises that would turn black and purple over
the coming week. But fortunately, possibly because of his youth or
an angel watching over him, he suffered only minor injuries. Detrick
raised himself from where he'd landed, wiping the dirt from his face
and hair. He stretched and ambled back over to his damaged
birthday present and broken dreams. As he gingerly stroked the
handlebars, tears welled up in his eyes. Wiping them quickly with

the back of his dirty hand, he realized he stood in the middle of a busy intersection.

"Get that thing out of the road before you get yourself killed!" an old man, slightly hunched over with thin strings of long, greasy hair attempting to cover the bald spot on the top of his head, yelled from across the street.

Detrick lifted the bent bicycle frame and pulled it along, keeping his head down. Ashamed of his clumsiness, but more importantly, humiliated, he could not hold back the tears. Detrick could not bear to face his friends. So, instead of taking his usual route home, he made a fateful decision and chose a longer way. It led him through the Jewish sector of the city. Neither he nor his family nor friends frequented this area, assuring him he would arrive at his destination without seeing anyone he knew.

Here the streets buzzed with vendors peddling their wares: old knives, pots, pans, and used clothing. But instead of German, they cried out to their customers in Yiddish. The sign outside the butcher shop read in German and in some funny letters that Detrick didn't recognize, "Kosher. All out of meat today." Detrick wondered what the word "kosher" meant.

Men bearing long, dark, curly sideburns and tall, black hats were deeply engaged in conversation and making wild gestures with their hands as they strolled along.

Brokenhearted, he stopped in front of a bicycle shop and peered into the window. Now remembering his happiness upon receiving his bike, he wept, and the tears mingled with the dirt and blood covering his face from the accident. The sorrow he felt extended beyond his own loss to his father, who would have used the bike to get to and from work, saving him commuting time. His father's anger would surely turn to violence.

Detrick steadied himself against the coming wrath. He'd been subjected to it before, but he would rather endure the lash of his father's belt a thousand times than see the hurt he knew would steal the joy from his mother's eyes.

Inside the Abendstern's Bicycle Repair Shop, Jacob Abendstern prepared for the *Shabbat*, the Jewish Sabbath. He hurried to finish his work so he could visit several of the food vendors before sundown.

Jacob ran a bicycle repair shop and had plenty of business. But Jacob was more than a bicycle repairman. He was a gifted man who could fix just about anything. With hyperinflation making cash nearly worthless, barter was the true currency of the land. Often, he received items that required repairs for cash or in exchange for bicycle repairs, and Jacob would fix the items and use them to trade for things he needed. Local businessmen knew that if they needed emergency repairs on equipment, Jacob would close up his shop and help them. The Abendsterns did not have to wait in line every morning to buy food. The neighborhood butcher, grocer, and baker all set-aside food for Jacob's family in the morning to either pay him for services rendered or to barter for the unique items he traded. In the event that Jacob had to pay cash, the items were reserved for him at morning prices.

There was much needed for the Shabbat dinner. This should have been his wife, Miriam's task, but she refused to leave the house. Since taking a fall on a mountain hike during the holiday had rendered their seven-year-old son, Michael, an invalid, Miriam spent her days at his side. It had been six months, and the boy showed no improvement. The Abendsterns' two other children—Karl, eight, and Leah, five—had learned to compensate for their mother's neglect.

Meanwhile, Jacob labored tirelessly to be a father and mother to all three of them. He understood Miriam's pain and shared it. But he would not forget, as she had, that the others still needed him. As time passed, it became apparent that Michael was most likely simple-minded. Had the accident caused this, or had the condition been present before? Jacob would never know.

As Jacob reached above his head to place a hammer back on the shelf, he caught sight of the battered child looking into his shop window. Although the clock on the wall ticked, pushing the day into night, Jacob immediately stopped his efforts. He stepped outside because he was concerned for the boy.

"Look at you. My God, child, are you all right?" Jacob thought he could not be more than seven as he looked at the soiled and injured child.

"Yes, sir, I'm fine." Detrick turned away.

"Wait. Hold on a minute." Jacob saw the battered bicycle and considered the boy's appearance. He knew there'd been an accident. "Come in. Please, let me help you." He could not bear to see a youngster suffer, and Detrick's tear-stained face did not slip past his observant eyes.

"Come in. It's all right." Jacob led Detrick into the shop.

"My name is Jacob Abendstern. And you are?" Jacob brought a stool into the center of the room and motioned Detrick to sit.

"I'm Detrick Haswell."

"Well, hello, Detrick Haswell. It looks to me like you took a pretty bad fall."

"Yes, sir. I guess I did."

"Let me help you. You shouldn't go home like that. You will scare your mother." Under his workbench, Jacob kept a first aid kit. He took it out and opened it, then cleaned the cut along Detrick's jaw and the scrapes on both his knees and elbows. "You aren't in too bad shape, just maybe a little shaken up. But that bike of yours, well, now that's a different story. It looks pretty bad."

"Yes, sir, I know. I guess it's done for." Detrick choked back the tears.

"Eh, not necessarily—maybe I can fix it."

"I'm grateful for your kindness and help with my scrapes, sir, but I don't have any money to pay you."

"Who said anything about money? Did I ask you for money? Of what good is money, anyway? You pay me in the morning, and it is worthless by afternoon." Jacob laughed, and his eyes twinkled with kindness. The warmth and sincerity of his grin reached out to Detrick.

"No, sir, but I would have to pay. I could not allow you to fix it without paying. My parents would never approve."

"Hmmm," Jacob stroked his beard. "I see. So, you must pay. You are not going to let me have a mitzvah on this Shabbat, eh?"

"I'm sorry, sir?"

"A mitzvah… a blessing—it is a blessing to help another. And on the Shabbat… well, that makes it an even greater blessing," he laughed, nodding.

"You've already helped me. My parents would be angry if I accepted charity."

"Ah, I see." Stroking his beard, Jacob studied the boy. "So, I have an idea. I am often in need of parts to fix the bicycles, and parts are hard to come by and so expensive, *oy vey*. Anyway, if you can find old, junked bicycles, bring them to me, and I will use whatever parts I can. And besides that, I could use a helper around here. I'm not as young as I used to be, and you look like a strong boy. How about you come and work for me until the repair is paid off? What do you say?"

Now this possibility opened a door. Here, Detrick found an option he could accept and a way to make things right again. Detrick felt relief flood his young body as if God himself had come down offering a blessing—and perhaps he had.

"Yes, sir, I would like that very much, and I know where to find some old junked bicycles that may have some parts you can use!"

"Good, but on one condition. You'll call me Jacob instead of 'sir,' yes?" Jacob planned to pay the boy for his work. He knew he would never take money from this child to fix the bicycle. Jacob's eye glimpsed the child's tattered clothing, and he felt sure that Detrick's family could not afford to pay for the repair.

"All right, I will call you Jacob." Detrick smiled all the way up to his eyes as his dimples came into view, and Jacob returned the smile, patting Detrick's shoulder.

The natural curiosity of a seven-year-old took hold of the boy. He inquired, "I hope I am not being too bold by asking, sir, I mean Jacob, but what is that you are wearing on your head?"

"It is called a yarmulke. I am a Jew." Jacob showed Detrick the black and gold skullcap.

"I don't think I've ever met a Jew before. I've seen a few but never actually talked to one."

"So, this is a first for you."

"Yes, and I like you very much."

"I like you too, Detrick."

Jacob's dark, kind eyes met Detrick's deep-blue ones as a bond like soldered silver forged between them, each trusting the other fully but not knowing why.

And so, unbeknownst to them at the time, began a friendship that would change both of their lives forever.

CHAPTER ONE

AFTER THE LOSS of the First World War, followed by the signing of the Treaty of Versailles, Germany plunged into a great depression. The country suffered both financially and psychologically. The people lost their jobs and their pride. Currency and food became scarce as the Germans searched desperately for a leader with ideas and conviction who would end their pain. The blow came down hardest upon the heads of the lower working-class men. Many of those men had served in the army and took the loss of the war as a personal defeat. With their inability to scrounge out a living wage, they grew angry and bitter, searching for answers and someone or something to blame.

Meanwhile, under the Weimar government, which was the government in place after the war, the country was making great strides in science and the arts. However, Germany seemed to have taken a hysterical descent into wild decadence. Vulgar entertainment and prostitution became commonplace. Political groups sprung up everywhere, promising a solution to the financial devastation but leaving the people vulnerable and confused. It was a time of extremes. The cry for a hero sounded like a lion's roar throughout the land until it fell upon the ears of one who had been quietly watching and waiting, like a spider in its web.

CHAPTER TWO

"ARE you still working for that Jew?" asked Konrad Klausen, Detrick's best friend since childhood, lighting a cigarette as they walked home from school together.

Charcoal-gray rain clouds hung angrily over their heads, threatening to storm.

"Jacob Abendstern is a good man. He is more of a father to me than my own father ever was, Konrad. And furthermore, what is this with you and the Jews? Why are you so filled with hatred?"

"My man, do you not see what is going on here? The Jewish bankers are the reason we lost the war. They take our jobs. They steal our money. Don't you realize that the Jews are the reason we're poor? Lying, cheating, no-good bastards."

"Konrad, you're my oldest friend, and I care deeply about you, but I won't stand by and listen to you talk like this about Herr Abendstern. He's my friend, too."

"He's your employer, can't you see? He owns the shop. You do all the work."

Detrick laughed. His dimples and full lips gave his otherwise chiseled face a boyish appearance.

"Oh, Konrad, you have no idea what you're talking about. Jacob pays me far more than anyone else would for the job I do. He allows me to make my own hours so I can attend track practice. And the man works far harder than he would ever expect or even allow me to."

They walked in silence for a few moments. Konrad had seen the anger flash in Detrick's eyes when he criticized the Jews, and for a split second, a finger of fear tickled his spine. Detrick could be a powerful force. Konrad had witnessed that a few months ago when the two had been in the park, and some older boys taunted Konrad. Without a trace of trepidation, Detrick confronted the boys, hurling several punches at one of them and sending the others running for cover.

Then he'd turned to Konrad, who was relieved that the fight had ended without his participation. "Bullies are only strong in numbers. As soon as one went down, the others backed off because none of them could truly stand on their own."

Konrad, never popular, had come to rely on Detrick's help. Since childhood, his clumsy body and lack of self-confidence had made him a target for the type of boys who group together and instinctively find the weakest child to terrorize. Only by torturing the pathetic do people of this nature find that they can hide their short-comings.

Because of Detrick's independence, gangs of angry, oppressive young men tried to recruit him. When they came offering friend-ship, Detrick just laughed, refusing. This flippant attitude ignited a strange jealousy in Konrad that he could not explain. Although these gangs of boys disliked Konrad and hurt his feelings as often as possible, he still vied for their approval, while Detrick came by it without any effort. Not only did they shower him with their accep-tance, but their admiration as well. Konrad often wondered how it was that Detrick never felt the desire to become a part of these groups of popular boys while he longed for their acceptance.

Carefully, Konrad spoke. "Detrick...tonight there is a rally in the center of town. I thought you might like to go. The speaker is a man, a new leader that everyone is talking about." He dropped the butt of his cigarette and smashed it with the toe of his shoe. "His name is Adolf Hitler."

CHAPTER THREE

WHEN DETRICK ARRIVED HOME, his father was slumped over the kitchen table with a half-empty bottle of beer at his side. Since losing his job, he guzzled the brew daily until he fell into a stupor. The entire family knew that Hans stole the money for his beer from the jug in the pantry that held Inga's meager savings. But when Detrick offered to stop him, his mother insisted he do nothing.

Helga and Inga stood at the sink, chatting quietly as they cut vegetables, preparing the evening meal.

The creak of the door closing awakened Hans.

"Look who's here." Hans laughed bitterly. "It's the Jew lover. He makes more money working for the kike than his father ever could... Don't you, Detrick?" A thin line of spittle sprung from his lips.

"Please, Hans. He is supporting us, and besides, he is your son." Inga glared at her husband. Hans had lost his janitorial job at the insurance company for drinking on the job.

Detrick laid his books on the table and, without looking at his father, went to his room to change for work. Sometimes, he avoided his father's gaze for fear he might lose control and hit the older man. Detrick knew this would devastate his mother, so he swallowed his anger and turned away. He looked forward to the time spent with Jacob. They sat at the workbench side-by-side, and Jacob listened as Detrick shared his dreams—how he hoped to go to the Olympics and prove himself a track star.

"It is not for me that I want to win," Detrick told Jacob. "It is for my family, especially my mother. She has had so little joy in her life. I've watched helplessly while she always makes sacrifices for all of us… And I guess I would like to give something back to her."

Over the years, Jacob had developed a particular affection for the boy equal to that he felt for his biological children. Some days passed as they worked in comfortable silence. On others, they would laugh and tell jokes. Often, Detrick came by the shop late in the evening after field practice. When Jacob saw Detrick's reluctance to go home, he purchased some food and stayed with him late into the night. It was on one of these occasions that Detrick revealed the revulsion he felt for his father.

"I don't want to hate him. He is my father. But when I see him drink all of his money away while my mother works so hard to make ends meet, I just find that I resent him. He raised his hand to her last week but didn't hit her. I am afraid that if he does, I will go crazy."

Jacob nodded. He knew how much Detrick endured to keep the peace and hoped the boy would not snap. Hans was out of work and pouring every bit of money he could scrounge into a beer bottle, so rather than give Detrick cash bonuses, he often sent food home with him instead.

Still, it was not enough. Detrick would never ask for more, so Jacob planned to propose an idea to help the boy. He knew that Detrick would never accept his offer of money. Instead, it must seem to Detrick as if Jacob needed his help. For weeks following the discussion, Jacob considered his plan. The older man sat at the bench, thinking about the best way to approach the subject as he repaired a bicycle chain. When Detrick arrived at work tonight, he would present it.

After Detrick changed his clothes and shelved his schoolbooks, he went to the kitchen to bid his family farewell for the evening. He prepared to leave the apartment without stopping to eat because Jacob always provided dinner at the shop. On nights like these, Jacob often brought luscious noodle kugels made from baked noodles with sour cream and raisins or apples. Sometimes, Jacob arrived with brisket sandwiches on sweet challah bread. Over the years, Detrick grew familiar with Jewish cuisine. Knowing the hardships the Haswell family faced and the appetite of a growing boy training to be an Olympic athlete, Jacob made sure that whenever the boy came to the shop, he had something to eat.

"I'm going to work, Mother."

"Going to see that Jew again?" Hans guzzled the remainder of his beer. "You know, there is a meeting tonight in the center of the city. I'm sure you've heard. The man who is speaking is going to save Germany. You watch and see. It's the stinking Jews that have ruined this country for all of us." After a loud belch, Hans set the empty bottle on the table.

"Stop, Hans. Enough!" Inga glared at her husband.

"Helga is going. At least, she has some sense. You? No, of course not. You'd rather go and spend your time with that kike."

"Goodnight, Father." Detrick felt his face turn hot, and he could not look at his father. Over the years, he'd grown bigger and stronger than Hans and had no doubt he could take him in a fistfight, but he would not. Instead, he kissed his mother and then patted his sister's shoulder. Helga looked up at him with eyes the color of the sky on a spring morning and lovely, long, wavy, golden hair the same color as hers.

"I'll tell you about the rally, Det."

"Thanks, Helga, but I'm not interested. I've heard all I want to hear about Hitler."

Detrick closed the door behind him. Hopping on the black bicycle, he headed to the little shop in the Jewish sector of town.

On the most unassuming day, on January 30, 1933, Adolf Hitler was appointed Chancellor of Germany. This singular event would change history.

It all began innocently enough, as most menacing threats do. Stormtroopers could be seen walking the streets, proud, in their brown uniforms. Occasionally, there was an incident against Jews. But the violent acts were so random that few paid them much attention. Most thought the Nazis would be little more than a passing political group, too radical to have any real power. So, among the small Jewish population in Germany, only a handful recognized the coming danger and fled while the rest of the population remained and hoped the Nazi Party would go away.

CHAPTER FOUR

KARL ABENDSTERN LEANED against a blood-red brick building in the alley, taking deep drags on a short, unfiltered cigarette. Three boys he'd been friends with since childhood accompanied him. Being a Jew in Germany singled Karl out as an enemy of the state, and with each passing day, he felt the hatred pointed firmly in his direction, coming from the eyes of his Gentile classmates. The rise in anti-Semitism poisoned the lives of Jews, young and old. Those Karl once considered friends now spit fiery hatred at their Jewish class-mates. What began as subtle, quiet, and almost discreet discrimina-tion quickly grew into a tree of bloody loathing. The branches continued to spread out, bringing more followers under their cover. Neighbors he'd known all of his life turned on families they'd shared apartment buildings with for years, and the division between Jew and Gentile grew as wide as a canyon.

"Karl, why are you fighting at every turn? What are you trying to prove? You cannot beat them single-handedly. After the fight, they only start again. Try to ignore them." Yussel shook his head at Karl's black eye and bruised cheek.

"One day, you'll see. We Jews will have our own state. Then they won't be able to treat us this way. Yussel, you should be proud of your heritage, and if that means fighting for it...well, so be it. When you let them talk badly about Jews, you give them the impression that we are all weak. When we establish Israel, they will have to stand back and see we are a people to be reckoned with." Karl stood up straight and looked directly into Yussel's eyes.

"Again with the Zionism, Karl? For now, we live here in Germany, and this is our home. And we are Germans first, and then we are Jews. So, let's make the best of it. You can't fight all of them. This will blow over; you'll see." Moishe wiped his nose with the back of his hand.

"Ah, Moishe, you are a fool. They hate us. They always have, but now Hitler gave them the right to beat the hell out of us and get away with it. We'd better retaliate now." Karl's eyes had turned dark with anger at the weakness in his friends.

"Who's going to retaliate? Me? Him?" Moishe pointed to Yussel. "We're not all fighters like you, Karl."

"So be scared—run scared. That will do you lots of good. Look at how controlling and strong they're becoming. They burned the Reichstag Building just to show that they were above the law and then turned around and denied they ever did it, laying the blame on the communists. Then, even more disturbing, they point the finger at us whenever there is trouble. The more they blame us Jews, the more the German people feel justified in their hatred and persecution of our people. Now, the Parliament has given Hitler the powers of a dictator. If we let them go on, they will only grow stronger. These Nazis are dangerous, I tell you."

"So go fight the world. I hope it works for you." Moishe crossed his arms over his chest.

Karl shook his head in disgust at his friend, threw the end of his cigarette on the ground, and turned away. Without looking back, he headed home.

CHAPTER FIVE

LEAH ABENDSTERN and her best friend, Dorothy Silver, prepared dinner for the family as her mother sat beside Michael's bed.

Their mothers had met early in their pregnancies. Both bearing the same swollen bellies, the women had shared afternoon walks. When the babies arrived a month apart, a ritual began. Every morning, the women met at the park, pushing their carriages slowly along the pathway on the grassy hills. As the two infant girls grew, a friendship developed despite the differences in their personalities. Leah, quiet and studious, loved to read and study classical music, while Dorothy, gregarious, sang American jazz and danced swing, entertaining Leah like a burlesque star. Dorothy's father worked as a bookkeeper but also sang in Hebrew, working as the cantor at the synagogue both families attended. There could be no doubt that Dorothy had inherited her beautiful voice from her father, but the style with which they expressed their art could not have been more different.

Leah learned to play piano at five and felt she grew up advantaged, so she offered free lessons to younger children who could not afford to pay. At fifteen, the kindness she'd been shown all of her life by Jacob came through in the way she treated others. Offering both

Jewish and Gentile children an opportunity to share her joyous love of music, Leah spent hours with those less fortunate.

However, Leah's happiest moments were spent with Dorothy. Sometimes, they giggled over secrets as they lay beneath the weeping willow tree dreaming about the future. Often, the girls amused themselves—Leah on piano and Dorothy crooning a bluesy love song—her raspy alto voice a strange contrast to her youthful presence.

They attended the same school and recently discovered an interest in the opposite sex. Whispering softly so that Leah's mother could not overhear, Leah and Dorothy gossiped about Lewis, clearly the most popular boy at school.

"I saw Lewis Shapiro today. Would you believe he's in my class? He glanced over at me, and I thought I might faint." Leah spoke so quietly that Dorothy almost had to read her lips.

Laughing softly, Dorothy looked over at her friend. Leah, modest in her mode of dress and shy with gentle eyes the color of maple syrup, could have been the prototype for a lovely and delicate china doll. While Dorothy, with her early-developing, womanly body and a head full of loose, auburn ringlet curls, evoked feelings in boys and men alike that gave her a power her young mind could not yet grasp.

"Leah, he is so good-looking and rich. I hear his family owns a house with a ballroom upstairs. His mother wears a white ermine coat. Can you imagine?"

"No, I can't. A ballroom right in the house! And he's handsome, too."

"Any Jewish girl would be proud to be seen with him and her parents. *Oy*, what *nachas*. How everyone would envy them. He sure is quite a catch." Dorothy laughed louder than she'd expected to.

Leah winked at her friend and smiled as she stirred the spaetzles: a blend of flour, eggs, onions, and butter that would first be boiled and then fried. The succulent aroma of chicken roasting and challah baking sent an enticing invitation throughout the modest house.

"You'll stay for dinner?"

"I'll have to go home and tell my parents, but then yes, I can come right back."

During the early part of Leah's life, her family enjoyed a comfortable life. Bicycles, the main mode of transportation for a long time until recently when automobiles began to enjoy popularity, had served the Abendsterns well. Over the past few years, the family's finances had been diminishing. However, Jacob still managed to provide a decent life for his family, largely due to his bartering skills.

Just as Dorothy was getting up to leave, the door opened, and both girls turned to see Karl enter. Even with his clothing disheveled and his eye bruised, he more than passed for a handsome man. He was tall and muscular. He also had thick, wavy, chestnut hair and penetrating eyes.

"Oh, Karl, you were fighting again." Leah shook her head in disappointment. "My brother... He's going to defeat Hitler all by himself. Of course, that's if he doesn't get killed first." She glared at Karl, who looked back at her—his eyes black with conviction.

"Leah, if we don't fight back, they will think they can do as they please with us, and they will. Not just the Nazis—all goyim. Non-Jews are Nazis in the making. They just don't know it yet. Just wait and see. We should get the hell out of Germany before they do something drastic."

"What will they do, Karl? They cannot do more than they already have. They boycott our businesses and treat us like dirt. If we just go along and ignore them, they will get bored with all of this and find something else to put their attention on."

"I don't think so, little sister." He grabbed a piece of *hamantaschen* from a china plate in the center of the table. At seventeen, Karl appeared more of a man than a boy.

"Hello, Dorothy, I'm sorry. I got so busy arguing with my sister here that I forgot to say hello."

"Hi, Karl." A slight blush crawled from her forehead to her neck, and she turned away so he would not see it.

"Go and clean up for dinner, please. Papa will be home in a little while. You look a fright."

"Yes, Leah." He bowed in mock servitude. "Excuse me, Dorothy, my sister commands!"

After he'd left the room, Dorothy whispered to Leah. "He is so handsome. Does he have a girl?"

"Are you kidding? Karl? A girlfriend? He is too busy trying to build a Jewish state and waging his own personal war on the Nazi Party."

Leah and Dorothy sat under a sturdy old oak tree the following afternoon, eating lunch. Fall's arrival seduced the tree to begin shedding her leaves, rewarding the ground with a multitude of rich colors. Their full skirts spread across the leaf-covered grass as the girls shared a bunch of grapes. Lewis Shapiro stood just a few feet away, talking with a group of boys, all wearing yarmulkes.

"He's looking over here. I see him glancing your way every few minutes."

"You really think so, Dorothy? Maybe he's looking at you."

"I don't think so. You should see his face."

Leah looked down at the camel-colored wool of her skirt, too shy to glance at Lewis. Her stomach fluttered nervously. "I don't know what to do."

"You don't have to do a thing, Leah. He is on his way over here right now."

Leah's nerves tingled, making her stomach churn, and she thought she might vomit. She tried to think of something to say, but words eluded her.

"Hello, you're Leah Abendstern. Am I correct?" His hair cradled his head in an ocean of blue-black waves. "I'm Lewis Shapiro."

"We know. Yes, her name is Leah Abendstern, and I'm Dorothy Silver."

"It's nice to meet you both."

"Likewise."

Leah still had not spoken. She'd opened her mouth, but no sound emerged.

"And you, Leah? Are you happy to meet me?"

Forcing a whisper, Leah smiled wryly. "I'm sorry, forgive me. I was thinking about an assignment for class," she answered sheepishly. "Yes, of course I am."

The school bell rang, indicating the end of the break period.

"May I walk you? I believe we share the same class."

"Yes, why not?" Leah felt as if every word she said sounded more foolish than the last.

Lewis swept up Leah's books, and after bidding farewell to Dorothy, they strolled silently back to the building.

CHAPTER SIX

WINTER RUSHED in with a flurry of white snow. Its frigid fingers forged their way into the school, and many times Leah and Dorothy wore their coats in the building during class. Lewis had moved his desk from across the room right beside Leah. Flattered, Leah watched as Lewis offered a few coins to the boy who had sat there previously to change seats with him.

One afternoon as school let out, Lewis asked Leah if he could walk her home, and she agreed. From then on, it became a ritual.

"I think my parents are giving me an auto for Hanukkah, which will make it easier for us to get around when it's cold like this."

"Yes, I suppose, but after sitting all day in class, I love to get outside and walk. I enjoy the fresh air."

"Well then, if you prefer, we will continue to walk and freeze." He smiled at her.

A week before winter break, Lewis scrounged up the nerve to ask Leah to have dinner with him.

This would be their first official date.

CHAPTER SEVEN

ON A CHILLY MORNING following a night of snowfall, Leah sat wrapped in a blanket.

Dorothy arrived unexpectedly and sat on the bed in Leah's room, where the girls had spent so much of their youth. Tears ran wildly down her cheeks, and she dried them with a handkerchief.

"What are you talking about? You are moving away?" Leah felt her face grow hot, and tears stung the back of her eyes.

"My father wants to go live with his brother in Chicago, Illinois, in America. He says the Nazis are getting too bold, and the anti-Semitism is getting too dangerous for us to stay here."

"Oh, Dorothy, I will miss you so much. What will you do there? You must learn English. Will you finish school?" Leah took Dorothy's hands into her own, concerned not only for herself but also for her friend's welfare.

"Yes, I plan to. My cousin, Hette, is only a few years older and works downtown in a store called Marshall Field's, selling hats. She promised that when I finish school, she will help me find a job there."

"I am so sad to see you go. Nothing will ever be the same."

"Oh, Leah, me too. I always thought we would grow old living down the street from each other, our children playing outside together, just like we did when we were little. I imagined them jumping rope as we sat, drinking tea and sharing recipes. This Hitler is a monster! He has changed everything in our world in so many ways."

Leah ran her finger along the embroidery on her bedspread. "When are you leaving?"

"Next week, on Monday. We're taking a ship."

An uncomfortable silence hung like a thick fog. Several minutes passed before Leah could speak.

"You will write?"

"Of course, I will. And you?"

"You know I will."

CHAPTER EIGHT

D ETRICK STOOD BESIDE THE WORKBENCH, a hammer held firmly in his hand, as he studied the broken handlebar on a customer's bicycle. Jacob had taught him to repair most problems, and he'd become astute at diagnosing what needed to be done. As he worked diligently, Jacob entered the shop with a platter.

"I brought some mandel bread. My daughter baked it this morning." Jacob set the platter on the table and sat down. "So, Detrick, how was your Christmas holiday?"

"Very nice. We took the train to see my grandparents. They are getting old, and it was good to spend time with them. My father didn't go, of course."

"*Ach*, well, don't be too hard on him. He is going through a lot."

"My grandfather gave me his pocket watch. It's been in the family for generations." Detrick showed the watch to Jacob. "It's real gold."

"It's beautiful, son. Wear it in the best of health."

"Thank you. I treasure it because my grandfather chose me, of all of his grandchildren, to give it to."

"That does make it special."

"Yes, very." Detrick's blond hair fell over his eye as he worked. Jacob secretly watched him and thought what a good-looking young man he had grown to be. His long, lean muscles, broad shoulders, and slim hips stretched over his tall, well-proportioned frame. Detrick stopped for a moment and reached beneath his bench. "I have a gift for you for Hanukkah." He placed a small, wrapped box in front of Jacob. A tear came to the older man's eye as he opened it to find a leather key chain with an 'A' for Abendstern made of sterling silver in the center.

"Oh, Detrick, it's beautiful. Thank you. I have a gift for you, too." Jacob walked behind the register and pulled out a brightly wrapped box. "Merry Christmas," he said, passing the box to Detrick.

Tears of affection threatened to fall from Detrick's eyes as he opened the box.

"It's a sweater. It should keep you warm."

"I love it, Jacob. Thank you so much...for everything."

"Listen, Detrick. I have a favor to ask of you." Jacob began to put his plan into action. He would help the boy and his family. He just had to be sure that Detrick never suspected he didn't really need him. "As I've told you, after sundown on Friday night, we Jews do not do anything. It is our religion, our day of rest. We cannot turn a light on or off, nothing. So, I wondered if perhaps you would come and do this for me. I will pay you well. A day's pay just to turn the light off on Friday night and another day's pay to turn it back on Saturday morning. What do you say?"

"That seems a great deal of money for just a half-hour's work. You don't have to pay me to turn your lights on, Jacob. I will gladly do it without payment. Why do I get the impression that you are trying to help me again? Jacob, I don't know what I would do without you. You have been a friend and a father to me. I don't know if I've ever thanked you for coming to all of my track meets. If you hadn't been there, no one would have been there for me."

"Yes, you've thanked me...a hundred times. So, you'll do it?"

"Jacob..."

"You'll do it. That is the way you can thank me."

Detrick nodded and smiled, shaking his head.

"And I insist on paying you. I don't want to hear any more about it."

CHAPTER NINE

WITH DOROTHY GONE, Leah thought she might die of loneliness. She'd begun to see Lewis regularly. Once, he'd planned a lovely evening, including a dinner at a fancy restaurant and a visit to the opera. Another time they'd shared a soda after school, he'd taken her for a ride in the new automobile he'd received from his parents for Hanukkah. But something about him left her unfulfilled. He always treated her respectfully but with an unspoken air of superiority and entitlement. She did not feel she could confide in him, and their time together never felt relaxed and comfortable. The warmth of familiarity was missing. Her middle-class home looked like a maid's quarters to him. He never verbalized his feelings, but the disdain showed plainly on his face, even with his attempts to hide them. Still, without Dorothy, Lewis passed for companionship.

"Would you like to meet my family? Perhaps you could come for Shabbat dinner this Friday night?" she asked, deciding it would be good for him to meet the rest of the Abendsterns and for them to get to know him.

Lewis glanced over at Leah. He found her exceedingly attractive, and strangely, she stirred his soul like none of the other girls he'd dated. She didn't fawn over him. Somehow, he felt he must continually work to win her affection, and the challenge appealed to him. An only child, Lewis knew that his parents would demand he marry within his own social class. They had pressed that point for as long as he could remember. Neither his father nor mother would approve of Leah. He was sure of that, but his desires made it impossible to walk away from this girl who exuded class and refinement. When he looked at her slender body with the grace of a doe, a passion within him stirred, and his hunger could not be denied.

"That would be very nice. What time is dinner?"

"At sundown—about six o'clock."

"I'll be there."

CHAPTER TEN

"WHAT A RALLY, Detrick! You should have seen them. Goering was there, and Himmler. When Hitler walked up to the podium, the crowd roared. What electricity! You could not help but be caught up in it. In fact, I joined the party."

"Konrad, the Nazi Party is all about hatred. I can't believe that's who you are."

For years, Konrad had secretly loved and hated Detrick. Konrad's admiration and yearning for his friend had sometimes taken the form of the serpent of jealousy. Why, he wondered, had he not been born like Detrick—strong, self-assured, and unafraid? Instead, Konrad was a small boy, almost feminine in his build. Sickly and with bad eyesight, he wore thick glasses that made him look like a fish in a bowl. The girls in school only talked to him in hopes of enticing Detrick. Konrad watched in disgust as they smiled and smoothed their hair, waiting for a glance from Detrick or the grace of his dimpled smile.

With a reputation of strength, which he never flaunted but had often been witnessed by his classmates in defense of the weak, Detrick had earned himself a sort of hero's status. This admiration had never been his intent, and it embarrassed him. Detrick only behaved as he did because he could not tolerate cruelty. It violated something deep within him. And for as dominant a fighter as he could be, Konrad had seen his gentle side, too. Detrick loved animals, and when the boys found a bird with a broken wing, Detrick set it gently and cared for the creature until it could be set free.

Konrad felt hatred and revulsion for weakness, and seeing that quality in others only made him more conscious of it. Instead of understanding the plight of those who shared his handicaps, he would seek to destroy them. If they ceased to exist, he perhaps could kill those qualities within himself and miraculously become someone else. Instead, he grew more pathetic through his attempts at bullying, causing those who would torture him to take notice and revel in his plight.

Konrad's feelings towards Detrick confused and frightened him. Once, he'd had a dream that left him consumed with alarm. He dreamed that he and Detrick lay together in what he considered a sin. As they coupled, Konrad felt loved for the first time in his entire life. When he awoke, he found himself soiled with semen. Immediately, he rose from the bed and vomited. Then he scrubbed his penis with harsh brown laundry soap until it grew raw and sore.

The following night, he stole money from his father's pocket and took off to visit the side of town known for prostitution. It was there that Konrad had his first sexual encounter. It was with a woman, a much older and worn-out female. She'd repulsed him as soon as he'd finished, and he ran from the room, leaving the contents of his pocket on her bed in payment. Outside the tenement building, he heaved until his stomach ached. Then, with tears in his eyes, he returned home.

Quickly, he undressed and scrubbed his skin until it bled, unable to purge himself of an invisible crust of filth that held fast to his body. Once thoroughly exhausted, he sat on the bathtub's edge, his face buried in his hands, and cried.

But the following week, he found himself, once again, in the district of the ladies of the night. He continued this behavior for several months until his father realized money was missing from his pocket. At first, the old man had assumed he'd spent the cash in a drunken stupor, but as he made an effort to be more aware, he realized he had not. Immediately, Konrad's father assumed his son had stolen from him. With anger too fierce for an explanation, he beat Konrad with a belt buckle. After that, Konrad never went back to visit the whores. He also never forgot the beating.

As the two boys continued walking home, Konrad kicked a stone down the cobblestone street and then looked back at his friend. Somehow, he must convince Detrick of what he believes to be right.

"Detrick, it is who you are, too. You are an Aryan! We are the master race! Don't you realize that we will rule the world soon? The Third Reich will last for a thousand years. This is just the beginning of Germany taking her place as the only world power."

"What propaganda you spew! And all of this is on the backs of the Jews, right?"

"Yes, right. Not only Jews but other unacceptable groups must be purged as well if we are to purify our race. Homosexuals, Gypsies… Don't you see that we must do this for future generations?" His face grew blotchy with conviction. He hated homosexuals; the very sight of them brought feelings of nausea.

"You are my best friend, Konrad, but you're making me sick to my stomach. No more talk of Nazis or rallies, understood?" Detrick's eyes narrowed.

A slight fear gripped Konrad. He would not argue with Detrick.

"Maybe sometime in the future, you will join us?"

"It's doubtful."

CHAPTER ELEVEN

LEAH WENT to Michael's bedroom and found Miriam, her mother, seated in a chair beside his bed. Her head bobbed with eyes half open as she set a novel on the night table. As an invalid, Michael's activities were limited to sleeping and eating. Books offered his only escape. Many times, Miriam or Leah would read to him for hours.

Michael, who'd almost fallen asleep, opened his eyes to see Leah enter. Although his body, paralyzed from the waist down, lay limp, his face lit up with a smile for his sister.

"Michael." She leaned down to kiss his forehead.

"Hello, Leah."

"I brought you some sugar cookies."

He reached for the platter and began munching. Miriam caressed Michael's head, fully awake now, never acknowledging her daughter.

"I love cookies, Leah." He giggled as the crumbs fell upon his chest.

"Mother, I have some news."

"Yes?"

"I've been dating Lewis Shapiro. If it is all right, he is coming for Shabbat dinner this Friday night."

"Lewis Shapiro?" She glanced up at Leah with newfound interest. Everyone knew of Dr. Shapiro and his eligible son, Lewis. Miriam could not contain herself. The Shapiros, considered wealthy by most standards, owned the nicest home in the area. Delight tickled Miriam Abendstern.

"Yes, I hope it's not inconvenient. I know you and Michael will be forced to dress up a little."

"No, not at all." Miriam thought that if perhaps Lewis married Leah, she might ask him for enough money to send Michael for treatment. Miriam lived her life consumed with guilt over Michael's accident. Almost every day, she thought of all the things she should have done differently.

It all began on a hiking holiday to the Bavarian Alps. Jacob had recovered a number of old, broken bicycles that had been discarded as worthless, built new ones from the parts, traded them to a travel agent, and surprised Miriam with a train ride to the Alps and two nights at a lodge for the family for a weekend holiday. The family was following a rustic trail up to a lodge, and Michael saw a red squirrel eating a nut on a branch down the slope just off the trail. Miriam was very thirsty and stopped to take a drink, not noticing that Michael was no longer with Karl and Leah. Before anyone knew he was gone, Michael had taken a bad fall from the trail and tumbled to the foot of a large walnut tree. Miriam then realized that Michael was missing and cried out Michael's name. Michael, in a weak voice, cried for his mother.

Jacob heard him and raced down the slope, falling and sliding, until out of breath, he reached his destination. The little boy cried out in pain. Jacob responded immediately, lifting him as if he were weightless. He carried him back down the trail and flagged down a policeman driving by, who rushed them to the closest hospital. Another police car picked up Miriam and the others and followed, arriving a few minutes later. It seemed like hours, but in reality, only forty-five minutes passed before the doctor entered the waiting room. Jacob wrung his hands and chewed the inside of his lip as he waited for the doctor's words.

"I'm sorry. We did all that we could. He severed a nerve in his spine. I am afraid Michael will be paralyzed from the waist down. Now, there are doctors who might be able to help…"

Miriam never heard another word that the doctor had to say— she fainted.

From that day forward, Miriam never left her son's side for more than a short period.

And so she sat beside him as he finished the cookies Leah had brought.

Leah lifted the empty plate.

"I'm glad, Mama, that you don't mind Lewis coming for dinner."

"A Shapiro? Of course, I don't mind. Why, I'll be the envy of every Jewish mother in Berlin!" The light that had so long been dim twinkled in her eyes for just a moment.

CHAPTER TWELVE

WHEN DETRICK SMILED, he illuminated the entire room. And so it was on that Friday afternoon when he arrived at the Abendstern bicycle shop. Jacob, who was in the middle of changing a tire, looked up and imagined he saw a glimmering white light surrounding the boy. It flickered for a second, then disappeared, leaving Jacob wondering if it had been there at all.

"So, you had a good day at school?"

"Yes, I suppose. An old friend of mine has joined the Nazi Party. It disappoints me more than I can say."

"Well, I think maybe lots of people are getting swept up in what they consider the promising future of this Third Reich. With luck, it will pass. Our friends, the Silvers, left Germany. I wonder if we should do the same. It is becoming unsafe for Jews."

"It is, I know. And whenever one of my fellow Germans foolishly takes up this cause, I am personally ashamed."

"*Ach*, Detrick, it's not your fault. You have no control over what the others do." Jacob patted his shoulder. "So listen, on a lighter note, you are coming tonight to do the lights for us, yeah?"

"Yes, and once again, thank you, sir."

"Stop with the 'thank you' and with the 'sirs.' You are like a son to me. So, you're coming for the lights. You should come early and have Shabbat dinner with us. My daughter, Leah, is an extraordinary cook. She makes a cholent that tastes like Heaven." Jacob glanced up from his work to wink at Detrick. "So you're going to come?"

Detrick smiled. "What would I ever do without you? Yes, of course, I will come. When should I be there?"

"At sundown. And by the way, you know what is a cholent?"

"No idea."

"It's like a stew, with potatoes, beef or chicken, sausage, barley, beans, and just a *bissel*, or a touch of goose fat for flavor. Once you taste it, I guarantee you're going to love it."

"If you say so, I believe you."

They laughed as Detrick drew his stool up to the long wooden workbench. He took down his box of tools and began to unscrew an axle. The men sat side by side as the afternoon drifted away. When four-thirty came, Jacob instructed Detrick to go home and get ready. Then he locked the shop and left to prepare for the Shabbat.

CHAPTER THIRTEEN

A WONDERFUL, rich aroma of bread baking filled the room as Jacob opened the door to the Abendstern home. The honey-colored wooden table stood in the center of the dining room. The places set with cream-colored china and crystal had been in the family for centuries.

Jacob kissed Leah. She wore her best black wool dress. It had a sweetheart collar and long sleeves. A thin gold chain with a Star of David hung delicately around her slender neck. The light in the kitchen illuminated her dark hair as she stirred the cholent. A plate of mandel bread, made with chocolate chips and nuts, sat on the counter covered with a white cloth napkin.

"Good Shabbat, Papa."

"Good Shabbat, Sweetheart."

Miriam entered the room. "Jacob, I need you to help me carry Michael to the table. I've set his special chair out."

"Of course, and good Shabbat," Jacob kissed his wife softly.

"Yes, it is a good Shabbat. Has Leah told you?"

"Told me what?" Jacob glanced over at his daughter, who blushed and looked away.

"Just that Lewis Shapiro is coming for dinner tonight. Can you imagine? Lewis Shapiro, interested in our daughter? *Oy!* What *mazel*, what luck."

"I was also going to tell you that Detrick is coming tonight, so set an extra place."

"The boy who works with you at the shop?"

"Yes."

"He's a *goy*, no?"

"He's not Jewish, but he is a wonderful boy and will turn on the lights for us tonight and tomorrow. Now, most importantly, I must talk to Karl. Is he here?"

"No, I don't know where he is."

"I'm afraid he will be insulting to Detrick. You know how he feels about non-Jews."

"Can you blame him, Jacob? They are constantly attacking him. He is fighting all the time."

"Yes, I know, but not tonight."

Miriam straightened her dress. She wore a simple high-collared beige knit with a matching silk scarf and high heels. Even after giving birth to three children, her figure remained slim and girlish. With their body type, mother and daughter appeared more like sisters. The only distinguishing feature was that Miriam's hair had turned almost entirely white since Michael's accident.

Jacob left the ladies to finish the cooking and went in to see Michael. Propped up with pillows, he smiled. His hair had been slicked back with water, and Miriam had dressed him for the evening's festivities.

"Good Shabbat, Father." Michael reached for Jacob's arm and squeezed it, smiling warmly as a bit of drool hung from his lips.

Jacob kissed his son's forehead.

"Good Shabbat, my son. Let me help you into the living room, yes?"

"Yes, I would like that very much. I love to sit with everyone at the table. It's my favorite time."

CHAPTER FOURTEEN

LEWIS ARRIVED WEARING a tailor-made gray pinstriped suit, a stark white shirt, and a black tie covered by a black cashmere overcoat. He brought Miriam a bottle of kosher wine and a bundle of pink roses for Leah. In the winter in Berlin, flowers carried a high price —as much, in fact, as a dinner for an entire family.

As he'd planned, the gesture did not go unnoticed. Miriam gazed at him, clearly impressed. Lewis glanced around the dining room. The house could not stand up to the luxury of the Shapiros' estate or any of the homes of close friends in the crowd Lewis had grown up with. Although he'd walked Leah home and seen the house from the outside, being inside sharpened the class differences between him and Leah in his mind.

"Good Shabbat." He smiled as Leah took the flowers and wine.

"Good Shabbat, Lewis. I am so glad you could come. She took a crystal vase from a cabinet and filled it with water. Thanks so much for the wine and flowers."

"You're quite welcome, my dear." He glanced at her approvingly. There could be no doubt that by any standards, she would be considered a beauty. His eyes took in the tiny waist and heart-shaped face. Her light brown eyes, specked with gold, offset her long, dark hair. Lewis felt the desire rise in him again, so he turned away, trying to settle down before he entered the dining room to meet the rest of the family.

"Papa, this is Lewis Shapiro."

"Good Shabbat, Lewis." Jacob extended his hand.

"Good Shabbat, sir." Lewis shook Jacob's hand.

"This is my mother."

"Good Shabbat." He kissed her hand, and Miriam's eyes looked as though they'd been sprinkled with glitter. She had not felt such an attraction to anyone since she'd first met Jacob. For a split second, she wished she were younger. She looked over at Leah. How wonderful to be young and carefree, to watch your future unfold. Her life had taken a bad turn, and now she could see no way back.

"And over here is my brother, Michael."

"Hello, good Shabbat, Lewis." A small line of drool trickled down the left side of Michael's mouth as he struggled to sit up. He stretched out his hand, wanting to shake hands with Lewis, who pretended not to notice. "I like it that you're here with us. It's so much fun for me to have company."

"Good Shabbat, Michael." Lewis could not help but be repelled as his eyes were drawn to the drool that settled on Michael's chin. He felt himself gag and had to look away, hoping to be seated far from Michael. He did not think he could keep from being sick. Lewis had never told his father about his revulsion for malformed faces and limbs and terrible nausea, and the threat of vomiting he felt when confronted with blood or mucus. Often, he wondered how he would ever get through medical school. And another thing plagued his mind—the boy, Michael, obviously both physically and mentally defective, could be reflective of the Abendstern genetics. If it had been a condition he had from birth, Lewis knew that as soon as his mother saw Michael, she would forbid any talk of a marriage between her son and Leah. So, not only would his mother argue that Leah had no money or class, but she also had a crippled brother who was simple-minded. Lewis speculated on the impossible feat of convincing his family that this delicate girl he longed to bed would make a suitable bride.

A few minutes later, Detrick knocked at the door. Jacob answered, expecting his friend. The outline of Detrick's well-toned physique was silhouetted through his black wool pants and white sweater. The fabric could not hide his broad shoulders and flat stomach, the strongly developed muscles in his arms and legs.

"Detrick, welcome. Good Shabbat, son."

"Good Shabbat, Jacob." Detrick smiled as he shook Jacob's hand, and then Detrick handed him a box of Jacob's favorite chocolate-covered cherries. "I know how much you like these."

"You went to the candy store. Thank you, Detrick."

Detrick's dimpled smile reflected the warmth he felt toward Jacob.

"Come meet my family."

As soon as he entered the living room, Detrick felt himself magnetically drawn to the beautiful young girl with maple-colored eyes. Leah glanced back at him. For a moment, the rest of the room disappeared. The noise of conversations and clattering of dishes were silenced as the two stood transfixed, their eyes locked on one another.

Then, remembering herself, Leah quickly looked away as a soft pink blush swept across her cheeks. Even as Jacob made the introductions, Detrick's eyes never left Leah, and her skin burned with the intensity of his stare.

"Detrick, sit here between my son, Michael, and me." Jacob indicated the chair, and Detrick sat.

"Hello, Michael." He turned to the boy, smiling.

"Nice to meet you, Detrick. My father always says such nice things about you. And it seems they are all true. My father said you are very good to look at, and you are." Michael giggled and reached out his hand to shake Detrick's. Detrick shook his hand heartily, which amused Michael, causing him to laugh aloud.

"And it's good to meet you, too. I'm glad to hear Jacob has pleasant things to say about me." He winked at Jacob and smiled.

When she was sure that Detrick's gaze had shifted to her brother, Leah peeked over at him. She could not help but be impressed by his stunning good looks—his eyes, deep like the ocean, and such an unusual color, a mixture of royal blue and sea green. The chiseled features of his face, high cheekbones, and strong chin, relieved by full, sensuous lips and the dimples when he smiled, made it difficult to look away.

They held dinner for Karl, waiting until nearly seven o'clock, but he did not arrive. So, Miriam lit the candles and began the prayers.

She covered her head with a white shawl, and with her hands, she pulled the smoke from the candles towards her as she closed her eyes.

Silence filled the room, save for the hauntingly beautiful Hebrew Shabbat prayer. The white candle cast a glow upon Leah's skin that made Detrick's heart ache with longing. Halfway through the prayer, the front door opened, and Karl came in, accompanied by a rush of snow.

"Sorry, I'm late. It's snowing." He stomped his boots on the mat by the door.

"And that's an excuse, Karl?" Jacob glared at his son. "Go, hurry. Get ready. You've already missed the prayers. We're having dinner, and we have company tonight."

The interruption disrupted the sanctity of the moment.

Miriam finished the end of the prayer quickly and then sat down. The anger on Jacob's face mirrored her annoyance at Karl's behavior.

She'd aspired to impress Leah's boyfriend, wearing her finest dress and using the best tableware. Now Karl had put a damper on things with his lackadaisical, selfish attitude.

Karl entered and took his seat beside his mother. She turned to him with eyes flashing like lightning bolts, not speaking.

Jacob made quick introductions. Then, to break the uncomfortable silence, Karl turned to Lewis.

"So, do you plan to attend the university?"

"I do, actually. As I am sure you are aware, my father is the head of surgery. I will follow in his footsteps, but first, I think I will take a year off and tour Europe. I've been before with my parents, but that is not quite the same. This time I will be on my own. My family has always stressed the importance of travel. It gives a person a rounded view of the world. I guess it will be my education before my formal education." He smiled, but even as he spoke, Lewis could not help but notice the blatant appreciation in Detrick's eyes as he gazed at Leah. And even worse for him, he caught her looking back.

"So you're a worker at the Abendstern shop, Derrick?" Lewis now turned his full attention to Detrick.

"It's Detrick, and yes, I work for Jacob."

"You aren't Jewish—not with that Nazi blond hair." He laughed and looked around, attempting to rally support amongst the rest of the family. Only Miriam smiled back.

"I guess you are part of that Aryan race they are all talking about," Lewis began again. "Personally, I feel these Nazis of yours have created this superior race as a means of giving the lower class a false sense of supremacy. When, in fact, we all know they are nothing but uneducated thugs. Now, Detrick, are you or are you not one of them?"

"I am not a Nazi, but I am not Jewish, either."

"Come now, Detrick, it is Detrick? All of you are Nazis. You all hate the Jews deep down in your hearts. And if you had the chance, you'd wipe us off the face of the earth. Of course, with my father's money and influence, I needn't be concerned with the likes of you, nor would anyone whom I chose to marry, or their families, for that matter. Jews and Gentiles hold the Shapiro name in the highest esteem alike. After all, even the Nazis need good doctors." He lifted his wineglass, smirking as he sipped.

Detrick's eyes narrowed, and his voice dropped to a low and menacing pitch. "You don't know me. You know nothing about me. You assume that all Gentiles are Nazis the same way they assume all Jews are thieves. So, does that not put you in the same category as the thugs you speak of?" Detrick tilted his head. "Now, because I am here as a guest in Jacob's home, I will not insult you and tell you what I really think of you, but only out of respect for my friend Jacob."

Lewis smirked. "Well said. Clever, aren't you?"

Karl studied them both. He didn't trust Detrick, being a *goy*, one of *them*, but Lewis's pretentious attitude disgusted him. And he had to admit that Detrick had guts. *Had Detrick been a Jew*, Karl thought, *they might have been friends.*

The following morning, when Detrick returned to the Abendstern home to rekindle the lights, he looked around, hoping to catch a glimpse of Leah. Although she hid in her room, she listened as Jacob insisted that Detrick have something to eat before going on his way.

For some reason, that made no earthly sense to her. She longed to see the blond-haired boy again and to revel in the hot desire that burned through her from the light in his eyes. The power she held over him intoxicated her. However, she knew encouraging any attention from Detrick would only mean trouble. He, being a Gentile, and she a Jew, would leave them both open to vicious gossip, followed by dangerous disapproval from the Nazi government. The less they saw each other, the better, she decided. So, she tried to focus her attention on Lewis, obviously a better choice. Wasn't he?

But when she heard the front door slam—an indication that Detrick had gone—she moved the curtain beside her bed just a fraction of an inch. Her heart beat faster as she watched the black bicycle and the golden hair as they disappeared down the road.

CHAPTER FIFTEEN

LATE ONE NIGHT in the early summer of 1934, Hitler, accompanied by his two closest friends, Goering and Himmler, carried out a treasonous plan. They murdered all the opposing leadership within their political party. This sinister event would go down in history as the Night of the Long Knives.

At the beginning of August of the same year, President Von Hindenburg of Germany died.

Hitler became the Führer.

By the end of August, Adolf Hitler had received a ninety percent vote of approval from the German people.

When Leah returned from school, she saw an envelope with familiar handwriting on the table nearest the door. The strangely colored postage stamps read 'United States of America.' As she tore the seal and opened the letter, she retired to the privacy of her room. Holding the paper in her hand, the loss she'd felt at Dorothy's leaving crept over her again, and she felt suddenly morose and lonely. Her hand caressed the pink lace bedspread as she sat down, and her mind drifted back to when she and Dorothy were children sitting in the same place. Dorothy's auburn curls had floated about her head as she chatted excitedly. Leah remembered how they had discussed their dreams for the future and how far those hopes had been from the reality they now faced. Their world had been altered forever. She unfolded the letter and read.

Dear Leah,

I miss you so much. It was a terrible boat ride. (The seas tossed us around violently, and I vomited until I thought my insides would come up.) Early one morning, I awoke as we sailed into the New York harbor. The fog of the harbor acted as a shroud, and when it lifted, the Statue of Liberty was revealed as if some grand magician had pulled back his cape as our ship made its way toward land. I thought my lungs would burst in awe from the majestic sight. It seemed as if everyone around me felt the same. I looked at the others, and their faces appeared so hopeful. This is the land of dreams, I guess. Although to be quite honest with you, my dear friend, my prayers are to return home to Germany, to you, and to everything I know so well. Sometimes, late at night, when everyone is asleep, my heart aches with the yearning to be at your side, to laugh and talk as we once took for granted we would do forever.

We took a train from New York to Chicago, where my uncle and his family live.

My father's brother, my aunt, and my cousin have been as accommo-dating as anyone could ask. But the four small rooms they share are even more cramped now that we are here. I miss our home and my mother's flower garden and our lovely furniture. I guess you could say that, here in America, we are amongst the poorer class.

There is a strange smell that I have been told is the smell of blood coming from the stockyards. It lingers in the air, but when the weather is hot, it is most nauseating. At first, the odor upset my stomach, and I could not eat. But I am starting to get used to it, and unless the wind blows up from the south, right in our direction, I don't smell it at all. My family does not purchase our beef from the stockyards. It is not kosher. We have a kosher butcher right here on the west side where we shop. It is only a few blocks from the apartment.

My uncle sells fruit and vegetables at the market, so we get all the semi-spoiled goods for free, but hard as he tried, my uncle could not find a position for my father to work with him. Fortunately, his friend, who owns a store that sells winter coats on Maxwell Street, had an opening, and my father took the job. He will keep the books for the owner, as well as selling. It is odd to hear how my papa has learned to negotiate with customers. This is so out of character for him. The pay is not very good—nothing like what he earned at home, but at least he is working. One afternoon, my mother and I took the L train to Maxwell Street to visit my father. The train goes up on a track above the city, and it feels like it will fall straight down upon the apartment buildings. Then it dives into a tunnel under the sidewalk, which is dark and lit by artificial lighting. The L roars loudly through the underground and shakes wildly as it does. What an experience, Leah! I had to bite my lip to keep from screaming.

Since we could not read English, my mother and I had to count the stops to be sure we got off at the right one. Finally, we walked several blocks as my father had told us to, and we were there. What a place! People on the street continually approach boldly, selling fake diamonds and phony watches. A man grabbed my arm and tried to pull me into an alley to sell me something. My mother started screaming, and he took off running. It is not a safe place for a woman alone, and I don't think we will go back again anytime soon. Papa and his brother leave very early in the morning and return late at night. The days are long, and the work is hard.

My relatives, like my parents, have only one child, my cousin, Hette. She is nineteen and beautiful. Can you believe she wears red lipstick and silk stockings? One day when she left for work, I tried her lipstick! It made me feel so glamorous, like an American movie star! Then I sang to myself in the bathroom mirror, wearing the lipstick, and wished you were here. I know how much it would have made you laugh.

Last week I started high school. The language is difficult for me to grasp, and reading and writing it is even worse. It is so different from German or Yiddish. So, I am stumbling through my classes, not doing so well right now.

My cousin promises to help me with my English, but she works so much I cannot imagine when she will find the time.

I miss singing with you at the piano. We had some good times, didn't we?

Please write to me soon. I am dying to hear from you. Let me know how things are going with Lewis. I don't have a boyfriend yet, and if I don't learn this language, I might never find one! And alas, I will be an old maid.

Goodbye, for now, my dear friend.

Love to you,
Dorothy

Leah refolded the letter, put it back in the envelope, wiped a tear from her eye, and laid it beneath her pillow. Then she got up and went to help her mother with Michael before preparing the evening meal.

CHAPTER SIXTEEN

WALKING around the school with Lewis beside her, Leah couldn't help but notice the envy on the faces of her female classmates. Handsome and poised, Lewis exuded an air of confidence. Unlike any other boys his age, he had an automobile that his father had given him for Hanukkah. After school the following day, he'd taken Leah for a ride. She felt uncomfortable when they drove by the front stairs of the school, where all of their friends congregated. It made her cringe when everyone turned to stare. Lewis enjoyed showing off and made a point of honking and waving. The vehicle's motion made her ill, so the following day, she told Lewis that she still preferred to walk after sitting in class all afternoon. Although disappointed, he joined her just to be in her company.

As they passed the main street in town, Lewis suggested they share a soda, and Leah agreed. He held the door as they entered the candy store. The decadent aroma of fudge filled the air. A group of students from the Gentile school on the other side of the city sat at the counter, staring in disgust, when they noticed Lewis was wearing a yarmulke.

Lewis tried to ignore them as he led Leah to a table and pulled out her chair. She sat and noticed that Lewis's hand trembled. His face had turned crimson as he took his seat beside Leah. From across the room, the boys taunted him.

"I smell pig, Ralph. Do you smell it?"

"I smell the stink of Jew pig."

The girls at the table laughed as one of the boys stood up. Putting his fingers behind his ears, he made loud oinking sounds.

Lewis felt shame at his fear and hoped Leah did not detect it. He looked away, avoiding her eyes. His weakness disgusted him. His voice was high-pitched and cracked when he spoke, so he grew silent. His usual self-assurance had been shattered. It bothered him. But knowing if he'd been challenged, he would have backed down bothered him even more.

After they had left, Lewis and Leah walked silently for several blocks. When he felt sure that they had gone far enough away from the Gentile group, his confidence returned.

"If you hadn't been with me, I would have beaten the daylights out of those creeps." Lewis pushed his chest out.

"Yes, I'm sure you would have."

"I didn't want you to get upset, so I restrained myself."

Leah just smiled, relieved to be far away from the dangerous situation.

Lewis and Leah continued to see each other throughout the school year. For the first time, she found herself searching for reasons to show up at her father's shop. She brought him cookies that she'd baked or an umbrella when it rained. Until the night she met Detrick, Leah had rarely gone to the shop.

Jacob took notice.

Whenever Leah came by, Jacob saw Detrick peek over at her from across the room. Although Detrick never spoke to Leah except to say hello, the attraction between the two lingered in the air, so thick that it covered them all like a blanket.

Detrick narrowly avoided forced public service when the *Reichsarbeitsdienst* or Reich Labor Service Act was enacted in 1935, conscripting all German males between 18-25 years old to either plant forests or dig ditches on farms. His coach wrote a letter and got an exemption for Detrick because he was training for the Olympics.

One Friday evening, when Detrick arrived at the Abendstern home to extinguish the lights, he saw Lewis sitting beside Leah at the piano in the living room. Her face lit up as if a candle flickered softly behind her eyes. With slender fingers, she moved about the keys, filling the room with glorious music.

"Your *Shabbat goy* is here. I guess it's time for lights out and me to go." Leah stopped playing when Lewis interrupted.

"Goodnight then, Lewis." She spoke to Lewis, but her eyes fixed on Detrick. His golden-blond hair had fallen over his forehead. Returning her intent look, he pushed the locks from his face. Detrick tried to look away, but he could not control his desire. He was bound as if by an imaginary rope winding itself tenderly around his soul.

Watching Lewis sitting so close to Leah that his thigh brushed against hers made Detrick miserable. His heart broke. He knew that he could never be with her because of the difference in their faiths. Religion meant nothing to him. Detrick had never been convinced of the anti-Semitic propaganda and would gladly fight anyone who challenged him. The problem, in his mind, was with Jacob. The man had been too good to Detrick for Detrick to risk hurting him. There was no doubt in his mind that Jacob cared for him, but the challenges a mixed couple would face might be more than the older man could endure. Not to mention the laws put into effect severely forbidding such behavior. A marriage between a Jew and a Gentile was now considered a criminal offense by the Nazi decree.

Detrick speculated whether Jacob wanted Leah and Lewis to marry. Lewis Shapiro. Detrick considered him for a moment. He was a Jew from a family of wealth and stature in the community. It seemed to Detrick he was everything Jacob would want in a son-in-law. Nothing would give Detrick more joy than to see Jacob happy. Detrick knew he should forget her, forget this crazy fascination. And yet, even knowing all the obstacles, Detrick could not avert his eyes from the lovely face that silently called out to him, haunting his sleepless nights.

On September 15, 1935, the Nuremberg Race Laws pertaining to the Jews came into being. Now, all Germans of Jewish descent lost their rights as citizens. Later, they would lose their rights as human beings. Aryan women could no longer be employed as household help by Jewish families. And the law clearly stated that marriage or sexual relations between a Jew and an Aryan were strictly forbidden and constituted a criminal act.

CHAPTER SEVENTEEN

DETRICK CONTINUED his training in track and field in hopes of being chosen for the Olympic Games that would take place in 1936. His coach encouraged him but did not feel he would reach his full potential until the next Olympics in 1940. It had come as a disappointment at first, but rather than quitting, Detrick worked harder. Because of the Nuremberg laws, Jacob could no longer enter the park to watch Detrick practice, so he stood outside the gate to offer support.

When Detrick saw his friend standing outside the metal bars, he felt a mix of emotions. It warmed him to know Jacob cared enough to support him in his efforts. But seeing Jacob denied entrance to the park filled him with anger and discomfort. No one from Detrick's biological family felt it was important enough to find the time to watch him practice. He believed Inga would have come had she not been burdened by the heavy workload she carried. Helga had developed a fascination with the SS (The *Schutzstaffel*, "The Protection Squadron"). The uniforms they wore and the way they walked through the streets exuding power held her captive to the idea of a lifestyle she saw as one of excitement and glamor. She'd become distant as she fell deeper into her dream of a different life.

Hans, on the other hand, would not have come regardless of time. In fact, Hans usually had free time in the evening when Detrick practiced. But his resentment towards his son had grown into an ugly hatred that separated father and son like an iron gate. Instead of facing his feelings of inadequacy, Hans poured another shot of whiskey.

But since that fateful day when Detrick had met Jacob, his need for a father had been fulfilled.

Once, in Detrick's youth, Jacob had taken him to a live play as a gift for his birthday. The two shared a special camaraderie as their laughter filled the auditorium. Detrick had never forgotten that night. The memories remained branded upon his heart. And Detrick believed that because of his surrogate father, he grew to be a better man. Now Jacob, by order of the law, could no longer attend the theater.

CHAPTER EIGHTEEN

IN FEBRUARY 1936, the German Gestapo was declared above the law! Outward persecution of homosexuals and others considered *undesirables*, as well as the Jews, began to be commonplace around Germany. The more the harrying continued, the more it became accepted as normal behavior amongst many of the population. And so, the violence that took place right in the streets became an everyday activity. Some were afraid to stand up, and others just stopped paying attention. But, amongst all this danger and turmoil, a few unsung heroes remained.

Lewis finally invited Leah to his home to meet his family. The power behind his desire for her had forced him to seek acceptance from his family. If he could only reach them, he could propose, and Leah would be his.

His mother planned to host a party in celebration of the opening of a new wing of the hospital. It took courage on Lewis's part to arrive with Leah as his guest. The potential of this bold action to bring great disfavor and consequences that could prove to be grave weighed heavily on his mind. Lewis's failed sexual advances toward Leah infuriated him, and his desires grew more obsessive each day. Because of this, he came to the conclusion that he must marry her. So, since his parents would be busy with their guests, he felt they would have little time to question Leah's background, making this the perfect time for an introduction. Later, after they must have recognized her loveliness and refinement, he was optimistic that they might be willing to look beyond her humble station.

After Lewis had invited her and she agreed to attend, Leah rushed home to decide what she would wear.

She searched her closet frantically. A frown came to her face as she studied her wardrobe. It clearly consisted of nothing suitable for a ball. In agony, she asked Jacob what to do. He suggested that she go into town and buy something new. His funds had decreased greatly since he'd been forced to stop serving Aryan clients, but he knew how to deal with Mrs. Lichtenbaum. Jacob had found an old grandfather clock case with no works that needed refinishing. He traded for the needed works and restored the old walnut case, making it a beautiful thing to behold. Mrs. Lichtenbaum had seen it and told him to call her if he ever wanted to sell it.

"Just go see Mrs. Lichtenbaum. She will take care of everything."

"Are you sure, Papa? I know how hard money is to come by right now."

"Of course, I am sure, my princess. What is money for if not for your family? So let me see that beautiful smile...eh? I will arrange everything, and you can stop after school tomorrow."

"Thank you, Papa," she said and gave him a hug.

Jacob stopped by Mrs. Lichtenbaum's dress shop on the way to work, and they concluded their deal.

The next day after school, a cold wind blew across the road, and a gust of snow whipped across her legs. Leah pulled her scarf tighter as she strode towards the ladies' garment shop. She hated to spend her father's hard-earned wages. Still, she could not attend such a fancy gala without something appropriate.

As Leah passed the bakery, she glanced across the street. A warm flush crept over her cheeks when she saw Detrick walking in the other direction. Accompanied by a short, slender man with thick

CHAPTER EIGHTEEN | 67

glasses, Detrick strolled slowly along the cobblestone sidewalk. Leah tried but could not force herself to look away before her eyes met Detrick's. The powerful magnetism of their attraction caused her knees to give way. She stood still, unable to move, mesmerized for a moment, and then began to tread quickly away, turning her head towards the store windows. Detrick's penetrating, endless blue eyes shook something deep within her like an internal earthquake, making her unsteady on her feet. A hot torrent of energy tore through her, and she no longer felt the cold.

What is this that I am doing? Thoughts and questions came rushing through Leah's mind. *It would be foolish to end things with Lewis, and it would be sheer madness to explore these wild feelings I have for Detrick because the law would forbid it. This entire situation is perilous. I must force it from my mind.* She realized all this, but try as she might, those blue eyes burned, imprinting her soul.

Across the road, Detrick and Konrad continued toward home, Konrad talking all the while.

"I am doing well with the party, Detrick. You should consider joining. Once we purge the world of Jews, homosexuals, gypsies, and other racial impurities, the Aryans like us will take our rightful place." Konrad's scarf had been blown away from his throat by a gust of icy wind. With a single twist, he re-wrapped the brown wool muffler his grandmother had knitted for him and then continued speaking.

Detrick did not hear him. Once his eyes caught sight of Leah, they could not be diverted from the vision that had captivated him across the street. His ears went deaf to Konrad's ramblings. Her soft features imprisoned him as his heart raced like a runaway train. His knees felt weak as he looked at her ivory skin, the color of blush roses from the cold.

"Detrick, you're not listening to me."

"What? I'm sorry, Konrad, what is it?" Detrick's tone bore his annoyance at being disturbed by Konrad's incessant chatter.

"I am trying to tell you that you should become a part of the new Germany. We are now in power."

"Konrad, I'm not interested in this nonsense. I don't know why you refuse to understand."

"I don't understand because Hitler has made it so that you, a true Aryan, can excel beyond your wildest dreams. You, my friend, can have all the things the Jews had. All of their money, their homes, and their businesses. They rightfully belong to you anyway because it is your birthright as an Aryan."

"Please stop already. It is not your right to take anything that doesn't belong to you."

"But it does. It belongs to us, all Aryans—people like you and me. That's what you don't seem to comprehend. All the natural resources of this country belong to us, the Aryans. They have stolen them. Now don't tell me you are still friends with that man you used to work for. Or are you still working for him? It is against the law for you to be employed by a Jew."

Since the passing of the Nuremberg laws, Detrick and Jacob had collaborated to keep his employment at the shop a secret. He had to slip in the back door, work in the back room and slip out the back when he left.

"No, I am not working there anymore. I've been spending most of my time trying to train for the Olympics."

"That's good. You will make Hitler proud."

Detrick looked away in disgust.

CHAPTER NINETEEN

"THAT DRESS IS STUNNING ON YOU." The meticulously groomed woman, well past her prime, smiled as she studied Leah in a deep-burgundy satin gown.

"You don't think it's too much. I mean, the color is so vivid." Leah frowned at her reflection.

"Do you want to look washed out? No, of course not. You want to stand out. *Oy*, your mother must be so proud her daughter was invited to the home of the Shapiros. Do you think maybe marriage is in your future?"

"I don't know, Mrs. Lichtenbaum. I realize he is quite the catch. Everyone has told me so, but somehow, I just don't feel the magic... you know?"

"Magic? Who needs magic? You've got a Shapiro, the son of a surgeon. And someday, he'll take over his father's practice, and you... Well, you'll be set for life." Mrs. Lichtenbaum adjusted a bobby pin in her neat gray bun.

"I suppose so. I mean, it would be good for my family. And he is a nice fellow, even if all he does is talk about himself constantly."

"So what should he talk about? That's the way men are. Don't fret. Just be your pretty little self, Leah."

Leah had known Esther Lichtenbaum as far back as she could remember, being a member of the same synagogue. Her father had traded things with Esther over the years to get dresses for his ladies.

Once, when the Lichtenbaums had an emergency, and there was no one to babysit for Esther's granddaughter, Leah offered her services as a favor so the family could attend a funeral.

"I don't know, Mrs. Lichtenbaum. I thought something in a midnight blue might stand out less."

"I don't know why a girl as pretty as you should want to hide in the corner, but… Very well. If you would be more comfortable, then let me show you what I have."

Leah settled on an indigo satin gown. With a sweetheart neckline and a straight skirt, it hugged her slender figure to perfection.

"Well, my dear. I must admit you're right. This is quite a sophisticated dress. I like how it looks on you."

"Are you sure?"

"I am."

"Me, too." Leah smiled, hugged the older woman, and went back to change into her own clothes.

CHAPTER TWENTY

DISAPPOINTED that he had not been chosen for the upcoming Olympics, Detrick resolved to put forth an even stronger effort. He practiced running track outside at the park daily, regardless of the cold. On the afternoons he worked, he stopped afterward to dash around the track a few times to keep up his momentum. Neither darkness nor weather would deter him. He'd failed to make it to the Olympics, which would begin in August. The others he'd been training with who had also been rejected had quit. But he charged forward with firm determination to compete in the next set of games that would take place in 1940. The exemption of government service his coach got him served to allow Detrick to work secretly for Jacob.

As Detrick finished working on replacing a bicycle tire one winter night, he decided to walk by the park on his way home and run a few laps. Detrick did not tell Jacob that he planned to train that evening. If the old man knew, he would have insisted he leave with enough time to finish before nightfall. Too often, the man had paid him for a full day and insisted that he stop work early so he could meet with his coach. Detrick knew how much Jacob cared for him and made a special effort not to take advantage of their shared affection.

The sunset made the frigid winds even more penetrating as Detrick ran, his breath turning white in the winter air. Common sense told him that he must stop soon, for darkness covered the park, and he could scarcely see his way. Just another half hour, he promised himself. But that turned into another hour and then two. So many others on his team had suffered the same rejection and no longer practiced. They'd given up, but Detrick would not quit. He harnessed all his inner strength, surpassing this failure, to become an even finer athlete.

Stopping for a moment, he rubbed his gloved hands together to warm them. He bent at the waist and stretched. Then, after taking a few deep breaths, he began to run again.

CHAPTER TWENTY-ONE

WHEN LEAH CAME out of her room, Lewis saw her, and it took his breath away. Stunned by her beauty, he could only stare with his mouth slightly open. She smiled at him and decided he appeared handsome in his black tuxedo. Jacob had just arrived home from work, and he watched his daughter in awe as the couple entered Lewis's automobile. *Perhaps the two will marry,* he thought. *It would be good for Leah. After all, Lewis had plenty of money.* However, Jacob's keen sense detected that something was missing in his daughter's eyes. If Leah married Lewis, would she be happy? Did she love him? Jacob sighed, unsure of the answer, as he watched the car turn the corner.

To reach the ballroom in the Shapiro home, Lewis led Leah up a winding staircase. When she entered, she stopped for a moment, allowing her gaze to fall upon the room, taking in the splendor. Never had she seen such opulence. The white marble floor was veined with silver gray. The entire room was lit by expensive crystal chandeliers and boasted a dance area the size of her entire house. Tables to accommodate one hundred guests had been set, surrounding a ten-piece orchestra of men and women all wearing black. Music played as white-gloved waiters passed hors d'oeuvres.

And the guests, magnificent in their exquisite attire, waltzed with the ease of those who attended these formal parties regularly.

Upon seeing her adored son enter the room, Mrs. Shapiro rushed to greet him. A brilliant but counterfeit smile plastered on her face contrasted the scrutinizing disapproval her eyes betrayed as she studied Leah.

"Good evening, Mother. This is Leah Abendstern."

"Good evening, Mrs. Shapiro. I am so honored to be invited to attend your party."

"Indeed. Well... Very well, then... Lewis, why don't you take your friend and get her something to drink?"

Lewis nodded. He knew his mother well enough to detect the true feelings that lay just beneath the surface of her demeanor, and they only formalized what he'd expected all along. She would not easily grant Leah entrance into their world. He'd orchestrated this meeting in feeble hopes of an unexpected outcome, but she'd responded as he'd feared she would. If only he had someone to go to who would understand, but his father brought nothing to the equation. Too busy with his professional life, his wife steered the family's social ship, and he gladly trailed along.

As Leah danced gracefully in his arms, Lewis came to a decision. This affair with Leah must end. Lewis had wasted far too much time not to seize the prize he'd worked so hard for. Tonight, following the celebration, he planned to bed her.

He smiled as he looked down at her brown hair, with its golden highlights sparkling in the light of the chandelier. The music stopped, and the couple finished dancing.

Lewis squeezed her just slightly. "I think they are calling us to dinner."

Pushing away gently, she held his hand, and they took their places at the table.

The dinner could not have been more scrumptious. The festivities, fine-tuned by Mrs. Shapiro's experienced hand, went off without a hitch.

Following an evening of grace and finery fit for a princess in a fairy tale, Lewis escorted Leah back to his automobile.

Although it felt much later, Lewis's watch read nine o'clock. He did not need to return Leah to her home until eleven. This gave him plenty of time.

On a side road, Lewis found a dark, deserted area where he parked the auto and turned it off. He reached for Leah and kissed her. She put her arms around him as one of his hands reached beneath her coat in search of her breast, and the other slithered up her thigh.

"Lewis, no. Please. I'm not ready."

"And when do you think you might be ready? We've been dating for a long time, and you've always stopped me. Not tonight, sweetheart. It's time we took the next step."

His hand slid into her panties. She moved away quickly. He caught her with his other arm and pulled her back so roughly that she felt her neck snap.

"I said no, Lewis!" Although she tried to sound strong and firm, her voice cracked with indignation as she fought to hide the tears that threatened to betray her weakness.

"Who the hell do you think you are? You are more than lucky to be seeing someone like me. I think you need to be reminded that you are nothing—a nobody—just a girl with a pretty face. No class, no background. There are millions like you who would be more than willing to solidify a relationship with a fellow like me."

"Date them, then. I will not allow you to talk to me in this manner, Lewis."

"And what do you think you can do about it?" He grasped her slender shoulder and tried pulling her toward him again. With all the strength she could muster, she shook herself free.

"Leave now, he hissed. Get out of my car!"

And she did. The car door squeaked open. Without looking back, Leah stepped out into the darkness. The freezing air slapped her face. Her heart sank as she looked down at her high-heeled shoes. Walking home would be difficult, but she could not, would not, get back into that car. She began to march towards home, trying not to slip on the icy patches, while Lewis, filled with fury, sped away.

Her anger gave her strength. Her floor-length dress now felt cumbersome as she fought the slippery, snow-covered walkways. Spots of ice lay hiding beneath the white powder. She slid, and catching herself, Leah looked around her. The arctic wind rushed across the landscape, catching her hair and slapping it back across her face. A shiver ran down her spine as she realized how difficult it would be for her to get home on foot. Gusts of snow began to fall from the dark, starlit sky. With Lewis's car nowhere to be seen, save for a few streetlights, the dark night enveloped her like a shroud. Leah felt completely alone, vulnerable, and lost. Fear now obliterated her rage, and she bit her lip as tears froze on her eyelashes.

Some of the homes she passed had dim lights shining safely within. Leah longed to be in her house with her family beside her instead of alone and abandoned on this unfamiliar street.

After walking a little further, the neighborhood park came into view. She felt some relief as she recognized the area. Only a few lights remained over the playground. The rest of the park lay covered in blackness, spreading out into an ominously empty and deserted area. The desolation around her touched a nerve, and she hurried to turn the corner. A soft voice whispered in her mind, "Hurry, Leah, it's not safe here." Her heart began to race. Sweat formed in her armpits. Now, there were no more houses, only open fields. She walked faster, and her heel hit a patch of ice. Stumbling and tripping, she fell. Fortunately, she'd fallen on a grassy surface. Nausea played havoc with her stomach as it accompanied the thumping of her heart in her eardrums. Something felt wrong.

Terror gripped her.

Then, as a shiver ran its fingers across her shoulder blades, she saw them, a group of three men in their early twenties. Their voices echoed through the eerie, quiet streets as they sang the popular tune "When Jewish Blood Spurts from My Knife." A thin line of smoke followed the cigarette one of the men puffed while the others passed a bottle wrapped in brown paper.

Then they noticed Leah. One of them let out a catcall while the others laughed. It became clear to her that they'd been drinking for a while and were now quite drunk. The one who'd made the vulgar sounds eyed her approvingly as if she would make a sumptuous meal. He nodded and motioned toward the other two, who followed behind him.

"Good evening, *Fräulein*. What are you doing alone in the dark and all dressed for a party?" Clearly, he was the person in charge. He smiled. His eyes, glazed over with drink, glittered at her. Then he grinned back at his friends, who offered support.

"She's a pretty one, isn't she?" he asked the other two.

"Yes, Reinhart, she's pleasing to the eye."

"We shall have some fun tonight, I think."

The others followed Reinhart's lead as they circled her. Leah's heart beat furiously, and despite the cold, sweat trickled down her face. With confidence she did not feel, she pushed the smallest of the bunch out of her way and tried to elbow through. Reinhart grabbed her arm and spun her around. She lost her balance as her ankle twisted. As she tumbled over, Leah heard her dress get torn. Then her palm scraped as it hit the cobblestone walk.

"Please," she begged, knowing even as she did that they enjoyed her fear.

Like predators who had conquered their prey, the boys fell upon her. One ripped the slit of her gown to her waist. Another tore the buttons off of her coat as he forced it open. With both hands, Leah tried to pull her coat closed. Angered by her resistance, Reinhart slapped her across the face. The sting of the slap caught her unaware. Instantly, she let go to reach up and grab her cheek. As she did, the smallest of the boys tore the bodice of her dress open. He smiled, licking his lips as he revealed her modest white bra. Then Reinhart pulled until the hooks at the back gave way. Shame now mingled with her terror. Leah had never been naked in the presence of a man. The tears poured out of her control as she fought to free herself, but this small girl proved no match for three strong men. At first, they found her struggle amusing. But as she continued, Reinhart became annoyed.

"Kill her when we're done. We don't need her going to the police," Reinhart ordered the two thugs, who he knew would honor his wishes.

"Police, you are not serious. Look." One of the men tore the Star of David from her neck. "She's a Jew. We can do as we please with her, and if she keeps giving us trouble, I will kill her—unless, of course, you want to kill her for the thrill of it."

"No, Helmut. Not yet. First, let's have some fun. Both of you, hold her down, pull her legs apart and make sure she doesn't move," Reinhart said.

Fat and sweating, Reinhart took Leah's coat and, using it to shelter his knees from the harsh stone walk, knelt above her. Leah fought, twisting against the force of the men, to no avail. With a single motion, Reinhart unzipped his pants and pulled out his hard member. Leah felt she might vomit as she smelled the alcohol mingled with his perspiration. She grew frantic and fought with her entire being, to no avail, and the grip of the others became even tighter. Until now, she dared not scream. Being a Jew, if she were to alert anyone, she would surely be blamed for what was taking place, and worse would fall upon her and her family. However, lying in the snow, held down, and about to be raped, she could no longer contain herself. A cry of fear escaped her lips and then another even louder. She shook her head from side to side. The rest of her body remained captive in their grasp. Reinhart took a pocketknife from his pants and cut her panties. The shrieks of terror consumed her as they filled the street.

"Shut this fucking bitch up! Stick something in her mouth," Reinhart commanded.

But neither of the men could silence Leah. Her head moved too quickly for them to gag her.

Leah clenched her fists, bracing herself for the pain. Soon, this disgusting pig would invade her body. Vomit rose in her throat. She turned her head away, unable to bear the sight of him. But she could not close her eyes. Then, there—across the street—she saw him, the familiar broad shoulders. At first, she feared she might be imagining it and thought that is what happens when one is dying. Then he was illuminated by the streetlight, the golden hair falling over his left eye. She gasped, panting, her breath ragged. She must draw his attention. As loud as she could, she let out a final shriek.

From where he stood, Detrick could not determine the goings-on. The sound of a tortured animal reached him. He did not see the girl, only the group of men.

Crossing the street, he approached to investigate further.

To his horror and disbelief, his eyes beheld his beloved Leah. Filled with the fury of a hundred men, he ran toward the attackers. On the side of the walkway, he saw a large tree branch. It would make an effective weapon. Wielding it, he hit the leader firmly in the stomach. With the wind knocked out of him, he toppled over like one of the fat punching dolls they sold at the children's store. With his pants down around his knees and his limp penis hanging unsatisfied, Reinhart rolled over, still in too much pain to stand up. When the confrontation turned violent, the others of his gang fled, leaving him to fend for himself. For a moment, Detrick considered going after them. He would have liked to make them pay. Instead, he turned to help Leah.

Ignoring the chill, Detrick removed his coat and covered her. Then, he turned to the culprit, who lay on the ground in shock, still trying to catch his breath.

"Get out of here before I kill you."

The man did not hesitate. His eyes grew wide. Stumbling, he got up. Then, as quickly as he could, he scampered away, trying to pull his pants back up.

Detrick turned his full attention to Leah.

"Are you all right?" Detrick took his hand and gently smoothed the hair away from her face.

"I think so." She clutched his coat where it covered her naked-ness. "I'm so glad you were here."

"So am I. Here, can I help you get up?" Detrick looked at Leah's coat. It lay smashed in slush where Reinhart had used it. She could never clean the dirt from the material. It was best to leave it where it lay.

She nodded, and he lifted her to her feet. Then he put his arm around her back and under her arms to offer support as he helped her home. Leaning her head on his shoulder, she inhaled the scent of peppermint. From this day forward, that fragrance would remind her of Detrick.

When they arrived at Leah's home, he escorted her in.

"Goodnight." He could not meet her eyes, afraid she might see how emotional he was.

"Please give me a moment. I would like you to have a cup of tea or hot chocolate to warm up. I didn't realize it, but I guess I used your coat all the way home. You must be freezing." Leah handed Detrick his coat.

"No, not really. I'm all right, but I would love a cup of tea."

"Sit, please. It's the least I can do." She smiled at him. "I'll be right back."

He nodded as he sat on the couch.

When she returned, she had washed her face and changed into a simple day dress. Even with the bruising that had begun on her cheek, he still found himself in awe of her beauty.

Detrick stood as she walked in, placing the cup of tea on the coffee table. He towered over Leah by a foot. Gently, he reached down and touched her cheek with his thumb. "Does it hurt?"

Leah allowed her eyes to drift up to him. "Yes."

The tenderness she felt towards him came rushing upon her unexpectedly.

"I'm sorry. I wish I could take the pain for you." He looked down at her, his heart beating like a tribal drum hammering out a tale of love.

"I can never express how grateful I am that you were there tonight. They would have killed me." Tears filled her eyes, and they glistened in the soft light of the lamp.

"Shhhh. You're safe now." He wrapped her in his arms, burying his face in her hair. "And if you allow me to, I will keep you safe forever." His voice came out hoarse. Detrick found himself shocked by his boldness. He could not tell her—must not tell her, lest he scare her away. But he knew at that moment, beyond a doubt, that he loved her.

She did not back away as he feared she might. Instead, she continued to look up at him, her lips slightly parted. A bolt of magical energy shot through them as their eyes held fast. Then his hand found its way behind her head. Tenderly, he caressed her hair and gently pulled her towards him. In awe and disbelief, Detrick thanked God that he held this jewel in his arms. Their lips met, and all the yearning they'd fought against for so long overtook them. Passion sped through their blood like a fast and wild wind. One kiss and then another, magical and sweet.

In the heavens, a symphony began to play as the angels smiled down at the lovers.

CHAPTER TWENTY-TWO

DETRICK CARRIED guilt like a boulder in his heart that weighed him down. He believed he betrayed Jacob each time he kissed Leah, but the love he felt for her consumed him. Nothing else brought him joy. No longer did his Olympic training fill his life. It had lost its importance. Only Leah mattered—her smile, her eyes—the look that came over her face right before he kissed her.

At first, the couple, blinded by love, took risks being seen together in public. It was hard for them to believe such hatred could exist in a world where the two had found such beauty and light. They rode bikes through the streets and into the park. Walking together holding hands, they visited the zoo in the Tiergarten, marveling at the lush trees and landscape surrounding them. Leah and Detrick ate in outdoor cafés, oblivious to the angry gazes that greeted them.

Detrick knew that he must talk to Jacob. Leah had completely separated from Lewis, and the disappointment that might have brought to Jacob worried Detrick. Since Leah had chosen to keep the night of her rescue by Detrick and all that had occurred a secret, her parents never knew what caused Leah to sever her relationship with Lewis. They were unaware of how he'd left her to walk home alone. In their eyes, Detrick believed Lewis would have been a perfect son-in-law. And here, Detrick, with nothing to offer, must tell Jacob that he loved Leah. He despised the thought of jeopardizing the friendship, but even worse, he could not bear to hurt his dear friend.

Detrick stood at the counter in the candy store. He planned to bring Jacob's favorites to the shop that night. It was a silly gesture but one that made him feel better.

After the box had been wrapped with a red ribbon, Detrick paid the woman and left.

A half a block down, Detrick saw Karl leaning against the building, smoking a cigarette. Until now, they had never conversed, but Detrick planned to offer his friendship.

"Hello, Karl."

"Stay away from my sister."

So Karl knew what had transpired between him and Leah. Detrick wondered if Jacob knew as well.

"Karl, I love Leah."

"I'm warning you, you fucking Nazi *goy*."

"Karl..." But before he could say another word, Karl sent a right punch into his face. Detrick's lip and nose spurted blood that fell upon the white box. But he would not raise his hands to hit Karl.

"Hit me... Go ahead! Go ahead, so I can beat the shit out of you."

"Karl... this is not what I want. I am not a Nazi. I love your sister. Your father is my dearest friend."

Karl hit him again and split his lip.

"Come on... let's go, tough guy."

But Detrick just stood there with the blood running down his face.

"Fuck you, coward." Karl kicked the side of the building, turned, and walked away.

The candy box was stained red with blood. Detrick threw it in the trash and headed back home to clean up before he went to work.

Jacob looked up from his workbench to see Detrick had arrived. His face was swelling, and the bruises Karl had inflicted were becoming visible.

"What happened to you?" Jacob rushed to his side.

"Another bicycle accident," Detrick smiled and winked.

"Are you lying to me? Who did this to you?"

"I got hurt while I was training."

"Detrick, you are a poor liar. Are you in some kind of trouble?" Jacob studied him.

"No." He would not tell Jacob about Karl. Even now, he hoped that someday, Karl would allow him to befriend him.

"So what is it?" Jacob asked again.

"I got hurt training. It's nothing. But there is something I must discuss with you."

Jacob sat down and motioned towards the bench beside him for Detrick to sit.

"Go on. I am listening."

Where to start? The thought of hurting Jacob unnerved him, but the dishonesty was far worse. Detrick hung his head. He could not meet Jacob's eyes. His stomach ached as he fumbled to find the right words. "You know how much I care for you. You have been like a father to me, and God knows I don't ever want to hurt you."

"Detrick, what is it? What are you trying to say?"

Detrick took a deep breath and sighed. Then he met Jacob's eyes with a serious stare. "I am in love with Leah. Although she has not said it, I believe she cares for me, too."

"Is that all?" Jacob laughed aloud. "Did you think I didn't know? What... Am I blind?" He patted Detrick's shoulder. "Come and have some strudel."

CHAPTER TWENTY-THREE

AFTER HE HAD LEFT DETRICK, Karl wiped the dried blood from his fist onto his pants. He lit another cigarette and slipped into an alleyway. It had grown dark, but he had too much angry energy surging through him to go home. He knew he must walk it off. If he didn't, this foul mood would never lift. Why had Detrick refused to fight him? Not for one second did Karl believe Detrick to be a coward. In fact, he felt sure Detrick would have beaten him. What made this goy different from the others? He shook his head. The blanket of darkness covered him like a friend, shielding him from a society that had rejected him, forcing him to fight like an animal for survival. For over two hours, he meandered, smoking a cigarette and lighting another as soon as he'd finished. He'd managed to secure a bottle of schnapps, which he gulped along the way. The worries that continually haunted him had now surfaced. How could he ever convince his family that they must leave Germany? They did not see the coming danger as clearly as he did. No matter what he said, they'd refused to believe him.

For the most part, this part of the city was quiet except when he passed the pub. Karl continued down the street into the non-Jewish sector of the city. Karl felt he might relax if he could find some Nazi and beat the shit out of him. Drunk, his body itched for a fight. He hated them, all of them.

Then up the road, he saw a group of pre-teen boys dressed in the uniforms of the Hitler Youth. They should not have been wandering the streets at such a late hour. Karl crossed the street. He would confront them and make them sorry they'd worn those despicable uniforms.

"Heil Hitler!" One of the boys addressed him.

"Fuck you and Hitler."

The boys looked at each other, appalled. The words of treason offended them.

"What did you say?"

"I said fuck you and Hitler and all of you fucking Nazis! I'm a Jew. Ya hear me? I'm a Jew!" The alcohol made Karl brash and brave.

"A filthy Jew. No wonder."

Just the words Karl had been waiting for. He smashed the bottle against the side of a building. Now, the broken glass became a weapon.

One of the boys hit Karl in the stomach, and he almost laughed aloud at the feeble attempt. Then two more attacked him from behind. Karl cut one of the boys across the face with the broken bottle. Then, as he turned, the glass found its way deep into the neck of another boy. It lodged there as the Hitler Youth fell to the ground, blood pouring as if from a garden hose onto his brown uniform. The other boys backed away. They looked at Karl. Until now, their anti-Semitism and hatred had been parroted from the sentiments of adults. They had never fathomed dying for it. A thick puddle of dark red blood pooled on the sidewalk. The dying boy that turned just thirteen a week before choked on his own blood as it ran down his throat. As he gasped and gagged, the struggle continued for several minutes, then the raspy noise stopped.

He was dead.

Karl had not expected to kill him. The drunken anger dissipated. Now all he felt was fear. If he were caught, they would punish him severely.

The bloody bottle dropped from Karl's hand, breaking into pieces on the street. He turned and ran. Expecting to be chased, he hid in alleyways, but no one followed him. Karl arrived home to find everyone asleep. He kept all the money he'd saved from his bar mitzvah in his top drawer. Placing that and a bunch of clothes into a suitcase, he headed for the door. Before he left, he reached into his father's coat, which hung on the rack. Inside, he found a small wad of cash. Karl took the money and left. Now, he could never return home. His presence would bring danger to his entire family.

Still watching and careful, he went to the train station. The next train out was headed for Warsaw, Poland. Karl bought a one-way ticket.

CHAPTER TWENTY-FOUR

HELGA HASWELL SURVEYED her closet with a discerning eye as she removed the pin curls from her long hair. Golden-blonde curls fell about her shoulders. Such an important dance and all she had to wear were hand-me-downs. Disappointment and frustration grew into anger as she flung the hangers from side to side. She'd been invited to attend a ball at the Nazi Headquarters. Finally, she felt she would have the opportunity to meet the right sort of men: men of power, money, and distinction. Men who could offer her the future she had dreamed of for so long. Back and forth, she shifted her dresses, unsatisfied with any of the selections. If she had more time, she would ask her brother, Detrick, to lend her the money for a new gown. But she had received the invitation the previous evening, and the dance would be held tonight. Such short notice!

A girlfriend, Gretchen, to whom she had become close over the last several months, had received two tickets and asked Helga if she would like to accompany her. Would she like to attend? My gosh, what a question. Of course, she would! When Gretchen had mentioned the dance, she had shivered with excitement, hardly able to catch her breath.

Again, she sorted through her things and finally settled upon a forest-green taffeta she'd purchased at a thrift store. Taking it from its hanger, she pulled it over her head to try it on and stood before the mirror. Despite the fact that she wore a second-hand dress, no one could deny her sparkling beauty. With full breasts, slim hips, and long legs accenting a tiny waist, she made a striking vision. After being satisfied with her appearance, a smile crept slowly across her lips. Helga giggled as she whirled about, the full skirts and petticoats floating around her. Then she sat down on her bed, eyes still glued to the looking glass. Folding her hands in her lap, she thought, *maybe my life is changing.*

In two weeks, on November 20, 1937, Helga Haswell would celebrate her eighteenth birthday. She tilted her head, pouting her lips in a mock kiss at her reflection. Soon, she would be a woman. Soon, she would make her own decisions. Her mother had discouraged her from accepting this invitation. Inga told her that the Nazis were not all she believed them to be. But then again, what did her mother know?

CHAPTER TWENTY-FIVE

THE BANQUET HALL had been superbly decorated with banners hanging from the ceiling bearing the likeness of the Führer. In the pictures, Hitler wore a serious expression as he gazed down at his followers with god-like power. Nazi flags stood over twelve feet tall, circling the dance floor. Large, sparkling crystal vases filled with an array of autumn-colored flowers appeared on each linen-adorned table. These flower arrangements reached so high that they obscured the vision of the guests on either side. The fine cream-colored china tableware had been carefully hand-painted with black swastikas in their centers. Around the perimeter of the dishes, tiny swastikas of 24-karat gold had been inlaid in a circular pattern to match the golden flatware.

High-ranking and lower-ranking officers strutted about, taking pride in their party and feeling accomplished in their uniforms. Many were alone, while others held the arms of attractive ladies in flowing gowns. A large group of uniformed men, army and SS, stood at the bar, sipping bitter, dark German beer.

Helga and her friend Gretchen inhaled the splendor, which exceeded all of their expectations. Chairs had been set up along the wall for single girls—wallflowers awaiting a dance partner. The two chose seats in the center. It took less than fifteen minutes for a young party member to ask Helga to dance. He approached, head bowed, in his pressed uniform and spit-shined boots. She could see by his medals that he held a lower rank. But Helga didn't care. She longed to dance. Her heart thumped with excitement when she followed him out to the floor. Everyone turned to look at the magnificent blonde in the gorgeous emerald dress smoothly gliding across the floor. From that moment on, she never sat down. Whirling like a princess in a fairy tale, Helga waltzed until the lights flickered on and off, indicating that it was time to take a seat for dinner. She turned, thanking the last man she'd danced with, and as she did, she saw a tall, high-ranking SS officer standing at the bar, staring at her approvingly. Helga turned shyly away while the blood rose in her cheeks as she followed Gretchen to their seats. When the girls were seated, Helga tried to catch another glimpse of him, but he had gone, so she assumed he had forgotten her.

After the speeches and a scrumptious dinner, Helga accompanied Gretchen to the ladies' room. On her way back, the handsome officer appeared to be waiting for her. With his raven hair slicked back from his angular face and his striking blue eyes accented by his shining black uniform, he made a stunning sight.

"Good evening, *Fräulein*. Is it *Fräulein*? Or is it *Frau*?"

Helga laughed nervously. "No, I am not married. It is *Fräulein*."

"And what is your name, *Fräulein*? Or shall I call you simply '*Fräulein*?'"

"Helga."

"Hello, Helga." He kissed her hand. "I'm *Haupsturmführer* Erik Schneider."

Helga could not find her voice. Her breathing momentarily stopped. Erik's charming smile and teeth, so white they seemed to have a violet tint, intimidated her. She'd charmed boys before, but this clearly was a man, and a captain in the SS, at that.

"May I have this dance?"

She nodded, and before she could say another word, he took her into his arms, and they glided across the floor to the final song of the evening.

Helga could not believe her voice as she heard herself agree to Erik's invitation to escort her home. He took her arm and walked her to his waiting vehicle. Then he opened her door and patiently watched as she arranged her skirt so he could close the door. Once inside his long, black automobile, Helga smelled the leather of the seats and the hint of an expensive cigar.

"Where do you live?"

Helga felt the shame rise, giving her face and neck a pale blush as she remembered her family's social position. What would this man think when he saw her home? Her mind raced, but she could not think of a lie. Biting her lower lip, she told him her address. Surprising Helga, Erik seemed unfazed. Even when he saw the apartment building with the women talking to each other through the windows across the courtyard, he did not flinch. Instead, he walked her to the door, and in a voice that penetrated right through her skin, he asked if he could see her again.

"Yes, I would like that very much." Helga wished she could stop the noise of her neighbors, people whose classless behavior embarrassed her. The voices of the women in her building carried across the walkway. Even at this late hour, the banter continued.

"My husband is out drinking again, Hilde—dirty, no-good lout. Get in here right now, Fredrik. You listen to me, or when your father gets home..."

"*Ech*... My husband too... the good-for-nothing bastard."

Although the clock read after ten, children with dirty faces, hands, and feet still played in puddles outside on the street.

"Would tomorrow night be too soon?" Erik seemed not to notice, his attention fixed on Helga.

"No, not at all too soon. I would love to see you," Helga replied.

"Good, it's settled then? Eight o'clock for dinner?"

"Yes."

Erik smiled, his teeth sparkling in the moonlight. Before he left, he turned back one time to take in the lovely girl in the green dress as she disappeared into the dilapidated apartment house.

CHAPTER TWENTY-SIX

THE FOLLOWING MORNING, two dozen crimson roses arrived in a long white box. When Helga opened the door to find the flower deliveryman, she stared at him in disbelief. None of the boys she knew would have had the finances or the inclination to orchestrate such a romantic gesture. Gently, she touched a petal and spied the small envelope. With trembling fingers, she opened it.

> *Helga, thank you for making the dance very special for me last night. I will spend all day looking forward to our dinner tonight.*
>
> *Erik*

Helga pressed the card to her chest and twirled around on her toes like a ballerina. Then a musical laugh escaped her lips.

Inga watched from the kitchen, and her heart ached. As Helga's mother, she hoped she'd been wrong about the world snuffing out her daughter's ambitions.

Inga thought that perhaps over-cautiousness caused this unwarranted worry. But, of course, Inga had every reason to be watchful.

After all, when she looked at what had become of her life, she cringed. She had been young once and at least attractive, if not beautiful. Hans had made promises, too. Now, he not only fell short of them all, but his failure to be the man she had once hoped he would be no longer bothered him. Often, she wondered if she still loved him. Once, she had loved him a great deal and admired him, too.

He'd been ambitious and filled with dreams, but poverty and daily failure had beaten him down and stripped all hope from him. Hans grew older, angrier, and miserable, while Inga's life became drudgery.

Although she never told anyone, Inga Haswell believed that her only way out of her wretchedness would be death. Sometimes, she thought she might welcome it.

Now she found it hard to watch her daughter being swept up in a mad love affair that might be her vision realized or result in a hideous disaster. So many mixed feelings surfaced as Inga thought of Helga finding herself in the same situation Inga was now suffering. Horror at the knowledge of how bad things could turn out made Inga overly cautious. After all, she'd seen things go wrong firsthand.

She had other concerns, darker, ugly ones that filled her with shame. Could she be envious of Helga? Would Inga allow her jealousy to poison her toward Helga's happiness? Inga despised herself for that thought, and confusion as to her motives worried her. Inga watched and listened as her daughter sang softly to herself. She combed her golden hair and carefully smudged a muted lipstick on her heart-shaped mouth.

Then satisfied, Helga grabbed her pocketbook and left for the bus that would take her to work. She had recently found a secretarial position at the local grammar school, but only part-time hours had been available. The pay left much to be desired, and she found that although it helped a little, the Haswell family remained poor.

At precisely eight that evening, Erik arrived. Crisp and polished in his uniform, the majesty of his presence caught Inga off guard. Instead of giving just a spoken greeting, he kissed her hand. Inga watched from the window as he opened the door to his automobile and helped Helga inside. Her daughter looked so beautiful that a tear came to her eye. After the car had pulled away, with a heavy heart, Inga went back to the washboard to work on the pile of dirty sheets she needed to finish for her customer by morning.

Hans did not come home that night until the tavern closed. When he entered the bedroom, Inga heard him. She could tell by the tune that he hummed that he felt amorous. She pretended to be asleep.

Erik chose a quaint restaurant with a lovely view of the city. Candles lit the tables, and a violin played softly. He ordered roast goose, sauerbraten, a green salad, potatoes with cheese, and a lovely strudel for dessert. Although her stomach rumbled, Helga could not eat. Her nerves made her feel clumsy as she sat across the table from Erik, trying to make clever conversation. He listened to her intently when she spoke. His eyes gazed into hers, soft with the emotion that stirred her.

"You were by far the prettiest girl at the ball last evening."

"Do you really think so? There were many pretty girls there last night."

"Yes… by far." His smile drew her in.

"Thank you."

"Please don't thank me. I am honored that you have allowed me to see you again. I hope you are enjoying yourself enough to agree to another date with me."

"Oh, yes. This is a lovely place."

"But you are not eating. Would you like something else? I would be more than happy to order anything you would like."

"No, please, this is more than perfect. And by the way, thank you so much for the roses."

"It is hardly enough."

She could think of nothing to say, so she looked down at her plate and moved the strudel around with her fork.

"Perhaps you will allow me to escort you to some of the finer ballrooms in town."

She looked at her dress. The sleeves appeared worn, and feelings of inadequacy robbed her as surely as a thief. "Yes, of course. I would love that."

He saw her lack of enthusiasm. "What is it? You don't seem to want to go."

"Oh, no. It's nothing, really."

"Come now, you can tell me." Erik's voice and mannerisms seemed so sincere that she felt at ease to express her concerns.

"Well, I… my dress is so old, and I'm just afraid people might think badly of me."

"Is that all?" He laughed aloud. "You just leave that to me." Such a simple problem with an easy remedy. Erik would simply purchase a gown and have it sent to her home.

After that night, the gifts began to arrive. Erik sent a dress of ivory satin, silk stockings, and an ermine fur stole. Every other day, a deliveryman climbed the stairs carrying the white box of red roses.

He bought her a hair comb with three tiny diamonds that sparkled like stars in her golden halo. Helga would see Erik for a week straight, and then he would leave on business for a few days. But as soon as he returned, he knocked at the door with a lovely trinket as an offering from his travels.

When Hans first met Erik, he radiated with pride. He made a point of telling his drinking companions at the local tavern that his daughter kept company with an SS officer. For a while, this knowledge kept him in an unusually jovial mood. Others respected and looked up to him for the first time in a long time. But after a while, the depression he'd suffered returned. Once again, he withdrew into the safety of the solitude of his own mind.

Detrick, however, had no such admiration for Erik. He found it difficult to keep his abhorrence of the Nazi Party a secret, even for his sister's sake. When he voiced his concerns to the SS officer for the future of a Germany ruled by a tyrant, his mother's face turned as white as parchment. She frowned at him in a warning. Instead of continuing the argument with Erik, he left the house.

As he walked down the street that night, his thoughts turned to Jacob and Leah, and he feared what the future would hold for all of them.

On occasion, Erik's sexual needs surfaced, but he seemed to understand that Helga's lack of experience made her reluctant to go to his bed. He never became forceful or insistent. Instead, he told her to take her time. Always kind and attentive, Helga came to believe Erik had fallen in love with her. His kisses grew tender as stirrings of desire manifested within her. When Erik looked at Helga, she saw that his eyes radiated sincerity.

They frequented ballrooms, waltzed the night away, dined at the finest restaurants, and laughed at shocking and decadent burlesque shows. Everywhere they went, Erik, wearing his black SS officer uniform, received the treatment of a crowned prince. Helga at his side drew the envy of females, young and old. Her fair-haired Aryan beauty radiated like the sunshine, and the couple seemed a perfect representation of the New Order of the Third Reich. The future of Germany!

Fall turned to winter, and winter to spring. Erik grew more reluctant to leave his government business, and he continually tried to find replacements so that he could stay with Helga.

They walked hand-in-hand through the park as the spring flowers began to bloom. The blossoms on the trees had just started to open. Erik turned to her; his eyes glassed over with feeling. She felt her heart skip a beat, and as he bent to kiss her lips, she sighed.

"I am falling in love with you." Erik touched Helga's face as his words sprung forth huskily with desire.

She swallowed hard and then looked up into his eyes. "I am falling in love with you, too."

They kissed and embraced for a long time. Helga felt Erik's powerful chest against her own. She could smell the fragrance of his cologne and the spicy odor of his cigars as they mingled with the perfume of the flowering trees. The passion mixed with the aromas left her intoxicated.

That night, following a lovely dinner at a quaint café, Helga agreed to accompany Erik to his room. She had given this much thought and decided that the time had come.

"I apologize for the condition of my apartment. I am traveling so much." Erik moved a decorative pillow onto his sofa.

"It's beautiful."

Every room bore the mark of tasteful and well-made furniture that had been carefully selected. Helga found no dirty dishes in the sink, as would be expected at a bachelor's apartment. The hardwood floors glowed with polish and harbored not a speck of dust. And when she entered the bedroom, she found the bed made up perfectly to military standards. However, the flat did not feel like it was lived in. The sofa, pure white cotton, bore not a single stain. In fact, the apartment gleamed with impeccable cleanliness.

When Erik left Helga to use the washroom, she curiously peeked in his closet. There she found a row of black uniforms, pressed and hung neatly. On the floor, shiny, polished shoes lined up at attention like a military platoon.

When Erik returned to the bedroom, he offered her a drink. Although Helga did not much care for the taste of liquor, she accepted. The liquid burned her throat as it trickled down, heating her body. She sipped it slowly. Erik took the glass from her hand and placed it on the dresser. He took her hand in his and kissed it. With soft, warm lips, he kissed each of her fingers. Helga felt the intensity of his breath as it fell hot upon her hand. Her heart beat faster as he slowly took her into his arms. When their lips met, she sighed. Then he backed away and took her hand, leading her to his bed. She followed, trembling with fear but filled with desire.

"This is my first time," Helga whispered.

He did not answer. Instead, he took her into his arms. While he kissed her, he unbuttoned her blouse, and his lips moved to her breasts as he reached behind her, unhooking her bra. She sighed as he took her nipple into his mouth. Helga felt her body warming, and she relaxed. When he entered her, she felt an initial pain, and then her body responded to his with equal passion. Twice that night, he took her, and she surrendered to his desires. After they were both spent, she lay beside him, and they slept. When he awoke, he gently nudged her.

"It's late. I'd better take you home."

His eyes could not meet hers. She reached up to kiss him, but he turned away. Then he left and went into the bathroom and got dressed. Helga slipped her dress back on and combed her hair. Then she sat on the edge of the bed, waiting for him to return. Something had changed; something felt wrong. When he entered the room, ready to leave, instead of a deeper intimacy between them, he'd affected a formal posture, almost as if she were a stranger.

"Erik?"

"What?"

"This was very special for me."

"Yes, for me, too." He looked away from her. "Helga, there is something I must tell you."

Her heart beat in terror at what he might say.

"I'm married. I do not intend to leave my wife. We had a good time, didn't we?"

She could not answer. Her throat had closed, and she feared she might vomit.

"I think we should say goodbye."

"But Erik… Why? What was tonight about? I don't understand. You said you loved me."

"Please, Helga, don't question me." His voice had grown hard, and she felt she hardly knew him when she looked at him. "Let's go now."

Erik drove her home in silence. Helga's heart had crumbled into a million tiny pieces. Although filled with questions, she could not speak.

When they arrived at her apartment, he got out of the car and opened her door. But unlike the other nights they'd spent together, he did not walk with her to the door, holding her and kissing her goodnight. Instead, he climbed into his vehicle, and without looking back, he drove away.

For a long time, Helga stood on the curb, staring at the street where Erik's car had been. Tears filled her eyes, and her face felt as if it had fallen a thousand miles. She could not believe what had taken place. It simply was not true. How could he have done this?

How could she have trusted him? Married? She saw no evidence of a wife in that apartment. Who and what kind of man had she fallen in love with? Helga looked down at her wrinkled dress and her twisted silk stockings. Then she turned away from the empty street and walked into the apartment building with her head down.

CHAPTER TWENTY-SEVEN

ALL NIGHT LONG, she thrashed about until her sheets became twisted and drenched with sweat. The following day, and for many days to come, Helga could not swallow her food. She continued to work but performed her duties in a daze, like one awakened from a dream, only to find herself in a nightmare. When her friends at work asked her to sit at their lunch table, she quietly declined. Helga had not yet found the words to tell the world of her betrayal and abandonment. Somehow, she continued to believe that she would arrive home to find the familiar white box filled with the blood-red roses that had awaited her so often this past year. It did not come.

Worse yet, neither did her monthly cycle. She awakened filled with nausea and felt the overwhelming need to vomit. However, she refused to believe that she could be pregnant.

When she passed her second month without her menses, she knew she must see a doctor. Since childhood, the Haswell children had been patients of Dr. Deisenhofer. He had been there at their birth. Now she must go to him and tell him of her plight. Regardless of Helga's shame and embarrassment, meeting with the doctor was unavoidable. *Perhaps,* she thought, *he might, by some miracle, be willing to help her to take care of the situation.*

The following morning, Helga arranged to take time off from her job. Instead of taking her regular bus, she boarded another going in the opposite direction to her doctor's office.

The nurse at the desk recognized her immediately and asked her to sit for a moment while she prepared the room. Because Helga had scheduled the earliest available appointment, she found the waiting room deserted. And she felt relieved not having to face mothers and children as they awaited the old doctor's attention.

After a short time, the nurse showed her to an examining room and asked her to remove her clothes and dress in the cotton gown. She did and then fumbled nervously with the handle of her pocketbook until the doctor entered.

"Helga Haswell, what brings you here today?" Dr. Deisenhofer smiled until he saw the tears that now stained Helga's face. With his right hand, he took the stool and pulled it closer to the examining table. Then he sat down and waited for her to speak.

The only sound that could be heard was the heels of the nurse's shoes as she set up the examining room next door.

"Helga?" He prodded gently. His old eyes had seen many distressed young girls.

"Doctor. You must not tell my parents anything that I tell you."

"Of course not, child, I cannot. I am a doctor. It is against my ethical code."

She took a deep breath. "I am afraid… I am afraid I might be pregnant."

He smiled at her, and the kindness in his eyes helped her to relax. "Well, before we go jumping to conclusions, let's just check this out and see what is what? All right?"

She nodded her head.

Dr. Deisenhofer examined her carefully and motioned her to put her clothes back on. He gave her a glass beaker with a cork stopper. "Please urinate in this bottle and give it to the nurse, then come back here."

Helga complied and returned to find the doctor waiting for her.

"Have a seat. The urine sample was because the government requires that I do a pregnancy test on all unmarried Aryan women who think they might be pregnant. They pay for it, of course, and the results won't be back for days. In the meantime, let me ask you a few questions to see if I can determine what is what." He eyed Helga and asked, "Have you had sex with a man?"

"Yes." Helga looked down.

"How long ago?"

"Two and a half months."

"Have you missed your menses?"

"Yes."

"How many times?"

"Twice."

"Were you always on time before?"

"Like clockwork."

"Is your body swollen or sensitive anywhere?"

"Yes, my breasts."

"How are you feeling?"

"I am nauseated every morning when I wake up. I get sick when I smell my mother cooking cabbage or cigarette smoke, and perfumes and colognes send me straight to the bathroom."

"Has your appetite changed?"

"I can't keep much down, can't stand anything greasy, and I absolutely crave ice cream and those little bitty fish in a can."

"Sardines?"

"That's it."

The doctor exhaled, removed his glasses, and rubbed the bridge of his nose. Then he collected his thoughts and spoke.

"My father died last year at a ripe old age and left me enough money to buy a brand-new auto. When I drive it, I see signs: signs to tell me how fast I can go, signs to tell me when to stop, what way is one-way, and how far it is to Magdeburg or Potsdam or other cities. The signs tell me what is what."

Helga lifted her eyes to look into his.

"The government may have to wait for the *rabbit test*, but we do not. You, my dear child, have all the signs of a healthy young woman who is going to have a baby."

"But I am not married. My family will be shamed."

"Helga. I understand how you feel, but I have a solution that might be perfect for you."

She looked up at him hopefully. The idea of aborting the baby terrified her. Even some women who'd done so under medical supervision had died. But she would have to take her chances. If she were to have a baby, it would surely ruin her life.

The doctor looked directly into her eyes as he explained. "You may not know about the Lebensborn, so I will tell you. In 1936, Heinrich Himmler began a program to engineer a pure Aryan race for the future good of Germany. It's called the Lebensborn Program. Now, I must ask you before we go any further, who is the father?"

Red fingers of heat crawled up her face. "I can't tell you."

"Why not? Is he a Jew?"

"Oh, no." she laughed a little. "He is married. He is an SS officer."

"Oh, child, this is a good thing. It is entirely confidential. We won't tell your parents, but we have to know who the father is so the government can confirm his Aryan bloodline. If everything is confirmed, you will be accepted at the Lebensborn Institute. The requirements are that the father and mother of the future offspring be of pure Aryan blood. Both of you fit the qualifications. You will stay at the Lebensborn Institute, which is located in the highlands near Munich until the baby is born. Then the child is taken off your hands and raised by a carefully chosen family, who will raise him or her to be a good Nazi, to follow the *Führer*, and to take his rightful place as a future leader of the Third Reich. It is that simple."

"You're sure you won't tell my family or contact the father?"

"I promise."

"The father is *Haupsturmführer* Erik Schneider."

"Good," he said as he scribbled the name on a notepad.

"Ah, where was I? Oh yes, while you are at the home, you will be fed and cared for. In fact, you will want for nothing. From what I hear, it is a lovely place. Then, once the baby is born, you are free to go. No one is the wiser, and you can go on with your life. Besides, women at the Lebensborn receive the highest honors for bearing a child for Hitler. You see, you will be having a baby for the Führer."

"And my family... Do they have to know?"

"Not at all. I will send a note to accompany you when the test comes back, then I will send the test results to the Institute. The government will check to confirm your captain is in the SS. SS officers are all confirmed to be of pure Aryan stock. I know your family tree, so I will send a letter confirming your bloodlines. Now also, if you would like, your Nazi officer can be notified of your whereabouts, in case he should like to see you. So, shall I arrange it?"

She wiped the tear from her cheek with the back of her hand. "Yes, but notification to the father will not be necessary."

CHAPTER TWENTY-EIGHT

As ERIK DROVE HOME after his final encounter with Helga, his mind drifted. He could not help but feel sorry for her, although he knew he would never want her again. It seemed to happen this way all the time. First, he would meet a girl and be sure he'd fallen for her. Then, once they made love, his interest seemed to be like a candle that had been snuffed out. The smoke lingered, but the fire was gone. Erik lit a cigarette and rolled down the window. He craved fresh air.

His life had taken such turns. As a boy, he'd grown up poor, poorer than Helga. *She might have been surprised to learn that.* But like her, he'd been gifted with physical beauty. Erik bore the face and body of a Greek god, and that had saved him. He'd never gone out in search of prosperity. It just fell into his lap, and seeing the opportunity, he seized it.

When Erik turned twenty-two, he found himself without a trade or education. He'd dropped out of school and spent most of his life drifting through dead-end jobs.

After Erik had endured two weeks of employment making sodas and sweeping floors at the local candy store, she'd walked in.

Nadine, the daughter of the owner of a large company, escorted by a group of her spoiled girlfriends, had come for a late-night soda. Her thin, blonde hair hung limply on her ample shoulders. She wore expensive clothes to hide her clumsy, overweight body. When she spoke to her friends, she spoke rapidly, sounding like machine gun fire, so much so that he could hardly understand her. For some reason, she seemed to do everything too quickly.

But when their eyes met, he saw that the girl who always got what she wanted had set her sights on him. He studied her, trying to find something he could be attracted to, and found nothing. Nothing but her father's money, and to a boy from his background, that meant a great deal. When he asked her out, she immediately accepted. They went to dinner, and he found her overly domineering and demanding. *For someone so unappealing, she had a lot of nerve.* But he also knew that by marrying her, he would catapult himself swiftly out of poverty. No longer would he coast through life on meager wages. With her father's money and influence behind him, Erik would surely live the life he deserved. So, Erik set out to court Nadine. With what little money he earned, he took her to dinner and told her how lovely she looked. When he paid the bill, Erik reminded himself that every penny spent was an investment. When he called her pretty, Nadine smiled shyly. Erik knew Nadine did not hear those words often. He held her and kissed her, declaring his devotion. And once he saw that the feelings in her eyes had grown deep enough, like an actor on cue, he told her he loved her.

They sat at a corner table in an intimate restaurant when he asked her to marry him. She'd squealed with delight, loud enough to attract the attention of the other diners. As the others looked on, he fought the embarrassment he felt at being with her. With Nadine's pug nose, pink skin, and round, needy eyes, Erik decided she resembled a human who'd been born at least a half-pig.

Now, he must take on a far more difficult challenge. Nadine would introduce him to her parents. He must ensure they do not see through him to his real motives. At first, her father seemed to reject the idea of their marriage, but her mother, like Nadine, found him irresistibly attractive.

No matter how hard he tried, Erik could not win the acceptance of his future father-in-law. The man simply did not take to him, regardless of Erik's numerous attempts at charm and his overzealous compliments.

Without marriage, keeping company with Nadine seemed pointless. But Erik had put far too much time into this endeavor to give up now.

The following evening, Nadine and Erik had plans to have dinner together. That afternoon, he rented a hotel room where he brought flowers, champagne, and chocolates. Since he did not own a vehicle, she had picked him up in her black Mercedes. She wore a pink chiffon dress that, in his eyes, made her look like a hippo going to a dance.

After dinner, they got back into the automobile.

"I have a surprise for you." He smiled, and her heart melted.

"Oh?"

"This may sound strange, but will you trust me?"

"Of course."

"I love you."

"I love you, too."

He directed her to the hotel. Nadine felt a little uncomfortable passing the desk clerk on her way upstairs. She knew that Erik wanted to bed her, and she had qualms. The passion she felt for him had never been equaled by anyone before. Although she'd not been a virgin, she might as well have been. For Nadine, making love with Erik took her body to places she'd never dreamed existed.

After two months of wild sex, sometimes in the park, in the car, often in the hotel room, and once in the ladies' bathroom at a fancy restaurant, Nadine became pregnant. Now Erik knew that her father would be agreeable to setting a timely date for the wedding.

In less than three months, the ceremony took place at a magnificent cathedral, followed by an extravagant reception at the bride's home.

The wedding and Erik's introduction to his newfound social status proved more magical than he could have fathomed. More food filled the house than Erik's family consumed in a year and of a higher quality. Rose bushes had been placed along the walkway to escort the guests inside while table arrangements designed by Berlin's most renowned florist flowed over so much of the table that there hardly seemed room for the place settings. Nadine wore a gown of white silk embellished with cultured pearls. Even though she'd been to a hairstylist who had swept her fine, stringy locks into an elegant twist and had her cosmetics expertly applied, Erik still found her repulsive. On two occasions, he'd found himself drawn to one of the female guests, but he forced his attentions to stay fixed on his new bride—at least through the reception.

His father-in-law offered him a position where he earned far more money than he deserved. He'd stayed there until the Nazi Party had taken over, and when his father-in-law joined, he followed suit. The SS offered Erik more than just employment. It gave him respect, money, and access to women who fell willingly into his bed when they saw the uniform.

For a tedious month at the very beginning of the marriage, he remained faithful but grew mean and short with Nadine. Pregnant and newly married, she had expected things to go differently. The dreams Nadine had fostered about her life with Erik were now crushed. After she had cried to her parents, her father had a warning talk with Erik. It was then that Erik decided that he must not allow his wife to know his true feelings. Instead, to maintain his sanity, he must find his comfort elsewhere. Erik decided it would be wise to treat Nadine as kindly as possible. After all, his father-in-law, a powerful man, could send him right back to where he came from. Erik would take care to be discreet, but he would find women who satisfied his desires outside of his marriage.

At first, the girls had been few and local, forcing him to be worried and cautious. Overall, it had only amounted to a couple of one-night stands between the births of his two children.

When his daughter was born, the couple agreed to name her

Christine. As she grew every day, she took on more of the characteristics Erik detested in her mother. Erik clenched his fists, turning red as he forced himself to find patience with the child. As a mother watching father and daughter together, Nadine's awareness of Erik's dislike for Christine disturbed her. She hoped things would change as the child grew up. When Christine reached a year old, Nadine found herself once again with child. This time, she spent most of her pregnancy in bed, ill with morning sickness. Erik took on extra hours at work to avoid spending time with his family, but he did hire a nurse to help Nadine with Christine.

On a chilly morning in March, Siegfried pushed his way into the world. He was a strong and hearty little boy who won his father's heart instantly, as his sister had failed so miserably to do. As a sign of his affection, his father called Siegfried 'Ziggy.'

As the years passed, Ziggy went to school, where he proved to be a fine athlete. When he joined the Hitler Youth at ten, Ziggy excelled at making Erik proud. Ziggy had his father's good looks, and when the two walked together, heads turned. Erik loved his son as he loved no one and nothing else. He spent time at home with the boy. Watching Ziggy develop as a child, fearless and ready to face life, filled Erik with pride. He shared his delight with his in-laws.

Although Nadine's parents adored Ziggy, they were pained to see Erik reject chubby little Christine. She ran to her father with pictures she'd drawn for him, only to have him lay them down on a table without ever acknowledging them or her. And as Nadine endured more of Erik's indifference, the confidence she'd had as a young woman drained away. She no longer acted rashly and without thought or consideration for consequence. Nadine had come to realize that mistakes could cost her dearly. She still adored her husband, but she knew he had lost any attraction he might have once had toward her.

Once Erik joined the Nazi Party, the deterioration of the marriage only escalated. Under the guise of his work and his travels, he took a second room. Now Erik no longer slept beside Nadine. With the pretense of consideration, he told her that he felt his work might disturb her, and he thought it best that they sleep separately.

He said that sometimes in the middle of the night, he awakened, suddenly inspired to work on a project. She accepted his lie but knew that she had completely lost him. Now that the two no longer slept together, all intimacy between them ceased entirely. The emptiness in her heart grew with the feelings of abandonment. When she considered discussing her problem with her parents, she felt too ashamed, so she put off the inevitable.

In his travels, Erik met various women. But after a while, the ones who slept with him immediately bored him, and he found the ones who presented a challenge more intriguing. Until they lay with him, Erik chased them with abandon. During the pursuit, he felt alive and involved. Occasionally, he felt himself begin to develop feelings for one of the girls. However, the situation always ended in disappointment. Once he'd conquered a girl, he no longer found her alluring. But he secretly wondered if that might be because he knew he would never leave Nadine. An affair could help him pass the time and overlook a lackluster marriage, but without his wife's financial backing, he knew he would find himself back in a one-room apartment with hot water not readily available. Because the ropes that bound Erik to Nadine were wrapped around his neck and strangling him, he found that he lost patience with her easily. Rather than fight and perhaps be confronted by an angry father-in-law, he left the house.

On the day Ziggy turned fifteen, Erik received a telephone call instructing that he must leave for Berlin only a few hours following the birthday celebration. Erik hated to disappoint his son, so the father promised to bring his precious boy a special birthday gift. "A football, perhaps?" Erik asked Ziggy.

Ziggy smiled with ease and patted his father's back. "Don't worry, Father, I don't need anything. I have a football and anything else I need. I'll see you when you return." Erik started the car, and the boy waved as Erik drove away and looked back at Ziggy, who'd already put his arm around his mother and sister and headed back into the house.

When Erik arrived in Berlin, he was immediately flooded with meetings and work; he felt overwhelmed, but he could not shake off the loneliness. Although exhaustion slithered through every muscle and nerve in his body, he knew he must go to the party at the Headquarters. It was expected.

That night, he'd met Helga. The brightness of her smile and the sparkle in her eyes made him think she'd cast a spell over him. Erik couldn't wait until the following night to have dinner with her.

When he returned home, he thought about her constantly and could hardly wait to go back to Berlin. Helga was on his mind even when he played soccer with Ziggy. The magnificent girl with the golden curls possessed his every dream, and he worried that he might even become foolish and divorce Nadine to marry her. But he found that Helga brought life and youth back to his spirit. She made him smile. When they kissed, the jaded years of a loveless marriage dissipated, and he found himself dizzy with wonderful desire. He believed for the first time in his life that he might be falling in love. This girl kept him waiting longer to bed her than any of the others, and he took a strange pleasure in the pain of yearning. The night he'd taken her to his apartment, he believed things would be different with her, and while they'd made love, it had been true. But once he'd spent himself, he could not look at her. He wondered how he could have considered sacrificing everything for just another girl. His mind darted to thoughts of his beautiful home and extravagant possessions. Now, he looked at the sweet little blonde with the angelic, heart-shaped face and saw her as just another conquest. With all the wonder and magic dissipated, he felt guilty as he drove Helga back to her apartment. The end of the evening could not come quickly enough for him. His emotions were a confusing mixture of guilt and disgust with himself, but more importantly, of fear. He could not believe what he had almost done.

After Helga had left his car, Erik sped away without looking back. A chill ran through him. At least he'd come to his senses in time. He would go home to Ziggy. His son... the only joy that he counted on in his life. A smile tickled the sides of his lips. Erik knew things would be all right now.

If Erik had been able to see into the future, he might have seen what was to come. He might have known that because of Hitler's ambitions, one day, when his son had just barely become a man, Ziggy would lie dying far from his family in the arms of a beautiful Jewish partisan somewhere just across the Russian border. But, of course, Erik was not able to see into the future. He saw only as far as a single tomorrow.

CHAPTER TWENTY-NINE

THE SPRING of 1938 brought with it all the new blossoms of a regular spring. Somehow, Mother Nature had not been made aware of the turning of the tides in Germany. She filled the earth with beautiful bounty, and the warmth of her love came through in the fertility of the flowers in magnificent colors. The trees turned every shade of green, and the grass grew thick and plush, like an emerald carpet after the winter snow. The ponds began to thaw, and one could see the activity of the fish just beneath the surface. Mother Nature bestowed all of her gifts without a second thought and asked nothing in return. All seemed right with the world.

But it was not.

In the city, posters made by men, rather than God's foliage, covered the buildings. The drawings were anti-Semitic pictures and slogans full of hatred, and their presence grew daily by epic proportions. Nazi flags, arrogantly flaunting their black swastikas, hung from the tops of buildings. The rallies continued to remind the German people that their Führer worked daily to rid the world of the Jewish menace. Adolf Hitler could be seen everywhere—in print, in life, and in the sentiment of the people. His seed of ugliness had been planted, and like the flowers of the season, it, too, had come to fruition.

Leah and Detrick tried desperately to close their eyes to the world changing. Blinded, the two spent their days lost in the pure joy of having found true love. They continued to break the law and walk through the park together, although now they dared not hold hands. One morning, as the sun rose, they sat outside in the back of the bicycle shop.

"I used to think I couldn't live without my best friend, Dorothy. Her family moved to the United States when things started getting bad for Jews here. But now that I have you..." Leah squeezed Detrick's hand.

"You mean more to me than any friend I've ever had. Konrad and I used to be friends, but he's joined the party, and we've gone our separate ways."

"My father had to register the bike shop as a Jewish business yesterday. I am not sure what that will mean in the future, but it can't be good. We must all go and apply for identity cards. Detrick, I hope this all blows over soon."

He took her in his arms and held her. She sighed and looked up into his eyes.

"I am worried, too." He hugged her tighter. Their hearts beat as one.

"Karl is gone. We have no idea what happened to him. My father is distraught. We hear that the Gestapo might be looking for him. Apparently, he had something to do with killing a boy in the Hitler Youth."

Detrick trembled. He would not lie to her. "The night your brother disappeared, something happened between him and me." Detrick took a deep breath, and then he continued, "I had gone to the candy store to buy something for your father. After I'd left the store, I passed Karl on the street. I tried to befriend him, but he knew that you and I had seen each other, and he rejected any attempts I made at offering friendship. He was hostile and demanded that I leave you alone. I told him that would never happen. He hit me several times. I refused to fight back. I guess it made him angrier because he walked away in a huff. My purpose that night had been to unite us, not to divide. I hope I didn't have anything to do with the trouble he may have gotten into."

Leah gazed into Detrick's eyes and saw they had glassed over with potential tears. "It's not your fault, Detrick. Karl is filled with so much anger, and rightfully so. He has suffered the hatred of anti-Semitism... and... Karl is a fighter. I don't know what happened after he left you, but I would venture to say somehow that boy provoked him."

"Then you forgive me?"

"Forgive you for what?"

"For... I don't know, actually. But all I do know is that I would never purposely want to hurt you or Jacob." He took her hand. "Leah?"

"Yes?"

"I love you."

He looked into her eyes, and she felt her body melt like an ice cream cone surrendering to the warmth of the summer sun.

"I loved you the first time I saw you. And don't think it doesn't bother me that I can't tell the world or walk with you, holding hands. I'm ashamed of my German blood. If it were up to me, I would stand up to all of them and say, 'This is Leah Abendstern. She is a Jew, and she is the woman I love.'"

They embraced, and she held him tight as she pressed her face into his chest so he would not see the tears that fell upon her soft cheeks.

"I love you too, Detrick. I don't know what kind of punishment we might face for having these feelings, but I can't help it. I love you."

CHAPTER THIRTY

"I WANT to take you to the movies and to dinner. I want to show you off." Detrick looked at Leah in her new dress with admiration shining in his eyes.

"Detrick, it's unsafe. Jews and Gentiles are forbidden from seeing each other romantically. It's best we meet here."

"In the back of the bicycle shop? Leah, you deserve so much better, so much more. No one will know you are Jewish. Let me take you to dinner and dancing. I have some money put away. I want to spend all of it on you." He longed to make her happy, to give her everything he had.

"Detrick." She touched his face. "I'm sorry." She shook her head.

"I'm sorry, Leah. I am sorry and ashamed of what has been done to your people. I want to give you so much."

They embraced, and he kissed her, determined to show her how much he loved her.

When he left Leah that night, Detrick took a long walk, lost in thought. How different things might have been had Hitler never gotten into power? His friendship with Konrad seemed to have gone stale. The two boys who'd been such good friends now stood on opposite sides of the fence.

Helga ran away from home, disappearing without even a note. His mother was distraught with worry, but Detrick felt sure she had run away with her Nazi officer. Detrick had no idea where she had gone or why, but he felt somehow that the Third Reich was responsible.

Jacob lived in humiliation and under constant scrutiny, and that tortured Detrick. But most of all, Leah. How he hated to see the effect of the Nazi Party on Leah. His love for Leah had taken precedence over everything else in his life. Keeping their love a secret seemed like a betrayal to all he found beautiful and holy. In his life, Detrick had never imagined he would be so blessed with love. She answered every prayer and dream he'd ever had, and he had no doubt he would marry her if he could. As things stood, he could not even take her to a café without fear of being arrested. If the punishment were sure to fall on him only, he would gladly have faced it. But he would not, could not, endanger Leah. When Detrick thought of what the SS might do to Leah, he kept his anger and rebellion in check, but to see her hurt in any way tore him to pieces. If word got out about the relationship between the two of them, Leah might be sent to a concentration camp. Detrick had heard horror stories of the goings-on in those terrible places, and he knew he would fight them all to the death before he would allow them to torture her.

The walk did him good. It gave him time to sort out his feelings. The farther he traveled away from the city, the better he felt.

He passed an empty house at the end of a sparsely populated dirt road. Most of the windows had been cracked, and the grass grew wild with weeds. He walked to the door, which he found ajar. When he entered, he found the rooms ransacked. Everything of value had been taken or torn apart. In the middle of the floor, he saw a menorah. He picked up the silver candleholder with Stars of David for each of the days. From Jacob, he learned that this piece had a sacred meaning for the holiday of Hanukkah. With his fingers, he tenderly touched the candleholder, feeling the cool metal in his hand.

Without any warning, his stomach lurched with nausea. The room spun as Detrick sunk to the ground and sat on the hardwood floor. The reality hit him with such force that his head began to pound. Once, a family had lived in these rooms. Perhaps it had been a family like Jacob's, maybe even a girl like Leah. Tears came to his eyes, and this house brought out all of his innermost fears. Why had he been born now, during such a dark period in history, and why was he faced with such impossible choices? Where were the people who had once laughed, loved, and cried in these rooms? Had they run away? If so, would they have left their precious menorah? More realistically, they were dead or in camps. *My God, how many others had suffered and would suffer the same fate before this all ended? And how could it be that just like that—in an instant and for no reason at all—these lives had been erased, obliterated from the face of the earth?*

What could he do to protect Leah and Jacob? His heart felt heavy, and for the first time in his life, Detrick felt weak and helpless.

Before he left, he thought about taking the menorah to Jacob but decided it might upset him. Instead, he placed it up high on a shelf and left.

That night, as he lay in his bed, an idea came to him. Perhaps the old house would be the shelter for joy and love again. The following day, he dressed quickly and went back to the house, carrying with him a broom, mop, bucket, and some rags. All day he cleaned and polished the dusty rooms. After Detrick had completed his task to his satisfaction, he returned home to bathe and dress. He owned only one black suit, but when he put it on, he could have easily been on par with Errol Flynn or Clark Gable. Then he went into town and purchased flowers in a bubble bowl, bread, cheese, a sweet red wine, and a bunch of grapes the color of amethyst. In another store, he found candles and holders. Detrick wanted to make things special, so he invested in a phonograph and a black vinyl record that played a waltz by Strauss. After he had arranged all of these things in the abandoned house, he went to see Leah.

"I have a surprise for you." He winked at her.

"Oh? You look nice."

"Thanks, come with me."

"Detrick, where are we going?"

The twinkle in his eyes intrigued her. Night had fallen, hiding them in the safety of darkness as they walked alongside streets away from the main road.

When they got to the old, abandoned house, he opened the door for her. A breeze gusted in after them. She stood at the threshold in the shadows. First, he lit an array of white candles, and then Detrick wound the crank and placed the needle carefully on the record. Music filled the room as the candlelight transformed the empty house into a ballroom. Stretching out his right hand, he bowed, requesting a dance. Leah giggled slightly as she placed her hand on his. Together, they glided across the floor as one. Detrick held her tightly. She found him an excellent dancer. He moved with the confidence and precision of an athlete. Once the music ended, Detrick removed his suit jacket and placed it on the ground.

"Please, sit." He took out the wine, cheese, and bread and smiled at her. She returned his smile as she sat beside him.

For several moments, Leah stared down at the wine bottle. Then she looked up. The seriousness of her gaze caught Detrick by surprise.

"Is everything all right, Leah? You look upset."

"I'm not upset. I've made a decision." Her eyes were still fixed on his. "I want you to make love to me, Detrick."

His voice grew hoarse. "Are you sure?"

"Yes, very. I have thought about it for a long time."

"Leah… I'm unprepared… What if you get pregnant?"

"Then I will."

"I would never leave you. But the law will not allow us to marry. It's far too dangerous."

"I know, but I also believe you will not turn me away." She lay back on his coat. "Please, Detrick. Don't be practical for once. Just follow your heart." He stood up and removed his shirt, balling it up to make a pillow. Then he gently placed it under her head. With care, he kissed her and studied her eyes to reassure him that she wanted him as much as he wanted her. When he saw what he needed to see, he kissed her again. She reached up and put her arms around his neck.

"I love you, Leah. You are my every wish granted. I promise to spend the rest of my life taking care of you. Until the day that I die, I will put you before me. I will love you with my whole heart and soul, and if need be, I will die for you."

She sighed. "Don't talk about dying, not now." She touched his cheek, and their lips met again and again as he unbuttoned her blouse. The taste and smell of peppermint, so distinctly Detrick, lingered on her tongue. His warm breath covered her breasts as his lips caressed them. Leah had always wondered if she would be afraid the first time she lay beneath a man, but she had no fear, only a desire so powerful that her mind had gone blank. Detrick touched her slowly and with a tenderness she had never known. When he entered her, her body arched up to receive him. Almost instantly, the spark of pain turned into an ocean of pleasure that surged through her like a massive tidal wave.

Humbled by the intensity of his love, Detrick moved his body slowly and with care. Passion consumed him, and still, he would not surge forward until she had finished. Once he was positive she had reached her climax, he followed. Then he lay beside her, stroking her hair.

"You are so beautiful, Leah. The most beautiful woman I have ever seen."

"Then I should blind you right now before you find someone who is more alluring."

"That will never happen, sweetheart. There is no one for me but you. I knew that the first time I saw you. But I never believed you would love me, too."

For a long time, they lay on the floor, she with her head on his chest, looking out the window at the stars, which burned through the night sky.

Then, as she ran her fingers over the skin on his chest, Leah spoke. "I never thought I would get over my friend Dorothy leaving Germany. We had been best friends since we were little children.

Her family left after Hitler came into power. Until I found you, I thought I would be lonely forever."

"You will never be lonely again, not as long as I live. Remember the first time we met?"

"I remember... Lewis had come to Shabbat dinner, and Father had invited you as well."

"When he touched your hand, I thought I might go crazy with jealousy. But I felt I did not deserve you. He is so rich."

"You want to know a secret?"

"Of course... If they are your secrets, I want to know and share all of them."

"I think I loved you that first time I saw you, as well."

Their lips met, and the warmth of their feelings spread like magical butter over their entire beings...soft, sweet, and tender.

CHAPTER THIRTY-ONE

THAT SUMMER, the sun cast such a bright glow upon the lovers that it served to block out the reality all around them, which grew more threatening daily.

By late October, the cold wind had sent an invisible but bone-chilling message announcing winter's arrival.

Leah and Detrick met at the abandoned house as often as time would permit. Love spread through their hearts like a rosebud opening into a full flower.

Occasionally they took risks as young lovers do. Once, while walking past an arcade, they dropped in to take a picture. The photographer caught a shot of the two looking into each other's eyes, laughing at a man who'd passed by with a monkey carrying a tin cup.

Once, Detrick left Leah alone in the house while he rode his bicycle to the ice cream shop. He purchased a pint of golden vanilla, then, as fast as he could, he pedaled back to the old house. Once he arrived, he realized he'd only been given a single wooden spoon. The lovers shared the spoon, feeding each other the melted ice cream and thanking God for the precious gift of their love.

On the evening of November 9, Inga said she did not feel well and asked Detrick to see the druggist and bring back her prescription. When he returned, she asked that he stay with her. He agreed to do so, but first rode his black bicycle to the Abendsterns' home to inform Leah that he would be unavailable for the rest of the evening. Then he returned to find his mother curled up on her bed, hugging her belly. She complained of horrible stomach cramps.

All evening, Detrick remained at her bedside. As usual, Hans did not come home. While Inga cried in pain, Detrick held her hand, offering comfort. Then she became nostalgic, telling Detrick how she missed Helga and the worry that followed her every minute of every day. Detrick listened. With a cool washcloth, he sponged the sweat from his mother's forehead until morning, when miraculously, she began to recover. The pains slowed at first and then ceased altogether. Relieved, Detrick left the house to walk to the bakery, where he planned to purchase some fresh bread in the hope Inga might eat. As of yet, he had no idea what had happened the night before.

At the Abendstern home that night, Leah cooked a simple dinner for the family. As each of the Abendsterns prepared to retire for the night, they were frozen in terror by a thunderous crash.

CHAPTER THIRTY-TWO

A SHATTERING SOUND broke through the stillness of the night as if the world was coming to an end. The sky lit up with orange and red fire, following a booming, thunderous roar as the synagogue that the Abendsterns had attended for years burst into flames. Then came the crashing of clubs as the windows of the local shops fell in shards upon the streets. Cries of terror from the women and children filled the Jewish sector of the city and throughout the Reich. Men who'd been ripped from their homes lay on the ground, beaten and bleeding. Wild mobs ran in every direction, looting and destroying, forgetting all respect for human life. The Germans called it *Kristallnacht*, the Night of the Broken Glass. For the Jews who lived and worked in peace for centuries in this tiny community, Armageddon had begun.

Miriam screamed for Jacob as she covered Michael with her body. He came running into the room, followed by Leah. Together, the three helped to carry Michael to the closet, where they propped him up on several pieces of clothing. Miriam crowded in beside him as Jacob closed the door.

"Stay here. Don't move. When it is over, I will come for you. Leah, come with me." Jacob turned to his daughter.

Leah, her face as pale as parchment, gave Jacob her hand, and together, the two climbed into the closet in Jacob's room. There they sat, waiting and listening as the destruction continued throughout the night. Jacob's hands shook, and his heart pounded as he prayed for the safety of his family.

The angry horde of rabble-rousers never came as far as the Abendstern home, but the smell of the smoke from the burning buildings wafted through the air, choking Leah. She coughed and gagged as she huddled beside her father in the closet. Sweat from the stifling heat caused their clothing to stick to their bodies as they waited, gripped with terror.

CHAPTER THIRTY-THREE

I𝑇 W𝐴𝑆 N𝑂𝑇 until he entered the bakery the morning following *Kristallnacht* that Detrick learned of what had happened the night before. He heard the other patrons discussing the situation all around him as they nibbled on cookies and pieces of bread. The attack on the Jewish community left him stunned. He ran from the shop, dropping his purchase and pedaling his bike with fervor as if Satan himself rode on his tail. His legs could not move as fast as he willed them to. Dread filled his heart, for he did not know what he would find until finally, after what seemed like a long time, he entered the Jewish sector.

Where the synagogue had stood only a day before, now only rubble and ashes remained. The smell of burning and the darkness of smoke still hung over the streets. Windows had been broken out of all the shops, and the shops had been looted. He saw puddles of blood on the streets and buildings where the word "Juden" had been painted. Detrick thought he would vomit as he rode past the bike shop to see that it, too, had suffered destruction during the night. He could not stop to assess the damage—he had to get to Leah and Jacob as quickly as possible. Under his breath, he prayed as he rode,

"Please, God, I have not been to church, I know, but I beg you to forgive me, and please, let them be safe."

The house stood unmolested. Detrick breathed a sigh of relief. But he still could not be guaranteed they had made it through the night unharmed. He must see the family to be sure. Trembling, he raced up the stairs and rang the bell. Leah stood behind the door in her nightgown. She peeked through the peephole before flinging the door open. Her hair fell in wild waves about her head, and her eyes looked wide and fearful.

"Detrick!" She had not cried until she spoke his name. Now, the tears fell upon her face in full force. Detrick took Leah into his arms and cradled her gently as her entire body shook.

"Leah, my darling…what happened…are you all right? Is everyone in the family all right?"

The words could not form in her throat. Instead, she nodded her head as he patted her hair.

"Jacob!" Detrick cried out. "Jacob, are you here?"

Jacob descended the stairs slowly as if he had aged twenty years in one fateful night. Detrick saw the pain in his face but could offer no words of comfort. Both men stared at each other, knowing things had taken a frightening turn. The mob would suffer no punishment. From now on, Jews would not be safe.

Detrick hugged Leah tighter and kissed the top of her head. Then, he turned to Jacob. "When you're ready, I will help you clean the shop and put it back together." Then, he turned to Michael and lifted him up, carefully placing him back on his bed. "How ya doin', Mikey?"

"I'm glad you came. I was so scared, Detrick. It was very bad." Though red-faced from crying, Michael smiled through his tears at Detrick. "I like when you call me 'Mikey.'"

"That's why I do it!" For once, Detrick was glad that Michael was simpleminded. It made things so much less tragic for the child because he understood so little of the magnitude of what had taken place. "It's all right, Michael… It's gonna be all right." Detrick ruffled Michael's already tousled hair.

"Thank you. Thank you for coming. Thank you for everything."

Jacob closed the bedroom door behind Detrick. "It's best we are very careful from now on. You must never be seen in my shop again or be seen coming there. You will have to come to work early while it is dark and enter the shop through the back door and leave after dark. I will set up a place for you to work in the back room. Never come to my house unless it is after dark, and always leave before light." The older man looked at him with a seriousness Detrick had not seen before.

CHAPTER THIRTY-FOUR

HEIM HOCHLAND, Institute for the Lebensborn near Munich,
Germany, situated in the Highlands near Munich, the home for the
Lebensborn beckoned with the charm of a country castle. A warm
sense of homey comfort had been carefully orchestrated in every
aspect of the décor. Large wool rugs covered the hardwood floors.
Heavy plush furniture was scattered tastefully throughout. In the
main dining area, long tables stretched across an airy and open
room. In the corner, a large grand piano awaited the accomplished
player who entertained at mealtime. Outside, tables and chairs sat
under weeping willow trees. A tennis court, pool, and exercise area
provided recreation. Manicured lawns filled with flowering plants
surrounded the home. And, of course, Heim Hochland featured a
fully equipped and staffed medical care center.

Helga Haswell endured all the questioning and testing required
upon her arrival. Once approved and assigned to her room, she met
Hermina, her roommate. Hermina had grown up on a strawberry
farm not far from Heim Hochland. Like Helga, she'd aspired to live
a better life, so rather than be the wife of a farmer, Hermina had
ventured into the city. Unlike many rural women, she'd learned to
read and write. Her ambitions drove her to learn shorthand and

typing. With her experience, she readily acquired a secretarial position. She enjoyed the challenges of her job and the independence of living on her own. In need of a roommate to share the expenses, Hermina had advertised in the local paper. The answer had arrived in Helga, a petite girl with dark, bobbed hair. Helga introduced her to the single life. Together they had stayed out drinking until the early hours of the morning when they would quickly shower and go off to work. Sexual encounters became as commonplace as sharing a quick meal. Nameless men came through Hermina's life and bed until she missed her monthly period. As with Helga, her doctor recommended the Lebensborn home. Now pregnant and sober, she'd come to realize that perhaps she had taken some wrong turns.

"I ran away without leaving a note. It is only recently that I have written to my mother. I told her what happened. I don't know if she will write to me. I hope so. I miss my family. I hope they can forgive me. I tried to tell them that it was an honor to have a child for the Führer. I hope they can accept that. My father might have a hard time with it, but maybe he will come around." Hermina took the brush off her nightstand and began brushing her long hair.

Helga shared her story with Hermina. Helga told her roommate about Erik and even confessed that she prayed daily that he might contact her. She still loved him, even after what he'd done. Daydreams filled her head. In Helga's fantasies, Erik would return, realizing that he loved only her. He would divorce his wife and marry her. At night she would collapse, exhausted from the daily exercise the Institute forced the pregnant mothers to engage in, only to awaken an hour later. Once awake, the reality of her situation set in, and she grew anxious. Sometimes, she lay in bed bathed in sweat. Other times, the tears flowed, and Helga whispered Erik's name into the silent, darkened room.

Down the hall, Margot shared a room with Frances. The two had become friendly with Hermina before Helga's arrival. All three girls would have their babies within weeks of each other, and then they would leave the home. Helga would not deliver until almost three months later. When they could, her friends would drag Helga outside to sit beneath the trees. But for the most part, Helga chose to be alone. Food nauseated her, and memories crept into her daily life, haunting her into depression. If only Erik would realize what he had sacrificed when he left her. If only he would return. Because of her anger at having been jilted, she wanted to believe she would be strong enough to refuse to speak to him if he did find her, but she knew she was deceiving herself. Helga longed for his touch and the sound of his voice. Sometimes, she made herself believe that he searched for her and would be at her side if he only knew where she had gone.

Every day, Helga's body grew more cumbersome. Her breasts, painful and full, strained against the restraint of her brassiere. The large, hard abdomen she had grown sported a dark line down the center, and looking at herself naked in a mirror brought tears to her eyes. Helga's shiny blonde curls hung limp and straight; worse, her skin had become blotchy. All she had left, she decided, kicked, and squirmed inside her womb.

At first, she hated the baby and blamed it for all her misfortune. But as time passed, she'd come to know the indentations of the tiny feet and elbows as they jutted through her skin. The baby danced in its watery world as the piano player entertained during meals, and automatically Helga's hand caressed her abdomen, and a smile crept across her face. In the beginning, she had counted the days until the birth. But now she feared her reaction when the doctors took the child away from her, which, of course, she had agreed to when she had come to Heim Hochland. Once the baby was born, it belonged to the Lebensborn. It had seemed such a simple decision at the beginning. But now...

Winter came early that year, and although it was only October, the wind tossed about a light dusting of snow. Helga and Hermina walked the grounds together.

"My family is coming to see me on Sunday. I can't wait for both of you to meet them." Hermina smiled, her face lighting up with delight. "I finally got an answer to the letter I sent them. It came yesterday. I have missed them so much."

"That should be nice." Margot's family had visited several times, and both girls knew them. Her family had announced proudly that their daughter had made the highest sacrifice for the cause, and they wore it like a badge of honor. "My daughter is bearing a child for the Führer." Margot's mother had smiled and patted her daughter's extended belly on her last visit.

Helga wished her mother and brother knew where she had gone and that they, too, would come to visit. The loneliness she fought came upon her suddenly, and tears rushed to her eyes. Margot did not notice right away, but Hermina saw Helga's despair. Although they had never discussed Helga's family, Hermina knew that her friend felt the isolation.

"Come." Hermina locked her arm through Helga's. "Let's go back to the kitchen and ask the cook if we can have some hot chocolate."

CHAPTER THIRTY-FIVE

HELGA RETURNED TO HER ROOM, sat alone, and wrote a letter to Inga. In the letter, she explained why she ran away and about staying at the Lebensborn. Tears smeared the ink, but she wrote until she had told the entire story. Then Helga tore the letter into tiny pieces and tossed them into the trash.

She could not expect her family to understand.

Sunday morning, Hermina dressed in her prettiest pink wool frock. Her face glowed, and after sleeping the night in pin curls, her hair floated in fluffy waves about her head. A pang of jealousy shot through Helga, but she forced it away as she watched her roommate dress for the arrival of her family. Instead, Helga tried to force herself to share in Hermina's joy. Even if watching Hermina's reunion with her parents brought back the reminder of the pain of losing her own, Helga would wish her friend well.

When Helga and Hermina arrived at breakfast, Margot sat waiting for them. Margot grinned as she told Hermina that her family would be visiting today as well. Helga held back the tears that stung the back of her eyes as she chewed and over-chewed a small bit of sausage. Unable to swallow, she finally spat it into her napkin. The sadness Helga felt at the loss of Erik and her family sprang forth anew. *Perhaps rather than ruin the celebration, she might just go off alone*, Helga thought.

"I am feeling so tired. I think I want to go up and nap. Perhaps I will come down later." Helga folded her napkin and forced a smile as she got up from the table.

"I will come for you when my family arrives. I want them to meet you." Hermina stroked Helga's arm.

Helga nodded. She would try to think of some excuse to stay in her room when Hermina came for her.

Finally, she was alone and sitting on her bed. The tears poured down Helga's face. She had held them back for so long that they came accompanied by loud and terrible sobs. Her hand rubbed her abdomen as the baby moved in sympathy with its mother's pain. And the realization that soon, the child would be born and gone from her life resurfaced, and with it, an agony so great she felt she might die. Helga cried until exhaustion overtook her, and then she slept.

When Hermina came through the door, Helga's eyes automatically opened. She wished Hermina had not seen that she was awake. She would have preferred to have been asleep and perhaps avoided the meeting.

"Helga, my family is here. Come, sweetie, wash your face. They are waiting in the dining room. We will all have our meal together."

The smile on Hermina's face forced Helga to push her sadness away and follow directions. When Helga returned from washing, Hermina had laid out a dress of her own for her to wear.

"I know you have always liked this one, and it is the same blue as your eyes. Wear it for me today?" Hermina winked.

Helga smiled. "Are you sure?"

"Absolutely. It will look wonderful on you."

CHAPTER THIRTY-SIX

PEOPLE FILLED the dining hall on visitors' day at Heim Hochland. They always did, but until now, Helga had avoided partaking in the celebrations. Lively polka music filled the area, accompanied by loud, excited conversations. The table had been set with red-and-white checkered tablecloths, and the smell of luscious food radiated in the air.

"This is my roommate, Helga." Hermina smiled. "This is my mother, my father, my little sister, Marsha, and my older brother, Kurt."

Helga brought forth the best smile she could muster. "I'm so pleased to meet all of you."

Margot spoke to Hermina and Helga, "Of course, you both know my parents."

While everyone talked excitedly, Helga looked around the table. Although Hermina had been honest about her humble beginnings, Helga found herself surprised to see the simple farmers who claimed her friend as their own. Hermina's mother wore a scarf tied around her stringy hair while a full and colorful skirt covered her fleshy body. Flab hung from her arms, but her smile lit up the room.

Marsha, Hermina's little sister, wore her church dress and sat very still as if she had never been amongst such a large crowd before. The father and brother both wore clean denim overalls and white shirts with skinny black ties. Their big hands were strong and calloused.

Kurt looked up from his plate to find Helga studying him, and a slow and easy smile came to his face. The open sincerity that shone on Kurt's face forced Helga to return the smile. He looked about twenty years old, with short-cropped hair and a large, muscular body. Kurt's years of manual labor in the summer sun had left a permanent bronze stain upon his skin, which offset his light-green eyes. Helga could not deny that she found his rugged exterior pleasing, even if his clothing lacked the polished style she had come to appreciate.

During lunch, Margot's mother spoke with the bravado of the pride she felt in her daughter's contribution to the cause.

"These children our daughters will bear will rule the world. They are the pride of the Third Reich. Every child born here at Heim Hochland is of pure Aryan blood. And to think... We...all of us here at this table...are a contributing part of it."

Helga's eyes dropped. Would her mother ever feel that way? If she asked herself honestly, would she? Now that the infant had grown deep within her, she acknowledged that she wanted to keep and raise the baby. This child had her blood flowing in its veins and belonged to her. And because of an agreement she had made in desperation, the day would come when it would be ripped from her arms, and she would never see it again. Motherhood would be denied to her. The baby would take its first steps and speak its first words while someone else stood by. When the child laughed or called out, "Mommy!" another would answer. And who could she trust to comfort her little one when he was ill? These thoughts haunted her mind, and she forgot to eat. In fact, she did not even realize the others were conversing or that the music was playing. Although surrounded by friends, Helga sat wrapped in her own painful, dark world of loss.

Margot's family explained that they must leave early, as they had a long drive back home. Once the goodbyes had been said with hugs all around, Margot went to walk her family to their car.

A light snow had fallen earlier that morning, covering the rolling hills and dusting the trees surrounding Heim Hochland.

"Would you like to see the grounds?" Hermina asked her parents.

"Yes, of course. Go and put your coats on, girls. We don't want you to catch a cold," Hermina's father instructed her and Helga.

Hermina and her parents walked ahead, talking softly, while little Marsha played with the snow. Rainbows from the sun's rays cast diamonds upon the virginal white landscape.

Kurt and Helga lagged behind, allowing Hermina time to reconnect with her mother.

"I'm glad they are on speaking terms again. My mother used to cry all the time."

"I can understand." Helga wondered if her own mother cried for her.

Kurt glanced over at Helga and saw that she seemed to be upset. "I'm sorry. I hope I didn't make you feel bad."

The tenderness in Kurt's voice brought out such a rush of emotion in Helga that she felt her false attempt at strength shatter. All the tears Helga had hidden would no longer be repressed. She began to weep uncontrollably as she wiped her wet face with the back of her glove.

"I am so clumsy with women. I don't know what to say or do, and it seems whatever I say or do is the wrong thing. Forgive me, please, Helga." Kurt wrung his hands in distress.

Helga had never met a man so honest and willing to admit his inadequacies. She could not believe that he was willing to appear unsophisticated. All the men she knew had prided themselves on their power, finesse, and charm. How refreshing Kurt seemed in comparison. However, Helga refused to consider him as a possible suitor. He lacked everything she aspired to find in a lover. Kurt had no money, no power, no position, nothing. He was a country bumpkin, nothing more than a farmer.

They walked for a while in silence.

"My family has no idea where I am." Helga didn't know why she suddenly felt so compelled to share that information with Kurt.

Kurt nodded. "I understand. That must be hard."

"It is." It was nice for Helga to be with a man she felt no need to impress. It made it so much easier to talk to him, to get things off her chest. "I got pregnant by a man who had a wife and children. I didn't know it at the time. I guess you could say he deceived me." Even as the words left her lips, Helga felt the heartbreak over Erik start anew.

"I'm sorry to hear it. Well, I don't know what to say to make you feel better. It is a terrible thing to lie to someone. It is how people get hurt. I can imagine you must feel betrayed. All I can say is, I hope you know that it wasn't your fault."

"When he left me, and I found out I was going to have a baby, I came here because I couldn't tell my family. My mother would have died of shame, knowing I had gotten pregnant out of wedlock."

"He was a fool. If I ever had a girl like you, I sure wouldn't walk away from her. Some people just don't realize what they have. But then again, if he had a wife, he shouldn't have been seeing you in the first place. That is insincere in every way."

The words Kurt spoke touched Helga deeply, and she suddenly felt uncomfortable. "I need to be getting back," she said, and then she looked up into his eyes, and the slight twinkle of attraction she felt frightened her. Without another word, she turned and walked as quickly as she could without running back to the safety of her room.

When she arrived, she flung her coat on the bed and slammed the door. Helga did not understand the anger that seemed to have taken hold of her. But she took Erik's picture and threw it against the wall.

CHAPTER THIRTY-SEVEN

THE HAPPIER HERMINA seemed to be, the more resentful Helga
became. Helga fought against the ugly, selfish emotions, but they
continued to surface. It seemed to Helga that regardless of what
Hermina had done in her past, Hermina would be redeemed and,
when the time came, returned to her comfortable, if not wealthy,
farming life. It seemed now that Hermina had realized her mistakes
and changed her mind. She was convinced that a rural existence
could offer her far more than the city, with its treacherous pitfalls.

When Hermina's family returned the following Sunday, Helga
remained in her room. Helga felt it best not to stir feelings she might
develop for Kurt, a man she would never consider for marriage.
Instead, she sat alone, gazing out the window, and wondered if Erik
ever thought about her. The smells of food and the uplifting piano
music drifted from the dining area. Although she was hungry, Helga
did not want to see Kurt, so she sat, stubbornly refusing to leave her
bedroom. If she ever considered allowing another man into her life,
which she doubted she would, he must be rich and powerful. But
hadn't Erik been all she'd dreamed of and more? Look at where
that had gotten her. Confusion turned to anger and more anger.

Once the music had ceased and the laughter and conversations had died down, Helga knew the meal had ended, and she began to allow herself to relax. Soon, Hermina's family would leave to return home, and with them, Kurt. As she got up from her chair by the window to find her knitting, there was a knock on the door. Helga wished she could just ignore it, but she knew she must answer.

"Yes?"

"It's Kurt. May I come in?"

She dreaded seeing him, but she could not think of an excuse. "Yes, come in."

Kurt entered the room carrying a tray of food.

"I didn't know if you might be hungry, so I brought this. Of course… if you are not feeling well, I will leave."

She saw that his hands trembled as he clumsily put the tray on her night table.

As she studied him, Helga felt bad. He had made a kind gesture, and she could not rebuke him for it.

"No, please don't leave." She found herself surprised to be saying, "I am actually hungry."

A big smile spread across his face as he timidly pulled the chair out for her, and she took the offered chair.

"Thank you. It is very kind of you to bring this for me."

A blush came to his cheeks, giving him a boyish, open, and uncontrived appearance. Helga felt a tug at her heartstrings.

"May I stay, or would you prefer that I go?" Kurt kept his head down, ashamed that his face had turned red.

"I suppose you can stay."

He sat in the chair by the window while she ate.

"What do you think of this Lebensborn concept, Kurt?"

"Not much…really." Then he studied her. "Are you sure you want to know the truth?"

"Only if you want to tell me."

"I think it is a disaster… I think the entire Third Reich will be a disaster. It is a far too radical way of thinking."

"You mean the creation of a superior race?"

"Well, yes, that and the removal of all people that Hitler sees as unfit. When we have different types of people, we have a diverse and interesting world."

She turned her chair to look at him.

"Before all of this began, I had been attending the university. I had plenty of Jewish professors. Many of them were wonderful and intelligent teachers."

"But I thought you were a farmer?"

"I am, and I always will be. But I had gone to study agriculture. There is much to learn, and I hoped to increase my production."

The more they talked, the more Kurt opened up like the pages of an interesting and inspiring book. He had befriended gypsies when they passed through Munich and told her what he knew about their culture. His acceptance of all people and all things reminded her in many ways of her brother. As Helga listened to Kurt's views, she began to see him in a different light.

When the sun began its descent from the sky, turning day to dusk, Helga found she wished Kurt did not have to leave. She had not enjoyed a conversation as much in a long time.

CHAPTER THIRTY-EIGHT

HELGA BEGAN to look forward to Sundays when Hermina's family came to visit. She and Kurt spent their time talking. Sometimes, they took long walks. Other times, they sat in front of the fireplace. He talked to her about farming and the delicious, sweet taste of strawberries, fresh-picked off the bush. She told him about the city and the parties she had once attended. Helga had never enjoyed reading until Kurt began to bring her novels. He would tell her the beginnings of the stories in advance so that she could not wait to open the books and continue the stories.

Margot went into labor late one Thursday night. By the time the girls found out, everything was over. Margot had delivered the baby and left the home without saying goodbye. Rumors spread that the child bore a cleft lip and had been euthanized at birth. Therefore, contact between Margot and the others had been forbidden, lest she start a panic. Imperfections in newborns would not be tolerated. Those words had sounded much easier to Helga when she had first agreed to her contract at Heim Hochland. That was before this baby had moved within her, lighting her heart on fire with a need to protect it.

That Sunday, when Kurt arrived, Helga told him what had happened to Margot.

"You remember Margot? The girl we had lunch with the first day you came to visit?"

"Yes, I remember her and her family. Why?"

"I don't know for sure, but I heard she had the baby, and it was born deformed. They euthanized it." She sat across the table from him, but her voice remained a whisper. "It's dangerous for me to tell you this."

"Come, let's walk outside." He took her arm and helped her to get up.

"Let me get my coat."

It was less than a week to Christmas, and the winter chill had set in. Helga's cheeks took on a rosy hue as they walked.

"Now, what do you mean, they euthanized the baby?"

"If children are born defective in any way, they kill them. It is never discussed, but it is an unspoken fact."

"My God, that is atrocious! When will this monstrous behavior end?"

"What if my baby is not all right? I can't help but wonder." She turned to him, and tears dripped from her eyes. He took her into his arms, holding her as her body racked with sobs.

"I don't know, Helga. I don't know. I don't have an answer. I wish I did."

She nodded, and for a long time, he held her.

"Helga?"

"Yes?"

"You must realize that I've fallen in love with you?"

"Please, Kurt, don't love me. I'm damaged. I can never love again."

"I don't believe that. I think you love me, too. I can't give you the world the way your Nazi officer could. It is not that I wouldn't want to. You deserve the best of everything, but I don't have it. But what I can give you is my heart and my soul. You will never have to worry about other women. No other woman will ever mean to me what you do. And I will give you children, Helga, children we can keep, raise, and love. Please give me a chance."

The snow crunched beneath him as he got down on one knee. Out of his pocket, he took a small box. His hands, red from the cold, trembled as he lifted the lid. Inside, a small diamond ring lay against a black velvet background.

For a moment, Helga stood still. She sucked a deep breath of the cold air into her lungs.

"Kurt, oh God, Kurt. I don't know what to say... I'm so confused." She stared into his eyes, eyes that were filled with hope. Frightened, she shook her head and turned, running back to the house. She did not stop until she reached her room. When she did, she flung the door closed behind her, then turned the lock.

Kurt stayed on one knee for several minutes holding the ring box before he collapsed, kneeling into the snow, his tears freezing in the winter wind as they fell upon his face.

CHAPTER THIRTY-NINE

"I SHOULD HAVE BEEN HERE with you. I can never forgive myself."
Detrick could not escape the guilt he felt at not having been with
Leah on Kristallnacht.

Detrick and Leah lay on her bed.

"You could not have known." Leah smoothed the hair out of
Detrick's eyes.

"I should have known. Konrad should have told me."

"Isn't that your childhood friend who joined the party?" She
remembered Detrick mentioning him.

"Yes, it is. Konrad disappoints me so much. I cannot believe that
he has become the man he is. When we were young, we were best
friends."

"Lots of people joined the party we never thought would do so,
people I've known all my life." Leah shook her head.

"Yes, I know, and they are cruel to their neighbors. I see it all the
time. The world has gone mad, Leah, and we are caught in the
middle. I would give my life to save you if it need be so."

"Don't talk that way, Detrick. This will pass. It has to." It felt like
a long fingernail ran up the length of Leah's spine, and she shivered.

CHAPTER FORTY

CANTANKEROUS OLD FOOL, Karl thought, as he watched his boss, Mr. Mencher, count the money drawer for the third time.

"Are we short?"

"I don't think so, but one can never check too many times." He watched Karl out of the corner of his beady, accusing eyes.

If you haven't found anything missing, why keep counting? Karl wondered. *This,* he thought, *is what gives us Jews a bad name.* He shook his head as he wiped the glass countertop.

"Is there anything else I can do?"

"Clean. Keep cleaning until I am all done. Then you can wait until I say you can go. That is what you can do."

Because Karl seemed eager to leave, the old man slowly checked the drawer one last time. He counted out Karl's small salary and handed it to him.

"Now you can go. I'll see you in the morning, and don't be late."

Karl nodded as he tucked the bills into his pocket and headed to the tavern. In the corner, his friend Joseph waited, sipping a whiskey.

"Karl, over here," Joseph called out when he saw his friend enter.

The chair groaned as he pulled it away from the table and sat down.

"You're really late tonight."

"Yeah, the old bastard got the idea that his drawer might be short, and he counted it until his old eyes almost popped out."

The two men laughed.

"Have you thought about coming to work at the aerospace factory? I could pull for you. And besides, I really want you to come to a meeting of the Bund." The Bund, the Jewish socialist union, had begun to boycott all merchandise from Germany because of Hitler's regime.

"I like everything about the Bund, except that they don't believe in Zionism. They don't think we need a Jewish state. And I'm telling you, Joseph, without a Jewish state, we will never be a strong people. The Gentiles will always do what they want to with us. They always have."

"The *goyim*, you mean?"

"Yes, anyone who isn't a Jew."

"Do you really think they are all bad?"

"Now, don't you? I mean, haven't you seen how they treat us? They'd kill us all if they could. If we had a state of our own... a homeland... well, then we'd always have a place to go, somewhere to turn."

"But we live here now. Let's try to defeat them here and build strength for our people in Poland."

"I agree with you in that respect, and I will attend the meeting, but I still think we must aim for our own land."

"Even so, until Israel becomes a reality, Poland is better for us than Germany, yes?"

"Yes." Karl lifted his glass, and the two drank in agreement.

CHAPTER FORTY-ONE

THE SMELL of sweat permeated the air as the leaders of the Bund took the podium. A tall, heavy-set man with thick gray hair and a coarse gray beard came forward.

"Have any of you heard about what happened on Kristallnacht?"

A buzz of whispered conversation caused him to raise his hands in protest. "Quiet, please. Only one of us must speak at a time."

In the back of the room, a man stood. He wore a black suit far too big for his puny frame. "In Germany, the Nazi Party attacked Jewish businesses. People on the streets got hit with clubs, and the Nazis also shattered all the windows and burned the synagogue. From what I understand, all Jews must wear yellow armbands with the Star of David to single them out. The Nazis have set a curfew, and all Jews must register as well."

"How long ago did this all happen?" Another voice from the corner of the room chimed out.

"Only one year ago. But from what I am hearing, things are getting tough for our people in Germany, and there is talk that Hitler plans to expand his empire even further, maybe to Poland."

"I don't believe he will come here. Poland is too big and

powerful a country." Another man stood—his throaty voice rang through the hall.

By the end of the night, Karl could think of nothing but his family. He wished he could visit and be sure they had not been harmed.

As he walked along the dark and quiet streets of Warsaw, Karl felt overcome with loneliness. Without his family and with only a few casual friends, the world appeared vast and empty. Inside, he secretly longed for love, but the vulnerability it might cost him hardly seemed worth the price. Perhaps he would go to the aerospace factory and apply for a job. He'd grown tired of Mr. Mencher and his precious hardware store.

Late August brought occasional cool nights, but on this night, no breeze broke the sweltering heat, and Karl felt a ring of sweat form in the armpits of his work shirt. He wondered when he might risk going home. Although his relationship with Jacob had been strained due to his fighting and radical beliefs, Karl found that he missed his father the most. As a little boy, Jacob centered him, giving him confidence and purpose. Only once the Nazi takeover shattered their lives did Karl find his relationship with Jacob to be a challenge. Their differences made him angry, and instead of discussing his feelings, Karl shut his father out. He resented that Jacob still kept that *goy*, Detrick, with him, even though Karl saw Detrick as just another Nazi in the making. Now Karl smiled wryly. Regardless of their differences, he would have given anything to see his family again, especially his father.

Yes, tomorrow he will apply for a job at the factory. It was time for a change.

CHAPTER FORTY-TWO

IN MARCH 1933, near the quaint Bavarian town of Dachau, the first real concentration camp was established. At first, it housed primarily political prisoners.

This facility, built on the grounds of an abandoned munitions factory, would later be established as the model for future camps. Thirty-one thousand reported deaths are attributed to the Dachau camp, but the true death toll is thought to be considerably higher.

At a little after four o'clock in the morning, a shooting took place on the Polish-German border. On the 1st of September, under Hitler's orders, a group of Nazis rounded up prisoners from Dachau and dressed them in German uniforms. Then they transported the captives to the border, where they shot them, crying out, "Poland has invaded Germany!"

Now Hitler had his excuse, through another deception, as he declared war on Poland, and the German troops marched across the border to take over their neighbor.

Poland proved no match for Hitler. Germany attacked the northern, southern, and western fronts. Within a few weeks, on October 6, 1939, Poland surrendered, and the German occupation began.

CHAPTER FORTY-THREE

Wilfrieda thumbed through her magazine and puffed on a cigarette as she awaited the arrival of her next client. Konrad Klausen had proven difficult in his prior visits but well worth the effort and discomfort, at least financially.

Prostitution is an art, she told herself repeatedly. Men like Konrad only served to reinforce her conviction. She had found his quirk quite accidentally. He had come to see her several times and been unable to achieve an erection. She'd begun to wonder why he continued to frequent the district. On one occasion, she'd spoken with another girl Konrad had visited, and she had admitted that regardless of what she'd tried, his manhood had remained limp. Then, one evening, he came to see Wilfrieda following a fight with his superior officer. He insisted that she join him in a drink and then another until they both had become inebriated. The two had been laughing and embracing. Things felt warm and ripe, so she'd taken his manhood from his pants and placed her lips around it, sucking deeply. He had remained flaccid, but his attitude changed, and his face grew red with anger.

"You stupid, good-for-nothing slut! You ugly whore!" he spat insults at her, and as he did, he threw her against the bed frame.

With one hand, he tore her dress open and ripped her panties. Now fully erect, he entered her and pushed her hands up over her head, forcing himself inside of her roughly.

Once she learned what he needed, she knew how to play him. For a long time, the mock rape had satisfied him. But as of late, he had been requesting to tie her arms and legs to the bedpost.

Instinct brought a cold chill of fear when she considered the possibility, and until now, she had refused him. But he paid more than her other clients, and she wanted to keep him.

CHAPTER FORTY-FOUR

WHEN THE BOAT pulled into Ellis Island, Dorothy Silver thought her heart would burst with anticipation. Many of the immigrants waved homemade American flags, whooping and hollering. The new world lay just steps away. Soon, she and her family would disembark from the ship, and her life in America would begin. In many ways, she longed for the old familiar days she'd shared with Leah in Germany, but her youthful soul could not help but embrace the adventure. The sun cast a blinding reflection on the shining copper Statue of Liberty, which had oxidized to green in patches. The noise ceased for a moment, and silence fell upon the group as the immigrants realized that they had arrived. The American dream had gleamed like a diamond in their minds. Now it was a reality before them. If one listened closely, the thunder of anxious heartbeats would be heard above the rush of the roaring waves.

Dorothy lost track of the days before the release of the family from quarantine. The halls smelled of sweat, salami, garlic, and sausages. But finally, the Silvers took the ferry off the island and into New York City. She had never seen this many people with such diverse ethnicities. She wished they could linger and observe all the strange goings-on, but her father insisted they hurry to the train station, board, and speed off to Chicago, where they would meet Dorothy's uncle and his family.

Oscar Silver longed to see his brother again but also felt embarrassed at imposing upon his family. In Germany, he'd earned a nice living, not to mention the respect of the town when he volunteered as the cantor at the synagogue. Now, he depended upon his brother to help him find work to support his family and begin his life again.

The Silver family sat quietly, looking out the window as the train chugged along from New York to Chicago, each one lost in his thoughts.

Dorothy slept and awakened several times before they entered the station. As soon as they disembarked, she smelled the horrible odor she would later learn came from the stockyards. It would take time for the family to grow accustomed to the nauseating stench of blood and death.

From the train station, they took the elevated train along the rooftops of the city to her uncle's house. She sped past clotheslines filled with garments blowing in the breeze, men working on construction sites, wearing dirty, white, cotton tee shirts, and tramps sitting on the pavement outside liquor stores with bottles concealed in brown paper bags.

Dorothy's mother looked gray with nausea as the train bumped and jarred. Her father continually reassured them that they were all safe, although he did not seem entirely convinced.

Finally, they arrived at their stop, where they were instructed to take a streetcar to the west side. When they boarded the car, they found it crowded and had to stand with their luggage for the entire ride. Passengers shot looks of disdain at the foreigners. Dorothy took notice of how differently they dressed from the people of her homeland. She admired the women with their tight skirts and brazen made-up faces. The open trolley moved through the streets. They passed restaurants and dance clubs, where she heard bands playing swing music. These rhythmic sounds fell upon her ears, bringing a smile to her face. She had heard of swing, but Hitler forbade it in Germany.

When they arrived at Uncle Benjamin's apartment, she met her cousin Hette and Aunt Essie. They lived in a large brick building on the third floor. Dorothy shared a small bedroom with Hette while her parents slept on a hide-a-bed in the living room. The flat was small and cramped before. Now with an additional family, it was even more so. The luxury of hot water was unaffordable, and that meant cold baths. This would be all right in the summer, but Uncle Benjie explained that when winter came, they would boil the water before bathing.

Since Uncle Benjie worked at the fruit and vegetable market, the family had access to all the spoiling food which Aunt Essie used to make soups. Although he tried, Uncle Benjie found no success in securing a job for his brother.

"The economy is bad," they told him. "We have no room for another worker." And so, for a while, Dorothy and her family felt like dead weight in the home of their relatives. No one ever said a word, but the air grew thick with their annoyance as the newness of the visitors wore off, and the lack of space and rations became more apparent day by day.

Dorothy's father set out to comb the neighborhood every morning in search of work, and each evening he returned covered in grime, sweat, and disappointment. She watched at the evening meal as he ate less and less, growing thinner with each passing day.

Finally, just before Dorothy started her senior year at Marshall High School in the fall, her father arrived home with good news. For a moment, he appeared to be the man of so long ago, the one of whom neighbors in Germany had spoken so highly. He walked in the back door through the kitchen, grinning ear-to-ear, and with the loud and booming voice that had made him the most popular cantor at the shul, he called out, "Mama, Dorothy, come quickly!"

They both raced into the kitchen just in time to see him remove his hat and toss it on the table.

"I have a job! I am working selling men's and women's coats on Maxwell Street! I will do the books for the store, too. It is not as much money as I earned in the old days, but for the love of God, it is a start! We are going to be all right." He stretched his strong arms out, embracing them like a giant black bear.

CHAPTER FORTY-FIVE

DOROTHY ADMIRED HER COUSIN HETTE, who worked downtown at Marshall Field's and wore a hint of lipstick. Dorothy knew her father wanted her to finish high school, but she felt out of place. The other students dressed and acted differently than her friends in Germany. The girls shunned her. When the teacher called on her in class, and she tried to answer, the other students giggled at the sound of her accent. She learned enough of the language to converse but could not grasp reading in English. This made her schoolwork twice as difficult, and most days, she walked home alone and depressed. And even though she was Jewish, she was subjected to the national hatred and distrust Americans had developed for Germans.

The only pleasure she found in this new country came from the wild and exciting rhythm of swing music. When her cousin played it on her phonograph, Dorothy loved to sing along. Her voice could tap with the beat or croon with the blues. Often, she begged Hette to take her to a swing club where she could watch the dancers, but Hette just smiled and said, "When you get a little older."

One afternoon in early November, Dorothy's American history teacher asked her to stand and read from the United States Constitution. She stood and stammered over the words. Her accent made much of what she said undecipherable. The anti-German sentiment was exacerbated by her accent. Few students realized that Dorothy, being Jewish, was just as much an enemy of the Third Reich as they were. Instead, they called her a kraut and focused their hatred of Hitler on her, the girl with the German accent.

As she read aloud, one of the boys in the back of the room hit her with a rubber band. It stung where it made contact with her shoulder, but the pain it brought to her emotionally devastated her. Since she'd come to America, she'd felt out of place, alone, and friendless. Tears came to her eyes. She looked around the room. At that moment, she made a decision. With trembling hands, she gathered her books and walked out of the room. Behind her, she heard the teacher. "Dorothy Silver, where are you going? I have not dismissed this class. Do you hear me?"

Dorothy heaved the heavy wooden door open and left the school. Outside, she saw a large trash can where she dumped her books. Then, wiping her hands on her wool skirt, she put her handbag under her arm and headed for the elevated subway station.

Dorothy's heart raced with trepidation and excitement as she took her handkerchief out of her purse and wiped her face. Then she counted her money. She had almost a whole dollar.

She paid her fare and boarded the train downtown to Marshall Field's. Dorothy knew that Hette got off the train at State and Washington. So, Dorothy carefully watched the stops and listened to the conductor. When she heard the announcement for State and Washington, she stood ready at the automatic doors. After she had disembarked, she walked up the stairs to the street, where she saw the tall building with green lettering. It looked just the way that Hette had described it. She turned to an old woman sitting on a bus top bench.

"Excuse me, please." Dorothy pointed to the building she suspected might be her destination. "Is that Marshall Field's?"

The old woman nodded. "That's it right there."

"Thank you." Dorothy dashed to her destination.

On the first floor, to the left of the hosiery, Marshall Field's hat department boasted some of the loveliest headpieces in Chicago. Hette stood behind a glass counter, helping a woman secure a fedora with a hatpin. When she saw Dorothy, she smiled and walked over.

"Aren't you supposed to be in school?" Hette asked her cousin.

"I need a job."

"What happened?"

"I walked out. Besides, we can use the money."

"Yes, I suppose that is the truth. Your father will kill me, but let me see what I can do. When I go on my break, I'll go down to personnel and see what's available. Come back at two-thirty?"

"Alright, I will. Thank you so much, Hette."

Dorothy wandered up and down State Street for several hours. The shop windows were decorated like works of art. Dorothy was awe-struck, for she had never seen this many beautiful things. When she saw Grant Park, she bought a hot dog and then crossed a busy intersection to sit on a bench next to the art museum, where she ate lunch. At two-thirty, she returned to the store.

"I have good news. They want to see you." Hette gave her an orange-red lipstick smile.

"Where do I go?"

"Second floor. Take the elevator over there. Let me know what happens."

"I will."

CHAPTER FORTY-SIX

"Good afternoon. May I help you?" The girl at the desk wore a white cashmere sweater and a gray wool skirt. Dorothy loved the way the sweater fell loose, just showing a hint of the receptionist's figure.

"Yes, thank you. My name is Dorothy Silver. My cousin Hette Silver said that I should come here and talk to someone about a job."

The girl nodded and handed Dorothy a group of papers and a pencil. "Fill these out. When you're through, bring them back to me."

Dorothy sat down in the waiting room and tried to read the application. Her writing and grammar left much to be desired. The tiny print was impossible for her to grasp. It seemed as if there was so much to read, but she hoped her enthusiasm would make up for her lack of competence in the English language. She reread her application twice, sounding out the words and trying to comprehend the meaning at the same time. Over and over, she erased and corrected until the paper tore. Then, she finally got up and handed the document to the receptionist.

After Dorothy waited twenty minutes, a well-dressed woman

with bottle-red hair in perfect finger waves appeared. The receptionist handed her Dorothy's papers, which she glanced over quickly.

"This way, my dear."

They walked down a long corridor surrounded by desks on either side. The clicking of typewriters filled the halls. Finally, at the end of the hall, they entered an office. The fire-haired lady closed the door and motioned for Dorothy to sit.

"Hello, my name is Gloria McMillan. I am the head of personnel here at Marshall Field and Co. Your cousin speaks highly of you."

Dorothy smiled.

"Cat got your tongue?"

"I'm sorry?"

Dorothy wasn't sure what that statement meant. She looked at Gloria McMillan blankly.

"It's just an expression." Mrs. McMillan smiled. Once she'd heard Dorothy's accent, she realized the girl had no idea what she'd said.

"So your name is Dorothy Silver." She studied the application. "It seems to me that you have difficulty reading and writing English. I am afraid this is a very necessary part of the job you are applying for."

"I can learn. I will work very hard."

For a moment, Dorothy thought she detected a hint of sympathy race across Gloria McMillian's face. Then, rising from her chair, Mrs. McMillian walked to the window facing away from Dorothy.

"I am sorry, dear. I really am. But I don't think this is a good idea for either of us. I am sure you understand."

Tears stung Dorothy's eyes. She rose from the chair.

"Thank you." Before the interviewer could see Dorothy was crying, she left the room and walked as quickly out of the building as she could, not meeting anyone's eyes on the way.

The fresh air stung Dorothy's face as she raced from the department store.

Her heart ached with rejection. She could not return to

school after disposing of all of her books, so where was she to go? If her father learned that she left her education behind without any prospect of employment, he would be furious. Frustrated, she paced the sidewalks, not realizing how far she had traveled from her original downtown location. When she finally looked around, she realized that the neighborhood had changed. Some of the windows bore cracks where they had been broken, and others stood covered by protective metal bars. A large pawnshop occupied the corner of a busy intersection, beckoning the down and out to bring their possessions for a quick sale. Dorothy hurried along, eyes scanning the streets nervously in search of a bus stop, but finding one wouldn't help her. She had no idea which bus would deliver her back to her uncle's home. A man appeared from the dark recesses of an alleyway.

"Hello, little lady. Where you goin'?"

She turned away from the stench of alcohol on his breath and ran, with the vile echo of his laughter ringing in her ears. She was lost. The reality hit her like a boulder tumbling upon her head. How would she ever find her way? A wave of panic clutched at her. Her accent and inability to read English made her situation even more perilous. Whom could she trust to ask directions? She scanned the street for a woman, deciding it would be safer to talk to a female than a male. But dusk had begun to settle, and she found the street empty.

In the window of a tall building, she saw a sign. In an attempt to read it, she sounded the words out as she spoke them aloud.

"Singer wanted—one flight up." For a moment, she forgot her distress. Dorothy knew herself to be limited in her employable skills, but she also realized that if she had any talents at all, the one she could most assuredly count on was her voice. After taking a deep breath and crossing her fingers, Dorothy opened the door and began to climb the stairs.

When she reached the second floor, she saw at least ten women in worn evening gowns dancing, with their bodies pressed tightly to men who slithered close beside them. Some fellows hung on the girls, groping at the dancers' buttocks and barely moving to the music.

Dorothy found herself unable to take her eyes off the spectacle as she walked to the information booth.

"Excuse me. My name is Dorothy Silver. I read your sign downstairs that you need a singer."

"Where you from?" The girl with striking silver-blonde hair curling about her tiny face asked.

"I am from Germany."

"Oh well." She shook her head. "I don't think the boss is gonna wanna hire a kraut."

"Please, miss. Give me a chance. I need a job."

The blonde saw the tears filling Dorothy's eyes, and she nodded. "Yeah, all right, let's face it. I'm a sucker. Let me go and get the boss. I ain't sure what he's gonna say, honey, but you just sit right over there and let me go and find him."

Dorothy lowered herself onto a rickety stool. Until now, she had not been aware of the pain the heel of her shoe had caused when it cut into her flesh. It seemed she'd grown so fast that her shoes no longer fit. With her family's lack of finances, she had opted not to ask her father for money to purchase a new pair. All of her life, she and her father had been close, so close she'd felt his pain as her own. Now, she saw his struggle and would rather suffer than give weight to his feelings of inadequacy as a provider. And she knew if she asked him for money, somehow, someway, he would get it.

Mr. McGleason limped with his pant leg dragging over his shoe to the stool where Dorothy waited.

"Carol here tells me you need a job." He wiped the sweat from his forehead with the rolled-up sleeve of his white shirt. "Says you wanna be a singer? Hell, you don't look old enough to be in here, let alone to be out at night."

"Oh, but I am. I'm twenty-one," Dorothy lied.

McGleason let out a laugh that came straight from his large, rolling belly. "Yep, I sure heard that one before. Well, all right, I guess you can audition. Go on up on the stage and tell Jeb what song you want to sing, and he'll play piano for you."

Her knees trembled as Dorothy walked up the three stairs at the corner of the stage. She went over to the piano player and asked if he knew any love songs by the famous Helen Morgan. He smiled an almost toothless smile and whispered to her that he did. They decided upon a song, and Dorothy walked to the center of the stage. She took the barrette out of her long curls and let them hang loose to her waist. Then she unbuttoned the top three buttons of her blouse. When she opened her mouth and began to sing in her deep, rich alto voice, everyone in the club turned to pay attention to her.

Pleasantly surprised, Mr. McGleason winked at Carol.

After she had finished singing, Dorothy walked back down to where Mr. McGleason and Carol stood.

"You got yourself a job, kid," McGleason smiled. "You start tomorrow. Be here at 8:00 p.m. sharp. And listen, this is a ten-cents-a-dance club, so learn that song, huh?"

"Yes, of course." Dorothy stammered with elation.

"Hey, Fred," Carol called out to Fred McGleason. "I wanna go and get somethin' to eat. I ain't had no break all day."

"Yeah. Hurry up, though."

Dorothy and Carol walked down the stairs together and out into the street.

"I am sorry to bother you, but do you know where I can catch a bus back to the West Side?"

"Sure, why don't you come and eat with me, and then I'll show you?"

"I can't, I'm sorry."

"You ain't got no money, right?"

"Yes, right." Dorothy looked down, ashamed.

"Aww, kid, don't worry about it. It's on me." Carol put her arm around Dorothy.

After dinner, Carol walked Dorothy to a bench. "This here is where the streetcar stops," Carol told her. "Now listen. Take the 29 to the end of the line, cross the street, and get on number 57. You got that?"

"Yes, I think so, and thank you so much for dinner and…well, and for everything."

"Aww, kid, don't worry about it. You're gonna like it here at the club. It ain't Heaven, but hell, it's a living."

CHAPTER FORTY-SEVEN

"TEN CENTS A DANCE..." Dorothy sang slowly in the deep, throaty, bluesy style that had become her signature.

In less than a week, Dorothy's popularity began to climb. The clients asked if she would be performing when they purchased their tickets for dances while Carol proudly reminded everyone that she had discovered the new singer.

Dorothy sang on stage for forty minutes on, twenty minutes off, until the wee hours of the morning. Carol helped her to find suitable costumes. She wore evening gowns of sequins in bright, eye-catching colors, her rich, auburn hair hanging in tight curls at her waist. The womanly body Dorothy had developed, with ample breasts and wide hips, sent the male customers into a frenzy. Then Carol helped Dorothy to use lipstick and mascara.

On stage, Dorothy felt like a starlet. But late at night, as she snuck back home and entered the apartment like a criminal trying not to make a sound, she worried about her father's reaction, should he awaken and confront her.

Oscar Silver knew his daughter. At least, he thought he did. In his mind, he felt sure something had gone wrong. Every night, Dorothy left the house and did not return until he had fallen asleep.

His daughter, his pride and joy. Where did she go? What did she do?

One night, when the questions in his mind became more than he could tolerate, Oscar fought the overwhelming exhaustion he felt and decided to stay awake and wait for Dorothy.

Oscar sat in an old but large, overstuffed chair, gazing out the window as the morning light began slipping into the room. Dorothy had not yet returned. His heavy heart hammered with worry. He stretched his arms, trying to open his tightened lungs, to try to breathe deeply.

It was only an hour before he would rise to leave for work that he heard the key move in the lock. Dorothy entered, carrying her high-heel shoes in her hand. She locked the door. Then, turning, she saw the shadow in the shape of her father in the semi-darkness. He sat quietly watching her, and although he had not spoken a word, his anger filled the air like a presence. A shudder crept up her spine as he rose and deliberately walked to the light switch. The silence was so thick that she could hear every step he took as the floor creaked beneath his feet. Once he'd illuminated the room, the misery she saw in his face shook her.

"Look at you. A curva... a whore... my baby, my Dorothy! Is this what we came to America for?" He looked her up and down as if he had never seen her before. The mascara she wore had smeared under her eyes, and although it had worn off, the red lipstick stained her mouth.

"I am sick because of you. Sick, I tell you! Where are you going all night? What are you doing?"

His voice echoed through the night.

"Papa, I am a singer in a nightclub. I am sorry, but it was the only job I could find. You have to understand, Papa. You could not find work either. Not for a long time." She'd fallen to her knees as she took his hands into her own.

"*Oy*, what about school? A singer in a nightclub. Is this a place for a decent girl? A nice Jewish girl? Dorothy, I am ashamed. I am so ashamed." He pulled away from her and then sat down in defeat.

After falling back into the chair, Oscar Silver put his face in his hands. Then he sobbed, deep, heart-rending sobs. Dorothy stood, unable to move. She longed to go to him. No matter what the family had faced, he had never cried before. Her heart beat in terror as she watched him, helpless. The sound of footsteps in the hallway caused her to turn and look. There stood her mother and her uncle, her aunt, and her cousin.

Trembling in terror, Dorothy walked slowly toward him with her arms extended the way she had done as a child. She remembered when he had come home from work, how she ran to him, reaching for him.

"Papa," her voice cracked, barely a whisper. "Papa, please," she begged him with all her heart. "Please forgive me. Try to understand."

He stood and walked towards her. Dorothy held her breath. Then, he turned away. "Go away from here and never come back! You shame us all! Go!"

"Papa!" she cried as the tears poured down her face. "Papa! Please!"

"Go!" The anger had gone from his voice, but he did not look at her as he walked through the grouping of his family and back into the room in the rear of the apartment. The door slammed, and the house was silent.

No one spoke. They all dispersed, leaving Dorothy standing alone, her arms still extended in the empty air.

CHAPTER FORTY-EIGHT

THE SUN HAD BEGUN to rise as Dorothy boarded the L train. She would ride until the club opened, and then she planned to talk to Carol about sharing her apartment. Dorothy rode from the end of the line at the north side of the city to the other end at the south. Occasionally, she slept for a few minutes, then awoke, frightened by the reality of what had happened the night before.

The club opened in the late afternoon. Although a few clients came in early, most of the first hours were spent preparing for the evening.

Dorothy arrived, disheveled, still wearing the dress she'd worn the night before. Her makeup was smeared across her face, and her tangled hair had been pulled back into a ponytail and secured with a rubber band.

"Holy cow, kid! You look a mess! What happened?" Carol put her arm around Dorothy's shoulder.

"My father threw me out. I have nowhere to go. I rode the L all night."

"Tough break."

"Yes. I don't know how to ask you this, but…would you consider a roommate? Of course, I will pay half the rent, and I am very clean and..." Tears rolled from her eyes.

"Dorothy, come on, kid, don't cry. Yeah, sure, you can stay with me. At least, 'til you get on your feet, all right?" Carol squeezed her shoulder. "Come on. Let's get you cleaned up. You can't go on stage like this."

Dorothy agreed, and they went backstage. Carol, a wizard with cosmetics and hair, pulled Dorothy together in no time.

That night, they took the streetcar back to Carol's small but clean and comfortable apartment. With only one bedroom, Carol made the couch into a bed. As soon as Dorothy lay her head down, she fell into a deep slumber.

CHAPTER FORTY-NINE

At first, Dorothy felt out of place and missed her family. But as the weeks turned to months and the Chicago winter crept in, she found herself adjusting. Each day, she and Carol took the streetcar to work together. She learned that Carol and Fred McGleason kept company. When Fred came to the apartment, and he and Carol disappeared into the bedroom, Dorothy took long walks to give them some privacy.

One morning in the dead of winter, Carol awoke with a terrible cold. She sneezed, coughed, and sniffled. With red eyes and a running nose, she told Dorothy that she would not be going to work and asked that she explain the situation to Fred. Dorothy agreed.

Snow and ice covered the ground as Dorothy waited for the streetcar. Watery-gray slush splashed under the tires of automobiles and buses as they sped by. Before Dorothy could back away, a large black car turned the corner, covering her with dirty water and ice.

"Damn!" she spat the word.

The vehicle came to a halt as the window in the back seat opened. "I am so sorry." A gentleman with blue-black hair slicked back from his face appeared. "May I give you a ride?"

"No." Still brushing the wet snow from her new white coat, she looked at him angrily.

"At least allow me to pay the cleaning bill."

"No, thank you."

He wore a black pinstriped suit and shiny gold jewelry. The driver wore a chauffeur's cap.

"My name is Anthony Salitano."

"Good for you, Anthony Salitano. You're holding up traffic."

The streetcar had come down the street and stood behind Salitano's car, waiting for him to move. Dorothy walked around the vehicle and hopped on board.

When she arrived at work, she informed Fred of Carol's condition, and he told her to tell Carol to take a few days off and rest.

The following day, as she waited for her transportation, Anthony Salitano appeared again. This time, he had a bouquet of flowers.

"Hello again. I brought these to say that I am sorry for yesterday. And please, won't you allow me to pay the bill for the cleaners?"

"Thanks, but no thanks." His confidence came off as arrogance, and she found him repugnant. Since she had begun working at the ten-cents-a-dance hall, her views on men had changed. She learned from watching them that they had only one thing in mind, and Dorothy decided that she would never be anyone's sexual toy.

Once again, the streetcar appeared, and she walked away from him.

Tony Salitano took pleasure in a challenge. Women came to him easily, and why not? He had money, good looks, and connections. What else could a man need? But this little redhead would not give him a second glance, and that only meant that he had to have her.

"Frank, follow that streetcar until the dame gets off," Tony told his chauffeur.

"You got it, boss."

CHAPTER FIFTY

A WILY GRIN crept over Tony's face as he took a seat at the back of the dance club and waited for the cocky little redhead. For a dime, he could hold her in his arms. A sardonic laugh escaped his lips while the girls entered the ballroom. He looked around but did not see her. Well, maybe this one took a long time to get dressed. He didn't mind. He'd wait all night if need be.

The piano player's nimble fingers moved briskly across the keys as the dancers took their places on the floor. Tony had an entire roll of tickets on the table in front of him. He decided he would be that little redhead's partner for the entire night if she would just come out of that damned dressing room.

"Ladies and gentlemen, the Diamond Room is proud to present the songstress, Miss Dorothy Silver," Jeb announced in a voice that sounded like a bass guitar, projecting through the dance hall from the microphone on the piano.

Dorothy sauntered to the center of the stage, taking the micro-phone with her. She shook her long curls back from her shoulders and smiled at the audience. Then she sang.

Tony sat spellbound as the haunting, melodious voice tapped into his innermost being. "So," he realized. "She is the singer. I shoulda known. She has too much class to be a ten-cents-a-dance broad."

Before Dorothy finished her set, Tony had disposed of the tickets. He did not want her to think ill of him. Instead, he would offer to buy her a drink. Then he would carefully explain his connections and how they might be helpful to a girl starting out on a singing career.

"Hey, who owns this joint?" Tony asked one of the dancers as she walked by his table.

"Fred McGleason. Why?" She flashed her most attractive smile.

"I wanna see him. Tell him I wanna buy the joint."

"Ya do?" Her eyes lit up.

"Go on and tell him."

In a few moments, Fred stepped over to the table, dragging a chair. He straddled the chair, moving it close to the table.

"Yeah, one o' my girls said you wanna see me about buying the place. Well, it ain't fer sale."

Anyone and anything can be bought for the right price. Even this clown, Tony thought as he studied Fred. *But why? Just to meet the redhead. That's all he really needed. His charm would take it from there.* Tony pulled a bill off the top of a roll of hundreds and laid it on the table. "I don't need to buy your joint, but I do have a little favor to ask, and I make a habit of rewarding those who do me favors."

"Yeah?" Fred eyed the money.

"I want you to introduce me to the singer. What was her name?"

"Dorothy? Dorothy Silver?"

"Yeah, bring her over here. And here's a little somethin' fer you." Tony pushed the bill over towards Fred's hand.

Fred picked up the money and stood, turning the chair and pushing it against a table. "Stay right here. I'll get her."

CHAPTER FIFTY-ONE

THE DRESSING ROOM, a noisy place filled with girls sprucing up their clothes and makeup, immediately went quiet when Fred walked in.

"Dorothy, I got a man out here who wants to meet you."

"You know I don't go for that, Fred. I sing, and that's all. I don't do no ten-cent dances or worse."

"I ain't askin' you to. Just go on out and meet him. Have a drink and then go back on stage. By the time you finish, he'll be gone. Come on, Dorothy, when you needed a job, I helped you."

She looked at Fred with affection. He had been there for her, and so had Carol. *Well, I can survive one drink.*

"You?" Dorothy looked at Tony, recognizing him from the street. "What are you doing here? How did you ever find me?" At first, she thought she might explode with anger at his following her, then looking at his expression, she could see how foolish he felt, and she laughed.

"Can I buy you a drink?"

"Sure. Why not?"

They sat in uncomfortable silence, sipping their drinks.

"How did you find me?"

"I'll tell you. Only you can't get mad."

176 | ALL MY LOVE, DETRICK

She laughed again. "All right, I promise."

"I followed the streetcar here. Then I bought a whole roll of dance tickets 'cause I was hoping you would maybe dance with me. But when you came out on that stage and you, well, you looked so beautiful. I asked Fred to introduce me."

"You know Fred?"

"We just met."

She laughed again. "You've made a lot of effort."

"I think you're worth it. I can tell."

"Well, that is certainly flattering." She felt the blush on her cheeks and was glad for the darkness of the club.

"Can I buy you dinner when you get outta work?"

"It would be more like breakfast by the time I'm off."

"Breakfast, then?"

"You want to stay here the entire night?" Dorothy was amazed at his persistence.

"Yeah, I do."

CHAPTER FIFTY-TWO

EVERY NIGHT for the next month, Tony appeared at the club. Sometimes, he stayed, but often, he came and left, only to return at the end of Dorothy's shift to drive her and Carol back to the apartment. Most nights, they dropped Carol off and went to eat at an all-night café.

On her days off, Tony took Dorothy shopping. He bought her a white ermine to make up for the coat he had splashed. As they left the store, she turned to him, kissing his cheek.

"You know, once a long time ago, when I lived in Germany, my girlfriend dated a boy whose mother owned a white ermine coat. I thought her the luckiest woman alive."

"Now you own one." Tony swelled with pride.

She smiled up at him. He put his arms around her, pulled her close, and kissed her.

"I like you a lot, Dorothy. I suppose you know that."

She smiled.

That night, they had dinner at a steak house. After the meal, Tony asked if Dorothy would like to see his home.

She knew he wanted to bed her and considered herself old enough. She just wished she felt more magic towards him, more passion, and more desire. There was no reason she did not. He had good looks, lots of money, and people showed him the respect he commanded wherever they went. They were seated at the nicest tables. The store owners bowed down with attention as he purchased expensive merchandise while the rest of the country struggled to eat. She could not figure out what he lacked…only that he did not excite her, not the way she wished he could.

Never had Dorothy seen such a magnificent structure. Tony's home looked more like a palace than a house. Far from the street, set off by a long path surrounded by well-manicured lawns, the white house stood like a museum. They walked up a flight of stone stairs to a red wooden door. When Tony opened the door and flipped the light switch, Dorothy's mouth fell open with surprise and admiration.

"That gold you see there on the marble floor, well, that's real, authentic gold." Tony smiled. "And the faucets in the bathroom are gold, too."

Her heels clicked on the marble as she walked from room to room. The bedroom was larger than the entire apartment she had lived in with her parents and her uncle's family. A thick white carpet covered the floor. She removed her shoes and marveled at the softness beneath her feet.

"This is beautiful, Tony."

"You like it?"

"Yes, of course I do. How could I not?"

"Well, would ya like to live here with me?" He grinned.

"Oh, I don't know. I–"

"I guess I oughta tell ya. I'm married. But it don't mean nothin'. She and I don't live together."

"You have a wife?"

"Yeah. In name only. But you, well, you're my baby."

Dorothy was shocked. She'd never suspected. Tony had a wife.

Well, she thought, *in a way, it was good. At least he would not expect to marry her. And she had wanted to shake her virginity. Who better to choose than a man who could not commit, a man who could never endanger her career?* She looked at him. At least he'd been honest. And well, let's face it. She didn't love him, at least not in that way. Perhaps his age had something to do with her lack of desire. She found her feelings towards him to be platonic, as she would feel for a father figure rather than romantic. He always gave her anything she asked for and always proved to be more than generous and kind. So, what difference did it make?

"Tony?"

"Yes?" He almost wished he hadn't told her. If she left now, he would surely lose her forever. A cold chill crept across his shoulders.

"Let's make love." She took his hand and led him to the bed.

CHAPTER FIFTY-THREE

CAROL WIPED her tears with an embroidered hanky when Dorothy told her she planned to leave, then gave Dorothy a big, lipstick-stained kiss on her cheek and wished her luck. Dorothy gave Carol a tiny gold heart she'd purchased with money Tony had given her.

Although making love with Tony left much to be desired, Dorothy tolerated the moments of intimacy in exchange for all the gifts she received.

Life for Dorothy became a magical voyage through a fairy-tale land. Money, which had been denied her for such a long time, now flowed to her freely. She purchased whatever suited her fancy and went to the beauty salon twice a week for hairstyling and a mani-cure. The masseuse arrived every Monday evening when the ten-cents-a-dance club closed, and she and Tony both enjoyed one-hour massages. Instead of cooking, they frequented the finest restaurants late at night after her performances. One evening, on Dorothy's night off from the club, they sat in a large corner booth at a popular steak house.

"Dorothy, why don't you quit that joint? You don't need that no more."

"Tony, I love to perform. I want to sing."

"But Doll, not there, not at no ten-cents-a-dance joint."

"Those are my friends, Tony. They have been my friends since I left home. They stood by me when nobody else would."

"Yeah. Well, how about I get you a job workin' at a top nightclub? How about I get you a job at the Chez Parée?"

"Really, Tony? You can do that?"

"I can do whatever I want to." He smiled at her. Even after living with her for six months, she still managed to keep him fascinated.

"I would love to sing at the Chez Parée." She moved closer to him and threw her arms around his neck, embracing him tightly.

CHAPTER FIFTY-FOUR

THE CHEZ PARÉE smelled like money. There were satin table linens, white-gloved waiters, gold silverware surrounded by crystal chandeliers, and girls selling cigars, kewpie dolls, and red roses. Coat-check girls waited in white gowns to take minks and sables for safekeeping while their owners danced the night away. Dorothy looked around in awe as she waited for Tony to arrange her audition.

The customers were elegant women in their expensive gowns, with diamonds dripping from their necks and ears, and men in expensive, tailored suits and custom-made tuxedos. They were the celebrities in music, sports, and art, all gathered to enjoy dinner or a drink. But more importantly, they came to see and be seen in the hottest spot in Chicago.

"Listen, she can sing," Tony told his friend Mickey, who knew the owner of the club and owed him a favor.

"For you, Tony…I'll get her an audition. And don't you worry, she's a sure thing. If not for the main act, at least to open. Would a couple of nights a week be enough?"

"Yeah, I want her around more, anyway. This is just to keep her happy. Ya know?"

"Sure, Tony, sure—I'll take care of it right away."

Tony smiled, self-satisfied. It paid off to be a member of one of the Sicilian Mafia families.

"Fred, I need to talk with you." Dorothy tugged on his sleeve when she arrived the following day.

"A'right, come in."

They went into the tiny mess he called his office.

"Sit. Now, what is it?"

"I'm sorry, Fred. Please, I hope you won't be angry. I know how good you and Carol have been to me. And believe me...I will never forget it. But I'm giving you my notice. I'll be leaving."

"Why? Are you goin' home, kid?"

"No, I am going to work as a singer at the Chez Parée."

"Holy cow! That's somethin'. I sure can't fault you fer that. Well, we sure are gonna miss you around here, but I wish you all the best."

"Thanks, Fred. I'm going to tell Carol."

"She'll be sad to see ya go, but she'll be happy fer ya, too."

And so, after two weeks, Dorothy left the dark ballroom where lonely men paid just a dime to hold a woman in their arms for just a few moments.

CHAPTER FIFTY-FIVE

DOROTHY DRUMMED her red lacquered nails on the tablecloth, wondering when Tony would return. It seemed he'd been gone for more than half an hour.

Finally, he sauntered to her table, carrying a red rose and wearing a big open smile.

"You got an audition. You ready?"

"Yes, I hope so. Do I look all right?"

"You, Dollface? You look beautiful."

When Dorothy heard her name called over the microphone, she suddenly felt dizzy and out of breath. This club was a long, uphill climb from the one she'd come from. Her knees quivered as she stood in front of the audience. Then, turning to the pianist, she said, "Can you play 'Lover Man?'"

"Of course, and don't worry. You'll do just fine. You're so pretty that no matter what you sound like, you're gonna knock 'em dead." James winked at her and began with a short opening on the piano.

And she did.

When Dorothy finished to a wild round of enthusiastic applause, she turned to thank her young accompanist.

"Thank you. I guess you know I'm Dorothy Silver."

"I'm James Harrington. And you got some voice." She thought him handsome, with his dark-blond hair slicked back from his forehead.

"Thanks. You're an excellent pianist as well."

He bowed his head in appreciation, then winked and smiled.

"You should see some of the big bands that play here. Why, we've had the Count and Benny, to name a few…"

"You mean it?"

"Sure…You'll see. This is a real hip joint." He laughed, and she laughed, too.

Then Dorothy left the stage. She walked back to the table where Tony waited, wearing a big smile.

"Well, you got it, kid. You're an opening act here at the Chez Parée!"

"Oh, Tony!" She reached up and embraced him. "I'm so happy. I'm a real singer now."

CHAPTER FIFTY-SIX

WITHIN MINUTES of the Chez Parée's opening each night, the
dressing rooms came alive. Dancing girls in extravagant costumes
carefully lined their eyes and filled out their lips with dramatic flair.
Dorothy no longer wore gold sequins. Now, her gowns of black silk
or satin fit her hourglass body like a second skin. She let her long
red curls frame her lovely face and used a delicate hand when
applying makeup.

Soon, Tony's business consumed him. He rarely attended her
performances, and she had begun to scowl with worry. When
Dorothy asked him what bothered him, he became irritable and
evasive. She knew something had gone wrong, yet she could not be
sure what.

But she couldn't keep her focus on Tony. Too much excitement
kept her riveted within the confines of her life. She enjoyed the pure
pleasure of performing at Chicago's top nightspot. When she
walked out onto the stage to heated applause, she felt the power of
the entire universe spin as she lifted the microphone.

Most evenings, Dorothy arrived early to find James practicing
his piano in the empty dining room. She heard the scales as she
entered and smiled at him. When he saw her, he began to play the

numbers they would perform together that night, and she sang along. One night, Dorothy came into the club hungry. The kitchen had not yet opened, so she asked James if he would like to accompany her to the diner down the street and have dinner before the evening began.

During dinner, they discovered that they enjoyed the same music. They laughed at the same things and found they had a great deal in common. From that day on, it became a habit that Dorothy and James spent much of their time together. With Tony preoccupied with his business, Dorothy found James to be a wonderful substitute. Both Dorothy and James loved to swing dance. And when they opened for one of the big swing bands, instead of relaxing through their breaks, they danced through all of them. By the end of the night, Dorothy and James were exhausted. When Tony's driver picked her up, Dorothy fell asleep on the way home.

On a Friday evening, Dorothy and James sat at their usual booth at the diner.

"Dorothy?" James asked as he cut a section of his pork chop. "Is Tony your husband?"

"No, just a friend."

"A romantic friend?"

"James? Why do you ask?"

"I don't know. It's none of my business."

"No, it isn't."

"I don't know how to tell you this. I don't even know if it's true… but you… well, you mean a lot to me, and I guess what I wanna say is, I think you deserve to know." He looked at her as if he were about to deliver the most terrifying news.

"Know what?" She studied him.

"I heard that he's married."

She burst out laughing.

"Is that funny to you?"

"I know, already."

"And you still stay with him?"

"You are asking far too many questions."

"Maybe so, but I thought better of you, Dorothy." He stood up and, taking a wad of bills out of his pocket to cover the restaurant check, threw them on the table and walked out.

She sat at the window, staring after him. Then Dorothy found she could not eat. After pushing the food around on her plate, she left.

Back in the dressing room, the girls giggled and chattered as usual, but Dorothy felt a strange heaviness in her soul. Had she fallen so far beneath her standards?

That night, her performance lacked the spark that made her exciting to her audience. She could not look at James, nor could he look at her.

For two days, they did not speak. When Dorothy lay in her bed beside Tony, her heart ached at the realization of what she had become.

On holidays, Tony went off to be with his wife and children. Dorothy spent the time alone. Until James brought it to her attention, she hadn't given it much thought. Now, she realized she had become what her mother had referred to as a *backstreet woman*. The thought hurt her deeply. When she remembered the Jewish holidays she'd celebrated with her family during her childhood, she thought she might cry. How Dorothy had loved hearing her father sing in the temple on the morning of Yom Kippur. And it had been a lifetime since she had last celebrated the Sabbath.

Quietly, she rose from the bed and went into the bathroom. She turned the light on and looked at her reflection in the mirror. The stain of lipstick remained smeared on her mouth, and a dark remainder of her mascara circled her eyes.

"Who am I? I don't even know anymore. Will I ever be married? Have children?" Her mind drifted back, and she remembered Leah. She reminisced about all the dreams they'd had and how they imagined their future would be.

Dorothy took time off for the following three nights, too upset to work, but when she returned, she found James waiting for her.

"I'm sorry. I had no business telling you how to live your life." He stood staring at her.

"I'm sorry, too."

"For what?"

"I don't know, James. For…?" She shrugged her shoulders. They both laughed.

"I missed you, Dorothy."

"I missed you, too."

She looked at the depth and sincerity in his eyes, and suddenly compelled, she put her arms around his neck and kissed him. Then she kissed him again.

CHAPTER FIFTY-SEVEN

WHAT SUFFICED for coupling with Tony could never compare to the intense lovemaking Dorothy relished with James. He pleased and satisfied her in ways she had never dreamed of. Her body harmonized with his, the way her voice accompanied his piano. They made love on her dressing room floor, against the wall, in the alleyway, and everywhere and anywhere they could find a moment to be alone. The memory of the taste of his salty sweat filled her with desire and shame. She could not meet Tony's eyes when he spoke to her, and when he touched her, she felt her body recoil with revulsion.

From what she knew of Tony, she felt sure that if he discovered her affair with James, he would surely kill him and possibly her. Day after day, she wrestled with the idea of ending the affair, and as soon as James touched or kissed her, she lost all sense of reality.

"I love you, Dot. I want you forever, every night, in my bed. You know we have something special."

"Yes. I do know that." She touched his face.

"Leave the old man. He's too old for you, anyway."

"I can't. Where would we go? He would find us and kill you, James."

"I'll take that risk. Let's go to Canada. He'd never find us there."

One night, between sets, James came back to Dorothy's dressing room to find her in tears.

"I have to go to the hospital. Tony has been shot. The doctors don't think he will make it."

"Do you want me to go with you?"

"Oh, no, please. That would be the worst thing you could do. Just stay here. I'll be back."

The hospital smelled of alcohol, and everything seemed white— the nurses' uniforms, the walls, everything. Dorothy ran to the front desk, her high heels clacking obscenely on the floor, and was directed to Tony's room. She raced upstairs to find him attached to tubes and needles on either side but dimly conscious.

"Hi, Doll." His voice came as a raspy whisper.

"Tony, what happened?"

He laughed, "Just a minor injury, sorta. Let's just say it's a little hazard of the job. But I'm gonna be just fine." Speaking seemed to drain what little energy he had. Dorothy sat quietly beside him, holding his hand in both of hers. Tears streamed down her cheeks until the nurse came and said she must leave. Visiting hours had ended.

"I need to speak with you," Tony's driver said.

"But visiting hours are over." The nurse insisted.

"I can't go until I tell you what I have to tell you, boss."

Tony nodded. "Let him stay for a few minutes, won't you, doll?" he said to the nurse. "I'd sure appreciate it."

The nurse nodded. "All right. But only one person in the room."

"I'm sorry, sweetheart. Can you wait in the car for just a few minutes?" Tony suggested.

"Sure, Tony. Whatever you want." Dorothy said.

After she left, Tony's driver leaned in and whispered. "I hate to have to you this boss. But I feel like if I don't, you are going to be mad at me."

"Stop all your dramatics and just tell me already. I'm tired."

"I caught your dame with the piano player. She's cheating on you."

Tony's face got red. He clenched his fists. "You come to my hospital bed to tell me this? You stupid jackass." Tony glared at his driver.

"I didn't know what to do. I thought you might wanna know, boss. Do you want me to kill 'em both?"

"Fuck, no. Did I tell you to do anything? I don't pay to you think. You only do what I tell you. And right now, don't do nothin' till I tell you otherwise, understand?"

"She's cheatin' on you, boss. And who the fuck does that kid think he is? He's just some lousy piano player, and he's gonna go up against the head of the mob?" Tony's driver began pacing the floor.

"Listen to me." Tony motioned for him to come closer. "Go to this lousy piano player and offer him some money to get the hell outta town. When he is far away from Dorothy, knock him off. Understand? I want her to think he left on his own and I didn't have no part in it. You got that?"

"Yeah, boss."

CHAPTER FIFTY-EIGHT

"HE'S BAD, James. I'm worried." Dorothy looked out the window.

"This is your chance, Doll. You run and get away with me now." James smiled at her. His smile always made her want to sleep with him.

"I don't know. If I leave now, it'll kill him. He has always been so good to me. I can't hurt him like that."

"You are such a foolish gal. This is your chance, baby. Do it now, Dotty, honey, before it's too late."

He sauntered over to her and took her into his arms. She felt herself weaken. All the muscles in her body grew limp with desire. They kissed. His lips tasted like port wine. They kissed again and again.

As HE WALKED towards the L train, James sensed someone behind him. When he turned, he saw nothing but a dark, empty street behind him. His head pounded, and he felt dizzy. Nausea caused his stomach to whirl like a tornado, and he gripped the building to remain upright.

An eerie sense of dread washed over him, and he wondered if someone had slipped a Mickey in his drink. Thinking back, James remembered that his vodka and tonic had tasted a bit off, but he had attributed it to the new bartender. Now, he wondered.

The streetlights reflected in round halos over the sidewalks, illuminating the streets only slightly. A chill ran up his spine, but he shook it off and continued toward the subway. When his stomach swished as if it had been filled with a pool of water, he gagged, expelling liquid vomit. Then, a clang that sounded like someone dropping a pan alarmed him, and he jerked his body around. Before he caught his breath, James felt himself being pulled into the alleyway. Four men stood in front of him with chains wrapped around their fists.

"Hello, James."

A scream escaped his lips as he felt his face turn to mush under a fierce punch.

"You been fuckin' the boss's broad. That ain't too smart, ya know?"

One of the men pushed James to his knees. A loud crack broke the silence of the night as James felt a pain shoot up his leg.

In an unfamiliar voice, he heard himself begging, "Please, let me go."

"We ain't gonna kill ya. Instead, we're here to give you a chance. Understand?"

James nodded, the blood dripping from his nose into his open mouth.

"I'm gonna be fair with ya, only 'cause the boss tol' me to. I'm gonna give you five C-notes to get the hell outta town and stay the fuck away from that girl. Understand? Now, if it were up to me, ya both would be lyin' at the bottom of Lake Michigan, but the boss don't want it that way. So, you take this cash and get your ass outta here. And you fucking make sure the girl don't find out that the boss had no say-so in your breakin' up with her. Make up some excuse, got it? We don't want to hear nothin' of you here in Chi-town! Understand?"

James nodded as the man threw the envelope at him. James picked it up, staining it with his blood-covered fingers. And in an instant, he found himself alone.

He wiped the blood from his face with the inside of his jacket. Then, with great pain, he held onto the wall and lifted himself. His back and leg ached, but he moved as swiftly as possible to find a taxi back to his apartment.

The following day, Dorothy arrived at the club. Roses awaited her in her dressing room. The note that accompanied them brought a stream of tears to her eyes.

Sorry, Doll. I got a phone call from my old girlfriend. We decided to give it another shot. I know you and me had something special, but I just don't think we were meant to be long term. It was fun while it lasted. Here's wishing you well.

James

She stared at the note in disbelief. The crack she felt growing in her heart seemed like it would never mend. How could she ever heal from such a betrayal? Tony had never hurt her like this. He had kept all of his promises. Everyone gossiped at the club. They said that James had a tendency to be a womanizer, but she never believed them. Now she did. Tears spilled down her face as she flung the vase against the wall. The crystal glass broke into a million pieces, and the flowers tumbled, scattering their blood-red petals about the floor. Then Dorothy washed her face and cleaned the smeared mascara under her eyes. After she was satisfied with her appearance, she called for her driver.

"Take me to the hospital," she told him. "I need to see Tony."

When she arrived, she found that the nurses had propped Tony up with pillows. The gray pallor had faded from his handsome face, and he smiled, never revealing what he knew about her and James.

"How do you feel?"

"Great, now that you're here, baby."

She would rather spend her life as the mistress of a married man who loved her than as a plaything for a single man who toyed with women's emotions.

Taking his hand, she squeezed it. "I love you, Tony."

"I know, and I love you, too, Doll."

CHAPTER FIFTY-NINE

JAMES BOARDED the first train headed to New Orleans the following morning. A void had settled in his chest. He loved her. He knew he did, but he hated physical pain and could not bear the thought of what they might do to him if he didn't run. So, he would travel down south to the home of Dixieland jazz, and there he would fill his empty heart with music.

If he hadn't been preoccupied with his sadness, James might have noticed the man in the black suit who'd followed him onto the train.

DOROTHY RETURNED FROM THE HOSPITAL, still brokenhearted but resigned. Her toes sunk into the plush pile carpet as she sat down at her dressing table imported from France, with its authentic twenty-four-karat gold handles.

Then she reached into the top drawer, removed her embossed stationary and expensive fountain pen, and began writing. Tears fell silently upon the paper as she told Leah of her years in America. With her heart in her words, she remembered her family and the loss she felt when her father sent her away. *Her friend would understand,* she thought, as she told Leah of the passion and love she had shared with James. Then she explained the betrayal and Tony's devotion, as well as the material comforts only he could provide.

How she missed Leah, how she wished that they could sit on her bed, laughing and sharing their feelings again; only her dearest friend could comfort her now, and she could not be with her. *Leah,* she thought, *what has happened to us? Why did things turn out this way? This was not how our lives were meant to be! This is not the way we planned it.* Dorothy sighed deeply as her hand wiped the tears from her face. Then she licked the envelope closed and took it outside to the mailbox. She squeezed the letter to her heart, then dropped it into the slot and turned to go back home. The letter would be returned undeliverable three months later. Leah would never receive it.

CHAPTER SIXTY

MIRIAM ABENDSTERN WIPED the crumbs from her kitchen counter. Leah had left a few minutes earlier to go to the shop. Jacob had forgotten his lunch, and Leah had decided to deliver it to him. After Miriam had finished reading Michael a short story, she noticed that he had nodded off to sleep. Now she finally had a few moments to herself. The ache in her slender, slumping shoulders had worsened over the past month. She attributed the pain to tension. Michael showed no improvement in his condition. If anything, he seemed to be getting worse. There was no doubt in her mind that he needed medical attention. But with the state of things in Germany, paying specialists had become financially impossible. Poor Michael ate very little, and his tiny body felt almost weightless when she turned him over to prevent bedsores. The bones in his chest and hips jutted out like twigs, and sometimes, she fearfully imagined they would break apart and dissolve into powder upon his sheets.

Well, at least for now, he sleeps, she thought, her ears alerted to any sound that might come from his room.

After she'd filled the teakettle, she placed it on the stove on a low fire. Then, gazing out the small window above the sink, her eyes drifted to the old elm tree that stood in the yard. Its branches shifted softly in the breeze.

Memories of Karl surfaced. When he was a child, he'd climbed that tree and built a tree house. This worried her as she scanned the yard, calling his name. Finally, she had dropped to her knees in tears, thinking the worst. And out of nowhere, he'd called to her. She could not see him at first. Then she'd looked up, and there he stood in the tree house he had built, with his hands on his hips, laughing.

Karl, her son—where had he gone this time? There was surely no easy explanation. Once again, she had lost him; only this time, she knew he could not be found on the old elm. Without realizing it, she touched her face to find she had been crying. It seemed to the rest of her family that she cared only for Michael. Although they never understood it, she loved all of them. Michael just needed her the most. Miriam dried her face with a kitchen towel.

Please, God, let my Karl be alive and safe wherever he is.

She ran her hand through her thin, oily hair, which had once been thick and healthy. Since Michael's accident, she'd aged. She knew she'd lost her youth and, with it, her beauty. She was lost in thought, so the knock on her front door startled her and forced her back into the present.

Quickly, she dried her hands, straightened her hair, and opened the door, forgetting to use the peephole. A man of slight build stood before her. He wore a dark suit, at least a size too big for his small frame, a white shirt, and a dark tie. Thick, wire-rimmed glasses covered most of his face.

"Mrs. Abendstern?"

"Yes?"

"Good afternoon. I am Doctor Vizelman. May I come in, please? I will not take up much of your time. I would just like to have a few words with you."

A stir of apprehension darted through her and then quickly passed. Miriam studied the man. He appeared to be refined, unassuming, and soft-spoken.

"Come in." She motioned to him. "Sit down, please."

CHAPTER SIXTY | 201

Taking a seat across from him, closest to Michael's room, Miriam waited, listening.

"I've come concerning your son, Michael."

"Michael?" She looked at him, wondering what he could want with Michael.

"Yes, Mrs. Abendstern, I have good news for you."

Miriam heard the pounding of her heart, forcing pulsating blood to flow into her eardrums.

"You see," he began again with a warm, sincere smile. "Our Führer is a good man. He wants to help those in need. And you see, madam, Michael would benefit greatly from proper medical attention. In fact, wouldn't it be nice if Michael could live a normal life? Find a job, get married, perhaps? It is Hitler's plan to make Germany a land of healthy, productive citizens. He feels that this will restore Germany to its rightful place as the most powerful country in the world."

She wondered if the doctor knew that the Abendsterns were Jews. She opted not to tell him.

The teakettle let out its high-pitched, piercing whistle. Within a second, Miriam ran to stop the noise before it awakened her son.

"Excuse me, how rude I am. Would you like some tea?" Miriam asked.

"That would be lovely, thank you."

As she prepared the tray, her hands trembled. Could this be the answer to her prayers? Every night, she prayed that the family would somehow find a way to afford the proper medical help for Michael.

When Miriam returned to the living room, she placed the tray on the coffee table and began to pour, spilling a large circle of the brown liquid.

"Excuse me. I am so sorry. I, well, you have caught me off guard. I guess you could say I am a little stunned." She wiped the mess with the towel she had tucked into her apron. "Herr Doctor?" She looked into his eyes with hope restored in her heart. "What is the cost of this treatment?"

"There is no cost, Mrs. Abendstern. This is part of the New

Germany. Michael would be sent to a facility set up to provide the necessary care to cure his condition. It is a lovely hospital surrounded by the beautiful German countryside, the perfect place for medical recuperation."

"It sounds wonderful, but I cannot make a decision without my husband. May I have a day or so to discuss it with him?"

"But of course. I will return in two days. Will that give you enough time to make a decision?"

"Yes. Yes, of course, and I certainly appreciate your considering us for this program."

He carefully placed the cup and saucer on the tray, showing respect for her china. Then he shook her hand and left, closing the door quietly behind him.

After she had returned the tea to the kitchen, Miriam walked quietly into Michael's room. As she stood in the doorway, her heart sank as she observed his useless limbs suspended upon the bed and his head lying awkwardly to one side, drool running from his lips. Although she'd looked at him every day for years, right at this very moment, she saw him anew, and it was then that Miriam made up her mind.

CHAPTER SIXTY-ONE

Miriam decided to speak to Jacob before mentioning the treatment program to Michael. When Jacob arrived home from the bicycle shop to find Miriam's mood elevated, a state that had become non-existent in their lives for many years, he watched her with wonder and disbelief.

"Jacob." She kissed his cheek, and he smiled cautiously. "Come, eat. Dinner is ready."

After washing up, Jacob went to the table. Leah arrived just shortly after. "Has Michael eaten?" she asked Miriam.

"Yes, I brought his tray to him earlier."

Leah had always taken it upon herself to prepare dinner while Miriam spent her time at Michael's bedside, so to come home and find a hot meal already prepared, with Miriam joining them at the table, seemed pleasant but strange.

Once they'd finished eating, Miriam placed her napkin on the table. Then, looking from Jacob to Leah, then back to Jacob again, she began to speak.

"A man came to visit today…a doctor. He spoke to me about Michael." She cleared her throat and then continued. "Apparently, a program has been set up by the government to help those with severe medical conditions. Michael would be sent to a special hospital where he would receive the treatment necessary for him to live a normal life."

"And how much will all of this cost?" Jacob studied her face.

"There is no cost. This is Hitler's way of restoring Germany."

"And for Jews, they are restoring Germany?" Jacob shook his head in doubt.

"The doctor had no idea that we are Jewish. At least he never mentioned it."

"And if they should find out, then what?" Jacob raised his hands in the air in question.

"I don't know. I suppose they would send Michael home. But we can hope that they don't find out, at least until he has been cured. Jacob, it's our only chance. You said yourself that we can't afford to take Michael to specialists with the way business has been lately."

"I don't know. It's so far away, Miriam. Are you sure this is a good idea?"

"I am sure of nothing, Jacob, but if we don't try, then we know for sure Michael will be condemned to an unproductive life in that bed. Is that what you want?"

He shook his head and pressed his hands to his temples. Suddenly, he felt as if a weight had fallen upon his brain. "Do what you think is right." Jacob stared down at the tablecloth. He could not look up at her because he had begun to cry.

CHAPTER SIXTY-TWO

MICHAEL SLEPT. The motion of the ride had a tranquilizing effect on him. When he awoke, he found himself already on the grounds of the Hadamar Institute. He looked around as two orderlies wheeled his bed into the large steel doors. Due to his mental condition, it is hard to know if he would have taken note of the shards of broken glass covering the top of the wall that fenced the building in like a fortress. It had been put there to discourage curious onlookers from climbing to look over and witness what took place inside.

A strong odor of alcohol permeated the air as he entered the building through a tall set of steel doors. Inside, a smiling group of nurses dressed in pressed, white uniforms with their hair tied back neatly greeted Michael.

"Hello, you must be Michael Abendstern?" A thickly built nurse, exceptionally tall, with heavy, dark, wavy hair, smiled at him. Her teeth had yellowed from years of neglect.

"Yes, and I am very happy to be here." Michael beamed. "My mother said you are going to make me well so I can run and play and be just like Detrick."

The woman nodded but did not answer. Instead, she looked over at the other nurses, who stood listening.

206 | ALL MY LOVE, DETRICK

Once he was checked in, Michael was transported to the base-
ment, where he smiled eagerly as the nurses took numerous pictures
of him. While the necessary photographs had been taken, one of
the nurses noticed that Michael had worn a piece of jewelry.

"I'll take that for you and keep it safe, alright?"

Michael nodded, and the young nurse took the gold mezuzah
that he wore around his neck.

"We will keep this necklace for you, Michael, until you are all
better and ready to go home." One of the other nurses, a golden-
haired girl of nineteen, repeated as she smoothed the hair out of
Michael's face.

"Thank you for taking such good care of me." A line of drool
had dribbled down his chin. With pity in her eyes, the pretty, young,
flaxen-haired nurse took a handkerchief from her pocket and wiped
Michael's face. A tear had formed in the corner of her eye, but she
quickly wiped it away.

Once all the paperwork had been completed, Michael found
himself alone in a small, white, windowless room. For what seemed
like a long time, he waited. He began to feel afraid in his childlike
mind. Panic set in, and he began to call out.

"Help me, please, someone come. I want my mother. Please,
send for my mother. Is she here? I'm scared. I need my mother!"

The tall, heavy, dark-haired nurse entered, accompanied by the
young, pretty blonde whose eyes appeared red and bloodshot.

"It's time that you get some sleep." The heavyset nurse smiled
at him.

"I'm hungry. I want to eat."

"And so you will when you awaken. Right now, you must sleep."

"But I don't want to sleep. I want to eat."

The tone of his voice alerted the other nurses outside of the
room, and they entered, ready to strap him down if necessary.

"Now, Michael," the young blonde choked as she tried to
comfort him. "This is part of your treatment, a very important part.
Don't you want to get better?"

"Yes, I do. I want to get better."

"Well, all right then. This is just a tiny prick. It won't hurt for more than a second."

The young nurse held Michael's hand while the heavy-set one pulled the syringe from behind her back, where she'd been concealing it from him. When he saw the needle, terror-filled Michael's eyes, and he screamed.

"No. No needles! No!"

Two more nurses came in and held him down until the injection was complete. Within a few seconds, he lay quiet. His head fell to the left side with his eyes still open in horror, his mouth in a frozen scream.

"He is better off, you know." The dark-haired nurse who'd administered the hypodermic needle turned to the others.

"Yes, I suppose he is, but he was such a sweet one." The blonde tucked the blanket around Michael.

"Most of the simpletons are. But this is best for Germany. Besides, did you see the necklace? Not only was he an idiot, but he was a Jew as well."

"You're right. It is best for the Fatherland."

CHAPTER SIXTY-THREE

"KONRAD, you look incredibly well. Just look at you! All dressed up in your SS uniform, so grown up. It's been ages since you've been here to see Detrick. Sadly, I must tell you that he is not at home." Inga studied Konrad. She'd known him since he and her son played together as small children. Now, he stood before her, an SS officer, sharp and commanding in his black uniform. She trembled slightly.

"It is not Detrick I've come to see. It's you, Frau Haswell, and Herr Haswell."

"Of course, come in then." What could Konrad possibly want with her and her husband? Once again, she looked him over more closely. His uniform fit him impeccably and had been freshly starched and pressed. The silver death's head symbol on his hat sparkled, and his black leather boots shone so clearly that they reflected the light fixture overhead.

"Sit, please. Can I get you something?" Inga offered.

"No, thank you. I will only take up a few minutes of your time. As you can see, I'm working for the party now, and I have a good position. Up until the present time, I have been able to shield Detrick. You see, I owe him a great deal. He stood up for me as my protector when we were just boys. An informant of mine has told me that Detrick has been sustaining friendships with Jews. I have not passed that information along to others. I am afraid that if he does not cease this foolhardy behavior, it will become known, and the Gestapo will arrest him. So, I am coming to you in hopes that you will have some influence over him because I do not believe he will listen to me."

"Jews?"

"Yes, Frau Haswell, I am afraid so. It seems he is still in contact with his former employer, Abendstern, the Jew. Do you know of him?"

"Yes, I knew he worked for him long ago, but I had no idea that he continued to see him. There must be some mistake."

"I'm afraid not. And it must stop. I am putting myself at risk by coming here to help him. Do you understand me?"

"Yes, of course. I will speak to him tonight." Her hands shook so hard that she folded them together, hoping Konrad would not notice. "And Konrad, Herr Haswell, and I appreciate your taking time out of your busy schedule to speak to us."

"You know, it would not be a bad idea if Detrick considered joining the party. I am up for a big promotion soon, and if he changed his ways, I would be happy to put in a good word for him."

Hans placed his empty beer glass on the table. "That would be very good of you. Would that mean he would work for the SS?"

"Perhaps yes, and if he did work with us, it would also mean there would be gifts for his family. Plenty of good food, furniture—that sort of thing. You know that the party is very generous with its own."

"We will certainly discuss the situation with him and do all we can. Thank you for bringing this to our attention." Inga smiled weakly.

Konrad got up to leave. "Well, I am hoping to hear some good news about my promotion very soon. Farewell for now."

He walked out, closing the door behind him. It had been diffi-cult for him to put everything he'd worked for on the line, but he owed this much to Detrick. If, by some miracle, this meeting encour-aged Detrick to join the party, it would have all been worth the effort. Then things would resume between the two of them the way they'd been before the Nazi takeover, only better. In the past, Detrick had been the popular and better-looking one. Now he, Konrad, had the power and the party behind him. He'd proven himself worthy time and again, and he'd made friends with the right people. Yes, things would be better, much better.

Detrick hung his jacket on the coat rack when he arrived home early that evening. Then, he took a few reichsmarks out of his pocket and put them in the jar where his mother kept her small stash of emergency cash. Except for the chirping of crickets, he heard no noise. His father would be at the tavern, and his mother would probably be delivering laundry.

The book he had begun reading awaited him where he'd left it on his bed. He sat down and tried to read but found he could not concentrate.

Things had become increasingly worse for the Jews. Although Jacob still ran his business, the loss of Gentile clientele and the increasing popularity of automobiles and public transportation had hurt his income substantially. But Jacob insisted on keeping Detrick on and paying him the same salary. Although with the shortage of work, Jacob hardly needed the extra help anymore. Detrick worried about Jacob. Between Michael going off to the sanatorium and the constant rise in anti-Semitism, he'd aged.

The once-vibrant man now suffered from labored breathing, followed by exhaustion. And he worried about Leah, his precious Leah. How could he keep her safe in a world so infected with hatred?

It seemed that anti-Semitism was like a plague that spread wildly, infecting Germany and threatening to swallow the world. And Leah, being such a small and delicate girl, could never stand up to the angry mobs who threatened her very existence, who wanted to take away her God-given right to walk upon this earth. Detrick shuddered. He thought of her tiny, delicate hands, the softness of her creamy ivory skin, and the warmth of her sweet, gentle smile.

He swallowed hard. For a moment, he wondered what his life would have been like if he had never seen or fallen in love with her.

From the first time he'd looked at her, she'd become his entire life, and because of the depth of his love, there was a constant risk to his whole family. And even worse was the risk to Leah herself. He didn't care about his safety, but he could not bear the thought that Leah might suffer and that he would be powerless to help her. The thought taunted him and even drove him to madness. But then Detrick looked at the small picture he kept of Leah and realized that if he had not loved her, he might as well never have been born. This was who he was and what he was meant to do.

Jacob had suggested that he stop his daylight visits to the house or the shop and only come by after dark. Gentiles seen with Jews put themselves in real danger. The possibility of being turned in by a friend or neighbor was ever-increasing. No one could be trusted.

When Detrick came to the house late in the evening, he would ask if Jacob needed any of the heavy mechanical work done to be as useful as possible. If something needed to be addressed, Detrick went to the shop well after dark. Most times, Jacob did not have any work for him to do. So, Detrick just stayed at the house, close to his friends and Leah. During the day, the shades had to stay drawn lest anyone see Detrick at the Abendsterns.

And even as he sat thinking of all the reasons he should not be in love, and even with all the dangers he faced, still, he longed, yearned, for nightfall, when he would make his way safely to the Abendstern home and into the arms of his beloved.

CHAPTER SIXTY-FOUR

INGA WONDERED how she would approach Detrick on the subject of joining the Nazi party. She knew how he felt about the Nazis, but she also knew that if he were a party member, they would all be safer, especially Detrick, her dearly loved son.

As she suspected, Detrick had not left for the Abendsterns when she arrived home. Inga knew where he went. She knew everything, far more than he realized. The sun had just begun to set, and he always waited until total darkness before making his way to the Jewish sector.

"Detrick, I'm so glad to find you at home. It has been such a long time since you and I shared a cup of tea. Let me see here. I believe I have a few cookies. Shall we indulge?" Inga brought out a round ceramic jar.

"Yes, mother. I would enjoy a chat with you. It has been far too long." He took a cookie and began to nibble at the edge.

After putting the teakettle on the stove, Inga sat at the table across from her son. She wiped her hands on her apron. She smiled at him and suddenly realized how much she needed to talk to her son.

"I often wonder where Helga has gone."

"I know, Mother. So do I."

"I hope she is all right. Perhaps she is with that Erik? I think that maybe they are married somewhere. However, it seems to me that she would, at least, have let us know. These are such strange and terrible times, my son. I constantly worry about the safety of my children." She shook her head. "With Helga gone, you are all I have left."

He nodded. There was precious little he could offer. "And so I must discuss something with you." The teapot whistled. Removing it from the stove, she poured him a cup of tea. After placing the kettle on a mat, she sat down. Then she lifted his chin so that she could look directly into his eyes. "As I said, these are dangerous times we are living in. And, well, I know you are very fond of the Jewish shopkeeper and his daughter. They have been good to you and good to us, too. However, Detrick, we live in treacherous times. I know that you realize that the law forbids this friendship, and the fact is that you are endangering us all, but most of all, yourself."

He knew he had put himself in harm's way, but until now, he'd tried not to consider the real problems he might cause Inga. It had been a long time since he had really looked at his mother, and now that he did, he saw that she'd developed a slight hump in her back. Although she'd always been slender, the strain of the years of Hans not helping out, her grief over the sudden disappearance of Helga, and the fear of Detrick being arrested with the Jews were like crushing weights on her shoulders, making her old before her time. "I'm sorry, Mother, I will leave here. I will move away. God knows I never wanted to hurt you or Father."

"There's no need to move away. In fact, it is probably best that you don't. If you leave, it might cause suspicion and make things worse for all of us. No, I have another idea. One that you will, I am sure, find a bit repulsive. However, I think it would help to guarantee the safety of your Jewish friends, as well as your family."

Detrick leaned forward, listening intently.

"I think it would be wise for you to consider joining the party."

"The Nazi Party? Are you serious, Mother? You know how I feel about the Nazis!"

"Yes, and that's precisely why I think this might just be the answer. As you can see, more of our Jewish neighbors are being arrested every day. What are you going to do when they come for your friends? There will be nothing you can do unless maybe you are a party member. Can I ask that you should at least think it over?"

"I will, Mother. I will."

CHAPTER SIXTY-FIVE

Detrick had ridden the bicycle in the dark on previous nights. Tonight, however, he chose to walk and think. His mother's words resonated with the truth. There was no denying the arrests. He'd seen and heard the black autos belonging to the Gestapo as they turned corners, their horns blaring, filling him with fear and dread. Thoughts of terror had come upon him at night as he slept, and he'd awaken, sweating with worry, wondering if the Abendsterns had been arrested. He needed to ensure the safety of his friends. Until now, joining the party had not occurred to him. The repugnance of it still appalled him. But if it was his only choice, the only way he might protect all he held dear, well then...

And what had happened to Helga? he wondered. Where had she gone? Was she alive? Was she all right? Did her Nazi boyfriend insist they be as far away from her traitor brother as possible? Or had she come to harm? Had he, in some way, been responsible? There were so many questions and not a single answer. A wave of guilt punched him in the stomach. Rather than see anyone else suffer for his choices, he preferred that he alone be subjected to the punishment for his behavior. His mother must not be forced to pay the price for his acts against the Nazi Party.

The wind rustled through the leaves of the trees as Detrick inhaled the sweet night air. If he continued as he had been, more problems would certainly follow. Perhaps his mother would be taken to a work camp. A shiver ran down his spine. She was so old and broken, barely surviving in her small flat. How would she fare under hard labor? To think of her being beaten, with him to blame, made him ill.

Careful to avoid the streetlights and automobiles, lest he be caught walking through the Jewish sector, Detrick hid by taking side streets and alleyways whenever possible.

What should he do? What could he do?

With his head heavy and spinning like a top, he ducked into an alleyway and leaned against the side of a building. Sinking down to his knees upon the pavement as the stars twinkled above him, Detrick prayed beneath the silvery light of the moon.

Dear God, I don't know what to do. I am confused, frightened, and trapped. Why me, God? Why have I been chosen to carry this burden? Why?

It had been at least half an hour that he knelt alone in the darkness, his knees aching against the cold cement, staring out into the empty alleyway before an idea began to take shape in his mind.

CHAPTER SIXTY-SIX

As ALWAYS, the soft illumination in the Abendstern home called out to welcome him as he turned the corner of the block.

After climbing the front porch stairs two at a time, Detrick knocked at the front door. Jacob opened it and took him in, greeting him with a bear hug.

"Are you hungry? Come, eat."

"No, really, I'm fine."

"Come, eat. You have to eat. How can you resist? Leah made matzo ball soup, and she baked challah. Come, you'll eat. It makes me feel good."

Detrick laughed. He loved the old man.

Leah stood in the kitchen. When Detrick entered and saw her, his heart fluttered. She had a special magic, like a spell that rendered him helpless.

Jacob left the room, knowing the couple would want to kiss, but would refrain out of respect for him.

As soon as they were alone, Detrick took Leah into his arms. Tiny, like a dove, she surrendered softly to his might, and he tenderly kissed her lips. For a long time, he held her, his heart swelling deep in his chest. He wondered how this love that he

218 | ALL MY LOVE, DETRICK

thought was all-consuming and as great as any love could continue to grow even stronger with each passing day. His hand smoothed her hair, and she shivered with desire.

"Can we be alone later tonight?" he whispered in her ear.

"I don't know. Let's wait and see when they go to sleep."

"My sweet darling, I want you. I want you so badly. I feel like I am dying of thirst, and you are my wellspring of sweet water."

"I want you, too. All day, I think I can't wait until Detrick arrives."

"I know, love. I know."

CHAPTER SIXTY-SEVEN

LEAH AND DETRICK lay naked in her bed as the stars sent bits of light through her window. She curled around him, her head bent against his chest, her leg over his. When they held each other like this, she felt nothing could ever hurt her. The strength of his body enveloped her in its warm, protective cocoon. The love they shared bathed them in intense light and joy.

"Sweetheart?" his voice always grew quiet and a little hoarse after making love, as if the intensity of their coupling rendered him weak by the sheer awe of it.

"Hmm?" she purred back at him, contented, inhaling the pleasant smell of peppermint.

"Several months ago…" He squeezed her shoulder gently. "A friend I knew from school came to me. His family owns a home with a large attic. He knew about my relationship with you. And well, he offered to hide you and your family. I would pay him, of course."

"Hide us in the attic? Where would you get this money? Do you really think things are that serious?"

Again, he squeezed her shoulder. "I'm afraid so, sweetheart. I know that Jews are being arrested without reason and sent to work camps. I can't allow that to happen to you or your family."

"How much money? With Father in hiding, the business would be closed, so how would you get it?"

"Well, that's what I need to talk to you about." He looked down at the back of her head, her dark hair catching tiny specks of starlight, and his heart broke a little. "I am going to join the Nazi Party. I will work for them and use the money to pay for your protection."

"Detrick, seriously. That is far too dangerous."

"Perhaps, love, but we have no choice. I will not sit by and wait until they decide to take you away. Cooperate with me, please. And tomorrow, I will have to convince your father."

"Detrick, I don't know. We would be leaving our home: everything we have, everything we know."

"Yes, but it will only be until this Nazi threat is over. It can't last forever. Better that you are safe than at their mercy. Let's face it. Kindness is not the strong suit of the Nazi Party, right?"

She nodded. "Yes, of course, you're right."

"And their sentiments toward Jews, well, they terrify me. So, please, Leah, do as I ask."

She moved away from him to look into his eyes and saw his determination. The enormity of the situation suddenly became real to her. "And how do we know we can trust these people? These friends of yours with the attic?"

"We don't, love, but we have to try. They are our only hope. I will pay them well. That should keep them satisfied. I will give them all that I can. They are not rich, and I know their sentiments are anti-Nazi. So, that should help us, too."

"All right, Detrick, I'll do as you wish. We will talk to my father together tomorrow night. My mother might not be willing, though. Every day, she is waiting to hear news of Michael or Karl."

"We must try to convince her."

"She may decide to stay."

"Well, if she does, then so be it. I can only offer. I can't force her. I only hope that if she decides not to go, your father will go without her."

"I don't know what he will do. If she refuses, chances are he won't leave her here alone. And quite frankly, I don't know if I could do that either. Let's just wait and see what happens when we talk to them tomorrow night. You better get dressed and go. It's almost daylight."

"I know. I will be back tomorrow night."

Kissing her lips, he whispered, "I love you more than life itself, my darling, my Leah. As soon as we talk to Jacob, I will begin to make arrangements."

He dressed quietly as she watched him. "I love you, Detrick."

CHAPTER SIXTY-EIGHT

A YOUNG BOY wearing short pants and a short jacket with a swastika armband rang the doorbell to the Abendstern home. Miriam opened the door and recognized him as John, the letter carrier. He handed her a plain manila envelope addressed from the Hadamar Institute and rode away on his bicycle. Jacob would not be home from work for several hours, and Leah had just left to see one of the children who partook in her piano lessons.

Miriam had been waiting for news. She tingled with the hope that this message she held in her hand would be the one to alleviate all the guilt and worry she'd been suffering. At this moment, anything seemed possible. By the postmark, she knew the letter originated at the hospital where Michael received treatment. Perhaps he'd begun to walk. Perhaps...

After she had closed the door and turned to sit, she opened the letter. It read:

> *Herr and Frau Abendstern,*
>
> *It is with the deepest regret that we must inform you that your son Michael has passed away. He came down with a bad case of measles and*

died within two days. There was no time to send for you. You have our
sympathies.

The Staff at the Hadamar Institute

Miriam read the letter in disbelief. Then she read it again. Michael was dead. Gone forever, never to come home again. She walked to his room and looked at his bed. She lay her head down on his pillow and took a deep breath.

It had been her fault. If she had not sent him away, he would still be alive.

She'd killed him, her child, her son. She would rather have killed herself. How dare she live, eat good food, drink hot tea? While he lay cold, never to laugh again? Still holding the letter in her trembling hand, her face blinded by tears, and her mind stunned with shock, Miriam walked slowly back to the kitchen.

There, she took a knife out of the kitchen drawer. Then, squeezing the paper into a tight little ball, she cried out, howling in grief. The pain filled every inch of her body, and she swelled with it until nothing but anguish existed for her. Still crying out, she fell to her knees, unaware of the pain of the impact of her knees on the floor.

"Michael! Oh God! Why? Why my Michael?" Her hand shook violently as if it moved of its own accord. With her mind crashing with guilt and shame, she cut the lifeline of the veins in her wrist.

Red blood ran freely, and with its release came the release of her mental anguish. She laughed hysterically, glad to feel nothing but agony as she fell to the floor.

Miriam lost consciousness, and with it, her lifetime of self-blame melted away as her life spilled itself into a ruby-red pool on the kitchen floor.

CHAPTER SIXTY-NINE

AN EXPLOSIVE THUNDER raged through the city of Warsaw. In response, Mother Earth convulsed wildly, sending tremors rippling madly through the streets. Trees vibrated as their branches ripped off at their centers. Karl raised his eyes to see the air munitions factory ablaze with angry, orange fire. People scattered in all directions to avoid the shooting debris. The fleeing crowd, desperately trying to escape, knocked some of the other people down and trampled them underfoot. Billows of thick, black smoke poured endlessly from the broken structure, covering the street and making visibility nearly impossible.

The factory had been bombed. If Karl had not been out on an errand for his boss, he would now lay dead beside all of his former co-workers, lost in the rubble. But surrounded now by chaos, he could little afford the time to consider his good fortune. Instead, he found himself swept into the hysterical mass of people gripping their loved ones and running for their lives.

Things happened too fast. He could not determine how far he ran or for how long the building continued to burn. His eyes and nose ran profusely, and he coughed, unable to catch his breath. Finally, the crowd that had pushed him along by the sheer force of its numbers began to disperse. He stopped and held on to the post of a street sign while he attempted to catch his breath. Then, looking around him, he saw a child coughing up gray mucus on the side of the road, his mother cradling him with her hand on his forehead. On the other side of the street, a couple gripped each other tightly—blood had been spattered on the man's face. The woman moaned as the man held her, whispering words of comfort.

For the first time in his life, Karl Abendstern wished he were not alone.

Love could be risky—it could make one vulnerable. In the past, he'd never allowed another person into his life for fear it would weaken him. Now he wished for the comfort of holding someone in his arms and knowing that it mattered to another person if he lived or died.

Thoughts of his family haunted him. They came flooding quickly into his mind, but he forced them away, wiping his nose with the back of his hand.

The walk back to his apartment seemed long and tedious, but he felt a little better once he arrived and began to clean himself. With the factory gone, tomorrow would bring a new challenge. For now, he must find another position. The bombing had left him unemployed.

The following day, the streets remained littered with bits of brick, wood, and plaster. By noon, it had begun to snow, and the temperature dropped, chilling the windy air as it blew in torrents, lifting pieces of the wreckage and flinging them across the ground. Karl could not allow the cold to stop him. He needed a job. The factory had paid him so little that he'd been unable to save anything. Without an income, he would be homeless in a matter of weeks. He walked down the cobblestone street, going from door to door and asking the local businessmen for work. Each of them turned him away with the excuse that they barely made enough money to support themselves.

At the corner of a busy intersection, he saw a shop that said, 'Grzegorz the Shoe Maker.' With no knowledge of this trade, he knew he offered little to the owner, but desperation forced him to try.

The rich smell of leather filled the shop. Grzegorz Novitski sat on a wooden bench and looked up when he saw Karl.

"How can I help you?" Grzegorz's brown and gray hair circled his head like the hair of a monk, leaving the top shiny and bald. His eyes, small and alert, studied Karl.

"I need a job. Do you have any work?"

"Not a lot," Grzegorz laughed, "but enough. Perhaps if you don't expect to be paid too much, I can use you. You're young, and you look pretty strong."

"I am strong, and I will work for whatever you can pay me."

"Hmmm… Perhaps we can come to some kind of agreement."

CHAPTER SEVENTY

GRZEGORZ TURNED out to be a fair boss, appreciative and undemanding. He marveled at the way Karl had advanced in his trade.

"A find you are, my boy!"

Karl just smiled. He'd developed an affection for the old man, and they worked together as if they were family.

Grzegorz Novitski and his wife lived above the shop in a small apartment. Their only son had married and moved to Paris to study art more than ten years earlier. Often, they invited Karl to join them for their meager evening meal. The couple enjoyed having the help of this strong and capable young man. Whenever he came for dinner, Karl tried to make himself useful by fixing things that had broken in the Novitski's flat.

Even with all the anti-Semitism since the Nazi occupation of Poland, Karl continued to wear a Star of David necklace. He refused to hide his background, infuriating the neighbors who lived and worked beside the Novitskis.

"Karl, I don't care that you are a Jew. It makes very little difference to me. But people on the street are making mention of it, and I am worried about you. You think maybe you should take off the necklace?"

"I can't. I am who I am, Grzegorz. I have been fighting all of my life with pride to be a Jew. I can't stop now."

Grzegorz just nodded his head, attributing Karl's stubborn behavior to his youth.

Winter's harsh and frigid weather gave way to a wet and slushy spring. Although he received looks of disdain from the Gentiles, among whom he lived and worked, Karl had settled into a groove. The relationship he'd developed with old man Novitski made his workdays easier. And the nagging obsession he'd had with the loss of his family seemed to subside a little. Other than Grzegorz and his wife, Karl had no friends.

On his day off, he stayed in his small apartment or had a beer alone at a local tavern. He preferred to work and stay busy than to spend his time idly.

Days turned into weeks, and weeks into months. The spring turned to summer, and the summer to fall as time ticked on.

A crisp chill settled into the air as fall gave way to early snow. Karl felt grateful that he'd purchased a warm coat and pulled it tighter around his large frame. Grzegorz kept the shop as warm as he was able to, but both men wore winter clothing as they worked. Humming softly, Karl sat at the workbench, tanning a large cutting of fine leather. Earlier that morning, a beautiful woman had come in, placing an order for a pair of fine, well-made, high-heeled pumps. She'd smiled at him, winking when she thought Grzegorz did not see. All day, her face stayed in his mind. The black cashmere coat she wore had hung open, revealing a scarlet silk dress that clung to her womanly shape. He could not help but wonder what wonderful mysteries lay beneath that frock.

Karl decided hers would be the finest pair of shoes he'd ever made.

CHAPTER SEVENTY-ONE

"HELLO, I am Claramond Bauer. I have a pair of shoes on order, black pumps." Her eyes glittered, and she smiled a knowing smile. There could be no doubt of his fascination with her. His eyes traveled over her body, out of his control.

"Yes, I recall." Karl heard himself speak and decided that his voice sounded a few octaves higher than his usual baritone. Embarrassed, he cleared his throat.

She laughed in response. "Do I make you uncomfortable?"

He laughed a nervous laugh. "No. I mean, perhaps, a little."

"I'm sorry. If you will just hand me my shoes, I will be on my way."

With that, he turned away so she could not see that the blood had rushed to his face. He walked to the shelf that held finished orders. It did not take much for him to find her name. He'd looked at it every day since she'd last been in. Once more, he studied the shoes. Satisfied with having done a perfect job, he brought them proudly to her.

Picking one up, a slow smile spread across her lips.

"Nice, very nice."

Not looking up, he pulled her receipt out of the register. Showing her the amount, he waited while she counted out her cash.

"Well, I thank you then, and I will be going." She began walking toward the door.

If she left now, he knew he would never see her again. "Mrs. Bauer?"

"Yes?"

"If you need any more shoes, please keep us in mind."

"I will." She stopped and strolled back. "Would you like to take me to lunch?"

He couldn't believe he'd heard those words come out of her mouth. "I would, yes. Let me go and tell my boss I am going out for a while."

"It's only ten in the morning." She laughed, "A bit too early for lunch, wouldn't you say? Perhaps you could meet me at the restaurant down the street at noon?"

"Yes, I could. I mean, I would like that."

"KARL, this is a married woman you are playing around with, and a Gentile, too. Have you gone mad?"

"She is so beautiful, Grzegorz. I sat across from her at lunch, and it was hard to believe that a creature so lovely could be real."

"This is not safe, Karl. Did anyone see you?"

"I don't know. I don't care, Grzegorz. I want to see her again and again. She is trapped in an unhappy marriage. It is only money that keeps her there. She told me all of this. We have plans to meet next week on Wednesday."

"Karl... What am I ever to do with you?" *Young and foolish,* Grzegorz thought.

"Be my friend?" Karl hugged the old man with vigor as he thought ahead with pleasure at the prospect of lunch with the beautiful woman.

CHAPTER SEVENTY-TWO

A GESTAPO CAR alarm signal blared rhythmically through the narrow thoroughfare, demanding attention. The automobile had been waxed to a brilliant onyx, mirroring all it passed in its glossy frame.

The sound reverberated in a deafening roar. Outside the small shops, people congregated on the sidewalks, staring, waiting, and wondering. What brought this black crow upon them?

Inside Grzegorz's little store, Karl worked tirelessly. At the beginning of the week, they had received an order for three pairs of boots. The patron had requested that they be finished as soon as possible.

Grzegorz had been unable to tolerate the long working hours. He'd developed arthritic pain in his shoulders and arms. Karl hoped to stay late, completing as much as he was able to. Since he planned to be off on the following day, when he would meet with Claramond, he wanted to leave a light workload for Grzegorz. While Karl worked, he thought of the day he had spent with Claramond.

He remembered her soft voice. How she had said, "Call me Clara." She had taken his hand in hers. Then she'd smiled and asked, "Would you like to kiss me?"

He hadn't been able to answer, only to nod. Then she'd pressed her lips to his, and the sensation had sent him reeling. Even today, as he remembered it, the sweet fragrance of her rose perfume still lingered in his nose.

Karl had held her for a few precious moments, rejoicing in the feeling of her body pressed against his own. While he was lost in the embrace of Clara, Karl was lost in the memory of her, oblivious to anything else. He was even oblivious to the sound of the sirens outside. But when three men in black trench coats and hats opened the door and walked into the shoe store, Karl was awakened from the reverie and returned to the present moment. It was the Gestapo. The leader, a man with a receding hairline, a dark, thin mustache, and a cruel expression, approached Karl.

"Karl Abendstern, you are under arrest," said the leader with a sadistic snarl.

Before he realized he'd been arrested, three strong men had forced him into handcuffs. He glanced out the window and saw Clara watching from across the street. She was crying.

Grzegorz, Karl's boss, who had been lying down in his upstairs apartment, raced into the shop.

"What's going on here? This is my employee. He has done nothing."

"Shut your mouth, old man. He is a Jew. You should not be employing Jews. You are lucky we don't arrest you."

"Wait, please! I have money. I will pay you to let him be."

Grzegorz reached into the cash register and pulled out a fist filled with German reichsmarks. He rushed over, trying to stuff the currency into one of the men's pockets. One of the police officers backhanded Grzegorz across the face, and he flew into the wall. His nose and upper lip leaked thick, dark blood. The officer took the money, shook his head, and looked at Grzegorz.

"Stupid old man—don't make this mistake again! You hear me?"

Grzegorz did not answer. He lay against the wall, knowing they would kill him if he tried to fight.

Karl had begun to kick as soon as he saw what had happened to

Grzegorz. Anger came pouring out of him like lava spewing out of an active volcano.

"Be still, Karl! They will surely kill you if you do not. Whatever they want, I am sure you can explain. You will be out in a few hours."

The men threw Karl into the back of the vehicle, and the loud alarm blasted through the street as they rode away.

With his hand on his heart, Grzegorz rose from the floor and wiped the blood from his face with the back of his hand. Outside the window, he saw the satisfied faces of other business owners who shared the block. Otto, the baker, saw Grzegorz and smiled at him as if to say, "Well, you got what you deserved."

Grzegorz could not bear to see the cruelty sparkling in Otto's eyes, and he pulled the shade closed. Then he sunk to the ground and wept.

CHAPTER SEVENTY-THREE

DETRICK HAD SPOKEN to the Muellers. For the right price, they agreed to hide the Abendsterns. Certain that he had secured a safe place for his friends, he planned to discuss the situation with Jacob. Once Jacob agreed, he would contact Konrad, join the party, and apply for work.

That night, when he arrived to find the Abendstern home dark, he felt a wave of panic. He feared he'd acted too late. Perhaps the Gestapo had come and arrested them.

Then Jacob opened the door, his eyes red and his skin gray.

"What's going on here?" Detrick entered, some of the alarm subsiding as he slammed the door shut and locked it. "Where is Leah?"

"She's here. She's fine. It's Miriam, Detrick. Miriam is dead, Michael, too."

"What? How?" He sank onto the sofa as Jacob handed him the blood-spattered message about Michael's death.

"Miriam was alone when this letter came this afternoon. She killed herself."

He read the paper and sprang up.

"Leah. Where is Leah?" With his heart pounding, he raced to her room to find her lying on her bed, facing the wall.

"My mother is dead, Detrick. My mother is dead."

"I know, sweetheart. Your father told me." He lay down beside her. Gently, he smoothed the hair out of her face. "I am here for you. I love you, Leah."

Suddenly, great sobs came from a place deep within Leah Abendstern. Detrick took her into his arms and held her, kissing the top of her head.

"My sweetheart." As she cried, he felt the pain firing through his own heart. The two were one.

They lay like that all night until finally, as dawn broke, Leah slept.

Jacob, still filled with grief, had been reluctant to accept Detrick's proposal. Finally, when confronted with the issue of Leah's safety, he had agreed, and the arrangements had been made.

Helma and Ebner Mueller had two daughters: Adelheid, fifteen, and Rebekka, twelve. Their son Gaufid and Detrick had formed a friendship when they had practiced on the same track team. It had quickly come to Detrick's attention that Gaufid shared his feelings concerning the Nazi Party and anti-Semitism. For a while, Gaufid had kept company with a Jewish girl they both knew from school. Now Gaufid was in the army, and it had been months since he'd been home. Although he was aware of the hazards, Detrick knew that he must put his trust in these people.

With open, honest faces, the Muellers assured Detrick that they meant to help. And there could be no doubt that the money he would provide would bring creature comforts to this otherwise impoverished family. They seemed grateful for the opportunity to earn money that would enable them to live a better life, although there was risk involved.

If his home had been spacious enough, Detrick would have attempted to keep Jacob and Leah there. But he lived in a tiny apartment with no area suitable for hiding.

Back when Gaufid had made the offer, he'd told Detrick that the old house he inhabited had been in the family for generations. With

a large attic that appeared to be closed off and completely unde-
tectable to anyone unaware of its presence, the house seemed a
perfect choice. At the time Gaufid had made the suggestion, Detrick
had felt the Nazi threat would pass. Now, he concluded that it would
continue and perhaps grow even more threatening.

After Detrick spoke with Jacob and felt secure about going
forward with the plan, he sought Konrad out immediately. The
entire operation rested on Detrick's ability to find employment.

CHAPTER SEVENTY-FOUR

DETRICK FELT his stomach twist as he waited in the lobby of the Nazi headquarters. He'd given an aide his name and told him he would like to see Konrad.

"And may I tell him what this is about?"

"Yes, of course. Just tell him his old friend, Detrick Haswell, is here to see him."

"Very well. Please take a seat."

Konrad walked into the room and raised his hand. "Heil Hitler."

"Heil Hitler," Detrick answered.

"Detrick! Good to see you! It's been forever since we've spent time together. How have you been?"

"Good, Konrad. You're looking well."

"And so I should be. I've just been promoted! I got a new position managing the punch cards for the new computer machine. Helps us keep track of the Jews and all of that. And you, what are you up to these days?"

"Well, that's what brings me here. I don't actually know how to put this."

"Let me help you. You are in need of work?"

"Yes." Detrick looked away.

A smile tickled Konrad's lips. "Well, you realize, of course, that to work here at headquarters, you would be required to join the party."

"Yes, and I am ready to do so."

A laugh of joy and triumph escaped from Konrad's throat. "I've been waiting and hoping you would come. After all, it is your true place as an Aryan to stand among us. We, you and I, are members of the most powerful race on this earth."

He stood up and walked over to pat Detrick's shoulder. "I'll find you something. I'll recommend you to my superiors. You will work under me."

"I appreciate everything, Konrad. I'll wait to hear from you."

After Detrick had left, Konrad lit a cigarette. He tingled with anticipation from the top of his head to the tips of each appendage. Things between Detrick and himself would return to how they used to be. He would be reunited with his best friend, sharing good times. Only now, instead of Detrick being the top man, the most popular and desirable, Konrad would be the king of the hill.

He licked his lips, tasting the very idea. Then, he took a deep puff of his cigarette and went to speak to his superior officer.

CHAPTER SEVENTY-FIVE

BEFORE HE BROUGHT Leah to the Mueller's attic, Detrick spent a day clearing spider webs and cleaning dust from the area. No one had opened the door to the musty rooms for years, and he lit a candle to clear the smell. It broke his heart to know that Jacob and Leah would live under such conditions, but he also considered the alternative. The arrests increased daily, and the sooner he secured them in this hiding place, the better he would feel.

Before he left for training, Detrick settled Leah and Jacob in the Mueller's attic and paid Herr Mueller for the first month out of his enlistment bonus. Even though Jacob and Leah were still distraught over their loss, they moved into the Mueller's attic at midnight. It was not until the following evening, when Detrick arrived, that the entire Mueller family came upstairs to meet their houseguests.

"We want to welcome you. We realize how hard this must be to leave your home and be displaced in such a place as this. As you can see, we don't have so much, but we will do what we can to make you comfortable," Herr Mueller said, speaking for the family.

"My daughter Leah and I thank you for inviting us into your home, and we, too, realize that you are taking a great risk. I don't know how we can ever thank you, but we are grateful from the bottom of our hearts."

Leah smiled at Adelheid and Rebekka. She hoped to befriend the girls. Even though they were younger, it would be nice to have them to talk to during the long, lonely days while she awaited Detrick's return from basic training.

"Herr Mueller, I will send the payments every month while I am away at basic training. Please watch over Jacob and Leah."

"Yes, of course. We will care for them."

Finally, the Muellers left to return to their own living quarters. Once they had gone, Detrick took tins of food out of his pockets and handed them to Jacob.

"I don't know how much the Muellers will be able to give you, so here is some extra food. I will bring whatever I can when I return without creating suspicion."

Jacob nodded. Then, putting the food down, he turned and hugged Detrick. A tear rolled down Jacob's face. Detrick turned to Leah. "Darling, I will be back again tomorrow night." He touched Leah's face.

Jacob turned away and began putting away what little possessions he had. They'd been unable to carry suitcases for fear of attracting attention, so Jacob and Leah had worn several layers of clothing. What they had on their bodies would have to suffice until Detrick could bring more or the end of the war came. Under their clothes, they carried personal items, like their combs and tooth-brushes. Jacob brought Miriam's wedding band and a picture of the family all together before Karl had gone and when Miriam and Michael were still alive. Leah had wrapped her gold Star of David and the few other pieces of valuable jewelry they owned and sewn them into the lining of her coat. Other than these few small items, they'd left everything behind.

Detrick spent the following night with Leah, kissed her goodbye, and left to bid his parents goodbye.

The next day, Detrick took the train to Wildflecken for six months of general military training. He had to write letters addressed to Herr Mueller for Leah. Because he was to work for

Konrad, his three months of service following his training and then his three months of theoretical training would all be at headquarters, working directly under Konrad. Konrad had advanced to the rank of *Sturmbannführer* (major) and had many influential friends. Detrick trained hard and concealed his political feelings, graduating training as a *Sturmmann*, lance corporal.

Detrick's first day working at the Nazi headquarters had stretched his nerves thin. Konrad had proudly handed him his new SS uniform.

"Go to the men's room and put it on, Detrick."

He'd obeyed without question. When he returned, Konrad sat at his desk waiting. "You look fantastic. It suits you."

Detrick smiled to conceal his distaste. Six months of training had disciplined him to the point where he could salute and 'Heil Hitler' with the best of them, pushing his hatred for them down, swallowing it like bitter gall. Leah, he had to behave himself for Leah's sake.

It tested his nerves when Konrad introduced Detrick to his superiors. He learned to discipline himself to keep his nervousness in check, lest some mannerism or nervous glance betray him to the other officers. *It was natural to be intimidated by the presence of officers. After all, he was only a corporal and wasn't expected to talk much in their presence.* He became accustomed to the constant greetings of his fellow workers with 'Heil Hitler' throughout the day. Though abhorrent to Detrick, he was learning to function without responding or reacting in a way that would betray him. Detrick had decided to use military training to discipline himself to play his duplicitous role.

When Konrad received his automobile from the party, he'd decided Detrick should be his driver and promoted Detrick to *Scharführer* (sergeant). Detrick happily agreed to be out and away from the office as much as possible. He knew it was easier to fool Konrad alone than an office full of SS officers.

CHAPTER SEVENTY-SIX

ONCE DETRICK HAD JOINED the party, as Konrad had promised, a rush of gifts arrived at the Haswell home. For the first time since Detrick's birth, his father took pride in his son. Gifts of boxes of fruit and chocolate, silk stockings, and fabric for Inga, as well as an offer of employment for Hans, gave his father pride in their family again. All came as offerings of friendship from the party. His mother had written him about the gifts while he was in basic training, along with the thank you note from Konrad for speaking with their son.

Now back home and alone in his room, Detrick assessed his situation. He combed his hair back, and it fell forward into a natural side part as he stood in front of the mirror. Self-loathing came over him as he considered the weakness he had begun to feel within himself. As much as he loved Leah, and God knows he did love her, he sometimes wished he had fallen in love with a Gentile. It would have been so much easier. And Jacob—the guilt and worry he carried over Jacob sometimes seemed as if it had taken over everything else in his life. He loved the man like a father but wondered why he had been chosen for this difficult purpose. Then, he thought of Konrad, his oldest friend. Konrad's smug self-assurance had begun to grate on his nerves. How could he be thoroughly convinced that his actions and behavior were perfectly acceptable? In Konrad's mind, his sadistic nature toward the enemies of the Reich only proved his superiority.

Detrick did not feel fortunate. In fact, he felt ashamed of his people and the blood that ran through his veins. *I should have been born a Jew,* he thought as he straightened the collar of his Nazi uniform. Another day he must carefully cover his true feelings. Another day he must live a lie.

After dark, he walked to Herr Mueller's house to visit Leah and Jacob for the first time since he had returned. Frau Mueller greeted him at the door. She was, at first, shocked, then smiled when she recognized Detrick. The curtains were drawn around the house, and Jacob and Leah joined them in the living room. Leah's eyes brightened at the sight of him, and Jacob greeted him as a long-lost son. Adelheid and Rebekka joined the gathering in the living room.

Adelheid glanced sideways at Detrick. She found him handsome, just the right age, and a truly desirable man. In his pressed black Nazi uniform with his blond hair wet down and combed away from his face, he brought out feelings within Adelheid that she'd never experienced. But the uniform had far-reaching benefits. Wearing it, Detrick found he could walk through the streets easily, regardless of the hour. So, he'd decided to wear it whenever he went to the Mueller's home. Adelheid watched him as he stood beside Leah and wondered how it would feel to have him stand beside her. She'd never had a boyfriend, although she'd begun to think a great deal about the subject.

CHAPTER SEVENTY-SEVEN

THE WARSAW GHETTO brimmed with dirt and disease. The small area, already overpopulated, grew as the Nazis brought more arrested Jews in daily. Four-story stone buildings stood on either side of the streets, each apartment housing more people than would be considered comfortable.

A group of Nazi guards stood at the train station making offers of bread and jam to anyone wishing to leave the ghetto to go to a work camp called Treblinka. Due to the lack of food and the madness of near starvation, some people agreed to the relocation.

The Nazis had a quota of Jews to be delivered to the camp each day. A group of Jews was put in charge of this operation by the Nazi guards. It was their responsibility to deliver a certain number of their own people to the waiting trains each day. Officially named the Warsaw Ghetto Jewish Council, these groups of Nazi collaborators were known by the other Jews as the *Judenrats*.

Anyone passing the train station could see the overcrowded cattle cars with people standing up, pressed together, and keeping each other from dropping with heat and exhaustion. They would remain standing through the entire train ride.

After his arrest, Karl was sent to the Warsaw Ghetto, where he occupied a two-room apartment with four other men of varying ages. Hunger motivated Karl to learn how to climb the rooftops and leave the ghetto during the night. On the outside, he found the black market where, for the right price, he bought food and supplies. Then, taking them back into the ghetto, he kept what he needed and sold the rest, enabling him to survive more comfortably than most.

News spread through the ghetto that a secret meeting was to be held. It concerned the trains, the food, the Nazis, and Eretz Israel. When one of his black market customers mentioned the meeting, Karl decided he would attend. Everyone stressed the importance of secrecy and insisted that the *Judenrats* be kept ignorant of the plan lest they deliver their fellow Jews to the Nazis and, once again, save themselves.

CHAPTER SEVENTY-EIGHT

THE MEETING WAS HELD in a small apartment on the third floor of a four-story building—it was a standing room only. With the scarcity of soap, the air reeked of the putrid smell of unwashed bodies. A few attendees had purchased cigarettes on the black market, and the thick smoke made breathing difficult. Karl fought the urge to gag as he entered. A tall, bearded, large-boned man stood upon a chair at the front of the room, which enabled even those standing at the back to see him. He stood so tall that his head brushed the ceiling. Paint crumbled off the ceiling, splattering his curly black hair with white specks.

"Quiet, everyone. Quiet, please!"

It took a few moments, but the room grew silent.

"My name is Yankel Finkelstein. Before I was caught, arrested, and brought here to the ghetto, I hid out in the forests. There I saw many terrible things. Now, because you are in this secluded place, you might not realize what's going on, what these Nazis are doing to our people in the outside world. It is imperative that you know and accept the truth. This may come as a terrible shock to you, but those trains going to the work camps. They are not taking people to work camps at all. They are taking them to death camps. The Nazis are systematically murdering us Jews."

Another man called out, "Before I was arrested, I escaped from a horror that happened outside of Kyiv at a place called Babi Yar. When the Germans were busy lining our people up, I turned and ran. I don't know how they didn't see me. I don't know how I got away, but I did. Then I watched from behind some thick brush and saw German soldiers forcing Jews to dig a deep pit. Then they forced them to strip off all of their clothes. I will never forget this if I live for a thousand years. Young men, old men, and women—children, too. The Nazi guards lined them up in front of the hole they dug and then shot them. Then they fell into the mass grave. One group after another. They lined them up and shot them dead. The mothers held their children tight to their naked breasts. Babies cried. I saw a child whose mother had shielded it from death with her body. One of the guards saw it too —a little girl still alive. He walked over to the side of the pit and shot three bullets into the terrified child. Horrible, I tell you. Horrible."

"I don't believe it." A heavyset woman crossed her arms in front of her chest.

"Me, either." A man in the front row shook his head.

"How can anyone believe that the Nazis would try to murder millions of people? That makes no sense. Wouldn't they profit more by using us to work for their effort?"

"Perhaps," Finkelstein said. "But they are choosing to eradicate us."

"This is not true. He is a rabble-rouser just trying to make trouble. The Nazis need us. Hitler has waged war on the entire world. Who will make their ammunition? Who will they use to make their uniforms if not us?" A male voice shot out from the side of the room.

"It is true what Finkelstein is telling you. I believe him." The woman's soft voice carried an air of authority.

Karl turned to see who spoke. A tall, slender girl with hair the color of new cherries returned his stare. He watched her as she took charge of the crowd.

"I understand how you feel. I, too, would like to believe that the Nazis could not be so cruel. However, I am afraid that the truth is they are. Perhaps it is time we considered organizing and fighting back. I believe that is why we are here tonight?" When she finished, the redheaded woman looked at Yankel, who smiled at her.

"Thank you, Ada, yes. That is the reason for this meeting here tonight. We must consider building our own army. We must fight our way out of here and then make our way to Eretz Israel. Our only salvation is there. I may die trying, but I would rather die fighting than surrender like a lamb."

Finkelstein continued to speak, and although Karl agreed whole-heartedly with his words, he had stopped listening. Instead, he watched, mesmerized, as the girl they'd called Ada gazed at Yankel, her eyes glazed over with admiration.

CHAPTER SEVENTY-NINE

ADA HAD IMPRESSED Karl the moment he'd seen her and heard her speak. Her presence had drawn a small pencil mark upon his mind that grew into an entire book of drawings as the week progressed. He gave a great deal of thought to what her life might entail. Could she be Finkelstein's wife or girlfriend? Karl thought he'd had contact with all the inhabitants of the ghetto at one time or another when he'd sold his black market goods, but he'd never seen Ada before. If he had, he would certainly have remembered. Everywhere he went, he kept watch for the lovely girl with the fiery-red hair. But he never saw her and could not even speculate on who to ask concerning her whereabouts. So, Karl continued to wonder.

One afternoon, Karl stood in the alleyway of his apartment building. In front of him, he'd put up a makeshift stand covered with the goods he had acquired on the black market the previous night that he planned to sell. A man with a familiar face approached him. Karl recognized him as Yankel Finkelstein immediately.

"I saw you at the meeting. I heard you speak," Karl whispered, to not arouse any attention.

"Yes, it was me."

"You spoke the truth. I think I always knew the truth about what was happening, but I didn't want to believe."

"Yes, it is all true. And I think all of us Jews feel the same way. After all, who wants to believe that the Nazis are systematically murdering our entire race? It's too terrible to comprehend." Finkelstein picked up two apples. "How much?"

"For you and your wife, a gift from me," Karl waited, hoping to hear news of Ada.

"Wife? I have no wife. But I do graciously accept your gift." Finkelstein smiled, tossing an apple in the air and catching it, then adding in a whisper, "I hope you will join us as we build a resistance army. You are young and strong as an ox. We need men like you."

"Will there be another meeting?"

"Yes. This one will be private. I will give you directions."

On the following Thursday, after the sun had set, Karl made his way through the narrow streets and up four flights of stairs, where he entered a room filled with friendly conversation. As he looked around, he spotted Finkelstein talking to a group. Then, he recognized the other man who had spoken the previous night, engaged in a heated conversation with a short young woman wearing a beret. He scanned the room but did not see Ada. Disappointed, Karl considered leaving. He was in no mood to listen to discussions. He was far too tired. In just a few hours, it would be necessary for him to climb the wall and bring back what supplies he could get his hands on. He longed to steal a few hours of sleep while the sun still shone, as tonight would surely be another exhausting ordeal. But before he could slip quietly out the door, Yankel Finkelstein walked over to him.

"Hello, my friend, and welcome. You know I never caught your name."

"Karl Abendstern."

"Come on over here. I want you to meet someone very special." Yankel put his arm around Karl's shoulder and led him to the other side of the room, where a young, attractive man stood drinking a glass of water. "Mordechai, this is Karl." Then Yankel turned to Karl, explaining, "Mordechai is our leader."

Mordechai reached out to shake Karl's hand.

"Welcome, I'm glad you came."

The door opened, and Karl felt his heart race as his eye caught a glimpse of the fiery hair. Ada had walked in.

"Ada, I have someone I would like for you to meet. This is Karl Abendstern."

"Hello, Karl. Welcome to our group." Ada smiled.

"Thank you."

"Mordechai, we should discuss securing weapons tonight. The Polish resistance has offered us some help." Ada turned her attention to Mordechai.

"Do you trust them?" Yankel asked.

"I don't know. But do we have a choice?" Ada waved a greeting to a woman on the other side of the room.

"That's true. We don't really have a choice. We need them," Mordechai said.

Ada caught the look of raw desire in Karl's eyes. He could not conceal his admiration. Flattered by his public attention, Ada met his eyes with an intense stare. Smiling, she licked her lips and winked. Ada's brazen behavior embarrassed Karl, and he turned away. Never had he met a woman so bold. Even the married woman at the cobbler shop he'd had a crush on had not been so open. Turning back, he tried to catch Ada's attention again, but she had changed directions. Somehow, she seemed to have completely forgotten him. Lost in a heated conversation with Mordechai, she never so much as looked Karl's way the rest of the evening.

That night, Karl learned of plans to create a resistance army, a secret underground society of which he was now a part had formed a group of fighters who, win or lose, would not go willingly to the death camps. The idea of fighting Nazis appealed to Karl. For as long as he could remember, he had tried with little success to influence his fellow Jews to be strong. Here, amongst this small band of rebels, he'd found a home. At first, he'd come to meet Ada, and his feelings for her had not changed. But once he'd heard the powerful speeches, he knew he belonged with this clan of Jews longing to build their own Jewish state in Eretz Israel.

After a date had been set for a follow-up meeting, Mordechai dismissed the group. Karl descended the stairs and walked out into the street. Jews were forbidden to be out after curfew, so the crowd dispersed quietly, slithering through alleyways. Karl ducked into an opening between buildings and lit a cigarette. Taking a deep breath, he looked out—watching, waiting, always careful.

Then he saw her.

"Ada."

"Karl." She walked over to him. "You should get home."

"Yes, I should… and you, too. It's not safe to be out on the street."

"Would you like to come to my flat? I live just a few steps from here. I have a little coffee, and perhaps we can talk a bit more."

"I would like that."

When they arrived, he saw that each of the three women Ada shared her two small rooms with had curtain dividers, affording them a little bit of privacy.

"I wish I could offer you something to eat. I am afraid we are very low on food, and my roommates and I are very frugal with what little we have. I just looked. I thought I had some coffee, but I'm afraid it's all gone."

He laughed. "I have plenty of food. I will bring you some."

"Plenty? How did you manage that? Don't tell me you're a Judenrat."

"Me? No! I've been dabbling in the black market. I guess you could say I refuse to starve."

She nodded in understanding. Then, walking over to him, she put her arms around his neck and kissed him full on the lips.

Karl, shocked, did not respond immediately.

"Is something wrong?"

"No… no… you just surprised me, is all." How could he tell her he had never been with a woman before? He'd been so busy fighting the world that he'd never taken the time to become involved with anyone. And just as he had thought he might have his first encounter with a woman, he'd been arrested.

"Don't you like me?"

"Of course. You're beautiful. I'd be a fool not to like you."

"Then, would you like to make love to me?" she whispered so as not to disturb the women who slept just feet away.

He nodded, unable to speak.

Slowly, she unbuttoned her blouse. When she removed her shirt, Karl felt dizzy, as if he might faint. In his entire life, he'd never seen such beauty or been so moved by anything. When she stood naked before him, he stared, unable to avert his eyes. Her small but rounded breasts stood high on her chest, and the curve of her hips rolled softly from her tiny waist.

"You are the most beautiful thing I have ever seen. You're like a statue of a goddess."

She laughed. "I'm very real, Karl. Come over here. Touch me."

He tried to control the trembling of his hand as he tenderly caressed her face.

"Are you a virgin?" she asked him.

"No." he lied. Then, looking deep into her onyx eyes, he whispered, "Yes."

"It's all right. I'll teach you."

In her arms, the strong man became weak and vulnerable. He held her close through the night, kissing and caressing the soft white skin that covered her like silk. The sweet smell of flowers drifted from her hair. Instead of eating one week, she'd traded some of her food rations for fragrant-smelling rose oil soap. Intoxicated by the fragrance and the moment, Karl lost himself in Ada.

Once she slept, he lay beside her, wondering if this had been what he'd searched for his entire life.

In the morning, when Ada awakened to find Karl watching her, she turned to him.

"Karl, listen to me. I have no time for love. We have only today…only this moment. At this moment, we must grab all that we can. For us, tomorrow may never come. Do you understand me?"

"No."

"Karl, no one is promised tomorrow. We Jews here in this ghetto, least of all. That is why I did not wait to take you to my bed. Before all of this began, I taught young children. My husband

254 | ALL MY LOVE, DETRICK

worked as a professor at the university. We lived quiet lives. Then, one morning, the Gestapo came and took him away. I have not seen him for years. I don't know if he is dead or alive. Funny thing is, I am not sure we could ever live as man and wife again. I have changed so much. In my other life, before the war, I could never have been so bold. Now, Karl, I live for the moment. For the moment is all I have."

"And your dreams...you have dreams...dreams of Eretz Israel, of the future. I know you do. I've heard you speak."

"Yes, Karl. When dreams are all we have, they become even more precious, but they also can weaken us and make us helpless. I have lost so much. So much. My husband, my parents, everyone, and everything."

"But what is the meaning of living if we never allow ourselves to dream or to feel? Ada, I know it is soon, but as you said, we are not promised tomorrow, so we must live at a faster pace than we once did. I am trying to say that I have more feelings for you than I've had for anyone ever before." He grew silent for a few moments. Then, although he felt foolish, he knew he must continue. "I think I'm falling in love with you."

She did not answer. For a long time, an awkward silence hovered over them.

"You should leave." Ada averted her eyes.

Karl didn't answer. He left the bed slowly and began to dress. A cold chill ran over Ada as she watched him. When he'd finished, he walked to the door. "This is what you want, so goodbye."

"Goodbye, Karl."

As his hand curled around the doorknob, Karl felt his heart sink.

"Karl, please. I'm confused. I don't know what I want. Will you please stay the night?"

He turned to see her holding the blanket around her body. The beauty of her curving white shoulders made him ache. He would not judge her or hold her fears against her. He felt them too, but he'd been alone too long. Without a word, he returned to the small cot, removed his clothes, and took her into his arms. He could not help but notice her face was wet with tears.

CHAPTER EIGHTY

THE FOLLOWING MORNING, Ada awoke and dressed.

"I have to leave. So, you must go, too."

"Can I come by and see you again? Later tonight, perhaps?"

"If you'd like."

He longed to ask her where she planned to go, but he dared not. If he possessed her too tightly, he feared she would turn away. So, he smiled, got dressed, kissed her cavalierly, and left.

That night Karl brought food as he'd promised. When he arrived, he handed Ada a basket filled to the brim.

"A small token of my affection."

Although Ada stood five feet, eight inches tall, she still had to reach up to kiss Karl.

"Thank you." She smiled.

"You are very welcome."

"Karl?"

"Yes?" He stroked her hair once again, touched by her loveliness.

"Please, don't think me ungrateful. I appreciate the extra food, and God knows we can use it. You see, one of the women I live with is pregnant. God help her. She hid it for a very long time. However, she is ravenous and eats almost all of our food." She laughed. "It annoys me sometimes, but I pity her. She is so alone and frightened. Karl, I don't know how to say this without sounding like an ingrate, but there is something I need even more than food."

"Tell me?"

"Well, I will pay you what I can."

"What is it, Ada? I didn't ask you to pay me…just tell me."

"Do you think you might be able to get pencils, paper, even books, perhaps?"

"For you, of course, I will find them. But do you mind me asking what you need them for?"

"Have you ever met Janusz Korczak? Or maybe you know him as Henryk Goldszmit? Perhaps you have seen or heard of him around the ghetto."

"The name doesn't sound familiar. Who is he?"

"He's a children's doctor who became a teacher and writer of children's books. Two blocks down from here, he has established an orphanage. After he'd taught me his teaching method, I began to work with him and the children."

"You see, you do have dreams." He touched her chin and bent to kiss her lips.

"Yes, I suppose I do, Karl. If we give up on everything, then what will be left? I just try to protect my heart. When I work with these little ones, I try so hard not to love them because they die, Karl. They are not strong, and the lack of food and disease claims many lives." She turned away from him. "If the Jews are to have a future as a people, it will be the children who will bring it about. I must believe, Karl. I must. Somehow, I must hold fast to the dream that these young people will someday live and work in a truly Jewish state where they will have no fear of being who they are. And when they get there, I want to be sure they know how to read, write, and do arithmetic."

Warmth and affection for her washed over him. For all of her attempts at remaining distant, Karl saw that Ada had a heart as big as all of Poland.

"I'll get the supplies for you. I'll go tonight."

CHAPTER EIGHTY-ONE

ON A GRAY DAY, light rain and a cold breeze blew outside the Nazi headquarters building. Konrad lit another cigarette. He'd smoked the previous one so short he'd burned his fingers. A new job had been created to instruct others on the use of the punch card machine. It offered a significant pay raise and would be considered a promotion. He wanted to be the one chosen for the position.

Detrick sat at his desk in the area adjacent to Konrad's office, looking over files and wishing the clock would move time along faster so he could be free of this workplace.

Another round of pathetic-looking Jews lined up outside to be checked in. Although it had not been openly discussed with him, Detrick knew that executions of innocent people were taking place. He shuddered to think of Jacob and Leah.

Their new home so far had proven to be as safe as could be hoped for. Although the living space in the attic had insect infestations, the Abendsterns were grateful for the refuge. Detrick and Leah did what they could to help keep the area as clean as possible.

"Detrick, come here," Konrad called to him.

"Heil Hitler." Detrick was careful to salute when he entered the office.

"Heil Hitler. Look, today you will check some of these Jews in and get them ready for transport to the work camps. I'm terribly busy and don't have the time for this. Therefore, I'm relying on you. Are we clear?"

"Yes." Detrick's stomach responded angrily with sharp, knife-like pain. But he smiled, not meeting Konrad's gaze.

"Good. Take care of it. I am involved in the making of some important plans."

"I understand."

Detrick walked outside. A slight headache began over his eye and traveled up the side of his head to his temple.

The job should have been easy. All that was expected of him was to sit at a table at the front of the line of Jews. As each family came before him, he had to ask for their information and then direct them to the line to be transported to the camp. Simple, right? Not for Detrick. He knew where the poor souls were headed and what awaited them when they arrived. Having knowledge of the fate of these fellow human beings tortured Detrick, but he knew he dared not speak out. Instead, he took the cards without asking questions. A pile grew upon the desk. His head pounded as if a hammer had drummed inside of it.

When he got up to pour himself a cup of coffee, Detrick saw someone he recognized standing at the front of the line. Although he was skinny, covered in open sores, and stripped of his fancy clothes, the man who stood before him could be none other than Lewis Shapiro.

The desire for revenge sparked like a flashing light of triumph in Detrick's mind. Once, long ago, this man had humiliated him, attempted to seduce Leah, and then proved himself to be less than a gentleman when she'd denied him his way. He'd left her alone to walk home in the dark of night. Now, Detrick held power over Lewis and his family. Taller by more than a foot, Detrick stood looking at Lewis. His black uniform terrified his prisoner. For the first time, Detrick wanted to show domination. Lewis's fate and his entire family, who stood with him, lay in Detrick's hands. If Detrick so chose, he could shoot them all right there. There would be no consequences, no one to answer to. A dark part of him entertained the idea.

"Do you remember me?" Detrick asked. The sound of his own voice startled him. For the first time, he sounded like a member of the Nazi Party.

A frightened look of recognition came to Lewis's face. He remembered. "I don't think so. Perhaps you have me confused with someone else."

"No, I don't think so. I am Detrick Haswell. Do you remember Leah Abendstern?"

"I'm sorry, I don't remember."

"Don't lie to me." Detrick's deep blue eyes blazed at him. "You do realize I have the power to decide if you live or die? I could shoot you right now." Then, upon hearing himself, Detrick's inner self protested. Regardless of what Lewis had done, Lewis was the catalyst that brought Leah to him.

"Yes, I know. I'm sorry about everything. Please spare us."

To hear someone begging him brought Detrick back to reality. He could not be cruel or sentence this man to death by his own hand. How many times had he wished he had the power to free all of them?

"Come into the office." Detrick turned to another guard. "Heinz, I will be right back. I have a personal situation with this group."

Heinz nodded.

A small workplace area had been established to be used by subordinate officers who did not have their own offices. Detrick took the Shapiro family inside the room and closed the door. He saw Lewis's hands and legs quivering and noticed the fraying on the sleeves and lapel of his jacket.

"I don't agree with the things you did, Shapiro, but I cannot kill you. It goes against everything I believe in. Although I'm not sure, you don't deserve it. That night you left Leah on the road in the dark to fend for herself—what kind of man does such a thing?" Detrick stared at Lewis, looking as if he'd eaten something foul. "However, I am going to set you free. You and your family will leave through the back door. I suggest that you do whatever possible to get out of Germany. Use your money—use whatever you have. Next time, I may not be able to help you."

Lewis nodded, relieved to be awarded another day of life. As Detrick looked down, he found that Lewis had urinated.

With a pity that Detrick had never thought he could feel for Lewis, he led him and his family out of the office.

"Follow me." Detrick directed the Shapiros to the back door. "Leave through here and disappear as quickly as you can."

Again Lewis nodded. Then, turning to Detrick, "I'm sorry. I'm sorry for everything."

"I know."

The family walked out the door, but before he left, Lewis turned to Detrick. "I know I shouldn't ask, but I must. Why are you doing this? Why are you helping us?"

"Because it's the right thing to do, Lewis."

Later, the Shapiro family would be rearrested and sent to Auschwitz. Detrick would never know of their plight. There they would all perish, but for today, they clung to life and to hope.

CHAPTER EIGHTY-TWO

THAT NIGHT, Detrick brought wood planks, paint, and a few of his books when he went to see the Abendsterns. He hoped to give them something they could do to fill the hours. "I brought you some crafting supplies. I thought you might want to whittle?"

"Do I look like a whittler?" Jacob laughed. "Detrick, we are grateful to you for everything, every day. You needn't worry about filling our time."

Remarkably, even after losing two sons and his wife, Jacob still managed to tell jokes and keep smiling, but the pain he endured was now reflected in his eyes.

Leah, like her father, never complained. Neither of them ever made mention of their home or the shop. No sad discussions of Miriam or Michael took place. Occasionally, Jacob wondered aloud about Karl's whereabouts, but other than that, the two were thankful to be together and to be alive.

Leah had formed a friendship with the two Mueller girls. They'd always wanted to learn piano, so she'd drawn a keyboard on the cement floor with chalk and taught them to play.

Adelheid, only a few years younger, admired the older and self-confident Leah. She wished she had the fashion sense and culture she recognized in Leah. But most of all, she wished she had Detrick.

When Detrick saw the drawing, he smiled. "A piano?"

"Yes." Leah laughed. "I'm teaching Adelheid and Rebekka to play."

"My sweetheart, you're so innovative."

"Is that what you'd call it?"

"Yes, I certainly would."

She giggled, and he kissed her. The two had not lain together as lovers since the move out of respect for Jacob. When their lips brushed, the passion within both of them ignited immediately. Leah gave Detrick a knowing smile and turned away lest he take her in his arms and make love to her right there.

"Here," Detrick reached into his coat pocket and brought out a small loaf of bread wrapped in a towel, a tin of fish, and an orange. "I thought you might like this."

"Oh, Detrick, you're bringing us your dinner? You should eat."

"I have plenty."

"We're fine here." Jacob smiled. "Eat."

"We can all share this now. Would that be all right?"

"Only if you promise not to do this again," Jacob began to tear the bread into three pieces.

The attic reached across the entire roof of the house. It was separated into two rooms. The large area in the front housed a small table with four chairs and a cot where Jacob slept. And a few feet away was the lavatory, and attached to it was a small closed-off room for Leah.

Once the couple heard Jacob's gentle snoring, they lit a candle and quietly slipped to Leah's room. There, they sat across from each other on Leah's bed, holding hands.

"How are you holding up, Detrick? I mean, really, how are you doing?"

"I'm fine, adjusting. Anyway, it's me who should be asking you how you're doing. Oh Leah, I wish every day that I could take you out of here and that we could live a normal life. Oh, that we could marry and make your father a grandfather."

"I know, my darling, and we will. This will all end. You'll see. Years from now, we'll tell the stories to our children."

She turned so he could not see the tears welling in her eyes.

"Yes, and they won't believe it because the world will have changed so much. Once the Nazis have been defeated, and everyone sees them for what they are, the entire world will shun them." Detrick smoothed her hair gently with his hand.

"Detrick?"

"Yes, love?"

"Do you think the Third Reich will really ever end? That Hitler will be defeated?"

"Of course, Darling." He cradled her in his arms and rocked her like a baby. "Of course he will," Detrick repeated it once again, trying to convince himself.

CHAPTER EIGHTY-THREE

MIDNIGHT HAD COME and gone when Detrick quietly descended the stairs out of the attic to leave the Mueller home. As he walked towards the door, a voice from the darkened hallway surprised him.

"I know you're not a Nazi, but the uniform becomes you."

Adelheid stepped out of the darkness.

"You startled me. What are you doing still awake?"

"My cat had kittens. I spent the evening with her. Do you want to see them?"

Exhausted, Detrick longed to go home and fall into a deep slumber, but he felt obligated to be cordial to this young girl who'd welcomed Leah with her friendship. "Yes, of course. Where are they?"

"Come in here." She led him through a short hallway to a small room where inside a wooden box lay a gray cat surrounded by six tiny, furry bodies. The cat purred loudly, satisfied with the accomplishment of motherhood as her kittens cuddled against her. Surprised by the feelings of tenderness the feline domestic scene brought on, Detrick found he had to smile.

"They're lovely." He gazed at the small, rat-like little bodies lined up and sucking fiercely at their mother's breast.

"Not yet, but they will be. Right now, they look like little mice, don't you think?" Adelheid bent over the box to get a closer look. "But in a few days, they'll open their eyes to the world, and they'll be beautiful."

"It is amazing, you know? That life goes on regardless of everything we are going through in the world. Like the war and the camps. I mean all of it, you know?"

"Yes, it is amazing, isn't it?"

He smiled. "Thank you for showing me the kittens. In a strange way, it did me good."

"Would you like one when they are old enough?"

"I don't have time to take care of it. Between my job and coming here, my days are full. I've even stopped my gymnasium exercises for lack of time."

"Do you think Leah would like one?"

"Yes, actually, I do. That's a fantastic idea and very generous of you, Adelheid. I also want to express my gratitude for how kind you have been to Leah and Jacob."

"You don't have to. They are such nice people. But Detrick, have you ever considered that you might choose to lead a more normal life?"

"How do you mean?"

"Perhaps with a girl who is like you, a German girl of Aryan blood? One you could go to the movies with, or even just take a walk." She looked away. "A girl like me."

"Oh, Adelheid, please don't develop feelings for me. I am in love with Leah and would not trade what she and I have for all the safety in the world. You are a young, intelligent, and very attractive girl. You will find a man of your own."

His words stung. This was not how she'd planned this encounter. For several minutes, neither of them spoke. They stood awkwardly, watching the kittens.

"I'd better be going. It's late. Thank you for everything, Adelheid."

"The offer of the kitten still stands."

He smiled. "I will tell Leah."

. . .

BEFORE DETRICK HAD a chance to remove his jacket and sit down at his desk, Konrad summoned him into his office. Whenever Detrick heard his name called, a lightning bolt of fear shot through him. His first thought always seemed to be, *they know. They have discovered what I am up to.*

After sucking in a deep breath, Detrick entered Konrad's office.

"Heil Hitler."

"Heil Hitler." Had they discovered that he'd allowed the Shapiros to leave yesterday? Had that been a reckless mistake?

"Sit down. I need to discuss something with you."

Detrick felt his legs go limp as he sat.

"There is to be a picnic for the officers this Sunday. And I have been invited. I have spoken to the proper authorities, and they approved your attendance as my guest. This is an important opportunity because there will be people there with the power to promote us to higher ranks. Frankly, I have even heard talk that the Führer himself may make an appearance. So, I've taken the liberty of inviting two girls to accompany us. They are perfect for this: blonde and Aryan. So, I expect you to make an excellent impression."

"Konrad. Thank you for the offer, but you know I am not good at these social things. I prefer to beg off if you don't mind."

"I do mind. I mind a great deal. I insist that you attend."

Detrick saw the power flash in Konrad's eyes and decided that arguing might cause a rift between them. He did not want Konrad to distrust him in any way. If Detrick brought suspicion upon himself, it would be likely that the party would pay more attention to his life outside of work. "Very well. I will do my best. Sunday it is."

"You are going to do just fine, my friend. And wait till you see these girls. They're real lookers."

Detrick nodded.

"And by the way, you'll be driving me today. I have a luncheon to attend."

"Of course."

It had all worked out according to Konrad's plan. Once Detrick left his office, he lit a cigarette and gazed out the window. Life was good. As a child, he'd followed Detrick in hopes of collecting crumbs. Now he'd far exceeded his friend in accomplishments. Who would ever have thought that he, Konrad, the withdrawn one, would be Detrick's superior? He turned to look out his office door. The light from the ceiling danced in Detrick's golden hair as he bent over a stack of papers that Konrad had given him the previous day to be alphabetized.

There could be no denying that Detrick had retained his magnificent physical appearance. But that hardly mattered anymore. Konrad smiled as he thought of all the women who strived for his attention. He remembered the past, how females had treated him, how they'd made him feel, and how he hated them. Whenever possible, he made them suffer.

Konrad discovered that all his wishes, hopes, and dreams were wrapped up in his advances in the Nazi Party. The picnic would prove very beneficial. If Adolf Hitler were to attend, anything could happen! A thrill tickled Konrad's spine, and a smile of satisfaction crept over his face.

CHAPTER EIGHTY-FOUR

ONCE AGAIN, Konrad insisted that Detrick sit at the front of the line and check papers. The morning had brought Detrick a stabbing headache as he attempted to send as many Jews as he could without being detected away from the horrible fate that awaited them. Walking the high wire was getting to Detrick, and his nerves were on edge. When the old rabbi appeared in front of his desk, wearing his black suit, long gray beard, and sideburns, a wave of pity that bordered nausea flooded through Detrick.

The rabbi handed Detrick his papers, and he glanced down at them. The other officer who usually worked beside him had gone to eat. Since he was all alone, Detrick knew he must take the risk of helping this old man to escape.

"Rabbi Stern?"

"Yes?"

"Come with me."

He saw the trembling in the bent body as the rabbi followed him dutifully to the back of the building.

"Rabbi Stern, listen to me. Get away from here as fast as you can. Find a place to hide yourself. I can help you today, but I don't know if I will be in a position to help you again."

The rabbi stared at Detrick in disbelief. The Nazis were known for playing cruel tricks, and the old man wondered if this could be one.

"Go find someone to help you hide."

Without another word, the rabbi ran as best he could. His left leg dragged behind, but he continued to run.

The vision of the decrepit man's efforts to escape haunted Detrick, and he made a decision.

"I would like to take my meal break now if that would be all right," he asked Konrad.

"Yes, certainly. Return in an hour so that you can take me to my meeting. You do recall the luncheon I am to attend?"

"Yes. I'll be here."

Detrick felt he must surely be insane. This act seemed purely irrational. But the vision of the broken, aged rabbi would not let him be.

It took him less than ten minutes to find the man. When he saw Detrick, Rabbi Stern looked like he had expected to be played for a fool. The old man assumed the Nazi had let him go just to give him enough hope to make his recapture even more horrific.

"Rabbi, you have no reason to trust me. But you also have no choice. I don't have much time, so I will tell you a little about myself with the hope that you will believe in me. I am in love with a Jewish woman whom I have hidden in the home of a friend. You must stay out of sight this afternoon. I will meet you in the alleyway between the bakery and the butcher shop tonight as soon as it is dark. Then I will take you to the safety of this house, where you will stay with my Jewish friends."

What made Detrick take such a risk? He could not say. God, perhaps. But as the rabbi looked into the depth of his dark blue eyes, he knew without a doubt that he could trust him.

"God bless you, my son."

CHAPTER EIGHTY-FIVE

"WHAT HAPPENED to that crazy old Jew?" Konrad asked Detrick as he drove him that afternoon.

Detrick felt the sweat beading on his brow. "I took him to relieve himself and then sent him to the transport."

"If the vermin had to take a piss, you should have shot him right there instead of leading him off to a lavatory as if he were a civilized human being."

"I didn't think—next time."

"Yes, be sure of it next time."

For the moment, Detrick was safe. Secretly, he agonized over the idea that someday he might be forced to kill someone to maintain his disguise. Just how far would he go?

The rabbi's conspicuous appearance didn't help the situation, Detrick thought, as he led the old man through the back alleys to the Mueller's home. By God's good grace, they arrived undetected.

Before Detrick could explain anything to Jacob or Leah, Ebner Mueller flew into the attic like a tornado.

"What is all this, Haswell? I didn't agree to this." He motioned to the rabbi with his thumb.

"I know. I am sorry. I had to bring him. He is old, and I knew they planned to send him to a work camp. Because of his age, he had no chance of survival."

"Do any of the Jews who are being sent away have any chance? Do they really? You cannot bring any more here, Detrick. It is too risky. My family is at risk, too. You must understand." Ebner looked over at the rabbi, who stood listening quietly.

"Ech, all right, Detrick, just this one, but no more. You understand? And I will require a few more reichsmarks for his keep."

"Understood, sir, and I appreciate everything. Of course, I will pay you extra. Thank you."

When Mueller left, Detrick glanced over at Leah to find her smiling.

"I guess I should explain." Detrick sat down. "I hope this won't make things too inconvenient. I realize you are living in a small space already, but…."

"Detrick, no need for any explanation. Welcome, Rabbi. My name is Jacob Abendstern, and this is my daughter, Leah. And this young man here, his name is Detrick Haswell. He is like my son. As you can see, we don't have much, but we are happy to share all that we have. Please make yourself at home. My daughter Leah will give you her room."

"No, I insist that she keep her privacy. A young girl needs her privacy. I can sleep out here on the floor. It is fine for me, and I would not have it any other way. I am deeply indebted to all of you. I never thought I would look into the face of a man in a Nazi uniform and say such a thing." The old rabbi's eyes glazed over with tears.

Detrick smiled. "The uniform and the job are my covers. I had no other choice. As you can see, I am no Nazi supporter."

"Of course. Even a blind man could see that, my son. Let's pray the Nazis never see it."

CHAPTER EIGHTY-SIX

Banners displaying pictures of Adolf Hitler and Nazi flags with swastikas hung limply in the summer heat. Detrick and Konrad arrived at the picnic early. Konrad insisted on promptness. The girls Konrad had invited stood beside them, eager to please their men. Both females had short, curly blonde hair and bright blue eyes. They wore traditional German costumes, displaying their ample bosoms.

German beer, the color of brown topaz, flowed freely. Waitresses carried platters of sausages on thick buns, sauerkraut, and over-flowing bowls of tart vinegar potato salad to each table.

"Come, ladies, let's get something to eat." Konrad winked at Detrick.

The girls were honored to have been chosen as SS officers' dates, and they fawned upon the men in appreciation. Konrad chose the prettier one for himself, and when she nuzzled him, kissing his ear, he laughed loudly in triumph.

Then, not to be outdone, Detrick's date put her arm around his neck and began playing with his hair. This felt wrong to Detrick, but he dared not stop her. If he did, Konrad would wonder why. The longer Detrick allowed her to continue, the bolder the woman became. She kissed his cheek, fondled his hair with her long painted nails, and with warm, moist breath, whispered a seductive suggestion into his ear, offering him a night filled with promise.

Detrick wondered how he would discourage the girl when the afternoon was over.

"Here, Detrick, my man, have another beer." Konrad handed him a glass just as the Führer's motorcade arrived at the gate.

Detrick's uniform felt heavy as the sweat trickled down his back on this breezeless summer afternoon.

Everyone attending the picnic stood up from his or her seat. An electric applause filled with exhilaration traveled through the park. Hitler's bodyguards surrounded the Führer's vehicle. From every direction, Detrick saw arms raised high in salute. The crowd cried out, "Heil Hitler!" in unison. Women fainted. Some were bent at the waist, holding their foreheads, and others were overcome with emotion. Others broke into tears, awestruck by the unrequited love they felt for their Führer. Among his people, Hitler had gained the status of an American movie idol.

As the group separated to make way, Detrick saw a small, almost shy-looking man walk through the crowd. There were photos throughout Germany depicting the man with his trademark toothbrush mustache, long nose, and straight brown hair. Now, here he stood, Adolf Hitler, in the flesh, behind a podium and smiling. He raised his arms in welcome. Then, with his fierce and direct tone, he honored them for their Aryan blood.

He guaranteed the Reich would last a thousand years, and they had begun it together. Their children's children would thank them for putting them back in their rightful place in the world. They were the Aryans, the ruling class, above all others.

A roar of approval came from the crowd.

Hitler's face had turned red with anger as he explained, "Germany has invaded Russia." The Third Reich must defeat the communists. The Bolsheviks and the Jews throughout the world posed threats to the Fatherland, Hitler told them. His face contorted, and his hands flew wildly as his voice thundered through the park. "These vermin will be destroyed!"

Detrick watched the crowd. They gave themselves, heart and soul, to the will of their Führer. The descent of individual human thought to a violent mob mentality left Detrick, without a doubt, frightened for the future.

After he had spoken, Hitler walked through the crowds, shaking hands and kissing women's cheeks. When he got to a small child with blonde hair grasping a doll, he lifted her into his arms and gave her a kiss. Her parents looked on, enthralled, as if God had chosen her.

Then, once Hitler reached his vehicle, he turned back one final time and raised both hands. A thunder of adoration followed. Then Hitler got into the back of his automobile, and he and his motorcade slowly drove down the street. The crowd continued to clap. The energy that had spread through the group took a long time to settle. For a long time, the picnickers talked of hatred of Jews and loyalty to the Führer, who had done so much to restore Germany.

While the horror of Hitler's presence filled the air, Detrick had temporarily forgotten about the girl who wrapped herself around him. Her arm circled his neck, and now she laid her head on his arm. Somehow, he must make it clear to the young woman that he had no intention of anything more than spending an afternoon lunching together.

Across the street from the park at the candy store, Adelheid Mueller stared open-mouthed in disbelief. Until he turned around, she could not be certain, but the silhouette of the uniformed man indeed resembled Detrick. She bit into her chocolate bar and watched. Adelheid perceived that the blonde seemed at ease in her affections with the SS officer, as if they knew each other well. It was crucial that Adelheid be sure of his identity. She crossed the street to have a better vantage point. There was no mistaking—it was Detrick. What would Leah think? So shocked she accidentally dropped her candy, Adelheid turned and ran home.

CHAPTER EIGHTY-SEVEN

WHEN ADELHEID ARRIVED HOME, she rushed to her room and shut the door. It was bad enough that Detrick had rejected her for Leah, but now he had another girlfriend. He was willing to date that blonde, so why not Adelheid? Was something wrong with her? Perhaps he found her unattractive. She'd always been impulsive, and now anger drove her to act. She raced up the stairs, risking the exposure of the attic. With a heavy hand, she pushed the door open.

Jacob sat across from the rabbi, playing chess, and Leah read a book. All three looked up as Adelheid entered.

"Leah." She was out of breath. "I must speak to you right away."

Leah put the book down, and the two entered her bedroom.

"I went to the candy store this afternoon, and I saw Detrick. He was across the street at a picnic for the Nazi Party. Adolf Hitler was speaking."

"I'm sure he was forced to go."

"That's not the worst of it. He was with a girl, a lovely blonde girl. She was kissing him, and he was holding her. I am only telling you this because we are friends."

Leah's face turned to a colorless mask, and her features hard-ened. "Are you sure, Adelheid?"

"Yes, absolutely."

"I'm sorry, please. I would like to be alone."

Adelheid nodded understanding. *Perhaps Detrick had not shown her any interest because of Leah's being in such close proximity. However, if Detrick and Leah ended their love affair, he might look at her differently. Then maybe, she hoped, he might see that they were both of the same blood, had a great deal in common, and were well-suited for each other.*

CHAPTER EIGHTY-EIGHT

THAT NIGHT, after sunset, Detrick arrived to find Leah in her room. After greeting Jacob and the rabbi, he knocked. When she did not answer, he became concerned and entered. Leah was lying on her bed, facing the wall. She did not turn to acknowledge him.

"Sweetheart?" he whispered. "Are you feeling well?"

"I'm fine."

"What is it? What's wrong? Did something happen?"

A heavy silence filled the room. When she finally answered, Leah's voice cracked like ice.

"I know where you were today, and I know what happened. What is it, Detrick? Have you become bored with me? I don't need your sympathy. Are you keeping up this façade because you feel sorry for us poor Jews? I'd rather go to a camp than suffer your pity. I know there is someone else."

"There is no one else, Leah. There has never been anyone but you for me. Never. For God's sake, Leah, I risk my life for you every day. If I wanted someone else, would I do that?"

"I don't know. I don't know what you're doing. You go out into the world, and I stay here like an animal in the zoo and wait for you to visit me."

"It's not like that, Leah. Not at all. I am doing all I can. Believe me, please."

But she could not believe him. Her heart ached. But what had he been doing kissing another girl?

"Go, Detrick. Don't come back to see me. If you want, just go ahead and report us. Then you won't have to do this anymore."

"Have you gone mad? I would never report you. I love you."

"If you love me, respect my feelings and leave. And please, don't come back."

Detrick was stunned. He felt lost and helpless because she would not listen.

"Leah? Please…"

"Go, Detrick. I beg you, go."

Detrick turned and walked out of Leah's room, closing the door.

"Detrick, what is it? What's the matter?" Jacob asked.

Detrick was unable to speak. He could not look at Jacob or the rabbi. He left the house, fighting back tears.

CHAPTER EIGHTY-NINE

DETRICK CONTINUED to work and pay the Muellers to ensure the security of the attic for Jacob and Leah. He decided that he would continue to do all he could, regardless of what had transpired between him and Leah.

But he adhered to Leah's wishes, and when night arrived, he did not force his presence upon her. Instead, he mourned the loss. Sleep eluded him. When he finally fell asleep, in sheer exhaustion, he awoke in a short time, covered in sweat and overflowing with anxiety. Food took on an odd, metallic flavor, and he could not eat. When he groomed his lush blonde hair, he found the comb full of fallen strands.

Detrick missed Jacob. He wished he could talk to the man he loved as a father. Jacob, wise Jacob—he would know what to do. If only Detrick could ask him.

He was obsessed with his love for Leah. With every cell in Detrick's body, every drop of blood, and every beat of his heart, he longed for Leah. Alone in his bed at night, he could no longer suppress the tears. Had he lost her forever? If only she would allow him to explain. If only he could make her believe him.

Jacob could not understand what had happened. He knew only

that something serious had taken place. The rabbi offered no specu-
lation, only watched and wondered if Detrick would turn on them
now that the love affair had gone sour. When Rabbi Stern discussed
his concerns with Jacob, Jacob only shrugged. He never doubted
Detrick's loyalty and assured the rabbi that Detrick would continue
to do everything in his power to keep them safe.

Leah refused to eat. She stayed in her room with the door shut
most of the time. When Adelheid brought the kitten to the attic one
evening, Leah accepted the gift with a sad smile. Adelheid tried to
press Leah for news of Detrick.

"I cannot believe Detrick has not tried to come by."

"No, Adelheid. I sent him away, and Detrick won't come back.
Thanks so much. He's a beautiful kitty." Leah cradled the orange
ball of fur.

"You've lost a lot of weight," Adelheid observed Leah, feeling
less jealous and almost sorry for the beautiful girl.

"I suppose I have."

"Detrick must be seeing that girl that I saw him with."

"Yes, probably."

CHAPTER NINETY

KONRAD'S AMBITIONS blinded him to Detrick's depression. Instead, he felt elated that he and Detrick spent each day together. His interest in sexual discipline with women ceased. In fact, he lost interest in females entirely. Although Konrad enjoyed the power his position gave him over Detrick, he enjoyed his old friend's company even more. It felt good to him to know that. Even though Detrick was undeniably more handsome than he was, Konrad's rank in the party gave him an edge. Konrad's boyhood dreams of having sexual encounters with Detrick returned. They came slowly at first but then became nightly events. Following the sentiment of the party, he hated homosexuals and fiercely denied his desires. The dreams, he told himself, were merely childhood fascinations that had not been erased. If he'd ever had a physical encounter with Detrick, Konrad was sure he would no longer experience the dreams. Then, he would know for sure that he could only be heterosexual. However, his pride would never allow him to even broach the subject. Besides, he feared Detrick would be appalled.

Since Konrad's promotion, Detrick's job changed. Now, instead of doing office work, he acted mainly as Konrad's driver. Konrad traveled, offering instruction in the use of the punch card machine.

Detrick didn't mind the open road. He loved rolling the windows of the automobile down and feeling the wind in his hair. But most of all, Detrick found relief in no longer being forced to witness the suffering of the Jews to be transported. Guilt that he could be more useful in helping to free victims at the transport station sometimes bothered Detrick. But he knew that in his new job, there would be far less opportunity for his superiors to discover his true motives. Therefore, he would be less likely to risk those he cared for most.

If his days were long, Detrick's nights were longer. At the end of the month, he dutifully delivered the payment to Ebner Mueller. It had been six weeks since he'd been in the same house and physically close to Leah. Although he could not see her, knowing she was only a few feet away made his heart cry out. He yearned to race up the stairs, take her hands, look into her eyes, and hold her, even for a moment. He could not go to her. She'd told him never to return. Perhaps she no longer loved him. So, Detrick reached into his pocket and handed a roll of reichsmarks to Ebner. Then, with an ache in his chest, he left and returned home.

From the picture window in the living room, Adelheid watched him go. She decided that next month, when he came to pay her father, she would go to him and offer her sympathy. Perhaps if he felt he could lean on her, it would help to engage his affections.

CHAPTER NINETY-ONE

"Rabbi, I must risk leaving the safety of this house and go to the Nazi Headquarters to talk to Detrick. Leah is getting sick. She is so thin. I am worried."

"Jacob, I understand how you feel, but you must not go there. Remember, you are a Jew. You will end up on your way to a camp. All we can do is pray that he will return and the two of them will somehow work this thing out."

"You are a wise man, and I know you are right, but if I don't go soon, I am afraid of what will become of Leah."

"You mustn't leave here, Jacob. If you do, you will not only put your daughter at risk, but you will also be endangering the entire Mueller family. May I make a suggestion?"

"Of course, Rabbi."

"Go to Herr Mueller. Ask him to go to Detrick for you. Tell him to tell Detrick that you must see him. Even if he refuses to come to see Leah, he will come to you. And then you will have an opportunity to talk to him and see what you can do."

"Although I hate to impose on Herr Mueller, I think you're right. Yes, it is the best way."

So Jacob waited until the next time Ebner Mueller brought their food into the attic. It was three nights before he arrived, carrying a small bundle meant to keep the group fed for the remainder of the week.

"Jacob, I brought what I could."

"Many thanks to you for everything, Herr Mueller."

"It's not much, I know, but we must share the rations between all of us, and as you know, they don't go very far." Herr Mueller threw his hands in the air. "I am afraid to risk the black market lest we bring suspicion upon ourselves. The very last thing we need is for the Nazis to start taking notice of us."

"True, yes. You're right." He hesitated for a moment, wondering how Ebner Mueller spent the extra reichsmarks that Detrick gave him for their food. Then, wiping the suspicion from his mind, Jacob asked, "Please, Herr Mueller, won't you sit down?" Ebner Mueller sat in the chair by the small table. "Now I know how much you are doing for us, and I am grateful. So, please, never think I am unappreciative, but I must ask you for a favor."

"Go on." Ebner Mueller raised one eyebrow.

"You know Detrick, the boy who brought us here? Well, he works at the Nazi Headquarters. I know it is a lot to ask, but can you go and see him and tell him I must speak to him?"

Ebner Mueller looked hesitant, as if some money should exchange hands when favors were involved. When Jacob realized that Ebner awaited a payment, he knew he had only one thing left of value. Jacob looked down at the gold ring on his hand. For a split second, his mind drifted back to the day of his marriage. Standing beside Miriam, young and filled with dreams, he'd stepped on the wineglass, shattering it into a thousand pieces. Their guests yelled, "*Mazel Tov!*" The memory brought a smile to his lips. Then Jacob slipped the wedding band from his finger and handed it to Mueller.

"Take this, please. It's twenty-four karat Italian gold."

Mueller nodded as his fingers closed around the ring. "I'll do what I can."

CHAPTER NINETY-TWO

AFTER A WEEK HAD PASSED without a visit from any of the Muellers and no news of Detrick, Jacob decided he must speak to Leah. Until now, he'd been careful not to pry into her private life. Tapping softly on the door to Leah's room, Jacob awaited an answer. When it did not come, he became alarmed.

"Leah?"

"Yes, Father?"

"May I come in?" Jacob wiped the sweat from his brow with the handkerchief Miriam had given him for Hanukkah, the year Karl, their first child, was born. She'd had it embroidered to read, "Jacob Abendstern, husband and father."

The kitten meowed as the door was opened. The light filtered into the room while tiny particles of dust floating in the air became visible. Other than caring for her pet, Leah had remained in the darkness, and unless he came out to eat or use his litter box, the kitten stayed at her side.

Jacob sat at the foot of Leah's small bed. "I don't know how to begin. I can see that something happened between you and Detrick."

"Yes. Oh, Papa, I miss him so much."

Even in the dimmest of light, Jacob could see her tear-stained face was red and swollen.

"I know. I miss him, too."

"But he doesn't love me anymore. He has another girl. I should have expected it, Papa. How could he not lose interest? Look at me? I have no pretty clothes or lipstick. I can't go with him to see a film or for a walk. There is no food for me to prepare a meal for him. All he can do is sit in this room with me, and he just... well, he must have just gotten sick and tired of it. I can't blame him. He's young and so good-looking. I'm sure the girls chase him all the time. Why would he want to continue something like this?"

"Did he tell you this is how he feels?" Jacob looked at her, disbelief reflecting in his dark eyes.

"No, not exactly. But I found out he was seen at a picnic where Hitler was giving a speech. He was with a girl. A blonde Aryan girl. Someone saw them kiss. Oh, Papa. What has become of us?"

Jacob did not know what to believe or what to say. All he could offer were his arms and his shoulder. Leah cuddled against her father and wept.

CHAPTER NINETY-THREE

When Detrick returned from driving Konrad to an early breakfast, he found a note from Ebner Mueller waiting on his desk. It read:

My friend,

My wife and I would like to invite you to dinner this Thursday evening, as you have always been such a good friend to Gaufid. Although Gaufid will not be present as he is off fighting for the Fatherland, our two lovely daughters will be here. I believe that Adelheid is just a few years your junior. The two of you should have much to talk about.

We look forward to seeing you.
Ebner Mueller

Detrick read the letter and then sat down at his desk. The letter lay open, and as Konrad walked by, he took notice. He picked it up and read the handwritten note.

"Well, well, my man. This is what happens when you put on a uniform. Everyone wants you as a potential husband for his or her daughters. Don't get trapped."

Detrick forced himself to laugh. He was secretly worried that something had happened to Jacob or Leah and that the letter had been written in code to bring him to the house.

"You look so gloomy. You needn't accept, you know."

"Yes, I realize that, but I will probably go out of respect for Gaufid."

Konrad nodded. "Yes, after all, he is holding up the front, doing a great service to the Reich. And by the way, I need you to drive me to a meeting this afternoon, so take an early lunch so you will be available."

CHAPTER NINETY-FOUR

IT WAS two whole days until Thursday. Detrick counted the hours
and could hardly contain himself. Crippling emotions filled his heart
and mind. He worried that something had happened and, at the
same time, was consumed with the need to see Leah.

The hours seemed endless while he was at work, and at night, he
sat staring out at the stars, unable to rest. Dark purple rings formed
beneath Detrick's eyes.

Konrad noticed and wondered if Detrick had begun staying out
late and with whom. Although Konrad wanted Detrick to feel the
power of being a member of the party and to experience all the
advantages it brought, he wished that Detrick would spend his free
time with him. For now, Konrad decided, he must be satisfied with
having Detrick with him every day at work. Later, well... Who could
say what could happen?

Detrick found himself looking up at the large, round clock on
the wall so frequently that only five-minute intervals passed between
each observation. Thursday morning remained uneventful, with
Konrad caught up in a telephone dispute that Detrick had no
interest in becoming involved in.

Instead, his mind continued to sift through the possible scenarios he might find when he arrived at the Mueller's home this evening. Perhaps Leah had asked to see him. Thoughts of her brought moments of elation. Then, icy fingers of dread ran up the back of his neck, and he prayed no ill had befallen Jacob or Leah. Another eight hours. Now, just another five… He waited for the evening the entire day with longing, anticipation, and fear.

With no need to hide his destination, Detrick arrived at the Mueller home before nightfall. He wore his uniform, looking distinguished and behaving as if he were on the way to visit family and friends. Greeted by Frau Mueller when he arrived, Detrick was escorted into the living room. She offered no explanation of why he'd been summoned, only that he must wait for Herr Mueller.

Detrick's hands trembled as he awaited Ebner's arrival. It seemed Ebner had worked later than usual that night. As Detrick sat staring out the window with his mind in a whirlwind, it took all the self-restraint he could muster not to run upstairs, fling the door open, and go to Leah. With her just a few feet from him, he thought he might go mad with the intensity of his yearning to be with her. He ran his fingers along the fabric of the sofa. It felt smooth and cool beneath his hand.

Finally, Herr Mueller walked through the door, carrying his metal lunch pail. He placed it on the counter.

"Detrick Haswell is here."

"Where?"

"I told him to wait for you in the living room."

Ebner Mueller entered the living room, and Detrick's heartbeat quickened.

"Detrick, I'm glad you came. I don't know what is going on with you and your friends, but Jacob asked me to go to you. He would like to speak with you."

"Is he all right? Is Leah… all right?"

"Yes, from what I can see, everyone is fine. I don't know how to tell you this, but even if you decide that you no longer wish to come to see your friends, I still expect to be paid for their keep. You do understand?"

"Of course, you needn't worry about that. Just take care of them, and you will be paid."

"Now, I suggest you wait an hour or so until it is dark before going up to see Jacob. The staircase is hidden, but if someone should be spying, who knows what he or she can see? I don't think anyone will be looking through the window, but still, we cannot be sure… and why take the chance?"

"Yes, I agree with you. I don't want to take any chances at all."

"So you'll wait here?"

"Yes, I'll wait."

Ebner Mueller left Detrick sitting on the sofa. When Adelheid and Rebekka came out of their room, they greeted him. Rebekka went to the kitchen to help her mother prepare dinner while Adelheid sat beside Detrick.

"How have you been? You've been away for such a long while."

"Yes, I know. I'm fine, and you?"

"Good. I'm doing well, going to school, the Band of German Maidens, you know, the usual stuff." She smiled, tossing her hair out of her face. "I have lots of boys asking for dates," she said, giggling, "but none as handsome as you are."

Detrick smiled. "Thank you, Adelheid, but I hardly believe that. You just see me that way because I am older." He tried to keep his mind on the present, but his focus drifted to when he would go upstairs and speak with Jacob. What if Leah became angry that he had come after she told him to stay away? It didn't matter. In just a few moments, he would be just steps from her room. Inches from her face, her eyes, her hair, her lips…

"No, it's true." Adelheid laughed.

"I'm sorry, Adelheid. My mind was wandering. What's true?"

"Oh, Detrick, it's true that you are the most handsome man I know."

"Well, then, all I can say is thank you." He smiled.

"I gave Leah a kitten." She craved his approval. He should be grateful and show her his appreciation. After all, she'd shown kindness to his friend. Instead, she found he grasped onto any conversation or word about Leah.

"How is she?"

Adelheid frowned. "She's all right, I guess."

"Is something wrong?"

"You mean with Leah or me?"

"Adelheid, please stop playing games. Is Leah alright?"

"Yes. She is fine."

Then, without another word, Adelheid stood and went to her room, slamming the door and leaving Detrick to wonder what he had done.

It seemed to Detrick that the sun taunted him, keeping him on edge and waiting. Slowly, so very slowly, it made its descent from the sky, leaving a crescent moon to rule the night.

Now that the time had come, Detrick hesitated. What would he find on the other side of the trapdoor?

His knees buckled as he climbed the hidden stairs. Then, he rapped softly and waited. When he heard movement, he announced himself.

"Jacob, it's me, Detrick."

The door opened, and before a word could be spoken, Jacob took Detrick into his arms in a hug.

"I've missed you! How I've missed you. How are you?" Without giving Detrick a moment to answer, Jacob looked him over and continued, "You look terrible. Dark circles under your eyes. You've lost weight. Do you feel well?"

"I've missed you, Jacob. I've missed Leah. God, how I've missed Leah."

"She believes that you are seeing someone else."

"There is no one else for me. There never has been, and there never will be. It's a misunderstanding."

Jacob nodded. "Talk to her. Go to her and explain."

Detrick knocked on Leah's door.

"Papa?"

"No, Leah. It's me."

The familiar voice made her dizzy, and their hearts pounded in unison, although a wooden door stood between them.

"Detrick?" It was all she could bring herself to say.

"Yes." He hesitated. "Please, may I come in?"

Somehow, whatever he'd done no longer mattered. She had to look into his eyes and see his golden hair falling softly over his forehead.

"Come in."

Across the room, he found her sitting on the bed. A candle illuminated the room, and he thought her more beautiful than he remembered.

Slowly, with his legs buckling, he approached her. Then, falling to his knees, he laid his head on her lap.

"I'm sorry if I hurt you. I never meant to. The girl you heard about was an arranged date. I was forced to take her to the picnic. Leah, I am living a double life. I cannot always say no to Konrad. I am afraid he will suspect something and somehow find you. That was the only reason I went. But never, not for a second, since the first day I saw you, have I stopped loving you. You are everything to me. The reason I get up in the morning, the reason I breathe. Leah, I love you. I always have and will forever, for the rest of my life and even after I am dead."

After he'd finished speaking, she tenderly ran her fingers through his hair.

"Do you still love me?" he asked, his voice hoarse and deep.

"I love you."

Reaching his arms around her, he looked deeply into her eyes. Then, taking her in his arms, he kissed her lips tenderly. Detrick worshipped every moment as his lips brushed-kissed her cheeks and eyelids. She bent her head and kissed his neck. Both lovers were consumed with the taste of the other's skin and the feel of the other's hair. With each kiss, the passion grew more intense until they were lost in the moment, lost in each other.

Detrick took a deep breath. He knew that he had to stop things before he was no longer able. He would not make love to Leah while Jacob and Rabbi Stern were only feet away. This would be disrespectful to Jacob; he could never do such a thing to the man he loved, like a father.

"Your Papa and Rabbi Stern are right in the other room. They can hear us," Detrick whispered in her ear, his breath heavy. It had been such a long time since they had lain together. "Because of our love for your father, we must not do this. Not like this, not here and now," he said, although exercising such self-control was almost unbearable for him. He was consumed with fear of how close they had come to losing this precious love, this blessing. He ran his fingers through her hair and held her as close to him as possible without hurting her. "You are my life," he whispered. Gently, he brushed his lips across her cheek and tasted the salty remnants of her tears.

"Stay the night with me," she said. "Just hold me in your arms."

He nodded and felt a single tear fall from his eye. "I'm here, and as long as you want me, I will be here. I will be yours. I've never loved anyone the way I love you. I pledge my life to you, Leah."

"Detrick." She touched his face. "I pledge mine to you."

He led her to the bed and got in beside her.

They lay together, wrapped in each other's arms. He smoothed her hair until she finally slept. But Detrick could not sleep; he did not want to sacrifice a single moment to sleep. Instead, he watched her as her breathing became slow and steady. "Leah, my Leah," he whispered, but he knew she was asleep and could not hear him. His body longed to join with hers, to become enveloped in that incomparable ecstasy that only happened when they joined as one. However, just holding her in his arms nourished his soul for now. For a few precious hours, he was able to forget the world that was descending to Hell right outside these tiny rooms, and that eased his mind all the way until the wee hours of the morning.

As the sun began to rise, Leah awoke and turned to Detrick. "You'd better go."

"I know. I will be back tonight. Leah?"

"Yes, love."

"Marry me. Be my wife."

"We're already married in our hearts."

"I know, but I want to make my vows before God and man. Will you marry me?"

"Of course, but how?"

"Rabbi Stern. He will marry us."

"He won't; you aren't Jewish."

"I'll become a Jew. I might as well. I've always been a Jew in my heart, at least since I met your father. Why not convert?"

"Seriously, Detrick?"

"Yes, love, seriously. We'll talk to him tonight."

The remainder of that night and all through the following day, the smell of peppermint lingered softly on Leah's pillow. She held the pillow tightly to her, inhaling deeply.

CHAPTER NINETY-FIVE

Had it been anyone other than Detrick making such a request to the rabbi, he would have been reluctant. But Detrick proved himself a worthy convert time and again, and the rabbi agreed to the plan. A short, intense course in Judaism required that Detrick spend an hour each day with the rabbi when he arrived. Although, over the years, Detrick had learned a great deal from his relationship with Jacob, the study period introduced him to the depth of the religion.

With a little effort, Detrick proved to be a quick study, impressing the rabbi with his ability to grasp concepts, ask questions, and remember. Although the rabbi wished he had the Torah, he realized that under the circumstances, he must make do with the available resources.

Once Rabbi Stern declared Detrick a Jew, plans for the wedding began.

They asked the Muellers to help Jacob by holding a tablecloth as high as possible to create a canopy. Frau Mueller agreed to bake a cake, which Detrick insisted on paying extra. Then Detrick brought a bottle of wine, and although they would use the Mueller's glasses for drinking, he acquired a special glass that he would stomp on and break into as many pieces as he could, each representing a year of marriage that the couple would share. The price of gold made wedding bands an unattainable luxury. Instead, Detrick purchased silver rings from the pawnshop. He presented the ring to Leah.

"Later, when this is all over, I promise to buy you the finest ring you could ever imagine in your wildest dreams."

"Detrick, this ring is lovely. I don't need another one. I need you."

"And you have me, forever. But I want you to have everything that any woman could ever want, and someday, Leah, I promise on my life that I will give you all of this and more."

"Baruch... Utah... Adonai... Eloheinu...." Rabbi Stern's melodic voice resonated through the room with the heart-wrenching tenderness of a violin. "Blessed are Thou, Lord Our God, King of the Universe."

Jacob's eyes shone with tears as he watched his daughter and the boy he loved as a son take the sacred vows of marriage.

A makeshift canopy had been constructed. Detrick bent to fit beneath it. Standing beside Leah in his white undershirt, his uniform jacket abandoned on the floor, Detrick experienced joy beyond any he'd ever imagined. He was finally able to make this dream a reality. Leah looked like the first rose of summer, wearing a blush-colored dress she'd borrowed from Adelheid, who stood sulking at the back of the group. It had been a difficult choice, but somehow, Adelheid had found it in her heart to loan Leah the frock because even though Adelheid had been hurt and rejected by Detrick, Leah had been a friend to her. Candles had been acquired at a high price and now illuminated the entire room in a golden hue.

The rings were exchanged once the rabbi finished the seven blessings and spoke about love and devotion to the couple. Detrick would leave his ring with Leah lest Konrad asks why he'd begun wearing a wedding band.

Then, the two sipped wine from the special wineglass Detrick had provided. After handing the goblet back to Rabbi Stern, who wrapped it carefully in a cloth napkin, it was placed on the ground in front of the groom. With one hard stomp, Detrick smashed the glass into tiny pieces as the Rabbi and Jacob cried out, "*Mazel Tov!*" (Congratulations!) and "*L'Chaim*" (to life).

Detrick turned and touched Leah's face with the tenderness one can only express for the most precious and sought-after gifts. His fingers trembled as he caressed the delicate white skin. Then, for the first time as man and wife, his lips met those of the woman he loved more than anything, even more than his life.

"Leah Haswell," he whispered in her ear, enjoying the sound of her new name. "I love you."

CHAPTER NINETY-SIX

ON JANUARY 20, 1942, a conference was held in a small suburb called Wannsee on the outskirts of Berlin. Reinhard Heydrich chaired it, with fifteen SS and government officials in attendance. A year earlier, Heydrich had been appointed to plan a program for the *Final Solution* to the "Jewish problem." The irony was there was no "Jewish problem." There was only a Nazi problem.

For a few hours, the men debated on how they might handle this situation. After all, the goal was to create a pure Aryan race, and they must do something to bring this about.

The conference members considered forced sterilization and mass deportation. However, neither seemed plausible. So, on this very innocent-seeming day, in this lovely cottage tucked away in the quiet little town of Wannsee, their decision would change the world.

The 'Final Solution' was the extermination, the mass murder, of an entire race of people. The end of all Jews: men, women, and children.

CHAPTER NINETY-SEVEN

TYPHOID SLITHERED through the Warsaw Ghetto, attacking and killing along its horrifying path. The illness ran rampant with over-population, lack of hygienic supplies, and almost no nutritious food. Ada's young and weak schoolchildren were vulnerable, and she watched, helpless, as the disease claimed them. First, the child would complain of a terrible headache, usually accompanied by a high fever. Then, a red rash on the chest and abdomen followed. Few survived.

Karl attempted to find medication on the black market but was unsuccessful. After exhausting all avenues, he did the only thing he could do. He held Ada, offering her a shoulder to cry on and a sympathetic ear.

The love that had grown between them had stifled their desire to fight in the resistance. Once, they'd both felt they had little to lose. Now, they embraced the joy and wonder of life. With love came the fear of loss, and although they hated the Nazis, an uprising would bring a quick loss of lives. Now that the United States had joined Great Britain and the Soviet Union to form the Allies, they hoped it would be just a matter of time before Germany's defeat. If they could just lie low until then, maybe they would survive.

With the extra money Karl earned from his black market sales, the couple found a small room offering them some privacy, which few in the ghetto enjoyed. As bleak as things had become, the two filled their days with hope and their nights with endless lovemaking. Much to Mordechai's chagrin, neither attended the meetings of the *Żydowska Organizacja Bojowa*, the Jewish Fighting Organization. Mordechai explained that he and his girlfriend were young and in love and had a great deal to lose, but they understood the importance of not hiding under the sheets. This situation would not just simply disappear, Mordechai explained. They—now—must address it with an uprising. For Karl and Ada, the words fell on deaf ears.

Winter's icy fingers clutched at the inhabitants of the ghetto. Without heat, many froze to death as the months inched slowly toward spring. Snow fell, covering slippery roads, making the walk from Ada's apartment to the orphanage perilous. Still, she insisted on going every morning, much to Karl's dismay.

"I can't disappoint the children, Karl. This is all they have, and they look forward to it so much."

"Ada, I know you love them, I understand, and I love the compassion that makes you who you are, but many of them are sick. They have lice, and lice carry disease. Besides, it's so cold outside that you could catch your death just walking. Every day, you put yourself at risk. I forbid you to continue."

"You forbid me, Karl? Since when do you forbid me?"

"Ada, please. You are a strong, hardheaded woman, but in this situation, I must insist that you do as I say."

"I will not."

"Ada, be reasonable."

"I established this school. I mean to continue it until this horror ends and these children can live normal lives. If you love me, Karl, step aside and allow me to do what I must do."

"Ada… Ada…" The conviction that shone from her eyes told him it was no use. "Please, be careful."

"You know I will." She kissed him and left.

Two children had died the previous night. When Ada arrived,

she received the news. It had been sudden. Neither had shown any trace of illness the day before. Anger and frustration came over her as she looked at the tiny bodies. A boy and a girl, filthy, covered in ragged, torn garments, barefoot against the winter chill, lay silent for eternity, awaiting burial. She refused to cry and would not allow depression to stop her. Instead, she fought the flood threatening the back of her eyes and forced a smile as she entered the classroom.

As the winter edged on, the deaths continued but came less often. Although the cold brought tremendous discomfort, it helped to kill the germs. So, for the time being, typhoid seemed to be held at bay.

On an early spring evening, Ada returned home tired and flushed. Removing her clothing before lying down, she looked at her torso. There, she saw the bright red spots indicative of the dreaded typhoid. Terror gripped her as she studied her body in disbelief. They had not seen an outbreak in weeks. She had thought herself immune. Now she knew better. Karl—she must inform Karl. If he stayed away, he might avoid the disease. Half an hour passed before the key turned in the lock and Karl appeared. When he saw Ada, he immediately knew that something was wrong. He raced to her side, but she pushed him away.

"Stay away from me. I'm sick, very sick. I don't want you to catch this."

"Do you think I care about that?" He forced her to allow him to take her in his arms.

Suddenly, she covered her face and began to cry.

"It's all right, Ada. I'm here. I'll take care of you," Karl whispered, but again, she tried to push him away.

"Go. I want you to leave here. Do you hear me?"

"I hear you, but I refuse."

"Karl, I have typhoid!"

His eyes could not focus. All around him, the room turned dark. He'd heard her words but could not accept them. Instead, he moved closer, taking her into his arms again.

"You're just tired. Lie down. I'll get you something to eat."

"I'm not hungry. Look at this." She lifted her nightgown to reveal the spots.

"Oh, my God! Ada, my Ada!" Much stronger, he forced her to allow him to hold her. "It will be all right. I'm here, and I'm not leaving."

The strength drained from Ada. She could not fight him. Instead, she lay shivering on the small bed. Karl covered her with all the blankets and spare clothing he could find. It grew difficult to lift her hands or her head. She could no longer hold a glass to drink.

Karl sat by her side, dipping a rag into the water and squeezing the liquid into her mouth. At first, she responded by swallowing, but as the night went on, the water just ran from the side of her lips, spilling onto her chest. A blinding headache brought on bouts of nausea, and Karl held her as she heaved violently.

At first, she tried to make it to the toilet but fell to the floor, covering herself with the contents of her stomach. Once he realized she could not walk to the bathroom, Karl gently cleaned her up and held her hair as she vomited into a pot. Panic set in, driving Karl mad as Ada grew delirious with fever. Fading in and out of consciousness, she called for her mother, whimpering like a child.

Karl begged, pleaded, and bargained with God, offering his life for hers. For months, Ada had given most of her food to the children, causing her to be painfully thin and weak, hardly able to fight such a horrible illness. As the early hours of the morning drew near, Ada became coherent. Although her eyes shone bright with fever, she spoke rationally, giving Karl hope. She sat up and asked for some soup, which he brought. While he held the spoon, she sipped slowly.

"You have been such a blessing to me."

"I love you, Ada."

"I know, and that makes me sad. Karl, I'm dying."

"No, you can't, Ada. Stop talking like that."

"Listen to me. Please always remember that I love you. Now, you must be careful after I'm gone. Don't take any crazy chances because when this is all over, you'll be reunited with your family. And you're young, Karl, you'll love again. I ask only one favor of you. Please, Karl, take care of the children at the orphanage. Look in on them occasionally. Please, promise me."

He took her hand and kissed it, holding it to his face. "I promise, of course, but Ada, promise me that you will not think of death. You must live, Ada. We must go to Eretz Israel together and build a Jewish state. Together, we will watch our children carve a homeland out of that barren desert, a place that will be safe for Jews forever."

"Yes, a Jewish state, a homeland…" She smiled. "I'm tired, Karl… I need to rest."

As she closed her eyes, he felt her hand go limp in his as the life quietly left her body. Like Moses, Ada would never enter the Promised Land.

Karl fell upon her dead body, crying like an animal shot in the forest. Grief overcame him as he continued to rock back and forth, wailing in mourning.

Midday had come and passed before Karl realized he must say goodbye.

Friends of the couple arranged the funeral. Karl attended, hazy and unfocused. He spoke to no one. Immediately following the burial, he left and returned to his room. Once alone, he lay down on the bed he'd shared with Ada, and again, he cried.

The months drifted by, and for Karl, life held no purpose. Sometimes, Karl forgot to eat or to bathe. His hair grew long and greasy, tangling into a black, curly, Medusa-like mass. His beard grew thick and unkempt. Often, friends came to look in on him, only to find him ornery and unwelcoming. With the money he'd saved, Karl purchased whiskey on the black market and began to burn the pain as the flame of liquor turned his feelings into ashes.

Winter turned to spring, followed by the scorching heat of summer. On a bright, sunny morning in early August, an old friend came to see Karl.

"Shlomie, it's been a long time."

"Yes, how are you? I shouldn't say it, but frankly, you look like hell."

"How should I be? I'm still alive, but I wish I weren't."

"You shouldn't say that, Karl. Life is a gift from God."

"Why did God take Ada? Why? Can you answer that question? I'm sick of all of you and your God, too. Where is God now? Tell me, Shlomie—why has he abandoned us?"

"I know you are hurting, and I don't blame you. You've lost someone, but you're not the only one. We've all lost people who were dear to us. But life must go on, Karl, it must."

"Eh... not for me."

"I didn't come here to help you to feel sorry for yourself. I came to let you know that the Nazis raided the orphanage last night. You know where Ada had that school of hers? Well, they took the guy who ran it and more than two hundred kids away. We know they are on their way to someplace in Hell that the Nazis built, where they'll probably murder them. Now, if that's not a reason to come back from the living dead and work with the resistance, I don't know what is."

"Shlomie, are you sure about this?" He remembered his promise to Ada.

"Yeah, I'm sure."

Karl stood up from the bed and walked to the window. He gazed out at the trees. Those children had been an important part of Ada's life. She loved them almost as much as she'd loved him. In the end, she'd died because she'd refused to discontinue teaching. And he'd vowed on her deathbed that he would look after them.

"When is the next meeting?"

"Tomorrow night. Mordechai's apartment at nine sharp."

"I'll be there."

CHAPTER NINETY-EIGHT

REBEKKA MUELLER ENVIED HER SISTER, Adelheid. Three years her junior and not nearly as pretty, Rebekka lived her life invisible in her sister's shadow. Both girls had been members of the Band of German Maidens since they'd turned ten. The Band of German Maidens put a strong emphasis on the ability to excel in athletics. Blonde hair and blue eyes, the pride of the Aryan race, were considered highly desirable characteristics. Adelheid possessed all these, much to her brown-haired, brown-eyed, clumsy sister's dismay. It seemed to Rebekka that no matter what, Adelheid outshone her, leaving little room for Rebekka to find any positive attributes she might possess.

Since the marriage of Leah, the Jewish girl in the attic, to the Aryan boy, Detrick, whom Adelheid had so fancied, Adelheid had changed. It began with her clothing. Dressing provocatively in tight skirts and sweaters brought whistles and catcalls as she walked down the street. Then she started coming home late at night, accompanied by various young men. From her bedroom window, Rebekka heard their laughter outside on the porch. The girls at school started to whisper, and the gossip humiliated Rebekka.

Before Detrick married Leah, Adelheid discussed her feelings for him with Rebekka. Now she would no longer admit to what she'd once felt.

"You still care for him, don't you? That's why you're running around acting like a tramp. This is doing you no good, Adelheid."

"Mind your own business. Detrick was a childhood fancy. He's no one. He means nothing to me. I have real lovers now."

"Do you have any idea what people are saying about you? They're calling you a tramp, and it's rubbing off on me. Everyone says since we are sisters, we must be alike."

"I don't care what they say. This has nothing to do with you, Rebekka, so stop sticking your nose where it doesn't belong." Adelheid had compensated for what she perceived as Detrick's rejection with a promiscuous lifestyle, proving her desirability to men repeatedly to herself in the hope of restoring her lost self-esteem. Sex seemed a small price for the adoration that made her feel beautiful.

Where once Adelheid had shared a friendship with Leah, she now avoided her and Detrick as well.

With the constant teachings of the Nazi doctrine forced upon them among their peers and in their classroom, both girls began to worry about the attic dwellers. They knew that hiding Jews was against the law, and their parents had firmly explained that they must never reveal their situation to anyone. Both Rebekka and Adelheid realized that the extra money Detrick provided improved the family's way of life. Tins of meat and vegetables replaced the former diet of bread and potatoes. When the girls needed clothing, they found themselves able to afford nice fabric, where once they'd remade hand-me-downs several times over. Sometimes, they were even able to shop for store-made clothing, a luxury once far removed from the Mueller's lifestyle.

Adelheid spent time with boys she'd met at gatherings of the Band of German Maidens, but she never allowed them inside her home for fear that somehow they might discover her family's secret.

CHAPTER NINETY-NINE

Emptied of the Jews, the streets of Berlin appeared distorted to Detrick. As he walked along, he saw that Gentiles now owned the shops that were once Jewish. Non-Jews occupied the once-Jewish residences. The bicycle shop where he had met Jacob so many years ago was now home to a new proprietor. For a long while, he stood on the sidewalk, staring at the building, memories passing through his mind. It was as if the entire Jewish population had never been there.

Because of his affiliation with the party, Detrick overheard talk concerning the *Final Solution*. It haunted him. If Hitler, by some horrible turn of fate, were to win the war, what would become of those he held so dear? He knew he must not lose faith. He must continue to believe that good will triumph in the end.

Over a year had passed since he'd married Leah. The U.S. had entered the war. Now Great Britain, the United States, and Russia pushed hard against the Nazis, and Germany appeared to be losing ground. Every day, Detrick prayed that his friends would remain safe until this nightmare ended.

Even with the world coming down around them, Leah and Detrick's love kept them from despair. As often as he could, Detrick went to the attic with extra food and supplies. The couple lay huddled together, hoping to be spared as the Allies bombed Berlin. The deafening, thunderous sound shook the little house through the night. Jacob and the rabbi remained awake, listening, praying. Rabbi Stern stood reciting sacred words, his body moving back and forth to the rhythm as the bombs shattered the night. Since the attack on Berlin, Jacob had developed a strange twitching on the left side of his face, which came and went sporadically. The cat, whom they had named Sammy, became nervous and skittish, often urinating in the corner of the room. Leah loved Sammy, so she cleaned the mess without complaint and gently offered her feline friend comfort.

One evening, as Detrick arrived later than usual at the Mueller home, Adelheid and one of her boyfriends came down the street. When the boy saw Detrick entering the house, he felt sure that he'd come to see Adelheid.

"Looks like you have company?"

Adelheid felt a tiny bead of sweat drip down the back of her neck. Quickly, she came up with an idea. "He's seeing my sister."

"Isn't she young for him?"

"Perhaps, but he's seeing her anyway. My parents approve. After all, he works for the party."

CHAPTER ONE HUNDRED

THE SMOKY ROOM, the enthusiastic voices—nothing had changed. It was as Karl had remembered it. Planning an uprising took effort.

"Welcome, Karl. We've missed you."

"Thanks, Mordechai. It's been rough since Ada passed."

"I know. I'm sorry. We've all known loss here. But we are glad to have you with us. We need as many as we can get."

"How many of us are there?"

"Give or take, about seventy-five."

Karl nodded as he looked around the crowded room.

"The Poles feel sorry for us, or they just want the help. Either way, it doesn't matter. They are supplying us with weapons."

"When do you think we'll be ready?"

"I'm not sure. Do you think you can get out of the ghetto at night and buy weapons?"

"Of course. I've been getting in and out since the beginning."

"Good. We're building underground bunkers. Can you help?"

"I can, and I will. I'm angry. I'm gonna kill as many Nazis as I can. I'm going to do it as revenge for Ada."

Mordechai nodded. He understood.

During the night, Karl joined the band of men, women, and

children, who faced constant peril to beg, bargain for, or steal to build an arsenal. They traveled over the rooftops and through the sewer systems, ducking out of the light and the vision of the guards. The Jewish Council, better known as the Judenrats, must never discover the plans as they were known to be collaborating with the Nazis.

But slowly, small piles of weapons and munitions lay hidden in underground bunkers. Bottle rockets, Molotov cocktails, pistols, rifles, a few pineapple hand grenades, and a handful of automatic firearms made up the armaments.

More people joined with the resistance daily as they realized that the Nazis meant to exterminate the entire ghetto. Two groups of Jewish defense were formed: the *Żydowski Związek Wojskowy (ŻZW)*, the Polish Jewish Military Union, led by David Moryc, and the *Żydowska Organizacja Bojowa (ŻOB)*, the Jewish Fighting Organization, led by Mordechai.

After much deliberation, the two groups reached a decision on the date of the attack.

CHAPTER ONE HUNDRED ONE

ON JANUARY 18, 1943, a frigid wind blew through the silent streets of the ghetto as the Wehrmacht guards began their roundup of Jews to be sent to the trains, taking them to Treblinka and their ultimate death. The noise of their boot heels clicked against the asphalt as their guttural language echoed through the streets.

Karl, accompanied by a handful of other ragged and angry people, waited hidden in alleyways. As the Germans turned the corner, the Jewish resistance came out firing. Immediately, guns were drawn, and the Wehrmacht fired back. The Jews fell to the ground in obscene numbers until, finally, the attack ceased.

That night, they held a meeting to discuss what had happened.

"There was far too much loss of life today," Mordechai said. "From now on, we will engage them in partisan warfare. Instead of meeting the Nazis in the open, we will spread out and shoot at them from high windows in various apartments. This way, they will never know where the shots will come from. It will make it hard for them to fight us."

A roar of agreement came from the crowd, and the fighters rearranged their plan.

Never before had the Wehrmacht been confronted by a Jewish

army. When gunfire attacked them from all angles, the Nazis trembled with fear, continually looking up and around every corner. Since the resistance had begun to fight back, the Nazis had backed down, entering the ghetto with caution. Now, the ŻOB and the ŻZW took control of the ghetto. The execution and imprisonment of the Judenrats began.

One evening in late February, another meeting took place, and the two resistance organizations planned the next attack. As the meeting began, a young woman with curly black hair walked up to the front. "I have a suggestion. This year, Passover falls on the night before Hitler's birthday. Why don't we give him a present he will never forget?"

The crowd roared with enthusiasm. A vote on the idea was taken, and a majority approved it.

On April 19, the evening of Passover, the holiday celebrating the angel of death passing the homes of the Jews, Hitler's henchmen would face a violent surprise. When the Nazis attempted to come through the streets with plans of liquidating the ghetto, they found themselves met by hails of bullets and Molotov cocktails. The assault came from every direction, from windows, from basements and alleyways.

Sweat poured down the back of his dirty shirt as Karl continued to fire. The acrid smell of gunpowder permeating his nostrils caused his eyes to tear and his nose to run. From the fourth floor of an apartment building facing the street, he threw a grenade that resulted in a deafening explosion as an enemy vehicle burst into flames. The Wehrmacht ran for cover. When informed of the battle, Hitler sent for Stroop, a commander familiar with partisan warfare.

The fighting continued in Muranowski Square. In addition, to Hitler's horror, a group of children climbed to the rooftop of the headquarters of the Jewish resistance. There, they raised the Polish flag and the ŻZW flag (a blue and white flag that would later become the flag of Israel).

In a rage, Hitler ranted to Stroop that the flags must be removed immediately. It took a large, well-equipped Wehrmacht four days to fight a handful of Jews before they could pull the flags down.

"David Moryc is dead," Mordechai announced as he entered the bunker where Karl had gone to replenish his ammunition.

"He was bombing a Nazi truck."

Karl shook his head.

"There will be more, I'm afraid, but we must continue. We'll say *kaddish*, our prayer for the dead, later."

Karl walked over to him, placing a hand on his arm. Then, swinging the rifle over his shoulder, he headed to another upstairs apartment to continue his attack on the Wehrmacht.

Karl fought fearlessly, for he'd lost all reason to live. At night, he stole weapons from dead German soldiers who lay out in the open streets. Even so, by early May, the provisions grew scarce. The Nazis stopped all food deliveries. Ammunition was in short supply, and the Jews began to worry.

Over the loudspeaker, Stroop announced a warning that reverberated through the ghetto. "Jews, surrender now! This is your last chance. Come out with your hands over your heads!"

While in the underground bunker discussing the situation and how to combat the lack of necessities, Karl heard a thunderous roar. Thick black smoke filled the area, catching in his throat as he coughed and gagged. Overwhelming heat engulfed him. He ran upstairs to catch his breath and see what had taken place. The entire ghetto raged on fire with orange flames. People flung themselves out of windows, falling to their deaths in the streets as the Wehrmacht maneuvered flamethrowers, blowing up buildings in their wake.

Sometime during the period when Karl had left the bunker, Mordechai was killed. When he returned to learn the news, Karl felt a pain in his heart for the young, idealistic Jew, who longed only for a Jewish state where he and his girlfriend could live peacefully.

The smoke grew thicker as the Wehrmacht set fire to basements and sewers. It became apparent that the Jews would be defeated. Now each person must choose whether to stay and fight, distracting the Nazis so their friends and families could escape, or run and hide, embracing life for another day. Earlier, they had built a tunnel that led out into the Michelin Forest. The plan had been that when all seemed lost, as many as possible would flee the ghetto, meeting in the woods to rebuild the resistance.

To stay meant certain death.

Karl decided to stay. He would be the distraction that would enable the others to escape. A handful of brave souls stood beside him.

After the larger group had headed out through the tunnel, Karl went off alone. Exhausted, he sat down there on the dirt floor of the bunker and spoke to Ada.

"I don't know if you can hear me. I hope so. I didn't protect your babies... your students like I promised." Tears mingled with the black soot that covered his face. "I failed you. I'm sorry. I love you... Your love was the greatest thing in my life. If there is a God, I will come to you soon, and I pray you'll forgive me. But there is something I must tell you. Someday, there will be a Jewish state. I am sure of it. You should have seen how strong our people were. We fought like the devil. Just a few ragged, worn out, starving Jews. We held them off. Those goddamned Nazis were afraid of us, Ada. Now it's ending. We knew we couldn't win, but we wanted to show 'em that they couldn't treat us like cattle. We wanted to give them something to remember us by, and it was really something to see!" With his fists, he rubbed the tears off his face and set his jaw with determination. "I won't go down without a fight. They'll never take me to a camp. I'm going out there onto that street shooting, and I'm gonna take as many Nazis as I can with me when I go. So, if you can see me, watch this, Ada. This is for you."

He took the last automatic machine gun from the pile. It had a full clip.

Then he motioned with a tilt of his head to the remainder of the group.

"Are you ready?"

A loud, hoarse chorus arose from the smoke. "Yes!"

"Then let's go kill some Nazis!"

And before Karl Abendstern took his last breath on the cobblestone street of the Warsaw Ghetto that day, he made sure a good number of Nazis would never kill another Jew.

CHAPTER ONE HUNDRED TWO

INGA HASWELL KNELT over the well-worn wooden washboard, wringing out white shirts for her new client, a member of the SS, when the doorbell rang. Slowly, she got to her feet, drying her hands on her apron, and then opened the door. Dressed in the crisp brown uniform with the short pants of the Hitler Youth, the mailboy handed her an envelope and quietly waited while she took a coin from her glass jar and gave it to him.

"Thank you, Frau Haswell."

"You're welcome."

Inga closed the door and stared at the familiar handwriting. "Could it be?" she asked herself. With shaky fingers, she tore the envelope open and read.

Dear Mother, Father, and Detrick,

> *I know it's been a long time since we last saw each other, but a day has not gone by that I have not thought of you. In life, we sometimes make mistakes that cost us dearly. This I have learned. But with the mistakes, often, God forgives us and gives us a reason to go on.*
>
> *When I left, I was pregnant with Erik's child. He abandoned me, and*

I had nowhere to turn. I was ashamed and afraid of causing you embarrassment, so I went to Heim Hochland, a home for the Lebensborn. The agreement when I entered was that I would surrender my child at birth to the Nazi cause. Early in the pregnancy, it did not seem like such a great feat. Before I carried the child within my body for nine months, it seemed to be little more than a burden to me. However, as the weeks passed, and I felt the small movements within my womb, the child became real to me, and with that, the pain of knowing I would never see it grow up tortured me. When the time came, giving up the baby proved to be the most difficult thing I ever had to do.

However, in the midst of this entire ache, there was a small flicker of light. It was here in this terrible place that I met my husband, Kurt. He is a good and kind man who truly loves me. We live a good and simple life here on his family's farm in Munich.

He has begged me to write to you for years, but I have been afraid. Now, the time has come to bridge this gap. I miss my family, and I realize that I will always be lacking something until you are again a part of my life, regardless of how happy I am. So, I want to invite you to come here and visit the farm, to meet my wonderful husband and his generous family. You will enjoy the fresh air, and we will see each other again.

It is my greatest hope that you will find it in your heart to forgive me for all I have done and come here. From the deepest part of my heart, I most humbly regret any pain I have caused you. I will wait in eager anticipation for your reply.

With much love, and missing you greatly,
your daughter and sister,
Helga

P.S. I have a surprise for you that I will tell you when you are here.

Inga carefully folded the letter and returned it to the envelope. Then she sat down at her kitchen table and took it out again to reread the words her daughter had written. Tears washed away years of fear that Helga had perished. Her daughter lived somewhere on a farm in Munich. Helga was alive. Inga would talk to

Hans and Detrick tonight. They must go to her. Inga began writing her response before confirming with the rest of the family. She told Helga that they would come to the farm. All of them would visit her in Munich.

Surprisingly, Hans agreed quickly. He would do well with a holiday out of the city, he said. But to her dismay, Detrick, the son she adored more than anyone, seemed reluctant. As they sat at the kitchen table, Inga marveled at how so many of their friends and neighbors had grown gaunt and sickly during the war. Detrick's favor, first with the Jews and then with the Nazi Party, kept him fed and well. His face had strong features, and his tall frame had shed any softness, leaving him lean, with hard, well-developed muscles.

"You really should come with us, Detrick. Helga is your sister, and it's been such a long time."

He agreed with his mother. Detrick missed Helga, but what he could not tell his mother was that to leave meant being away from Leah and his friends. Should any problems arise, he would be unable to step in from miles away. "Why don't you and Father go now? I am not sure I can get away from my work. I will arrange to go later in the year."

"Perhaps we can all arrange to go in late spring. I've heard that the strawberry season in Munich is lovely. If you speak to Konrad and explain that you plan to visit your sister, I am sure he will make arrangements to allow you to do so."

"I'll speak to him. Late spring is only a few months from now. I will let you know if I can leave."

"Tell him it would only be for a week or so. We would not stay long."

Inga knew Detrick's concern had little to do with his work, but rather than confront him at the table with Hans, she decided to wait for his final decision.

"Would you like to see the letter?"

"Of course." Detrick read his sister's words. Childhood memories came back to him, and he realized how much he'd missed her.

That night, as he walked through the streets, Detrick noticed that the winter had already begun to break. Frigid temperatures had been slowly rising, a few degrees at a time. The blossoms that had taken the place of icicles started to offer their faint fragrance to the air. Where the snow had covered the grass only a few months earlier, it now remained in sporadic patches while tiny, new green shoots rose from the ground. Illuminated by the streetlights, Berlin appeared as it once had when Detrick was just a child, but he knew it had changed forever.

Always attentive, always watching, Detrick entered the Mueller home. Then, slipping through the trapdoor to the attic, he took a small block of cheese from his uniform jacket and placed it on the table.

"Thank you, and God bless you, Detrick. Again, you didn't eat your lunch." Jacob hugged Detrick.

"I'm doing fine. I have plenty. Please share this with everyone, Jacob."

"God bless you." The rabbi nodded to Detrick as he took the slice of cheese Jacob gave him.

Then Jacob cut another for Leah, one for Detrick, and a small sliver for himself.

Detrick turned to Leah. "Take mine, too. I have plenty to eat."

"No." She laughed. "This is more than enough."

"What is the news out there in the world? How is the war effort going?" the rabbi asked.

"From what I can see, it looks like the Allies are closing in on Germany. There is a lot of whispering that Hitler is losing the war."

"We can only hope." Jacob smiled.

"I believe it's true. He weakened himself when he divided his army, fighting on two fronts." Detrick looked into Jacob's eyes. "I believe that soon Stalin will march his troops into Germany, and the war will be over."

"Then what happens to you?" the rabbi asked with genuine concern.

"Then all of you will be hiding me," he said, smiling.

"We will explain. We will tell them how you've helped us."

"I hope they will believe you, Jacob. Can you imagine what they will think of me in my uniform? It will be better for me if the Americans come first. I have heard that they are more compassionate than the Soviets. Perhaps they will understand my plight."

"We can only wait and see," the rabbi observed.

Leah took Detrick's hand and gripped it tightly.

"I will stand up for you. No matter what, Detrick, I will make them understand." Jacob's eyes met Detrick's as he offered reassurance. "Then we will all leave Germany together."

"Yes, Papa. All of us, together." Leah smiled as she gazed into Detrick's eyes.

That night, as they lay quietly, gazing at the stars, their hands clasped together, Leah's head on Detrick's chest, their hearts beat in perfect harmony. Tenderly, Detrick ran his hand over her soft hair and marveled at how it resembled silk.

"Sweetheart, a letter came today from my sister Helga."

"Helga! Oh, Detrick, that's wonderful. Is she all right? Where is she?"

"Yes, she's fine. In fact, she's living on a farm in Munich with her husband."

"She married that man she was keeping company with?"

"No, according to the letter, it is someone else."

Then, he went on to explain what Helga had written.

"You must go. Your mother is right."

"More than anything, I wish I could take you with me. I wish I could tell my family that we are married. Sometimes, I am so tired of this uphill climb. It's a constant fight to keep our love hidden. And it isn't fair, Leah. Why should something as beautiful as what we have be against the law?"

She could not answer, so she did not. Instead, she squeezed his hand. "Go with your family. See your sister. I will be here when you return."

A cold chill descended upon him, although the temperature of the room had not changed. "I am so afraid to leave that I'm getting goosebumps, but you are right. I must go."

He bent down and softly kissed her. She met his kiss with a

passionate one, and the tiny flame she sparked exploded into a blazing fire. His heart beat wildly with love for her. Turning her over onto her back, he covered her face and breasts with kisses. Their bodies molded together, fitting as perfectly as two puzzle pieces. With his blue eyes, deep as the ocean, locked on hers, he whispered.

"I love you, Leah. God, how I love you."

CHAPTER ONE HUNDRED THREE

KONRAD ENCOURAGED Detrick's trip to the country. It would be good for Detrick to get out of Berlin for a week or so and spend time with his family. In a show of generosity, Konrad even offered the use of an automobile, which Detrick gratefully accepted. The six-hour trip from Berlin to the outskirts of Munich in a private vehicle would afford the Haswells comfort they'd never experienced during train travel.

With excitement, Inga washed and packed enough clothing for the trip. For months prior to their leaving, she took in extra work to purchase small gifts to bring to her daughter.

As the date grew closer, even Hans seemed excited. Only Detrick grew more anxious, which he managed to hide from everyone except Jacob, who had a way of looking into his soul.

One evening, a few days before Detrick's trip, Jacob put his hand on Detrick's shoulder. "Sit with me a minute, Detrick."

They sat at the table. The rabbi tried to busy himself to give the two the privacy they seemed to need. When Leah came out of her room, seeing her father and Detrick engaged in a whispered conversation, she quickly turned back, closing the door.

"Jacob, you've always been more of a father to me than my own father. Watch her for me. I will be back as soon as I can."

"I love her, too, Detrick. After all, she is my daughter. But you must stay safe as well. I love you, too, Detrick. Don't take any foolish chances. We will be fine."

"I was planning to return early."

"You mustn't. You must return with your family. You must do nothing to draw attention."

"Yes, I suppose you are right."

"Every day when you go to that office, I worry. I am always afraid for you."

"I know, but don't be. I am careful, and I will continue to be. We will make it through this…all of us. You'll see." Detrick winked at Jacob with a confidence he did not feel.

The outskirts of Munich, adorned with its lush, green, rolling hills and ruby-red, blooming strawberry patches, made a strong contrast to the congestion of Berlin. The air smelled pure, embraced by sunshine, instead of the usual smell of automobile exhaust.

When the Haswells drove up the dirt road to the white farmhouse with its large red barn, Inga gasped. Surrounded by neatly fenced and planted fields, cows stood grazing under the shade of lazy green trees in an open pasture. A brown and white plow horse accompanied them.

An air of calm surrounded the homestead. Detrick carried his mother's suitcase and his own up the path to the house. Before they could knock, a healthier, more robust Helga burst through the door. Her body had filled out, bearing womanly curves she'd not had as a girl. Wrapping her arms around her mother, she laughed and cried tears of joy mingled with the pain of such a long separation. Inga cried, too, as she embraced the daughter she'd thought she had lost.

Kurt came to the door, smiling. "Welcome, please come in." When Helga finally released her mother, Kurt turned to hug Inga.

"I'm so glad all of you could come. I'm Kurt, your son-in-law." Then he extended his hand to Hans, who received it uncomfortably.

"Thank you, thank you for inviting us." Inga smiled as she wiped the tears from her face with the back of her hand.

"You must be hungry. Come into the kitchen. I would love for you to meet my family." Kurt patted Detrick's shoulder in welcome.

Introductions followed. Detrick could not help but feel isolated as he watched the easy exchange of laughter between Kurt's sister, Hermina, and Helga. The secret he kept of his pale and painfully thin wife grew bitter within his soul, as jealousy he'd never known before brewed like a strong pot of morning coffee. To his dismay, he was angry that he and Leah could not live an open and honest life. Instead, the woman he loved sat in the darkness of an attic, denied the God-given right of sunshine, fresh fruit and vegetables, and wholesome, clean air. As the rest of the family dined on the food picked that morning, the finest they'd ever tasted, Detrick, unable to swallow, excused himself.

Alone, he walked through the fields. Would he ever again stand outside with his wife, enjoying the summer breeze, unafraid? Would their children ever be permitted to attend school? Would they ever watch their children run free through the grass or ride a bicycle? All these questions were without answers. His thoughts brought on a dark, brooding mood so foreign to his nature that when he returned, his mother asked if he felt ill.

The days that followed brought him more unrest. Try as he might, he could not assimilate into the family gatherings. Mostly, he sat gazing out the window, absently watching the horse or the cows, while the open wound in his heart grew larger. Kurt attempted conversation and offered friendship. Detrick liked him. It was immediately apparent that he held no Nazi sympathies. But Detrick could not enjoy good food and drink, breathe fresh air, and flourish in the joy of family while he knew Leah and Jacob's predicament.

He watched as Hans sat outside, talking with Kurt's father. Even he seemed to be enjoying the trip.

CHAPTER ONE HUNDRED FOUR

REBEKKA MUELLER COULDN'T FALL ASLEEP. FAR too excited, she lay awake, her mind drifting, sorting through fantasies. Tomorrow evening, she will attend her first dance. From her bed, she could see the dress she would wear illuminated in the moonlight. It had taken her over a week of shopping to choose the perfect frock, a pale-pink lace over satin, belted with a matching satin sash. When she'd tried it on, she'd whirled around in the dressing room as the skirts circled her, deciding that, for the first time, she was truly lovely.

It had been a surprise when Warren had asked if he might accompany her. They'd known each other for years as members of the Hitler Youth and Band of German Maidens, but he'd been athletic and popular while she'd been reserved and quiet. Of course, she'd accepted without delay and had run to tell her sister. Together, Rebekka and Adelheid had not only picked the dress but all the accessories she would wear, from her white shoes to her tiny, gold heart necklace. During the preparations for the dance, it seemed to Rebekka that the relationship she'd shared with Adelheid before the Jewish influence in the attic had returned to its former state.

As she'd grown older, Rebekka found that she believed the Nazi party to be right in their stance concerning Jews. It seemed to her that everywhere that the Jews infiltrated her life, she'd experienced problems. If Detrick had not been involved with the Jewess, he might have paid Adelheid the attention she'd craved. Then surely her sister would have a good reputation instead of walking through the halls at school to the quiet echoes of *tramp* and *whore*. The Band of German Maidens proved correct. They'd taught her a truth her parents failed to accept. She wondered how her father could not see that the Jews had used their money to con the Muellers. That is what Jews do (Hitler himself had said it). They finagle and trick the good people. Why had her parents allowed these vermin to taint their lives?

Although she was not beautiful by any standards, Rebekka's skin glowed with the radiance of excitement when Warren arrived to escort her to the dance. At Herr Mueller's insistence, she reluctantly agreed to meet her date on the porch lest he hear or see anything suspect.

The dance hall overflowed with young people. Rebekka recognized most of the guests from school or the Hitler Youth or the Band of German Maidens program. With Warren beside her, all the popular girls befriended Rebekka. While the years of taunting and isolation drifted away, the warmth of belonging replaced them. The girls complimented her dress and her hair. Warren brought her cups of punch, smiling and telling her how beautiful she looked. Never before had Rebekka Mueller felt so accepted, so much a part of something.

It was a night out of a storybook until Warren stopped the car a few blocks from her house. He kissed her. At first, she welcomed the kisses. Then, the passion swept him up faster than Rebekka, and she asked him to stop. He pushed away, taking a deep breath.

"Your sister does it. Why not you?"

"Are you saying my sister is a whore?"

"Well, she did it with me and lots of other boys I know, too. If it's all right for her, why not you?"

She stared at him in disbelief. If she lost him, she would be diminished to the lonely girl in the back of the classroom again. It sickened her to know that Warren had made love to Adelheid and bragged about it. Again, Adelheid had stolen her light.

"I've never done this before." She didn't know what else to say.

"That's fine. There's nothing to it. I'll show you. Just relax."

It did not feel right, but she lay still and allowed him to do as he pleased. Once she completed her mission, she would be Warren's girlfriend, and all other classmates would continue to accept her. She would have friends and be popular. It hurt, and she counted to one hundred, first forward and then backward, to distract herself until it ended.

When Warren dropped Rebekka off at the door, he kissed her, his tongue probing her mouth deeply.

"Goodnight."

"Goodnight."

Perhaps we are in love. Maybe this is what people who are in love do. After all, Warren would know, being two years older.

CHAPTER ONE HUNDRED FIVE

ON MONDAY MORNING, Rebekka walked into her first class, greeted by jeers and whispers, "Slut and whore, just like her sister."

She turned to see Warren wearing a guilty smile. Then, overcome with humiliation, she ran from the classroom to the bathroom, where she vomited.

She knelt on the floor of the school bathroom and cried. Rebekka hated her sister, but more than her sister, she hated Detrick for destroying Adelheid and turning her into an embarrassment. Even more than Detrick, she hated the Jews who lived upstairs. If she looked closely at the problem, it stemmed from them. Just as Hitler said, it always stemmed from them.

For years, the Nazi Party had made it clear that if one's family broke the rules, one must report the offense. Now, Rebekka wondered what had taken her so long. If she'd gone to the authorities earlier, things might have been different. She would go to Nazi Headquarters now, with Detrick out of town. She would beg for a pardon for herself and her family, explaining that they'd been tricked. The officials would understand.

CHAPTER ONE HUNDRED SIX

"I'VE BAKED a strawberry strudel with the berries I picked from our garden this morning. Tonight is a special night. Tonight, I have something to tell all of you." Helga beamed, looking like a golden-haired angel. It was the last night the family would be at the farm. In the morning, Helga must say goodbye until the next visit. Her lovely, rounded face shone brightly with excitement as her eyes radiated happiness. "Well, Kurt and I have saved this special treat for your last day here." Helga turned to smile at her husband. "We are going to have a child."

"Oh, Helga!" Tears welled up in Inga's eyes. "When?"

"December. So, now, that's a reason to plan another trip here."

"Of course, we'll come. We must see the baby. How wonderful." Inga hugged her daughter.

Detrick found himself repulsed by his feelings of jealousy. Instead of allowing selfishness to consume him, he smiled, wishing the couple good luck.

But that night, as he lay in bed, he wondered if he and Leah would ever share the joy of building a family and sharing a home. He must stop these painful thoughts. He knew they burned a hole within him that only served to fill him with anger and hatred. Better to focus on his love. Soon, he would be home and could bury his face in her hair and taste the salty essence of her skin. When they awoke, the family would have breakfast and then depart for Berlin. They would arrive at home by late afternoon or early evening. He knew he must wait until darkness to go to the attic. With a smile he could not contain, he considered his feelings. Even after all these years, when he thought of making love to Leah, he could not catch his breath. The sheer intensity of his emotion held him captive. Yes, it was true. He'd been destined for a difficult path, but he would not have traded it for a room filled with reichsmarks. Regardless of the risks, dangers, pain, horror, and hope, he considered himself the luckiest man on earth. Soon, very soon, she would be in his arms.

CHAPTER ONE HUNDRED SEVEN

"THERE IS A YOUNG GIRL, almost a child, here to see you. She says her name is Rebekka Mueller."

"Show her in." Konrad lit a cigarette. Convinced that the Band of German Maidens girl had come again requesting an officer willing to attend one of their meetings as a guest speaker, he sat back in his chair. Perhaps he would agree to give a speech. The admiration he received always gave him a boost.

Rebekka Mueller entered, wearing a gray wool skirt and a white blouse with a cap sleeve.

"I'm coming to you because I was told you are Detrick Haswell's superior officer."

"That's correct." Could Detrick have slept with this young child? Konrad wondered. "Sit down, please." He gestured to the chair on the opposite side of his desk. Then he got up and closed the door.

Walking back to take his seat, Konrad studied the girl. Her nose, too short, left a large gap that curled upward to her lip. A sprinkle of angry red pimples covered her cheeks. Considering her small, darting, dark eyes and lifeless brown hair, Konrad wondered what had attracted Detrick to this ugly child. Then he considered the strange sexual experiences many men discussed, his own included. It seemed that when one had the power to act at will, without consequence, one indulged one's every whim. He settled back into the large, comfortable leather chair and waited to hear her story. Whatever Detrick had done to her, Konrad decided, he would give her some money to buy lipstick, and she would keep her mouth shut.

"If I tell you something, do you promise my family will be safe?"

He cocked his head, intrigued. "Of course. What is it, my dear Fräulein?"

"Well, you know Detrick Haswell? He tricked my family."

"Did he? And how did he do that?"

"He convinced them to hide three Jews in our attic."

Konrad sat up straight, his arms crossed over his chest. "What? When?" A bolt of shock shot through him.

"For the last several years. It is because he is in love with the girl."

"A Jewess?"

"Yes, her name is Leah Abendstern."

Leah. He remembered Leah. Detrick had been fascinated with her when they were in school. So, this is what he'd done. He'd kept her as his secret mistress—the fool. What woman could be worth your career, your life?

"Hmmm, it's good that you brought this to my attention."

"You must not tell my family that I told you."

"No, of course not. You did the right thing." He smiled as he escorted her out of his office.

Once Rebekka had gone, Konrad called for one of his men.

"Arrange an arrest at the home of the Muellers. Upstairs, in the attic, they are hiding Jews. Arrest the entire family and send them off to Bergen-Belsen."

"The girl who just left here? Her as well?"

"Yes, all of them. Except the Jewess, who is in the attic. Her name is Leah Abendstern. Send her to Ravensbrück with the following instructions. She is to be cleaned up and deloused, then sent with the next transport to the brothel camp in Gusen. Do I make myself clear?"

"Yes, perfectly."

"Go then."

"Heil Hitler."

"Heil Hitler."

Konrad would talk to Detrick when he returned and explain how he'd saved him from ruin. Then, he would arrange a visit to Gusen, where he would take care of that tricky little Jewess himself. When he's finished with her, she will wish she'd been exterminated, like the insect she was.

CHAPTER ONE HUNDRED EIGHT

SILVER DROPS of rain fell upon the hood of the black Volkswagen, evaporating into a puff of steam upon contact with the hot metal. In the distance, Detrick made out the formation of a rainbow.

"Why don't we stop for lunch until the sun shower is over?"

"Sure, Mother, if you'd like."

Hans had fallen asleep. When Inga nudged him awake, he awoke with a start.

"We are going to eat something."

Hans nodded. The country calmed him, and he realized he hadn't fought with Detrick once during the entire trip.

CHAPTER ONE HUNDRED NINE

THE BLACK SS vehicle rounded the corner and stopped in front of the Mueller home. Leah lay on her bed, reading a thick novel that Detrick had given her before he left. The rabbi slept, snoring quietly in an old living room chair, while Jacob whittled, forming the likeness of Sammy, the cat, out of a scrap of wood.

Even though they'd felt somewhat safe for a long time, when they heard the sound of several pairs of boots on the stairs to the attic, they were jolted back to reality. The hammering of heels against wood echoed in each of their chests, pounding with the quickened rhythm of their hearts. Each of them wanted to run, but they knew they were trapped. They had no choice but to wait for the door to open and the Devil's henchmen to enter.

Leah felt as if her body had frozen. She could not move, and she hoped, as did the rabbi, that there might be some mistake. It was Jacob who stood first. He knew they'd been discovered. They'd been betrayed.

As the decrepit wooden entryway rattled against the force of someone powerfully kicking to break the lock, the rabbi, an old and feeble man, threw his hands in the air in a pathetic gesture of defeat. Jacob rushed to Leah's side and took her in his arms. He held her close while she buried her head in his chest. Not fearing for himself, Jacob thought now only of Leah and Detrick. What would become of them? Before he had an opportunity to allow his mind to drift to the possible horrors they might face, the door burst open. Four SS men ordered the three to gather their things and follow the guards to the waiting vehicle.

CHAPTER ONE HUNDRED TEN

BECAUSE INGA INSISTED upon a leisurely lunch, followed by a short nap, the Haswells arrived home just as the sun set.

Detrick paced, waiting for the darkness of night when he felt safe to make his way to Leah. It seemed as if the hours did not pass until, finally, he dressed and readied himself to leave. Instead of attracting attention with the noise of the automobile, he decided to ride his bicycle. Pedaling fast, his legs still remarkably strong, even though he'd given up training years ago, he arrived in twenty minutes. As he rode up to the house, a chill came over him. It was far too early for the family to be asleep, yet the house stood in total darkness.

Unsure what he would find, he entered. Dishes lay in piles of broken glass on the floor. Pots and pans were strewn about and fell at odd angles around the room. With his heart beating loudly in his ears, Detrick raced to the attic staircase. Seeing the shattered doorway, he ran upstairs to realize his greatest fear: Leah and Jacob were gone. He fell upon Leah's bed, grasping her pillow. For a moment, against the dizziness that fought to overtake him, Detrick devised a plan.

As Detrick left the Mueller home, he checked around him to

ensure he had not been followed and then jumped on his bike and rode faster than he had ever ridden toward home. When Detrick arrived at his parents' apartment, he quietly gathered his belongings. He put everything of value into one of his mother's large cotton laundry sacks. Then he quickly loaded the car with his possessions, including his beloved bicycle, and drove through the streets, searching for a pawnshop that kept late hours.

CHAPTER ONE HUNDRED ELEVEN

THE PAWNSHOP OWNER had meant to close earlier but did not want to face another confrontation with his wife. He'd taken a lover, and she'd found him out. His lady friend, married as well, had called it quits. Now, he spent as much time at the store as possible rather than engage in another battle with his wounded and bitter spouse. Often, he wished she would just give him a divorce, but every time he broached the subject, she flew into another rage. When the attractive blond man came to his shop door, it seemed a good excuse not to go home.

"How can I help you?" The pawnshop owner ran a hand through his short, cropped hair.

"I have some things that I would like to sell." Detrick wore civilian clothes, leaving his uniform in the backseat of the car to help preserve his anonymity.

"Let me see."

Detrick laid his grandfather's pocket watch on the table beside his wedding band. Next, he placed a stamp collection he'd kept as a child and all of his soccer equipment.

The shopkeeper lifted the watch and turned it in his hand. Then, coming out from behind his counter, he studied the old black bicycle. It was obviously used but still saleable. Before he finished with a price, the pawnbroker looked at the wedding band.

"I'll give you one hundred reichsmarks for the lot."

"The watch alone is worth that."

"Take it or leave it. That's my offer."

"I'll take it, and I would also like to purchase a flashlight."

Although he had a key, Detrick had never dared enter head-quarters after hours. He knew Konrad occasionally brought women to his office to impress them and hoped that tonight would not be one of those evenings.

Detrick did not turn the lights on. Instead, he used the flashlight to navigate his way to Konrad's office. Relieved that Konrad had not chosen this night to make another conquest, Detrick entered the room alone.

Several piles of manila folders had been arranged neatly on Konrad's desk. Detrick knew these were documentation to be entered into the punch card system. Depending upon when the arrest had occurred, the Abendstern files might still be amongst them. Detrick prayed that they had not yet been processed. If Konrad had already finished and entered them, then locating the records would be far more difficult.

CHAPTER ONE HUNDRED TWELVE

PACKED wall-to-wall with desperate souls standing upright because there was no room for sitting, the train to Bergen–Belsen seemed airless. Unrelenting heat and the lack of water caused death amongst many of the elderly and sick in the compressed boxcar. A strong, permeating odor of urine, feces, and vomit prevailed throughout the trip. With only a small light peeking through the wood panels, Jacob lost track of the hours.

By the time the train reached its destination, he could not remember how long he'd been riding. He had no idea what had become of Detrick or Leah, and he hoped the two would somehow locate each other. If the Nazis meant to kill them all—and Jacob believed that they did—his final prayer would not be for himself but for those he loved. And so he prayed, with tears running from his eyes, that at least the lovers might face the end together and find comfort in each other's arms. The rabbi stood beside him, silent the whole trip. Neither could speak. Both men were lost in their own premonitions of what awaited them and all the Jews.

CHAPTER ONE HUNDRED THIRTEEN

With the "Jewish problem" under control and Detrick's return not due until Monday, Konrad prepared to attend a party to honor a high-ranking official that Friday evening. The situation with the Muellers and the Jews would require some disciplinary action. Detrick must realize the seriousness of his crime. Still, Konrad felt secure that he'd had the brilliance to resolve the entire fiasco without any higher-ups ever discovering Detrick's offense. Therefore, the punishment would be enforced and acknowledged only between them. No one else need ever know.

As he shaved the soft shadow of stubble from his chin, Konrad winked at himself in the bathroom mirror. He'd saved Detrick's life, and now Detrick owed him an even greater debt. Careful to wear a perfectly pressed uniform, he affected a smile guaranteed to push him toward another advancement in the party. Then, as always, picking up the black phone on his desk and dialing a number from his long list, he secured the perfect girl to appear as his date. After he had replaced the receiver, he marveled at how women willingly accepted his invitations at the last minute because he was a man to be reckoned with. It had never been clearer to him how much the

Third Reich had done to change his life. He had gone from the awkward, unaccepted boy to a man women and men aimed to please. Yes, the Nazi Party had been the best thing that ever happened to Konrad.

CHAPTER ONE HUNDRED FOURTEEN

JACOB WAS MOMENTARILY BLINDED when the doors to the train rattled open and the sunlight flooded in. He heard the harsh voices of the guards yelling, "*Beeilen, schweine!*" *Hurry up, pigs*, as the crowd rushed through the door. The force of their pushing swept him along with them. Once outside, Jacob searched for the rabbi, but the guards would not tolerate his hesitation, and one of them hit him on the back with a club, telling him to move along. A pain shot through Jacob's shoulder where the blow had landed as he followed the line that had begun to enter the barbed-wire enclosure. Once inside, the prisoners' heads were shaved. Then they were ushered to another line where they waited to enter a hot-air delousing machine. Standing in the broiling sun for hours, waiting, Jacob felt dizzy and drained. He continued to scan the large masses of people in search of the rabbi, but to no avail.

After the delousing, the captives, herded at gunpoint, received their uniforms and entered the already overcrowded barracks. The odors on the train had been horrific, but they could not compare to the stench that pervaded these rooms. Emaciated men slept on the floors without blankets. Their skin was stretched so tightly over their skeletons that it looked like the bones would soon pop right through. Anywhere Jacob looked, he saw people coughing or vomiting. In the background, he heard the guard instructing the newly arrived to find an open space. Again, Jacob tried to locate the rabbi but did not see him. Finding a small area between a teenage boy and a man appearing somewhere around forty, Jacob sat down.

"The man who used to sleep here died last night. We think he had cholera." The middle-aged man scratched his head.

"Thanks. I'm glad you let me know the good news." Jacob observed the crusty, sore, dripping blood where the man had scratched it. Then he realized that the man's entire skull was covered in red, angry bumps, some covered with scabs.

On the other side of him, the boy lay quietly. A pang of sadness shot through Jacob as he smiled at the youngster.

"Hello, my name is Jacob."

"I'm Benjamin, but my friends call me Benny. You know, like Benny Goodman."

"Ahhh, the American musician."

"Yes, right." Benny perked up. "You know American music?"

"A little bit, but not as much as I would have liked to. It became illegal to listen to it, and I didn't want any trouble." Jacob laughed. "I guess I could have listened. It seems I have trouble anyway."

"I guess we both do." The boy pointed to the yellow star on his arm. "If you're a Jew in Europe, you have trouble."

"Where are you from?"

"Poland. I was in Auschwitz for the last three years, but as the Allies are getting closer, the Nazis are moving us into camps in Germany. I don't think it will be too long before the end of all of this. The Germans know they're losing the war. I just hope I'm strong enough to make it to the end."

"You're young. You'll make it."

"I hope so. There's no food here and no water. It's filthy with lice, and everyone seems to be suffering from one illness or another. From what I understand, this camp was designed to be a sick camp. The Nazis were sending all the diseased prisoners here. Now, there are sick and healthy, all together. So, the healthy get sick."

"Well, you won't get sick." Jacob smiled. "You'll be all right." He patted the boy's arm.

After a time, the middle-aged man introduced himself, "I guess since we are going to be neighbors, I should tell you my name. I am Leon, from Hungary."

"Good to make your acquaintance, Leon. I am Jacob, from Berlin."

"German Jews. They think they are really something special, eh? Always putting on airs, you Germans, as if you are a higher class of Jew. Well, here you are, dying with the rest of us."

CHAPTER ONE HUNDRED FIFTEEN

"This is a work camp. Unless you work in the laundry or kitchen, you will have to make socks for soldiers in the textile factory or assemble rockets in the Siemens plant nearby. Rockets sometimes have defects, especially if the guards are not looking. The women make the toes and heels of the socks purposely thin so that they break down. We don't want the Nazi bastards marching at all, but if they do, we want their feet sore," Simza, the young gypsy girl, said.

"I thought they would have shaved my head," Leah said.

"Not everyone's head is shaved. Sometimes, they wait to see if they want to send you to Gusen, Austria, to the brothel camp."

"A brothel camp?"

"Watch your step. Being pretty is dangerous here. If you are chosen to go to the brothel, and the other girls find out about it, they will beat you to death," Simza warned as she gazed at Leah. "See that one over there?" Simza indicated a large, heavyset woman prisoner with a massive bulbous nose and thinning dark hair. Her small blue-green reptilian eyes darted around the room, looking for a victim. "That's Dagmar. She's the ringleader, and she is meaner than a hungry badger. Be careful to stay out of her way."

Simza ran her fingers through her long, curly black hair, her dark eyes studying the new girl who had been placed in the bunk beside hers.

"Why would anyone be jealous of someone being forced into a brothel? It sounds like the worst thing that could happen."

"Yes, I agree with you. But you see, the girls who are sent to the brothels are fed better food and treated much better than we are. A girl like Dagmar has no chance of being chosen. She is lucky they haven't done away with her yet. I think the only reason they even keep her around is because she dominates the others and keeps them all under control. Sometimes, I think she works directly with the guards."

"You're very pretty. Do you ever fear that you'll be selected?"

"Yes, of course. My biggest worry is that I will be sterilized. There is forced sterilization here, especially if you're sent to work as a prostitute. They don't want anyone to get pregnant. If that should happen, the girl is immediately forced to abort. One of my friends was married and already with child when she came here. She tried to keep it secret, but she started to grow a big belly. When the Nazi guards found out what was happening, they took her to the doctor, who performed a quick abortion. She died. Most of those who are treated here at the hospital for anything wind up dead. Try not to irritate the female guards. If you do, they usually send you for use in medical experiments. Those are terrible. See that woman over on the other side of the room? They did an experimental surgery on her leg, and now she can't walk without limping anymore. She tries to hide it, but I have seen where they cut her. It's red and swollen and getting worse every day. Soon, she will die."

Leah took a deep breath. She'd planned to tell Detrick when he returned from Munich that she carried his baby in her womb. Now, thoughts rushed at her with terrifying speed as she asked herself how she might protect that precious life from all the evil around her that could snuff it out.

CHAPTER ONE HUNDRED
SIXTEEN

Halfway through the stack of files on Konrad's desk, Detrick found one folder for Leah and another for Jacob. It surprised him that Konrad had separated them. But as he read further, he realized why. Plans to send Leah with the first transport to the brothel at Gusen were clearly indicated. Therefore, Konrad had sent her to Ravensbrück, the all-women's camp. It was from Ravensbrück that the females for sexual slavery were selected. Unable to breathe, Detrick continued quickly thumbing through the papers to discover Jacob had been sent to Bergen–Belsen.

With trembling hands, Detrick reached into Konrad's drawer, where he knew the letterhead paper would be kept. Then, placing the flashlight next to the typewriter, he picked out two letters, forged Konrad's signature, and sealed them with his seal. Detrick's knees buckled, and his chest tightened. Forcing himself to breathe, he grabbed the car keys, only to have them fall from his hand. Picking them up, he grasped them tightly, his knuckles white with force, and raced out to the car.

The stillness of night lay upon Berlin, causing Detrick to cringe as the sound of the car motor broke through the calm. Quickly removing his shirt, he replaced it with his uniform jacket. Then, with as much self-control as he could muster, Detrick steeled himself to refrain from speeding as he set out to Ravensbrück. First, though, he must stop at the Mueller's house and find clothes for Jacob and Leah.

Thoughts and terrors flew at him like runaway aircraft, crashing into each other in the midnight sky. All the *what-ifs* imaginable fought their way into his consciousness. How long had Leah been at Ravensbrück? Had they hurt her? Was she still alive? If she were dead, nothing mattered anymore. He would just as soon die, too. Detrick swallowed hard, pushing his feelings back. If he allowed fear to take over his mind, he would never be able to play the part he must, to do what he could to save her life.

CHAPTER ONE HUNDRED SEVENTEEN

"HEIL HITLER," the guard addressed Detrick as he entered.

"Heil Hitler. I am *Scharführer* Detrick Haswell. I've been sent here to retrieve a Jewess for Sturmbannführer Konrad Klausen in Berlin."

"Do you have documentation?"

"I do." Detrick handed him the sealed letter on Konrad's letterhead.

The man tore the envelope and read. "You have come so late at night?"

"Yes, I'm sorry. I was supposed to arrive earlier, but I got tied up. I must deliver the Jewess by tomorrow morning. As you can see from the letter, she is an expert pianist. My superior is hosting a special luncheon, and he wishes for her to entertain. My guess is I will be returning her to you tomorrow evening following the festivities." Sweat trickled down the collar of Detrick's uniform, but he continued to meet the man's eyes without wavering.

"There is no one here of authority to grant permission for this. Perhaps you should return in the morning."

"Impossible. He wants her to practice through the night. There are to be no mishaps at the gathering tomorrow. You have the letter.

That should suffice for your superior. Just explain the situation, and I will have returned her by nightfall. Besides, between you and me, what is one more Jewess?" Detrick laid a few reichsmarks on the table in front of the guard. "My job is at stake here. I need to be sure not to disappoint *Sturmbannführer* Klausen."

The guard laughed and nodded understanding as he stuffed the currency into his breast pocket. "Wait here. I'll have someone go and bring her back."

The white-faced circular clock on the wall ticked loudly. With each movement of the hands of the timepiece, Detrick felt his heart flutter. Above him, he saw a picture of Adolf Hitler and wondered how one man had started such a snowball of horror. Either the guard would return with Leah, or Detrick would be arrested, and soon he would find out. If he were arrested, Detrick worried that he would never know what had become of Leah. He ran a nervous hand through his golden hair.

CHAPTER ONE HUNDRED EIGHTEEN

SIMZA WAS ATTEMPTING to teach Leah to make dolls when the male guard entered the barracks.

"Shh... Stay quiet... These guards come here at night when everyone is gone and force themselves on us."

Leah and Simza curled quietly into their beds, hoping they'd not been seen or heard.

A gruff male voice called out, "Leah Abendstern. Is Leah Abendstern here?"

Leah's heart beat wildly.

"Shhhh... Don't answer," Simza whispered.

"Abendstern!" the guard called again, this time louder and more demanding.

"She's over there." Dagmar stood, resembling a hippopotamus, as she indicated Leah's bunk.

The hard clank of the guards' boot heels hitting the cement floor terrified Leah, and her eyes filled with tears.

"This one." By one arm, he lifted Leah entirely into the air.

"Yes," Dagmar answered.

"*Gut.*"

Dragging Leah from the room, he pulled her through the mud outside and all the way to the main office.

A door slammed, unnerving him, and Detrick jumped.

"*Scharführer* Haswell, is this the one?" He roughly pushed Leah forward, and she tripped. Detrick's heart broke as he saw her fall to the ground. It was all he could do not to pick her up and take her into his arms, not to knock this man into the next world. But he knew if he were to save her life, he must continue with this masquerade.

"Yes, I believe it is, from the photographs I've seen. Thank you. I will have her back here before nightfall tomorrow. You need not even mention it to your superior. By the time he notices she is gone, I will have brought her back."

"That's a good idea." The guard winked at Detrick as he massaged his breast pocket where he'd placed the bribe.

Detrick took Leah's arm and feigned authority. "Let's go. Quickly."

Leah could barely contain her joy at seeing him. When they got into the car, she wanted to kiss him, but he told her to sit in the back in case anyone looked out the window. Then, he drove off.

"Sweetheart. Are you all right?" The tightening in his chest finally began to give way.

"I wasn't, but now I am, now that you're here."

"My God, Leah. I was so afraid. I was so afraid they'd hurt you or worse."

"Detrick, I want to kiss you. I want to hold you."

"Soon, darling, soon. There is a pile of clothes on the floor, under the seat. Change from that uniform. Then, when you are in regular clothes, I am nothing more than a Nazi officer out for an evening with my girl. It will look less suspicious if we are stopped. And once we get to the Swiss border, I will tell them I am taking you with me on special business concerning fine art. The Nazis are hiding stolen art in Switzerland. The border patrol is aware of it, and they know not to ask questions." He handed her a bag filled with bread and cheese. "Eat this. You must be starving."

"Papa is in trouble, Detrick."

"I know. I have it all under control, Love. Do you trust me?"

"More than anything or anyone in the entire world."

Leah fell asleep in exhaustion with the motion of the car as they sped towards the Swiss-German border. She awoke just as the guard gave them the right to enter Switzerland. Although it took a mere second to cross, the intensity she and Detrick felt made them both think their lungs would burst as they held their breath. Then it happened. As the wheels of their car crossed into Switzerland, they were free of Nazi rule.

Detrick drove through the little border town, found a small hotel, and paid for the entire month. Then, he took Leah up a winding staircase to a small room on the second floor. Although the cost had proved substantially higher, he had insisted upon a private bath within the room rather than using the communal one at the end of the hall. Once inside, he began to run the water, filling the tub.

"I thought you might like a warm bath."

Grateful, Leah did not say a word. She just nodded. She shed her clothes and stepped in. Detrick knelt beside the tub and soaped up a washcloth, gently running it across her body. Bathing her like a baby, he took the soap and shampooed her hair, rinsing it carefully to avoid her eyes.

"I've never had anyone give me a bath before." She smiled.

"I wanted to make you comfortable."

"I know. You always do so much for me, Detrick."

"I love you."

"I love you."

He lifted her into his arms and covered her with a towel. Then he carried her to the bed. Tenderly, he kissed her.

"When I got to the house and saw you were gone, I thought I would die."

She could not answer. Tears streamed down her face.

"I found you, my darling, my love. I give thanks to God that you are alive." He kissed her again and again, the passion of their feelings bringing them together as one.

After they'd finished, he held her close for a long time. Their hearts beat in unison, and their breaths were synchronized as they lay wrapped in each other's arms on the little bed. Outside, light rain fell, the cold drops dribbling down the windowpane.

"I'm pregnant, Detrick."

He moved his body down to where his eyes could meet hers, so full of emotion he could not speak. Instead, he kissed Leah and held her face with his hands. A single tear fell from his eye into her drying hair.

"Leah," he whispered, hoarse with emotion. "Leah. My God, I am so happy."

CHAPTER ONE HUNDRED NINETEEN

"HEIL HITLER."

"To the Führer."

"To the Führer."

"To the Reich."

"To the Reich. May it last one thousand years."

The toasts continued through the night. Konrad drank far more than usual, and the alcohol had begun to take effect. By four in the morning, he knew it would be necessary to request a driver to take him home.

CHAPTER ONE HUNDRED TWENTY

JACOB SEARCHED TIRELESSLY for Rabbi Stern and the Mueller family but found only Ebner Mueller.

"The women were separated from us when we got here." Ebner bit his fingernail.

"I know. I saw them send a group of females to the other side when we first arrived. I think there is a women's camp there."

"Yes, I believe you're right. I wish I hadn't agreed to this. I didn't think we would be caught." Herr Mueller sat with his arms crossed over his chest. "I've destroyed my family, and for what?"

"I could say I am grateful to you."

"Don't bother. I would rather you just leave me alone. When I look at you, I think about what I've done and feel sick."

Jacob nodded, got up, and went back to his space.

He could not help but wonder where Leah had been taken, if she lived, or if they'd killed her. And Detrick—Jacob knew his crime was punishable by death. He shook his head in despair. Jacob sat in his tiny corner in the dirty barracks of Bergen–Belsen, powerless.

CHAPTER ONE HUNDRED TWENTY-ONE

ALTHOUGH TIME TICKED AWAY AND, with it, the precious moments of safety, Detrick could not bear to awaken Leah. She was exhausted. The ordeal had taken a toll on her. But he knew if he were to succeed in his mission, he must leave soon. Once again, he studied her face. She was relaxed, and the pain he'd seen earlier was now diminished. Careful not to awaken her, he loosened himself from their intertwining limbs. He stood up and stretched, fighting the need for sleep. Then Detrick went over to the desk, sat down, and began to pen a letter.

After he'd finished, he folded the paper and sealed it in an envelope he found in the desk drawer. Then, regretfully, he knew he must rouse Leah.

A gentle kiss on her cheek and a loving hand across her hair awakened her. She smiled and pulled him to her. They kissed, but before the passion could consume him, Detrick pulled away. He could not stay any longer.

"Leah, darling, listen to me." Detrick took her hand, caressing the pale skin with his thumb. "I must go. Your father is in Bergen–Belsen. I found the files in Konrad's office."

Ashamed, Leah looked away. For the last few hours, she'd been so happy that she'd forgotten Jacob. Now Detrick planned to leave her and re-enter Nazi Germany. The risk to his life would be grave. Selfishly, she longed to beg him not to go, to stay with her, here in the safety of this little room that had come to represent heaven. Right now, he stood before her, his body within her grasp, his eyes fixed on hers. Once he walked out that door, she would wait, consumed with distress, until he returned.

But her father, her kind and loving father, remained a prisoner in a horrendous concentration camp. The Nazis could very well be torturing him right now. The nausea she'd felt for the last several weeks after realizing she was pregnant flooded her. Swallowing hard, she tried to avoid vomiting, but in the end, she knelt over the toilet with Detrick holding her hair.

After she had emptied her stomach, he helped her back to the bed, where she sat down with him beside her.

"I'm terrified, Detrick. I want to beg you not to go, but I can't. Oh, Detrick. Oh, dear God." She wept and wept. The tears filled her face and dripped down onto the sheets. As he watched her, his heart broke into as many pieces, like the glass he'd shattered during their wedding ceremony.

"Leah, what can I do? I must save your father if I can. We could never be happy and enjoy our child if we let him die there."

She nodded, her hands covering her face.

He gently pried her fingers away from her cheeks and lifted her chin so their eyes met.

His eyes, as blue and deep as the ocean, looked into hers with serious intent. "I love you, Leah. I want you to tell me that you know that I love you."

"I know, Detrick. I know."

"I've left a letter on the desk. Beside the envelope, you will find a good sum of money. I took a few reichsmarks with me to bribe the guards at Bergen–Belsen. Otherwise, that is everything I have. Wait several days. If I do not return, open the letter and read it."

"Detrick, I love you."

They kissed. He held her so tightly that she stopped breathing for a moment. When her breath resumed, she inhaled the sweet, fragrant peppermint. Tears filled her eyes, threatening to spill over her face. Then he released her. He smiled, and she felt the emptiness begin when she saw that familiar blond hair fall over his left eye as he walked out of the hotel room.

CHAPTER ONE HUNDRED TWENTY-TWO

DETRICK RACED the car at top speed until he reached his destination. As he received approval from the guard, he entered the barbed-wire fence and drove directly to the main building. On either side of him, Detrick saw broken men wearing gray-striped uniforms, their eyes vacant as if they were already dead. Since it was Sunday, the odds that the officials at Ravensbrück had already contacted Konrad were slim. Sometime tomorrow, the telephone call to Konrad would be made, and Detrick's actions would be uncovered. But if all went according to plan, he and Jacob would be well across the border by then.

Behind a large steel door stood the guard he would have to convince to release Jacob into his custody. Once again, as he did for Leah, Detrick steeled himself and entered the office building.

"Heil Hitler." A perky blonde with wavy hair, like an American sex symbol, sat at the desk smiling a white-toothed smile, clearly attracted to the young sergeant. "How can I help you?"

Detrick assumed his most charming grin. "I have a letter here from my superior, *Sturmbannführer* Klausen. He is giving a bicycle race in honor of the Führer next week. I have been sent to retrieve a mechanic who is known to be a wizard with bicycles. *Sturmbannführer*

Klausen wants to keep him on hand throughout the race in case any of the machinery breaks down."

"That's an excellent idea. What's the prisoner's name?"

Detrick opened the paper and pretended to read the name. "Jacob Abendstern, from Berlin?"

"Any idea when he might have arrived here?"

"Quite recently, I believe."

She took the paper from Detrick's hand. "I will have to get approval to release him. It may take several hours."

"Must you? I am in a terrible hurry. Can you just send for him, and later, give the letter to your superior officer? I'm sure there won't be a problem."

"Well, I don't know. I mean, I don't think I should."

"What's your name?"

"Lydia, and yours?"

"I'm Detrick. Lydia, perhaps if you would help me, I could drive this prisoner back to Berlin, and then once I've delivered him, I would like to come back here and take you to dinner as a thank you for your cooperation. You see, my promotion is involved."

"Oh, I understand. But I don't know, Detrick. I don't want to get into trouble."

"You won't. A girl as pretty as you? What kind of boss could stay mad at you for very long? I know I couldn't."

She smiled.

"Come on, please, help me get this promotion. I promise you a lovely evening in exchange, *Fräulein*." Detrick could not believe the words that came from his mouth.

"Oh, very well." She lifted the telephone receiver. "Send the prisoner Jacob Abendstern to the main office immediately."

When Jacob walked into the room and saw Detrick, joy came over him, the likes of which he'd never known before.

"Get in the car, Jew." He turned to the girl. "Goodbye, Lydia, and thank you. I will contact you in the next few days, and we'll have that dinner."

She nodded, watching as Detrick's hair fell over his eye.

Detrick grabbed Jacob's arm and forced him into the back seat.

Then, jumping into the front, he turned the key in the ignition, forcing the auto to spring to life.

Jacob breathed a sigh of relief as Detrick waved to the guard who opened the gate, allowing them to pass through the door and out of Bergen–Belsen.

"Are you alright?"

"Yes, yes, I'm fine. Have you found Leah?"

"Yes, she is in Switzerland awaiting our return."

"Praise God."

"Change into the civilian clothes that are under the seat. Then, look for a small paper bag. You'll find a hunk of bread and some cheese inside the sack. There is also a canteen filled with water. I'm sure you're hungry."

"Yes, very, but now, even more than I am hungry, I am happy." And he was grateful to be alive, but nagging guilt fluttered like a bumblebee in the back of his mind. Jacob could not forget the face of Benny, the young boy who lay starving beside him in Bergen–Belsen, or the memory of the Mueller family and how distraught Ebner had been when he'd last seen him, or even the bitter old Hungarian who'd accused him of thinking himself superior. And the rabbi, what of the rabbi? What would become of them? Try as he might, he could not push the images of them from his mind.

In his haste, Detrick had forgotten to include a hat, and when he saw Jacob's head had been shaved, it concerned him for a moment. But once Jacob had exchanged the uniform for a simple shirt and slacks, he looked no different from any other German father accompanying his son.

As they drove silently, Jacob seemed lost in thought, gazing out the window.

"You should not have come back for me. You and Leah were safe and together. You know I wanted that."

"I had to. You have been my real father ever since that day, so long ago, when you fixed my bicycle."

"I remember. You were little and scared."

"And you rescued me."

Jacob smiled at the memory. "And now you've rescued me."

They both fell silent for several minutes as they recalled that fateful day many years ago.

"Jacob? I have something to tell you."

"Yes."

"You're going to be a grandfather."

Tears fell from Jacob's eyes, and he wiped them with the back of his hand. He was so overcome that he could not speak.

CHAPTER ONE HUNDRED
TWENTY-THREE

AFFLICTED WITH A TWO-DAY HANGOVER, Konrad felt like a demon had played drums inside his head. He'd slept most of Saturday and finally awakened late Sunday afternoon. The gathering on Friday night had given him the opportunity to meet and mingle with more important party members than he'd anticipated. Therefore, he'd deemed it a success.

Konrad slowly sipped on a glass of water. Perhaps a good meal would diminish this powerful headache. Rather than eat alone, he telephoned a friend and invited him to a local restaurant. They arranged to meet for an early dinner. Then, still feeling under the weather, Konrad regulated the water in the shower to lukewarm. As the rain-like mist sprinkled over his head, Konrad felt self-satisfied as he considered how far he might advance due to this weekend's newly acquired connections. He quivered with the possibilities. The future would see him as a high-ranking officer, not only filthy rich but admired and respected—a dream realized.

The tiny two-letter word, 'if,' is often the most important in the human vocabulary.

If the water had not been running, if his mind had not been so preoccupied, and if he had felt better, Konrad would surely have heard the phone ringing. But as fate would have it, he missed the call from Ravensbrück, and by the time they tried to telephone again, he'd already left for dinner.

CHAPTER ONE HUNDRED
TWENTY-FOUR

THERE WERE ONLY a few miles left to the Swiss border. A bead of sweat formed on Jacob's brow. Soon, they would cross into Switzerland and into safety. Detrick glanced over to see Jacob studying him.

"You have been my dearest friend. My true son."

Detrick reached over and squeezed Jacob's hand. "We'll make it through this. And someday, when the baby is older, we'll tell the child all about what we did today."

"I don't think I'll ever forget it. No matter what happens, Detrick, I've always loved you."

"I know that, Papa. And I have loved you, too."

They pulled behind a short line of cars at the border patrol station. Jacob smiled reassuringly, but Detrick saw his hand trembling as they waited.

CHAPTER ONE HUNDRED
TWENTY-FIVE

THE HEAVY BLACK telephone rang out as Konrad turned the key in the door. He rushed to pick it up.

"*Sturmbannführer* Konrad Klausen?"

"That's correct."

"This is *Unterscharführer* Hauptman. I am sorry to bother you at home on a Sunday, but my superior insisted that I telephone to make sure all had gone well for you."

"I'm sorry, I don't understand."

"With the Jewess—feel free to keep her as long as you need to. We just wanted to check in and get an estimated time when you plan to return the prisoner."

Confused, Konrad listened but could not make sense of the call.

"Excuse me, please. It's been a rather long weekend. I'm not sure what you're talking about. Explain?"

"On Friday night, you sent a driver to retrieve a particular prisoner. The Jewess, one Leah Abendstern, you'd selected to play piano at your luncheon. Do you recall now?"

Leah Abendstern, Detrick... The puzzle pieces began to fit together. What had Detrick done? The headache Konrad had almost defeated had returned with a vengeance. Detrick had now put them both at risk again. If Konrad tried to protect Detrick this time, he might lose his position or worse. But before he was willing to lay his friend's head on the block, he had to make sure beyond a doubt that Detrick had committed the crime.

"I'm sorry, someone is at my door. Let me get back to you."

For a moment, Konrad racked his brain. He could not remember where he'd sent Jacob. Then it came to him. He lit a cigarette and called Bergen–Belsen.

Konrad hung up the phone. In desperation, he cried out Detrick's name. The sound echoed through the empty house. "Why, Detrick, why?" He called out again. Sick to his stomach, he fell to his knees. Bent over, he held his midsection as the pain shot through him. It had been years since Konrad had cried, but he did so now. He knew what he must do and even found he could easily guess Detrick's next move. Picking up the phone, he called his superior, *Standartenführer* Brandt.

"Close off the borders to Switzerland." Then he explained why. Once the betrayal went into action, the power to stop it was no longer Konrad's. His stomach grew sick from the rich dinner he'd just eaten, and he ran to the bathroom, where he vomited. Once he'd finished, he splashed cold water on his blood-red and feverish face. Then he scrubbed his hands with soap until they bled. For the rest of his life, he would wash his hands, like Pontius Pilate, compulsively trying to cleanse his guilty heart.

CHAPTER ONE HUNDRED TWENTY-SIX

JUST A SINGLE AUTO ahead of them to go, then Jacob and Detrick would be free. Detrick gripped the steering wheel so tightly that his knuckles turned white. They glanced at each other. Knowing that this could be the end. They waited.

"Name?"

"*Scharführer* Detrick Haswell. This is my father, Hans Haswell."

The officer gazed at the two. "What is your business across the border?"

"I am here to do some work for the Reich, and at the same time, my father and I plan to take a short holiday." Detrick felt the collar of his uniform tighten like a noose around his neck. It had been days since he'd slept, and dark circles had formed beneath his heavy-lidded eyes.

"Very well." Just as the guard was about to open the gate, the phone in the booth rang. "Excuse me. I must answer this." The guard turned to Detrick.

Detrick nodded, but he felt something had gone wrong. He turned to Jacob, who felt it too. If he crashed the auto through the gate, the metal bar would decapitate them. Detrick looked back at the guard. By the expression on the guard's face, Detrick knew for

372 | ALL MY LOVE, DETRICK

sure they'd been found out. Turning to Jacob, he squeezed his hand. "Open the door and run, Papa. I am right behind you."

They both opened their car doors and took off as fast as they could. It was only one hundred yards to the safety zone.

When the gunshot rang out, Detrick turned and saw Jacob fall. Instead of crossing the line, he ran back to hold the old man as he died.

"Jacob, I'm here."

"I know, I know... You should not have come back. Not now, when you were almost across the border or when you were safe with Leah."

"Shhhh, don't talk."

"Before they come, I want to say goodbye. I tell you, go now, leave me here. Go. Run..." Jacob closed his eyes.

Detrick felt for a pulse, but none remained. He got up from the blood-covered street, but before he could move, two guards held him at gunpoint.

"Move! Get into the booth!"

Detrick wanted to fight but knew that they would shoot him. Instead, he followed.

A call was made.

Then, a car arrived, which took Detrick to the closest headquarters. There, a high-ranking officer met him.

"Not only do I hate to be disturbed on a Sunday night, but this behavior is appalling. What do you have to say for yourself? A good Aryan boy going against his own for Jews."

"I have nothing to say."

"That you are sorry would be a beginning." The man took a club from a holster and hit Detrick across the shoulders. A loud crack, followed by shooting pain, indicated to Detrick that a bone had been broken.

"I'm not sorry."

"Courageous, aren't we? Well, what else should I expect from a pure Aryan? After all, we are the superior race. It's just a shame you aren't smarter. To betray your own people for these vermin was truly a foolhardy mistake. Don't you realize that they are filth and they were destroying Germany?"

Detrick did not answer. Once again, the officer hit him. This time on the other side of his body.

"Apologize! Say you were tricked. And perhaps, just perhaps, I might let you live."

"I am sorry, but not because I helped the Jews. I am sorry I was born one of you. It sickens me what the Nazis have done."

"You stupid man. You fool." He hit Detrick across the face, breaking his nose. Blood shot across the room and splattered onto the wall.

Detrick's entire body was filled with pain. "Call me what you will. I will never regret helping my friends. Never."

Now, the officer grew even angrier, and in his rage, he swung the steel pipe across Detrick's knees. Again, the deafening crack was followed by terrible pain, and Detrick knew his knees had been destroyed.

"Say you are sorry. Say the Jews are nothing but lice, and I will send you to a hospital where you will get help."

Detrick's voice had gone hoarse from the pain. He looked up into the SS officer's pale blue eyes, and a last flood of bravery came over him. "I am a Jew. I converted. My wife is a Jew, and my child is a Jew."

With that, the Nazi officer slammed the steel club across Detrick's skull with all his might. Blood poured like a river. The guard held the weapon in front of Detrick as he paced around him like a panther, continuing to make demands.

But Detrick no longer heard him. His mind had mercifully silenced the malevolent words. Now, as his eyes closed upon the world, all he saw and heard was Leah. She smiled as she told him she loved him. A vision of the future came to him as clearly as if it had happened right before him. He saw a little blond boy in his wife's arms. They sat by a fireplace, and she kissed the child's forehead. In his heart, Detrick felt contentment, and knowing that they would be all right, he allowed himself the escape of death.

CHAPTER ONE HUNDRED TWENTY-SEVEN

ON APRIL 30, 1945, Hitler and his wife Eva Braun committed suicide. Only a few days later, the Nazis surrendered. The war was over. The Allies marched into the previously occupied territory and liberated the concentration camps. The soldiers were sickened by the horrific conditions they uncovered. In May 1948, Israel became a state. Although its Middle Eastern neighbors attacked the tiny Jewish country countless times, it prevailed through the sheer will of a people who gave everything to build a dream. And today, the Jews have a homeland.

CHAPTER ONE HUNDRED TWENTY-EIGHT

REGARDLESS OF WHAT HE TRIED, Daniel Joseph Haswell could never keep his hair from falling over his left eye. As he stood before the mirror, he ran a comb through his stylish, long, golden mane. Today, he would marry.

In the room across the hall, his mother, Leah Haswell, dressed for the occasion. She laid the maroon dress with the paisley flowers across the bed. This gown would not have been her choice, but Sarah, her future daughter-in-law, loved it. So, who was she to spoil their wedding day? Leah just looked at the dress and laughed a little. *Just let them both live long, happy, and healthy lives*, she thought. Then she went to her dressing table and carefully applied her makeup. Twisting her graying hair into a simple knot, she studied her image in the mirror. Satisfied, she went to her small jewelry box. Inside, she found the well-worn, yellowed paper. Today, she would allow her son to read the letter. It was time he read the words his father had written on that last day she'd seen him. She remembered the first time she'd opened the envelope and read the final words Detrick would ever say to her. It had been almost an entire week before she accepted the fact that he would not return. She'd paced the tiny hotel room from morning until night, unable to rest. Yet somehow, she knew that Sunday night that he had died. At first, Leah refused to believe that Detrick had left the earth, but she had known in her heart just when it happened. She'd felt it. She'd seen his face in her mind and heard him whisper, "Take care of our child."

Sadly, she also knew Jacob had perished, and she would now be on her own. She'd named her son after them both. Daniel for Detrick, Joseph for Jacob.

Leah had never remarried. Not because there had not been ample opportunities but because she never stopped loving Detrick. There had just never been room for anyone else in her heart. All the love and affection within her she'd used to blanket Daniel from a cruel world. It had not been easy. Sometimes, she'd missed Detrick so much that she felt she might perish with the loneliness. However, sometimes, Leah found solace in talking to the small picture the two had taken at the arcade so long ago.

Financially, Leah and Daniel's lives had been a balancing act. At first, she used the money Detrick left to get situated. It had been just enough to move to Geneva and purchase a second-hand piano. After that, she'd earned their way by giving music lessons. Sometimes, money did not flow as freely as she would have liked, but every day, she thanked God for this precious gift, this child created from love so great that even death could not destroy it. The little blond boy, with his father's dimpled smile, kept her going.

"Mom?" Daniel interrupted her thoughts.

"Yes, dear?"

"I can't find my tie."

"I thought you put it in your top drawer."

"That's right. I guess I'm so nervous that I forgot."

For a moment, Leah remembered her own wedding. She and Detrick had stood there in that dark attic room, and he'd thrown the jacket of his Nazi uniform on the floor and taken her hand as they walked together beneath the makeshift canopy.

"Sarah wanted me to give you this. But it's really from both of us." Daniel entered her room and handed her a small white box.

Smiling at him, she opened it. Inside, she found a gold heart. It was a little larger than an American silver dollar.

"It opens." Daniel smiled.

With care, she pried the locket apart to find a small photo of Daniel and Sarah.

"This is lovely. Thank you."

"Read the back. That's the part from Sarah."

Leah reached for her glasses and turned the piece onto its back. The inscription read, "Thank you for raising a wonderful son."

Tears filled her eyes as she looked at the beautiful boy who stood before her, so strong, so confident.

"What's that paper?" Daniel noticed the letter that lay on the bed.

For a moment, she considered not showing it to him. After all, why bring this up on his wedding day? "Never mind, it's nothing."

"I can see by your face, Mom, that it's something important. Are we in financial trouble? Because I want you to know that, even though I am getting married, I will help you if you need it."

"No." She laughed aloud. "I'm fine. Your responsibilities are to your new wife."

"Then what is that, Mother?"

"It's a letter. The last letter I ever received from your father. He left it with me when he returned to Germany to try to save your grandfather from Bergen–Belsen. I was not to open it unless he did not return."

"Can I see it, please?"

She handed him the letter. Sinking onto her bed, he read the words Detrick had written before his birth:

My Dearest Love,

If you are reading this, fate has it that I am dead. It breaks my heart to leave you behind, alone and with our child. More than I can ever say, I wish I could be beside you, to love you, and to help you raise this precious life within your womb. Tell our child how I would have loved him or her with my whole heart, the same way I have always loved you. Share our pride in our Jewish heritage with the little one. Make sure that he or she knows how much our people have sacrificed to be Jews. I guess one would agree that I, too, have sacrificed to be a Jew, even though I was not born into the religion.

Now, I must tell you that you have been the greatest joy of my life, my reason for living. Every precious moment we spent together, I have cherished more than you will ever know. So often, in my mind, I go back over every-thing we've shared, and I think, "I have truly been a lucky man. I have truly been blessed." Even though this has come to a tragic end, I have no regrets. My love for you was my light in the darkness, and my darling, it burned so very, very bright, bright enough to illuminate an entire world.

God bless you and our baby. May you both live in safety and in peace.

All my love,
Detrick

"Mom, I don't know what to say." Daniel looked at Leah, his face stained with tears.

"There is nothing to say. Your father loved us very much."

Daniel nodded, handing the letter back to Leah. Then he went into his room, where he went into the box where he kept the things he cherished from childhood. Once, when he was just a boy, his mother gave him a Star of David necklace. It had been years since he'd worn it. Carefully, he took it out of the box and put it on. He would wear it in honor of his father and his people today, on the most important day of his life.

Leah sprayed a single spritz of cologne as a finishing touch before leaving for the synagogue. Soon, Daniel would be married, and she would be alone in this apartment. She sighed, wondering how can someone be so happy and so sad at the same time?

Then, as she turned the light off in her room, she heard a familiar voice in her mind. A faint hint of peppermint drifted through the air.

"You're never alone, my darling. I'm always here. My body may be gone, but my spirit has never left you. Don't be sad. I'll stay by your side while you are still on earth, and when the time comes for you to join me, I will be waiting for you with my arms open." She felt Detrick's hand warm on her shoulder. "Come, my love, let's go and take our son under the canopy. It's a good day for a wedding. L'Chaim."

"L'Chaim," she whispered.

The End

AUTHORS NOTE

I always enjoy hearing from my readers, and your thoughts about my work are very important to me. If you enjoyed my novel, please consider telling your friends and posting a short review on Amazon. Word of mouth is an author's best friend.

Would you like to find out what happened to Dorothy? Join my mailing list, and you will receive *Little Song Bird*—a **free** short story about Dorothy—along with 2 other **free** short stories, and my USA Today award-winning novella, as my gift to you! To sign up, just go to my website at www.RobertaKagan.com.

I send blessings to each and every one of you,
  Roberta
  Email: roberta@robertakagan.com

ABOUT THE AUTHOR

I wanted to take a moment to introduce myself. My name is Roberta, and I am an author of Historical Fiction, mainly based on World War 2 and the Holocaust. While I never discount the horrors of the Holocaust and the Nazis, my novels are constantly inspired by love, kindness, and the small special moments that make life worth living.

I always knew I wanted to reach people through art when I was younger. I just always thought I would be an actress. That dream died in my late 20's, after many attempts and failures. For the next several years, I tried so many different professions. I worked as a hairstylist and a wedding coordinator, amongst many other jobs. But I was never satisfied. Finally, in my 50's, I worked for a hospital on the PBX board. Every day I would drive to work, I would dread clocking in. I would count the hours until I clocked out. And, the next day, I would do it all over again. I couldn't see a way out, but I prayed, and I prayed, and then I prayed some more. Until one morning at 4 am, I woke up with a voice in my head, and you might know that voice as Detrick. He told me to write his story, and together we sat at the computer; we wrote the novel that is now known as All My Love, Detrick. I now have over 30 books published, and I have had the honor of being a USA Today Best-Selling Author. I have met such incredible people in this industry, and I am so blessed to be meeting you.

I tell this story a lot. And a lot of people think I am crazy, but it is true. I always found solace in books growing up but didn't start writing until I was in my late 50s. I try to tell this story to as many people as possible to inspire them. No matter where you are in your life, remember there is always a flicker of light no matter how dark it seems.

I send you many blessings, and I hope you enjoy my novels. They are all written with love.

Roberta

MORE BOOKS BY ROBERTA KAGAN

AVAILABLE ON AMAZON

Margot's Secret Series

The Secret They Hid

An Innocent Child

The Blood Sisters Series

The Pact

My Sister's Betrayal

When Forever Ends

The Auschwitz Twins Series

The Children's Dream

Mengele's Apprentice

The Auschwitz Twins

Jews, The Third Reich, and a Web of Secrets

My Son's Secret

The Stolen Child

A Web of Secrets

A Jewish Family Saga

Not In America

They Never Saw It Coming

When The Dust Settled

The Syndrome That Saved Us

A Holocaust Story Series

The Smallest Crack

The Darkest Canyon

Millions Of Pebbles

Sarah and Solomon

All My Love, Detrick Series

All My Love, Detrick

You Are My Sunshine

The Promised Land

To Be An Israeli

Forever My Homeland

Michal's Destiny Series

Michal's Destiny

A Family Shattered

Watch Over My Child

Another Breath, Another Sunrise

Eidel's Story Series

And . . . Who Is The Real Mother?

Secrets Revealed

New Life, New Land

Another Generation

The Wrath of Eden Series

The Wrath Of Eden

The Angels Song

Stand Alone Novels